Early Praise for *Bad Blood*

'Incredibly gripping. A triumph'

Claire Douglas

'A dark, twisted thriller from a compelling new voice. Part law-room thriller, part psychological family drama – this had everything I expect from a pageturner and more. An absolute belter!'

Russ Thomas

'Excellent debut psychological legal thriller. Flawless structure. Taut, intelligent, and shockingly gripping. Loved the mentions of Kintsugi, the epistolary flourishes and the descriptions of barrister life. BRILLIANT'

Will Dean

'A beautifully written, atmospheric thriller with a killer twist – I loved it'

Catherine Cooper

'A satisfyingly complex twisty and twisted thriller that takes you in all manner of unexpected directions. Sarah draws her characters with great skill and a knack for pacing that would put many a seasoned writer to shame, let alone a debut'

James Oswald

'Sarah Hornsley takes us on a well crafted journey full of tension and twists. Claustrophobic and unsettling in the best way – *Bad Blood* is sure to be the thriller of 2025'

Roxie Cooper

BAD
BLOOD

About the Author

Sarah Hornsley started her career in publishing in 2012 at Orion Books, followed by a short stint in script development before becoming a literary agent in 2015, joining PFD in 2021. She was selected for *The Bookseller* Rising Star list in 2019. She lives in Essex with her family, and writes alongside working as an agent.

Bad Blood is her first novel. Rights have sold in multiple territories and it has been optioned for television.

BAD BLOOD

SARAH HORNSLEY

HODDER &
STOUGHTON

First published in Great Britain in 2025 by Hodder & Stoughton Limited
An Hachette UK company

1

A CIP catalogue record for this title is available from the British Library

Hardback ISBN 978 1 399 72587 3
Trade Paperback ISBN 978 1 399 72586 6
ebook ISBN 978 1 399 72588 0

Typeset in Sabon MT by Hewer Text UK Ltd, Edinburgh
Printed and bound in Great Britain by Clays Ltd, Elcograf S.p.A.

Hodder & Stoughton policy is to use papers that are natural, renewable
and recyclable products and made from wood grown in sustainable
forests. The logging and manufacturing processes are expected to
conform to the environmental regulations of the country of origin.

Hodder & Stoughton Limited
Carmelite House
50 Victoria Embankment
London EC4Y 0DZ

The authorised representative in the EEA is Hachette Ireland, 8 Castlecourt
Centre, Castleknock Road, Castleknock, Dublin 15, D15 YF6A, Ireland

www.hodder.co.uk

For my parents, Val and Berni,
for teaching me that no dream is too big.

Chapter One

I was seven when I learned aloe vera plants are the best remedy for burns. I'd been watching my mother from the kitchen doorway as she sliced the plant in half with a knife before scooping out its wet flesh and applying it to the top of her arm. Her burn had taken almost three weeks to heal, first turning a sloppy yellow in the middle before leaving a perfect circular scar I noticed every summer after. I never mentioned it; had jumped out of sight when she turned from the kitchen counter.

This is how I know the defendant is lying about the burn. I scribble it down on a piece of paper and pass it to where Charles Cole is standing midway through his cross-examination. He glances at it and then to me. I can see he's confused but he trusts me. I am his rising star and so, after only a moment's deliberation, he indicates for me to stand and makes his way back to the prosecution desk.

He is handing the court – our stage – over to me.

'Mr Jackson.' I smile at the defendant, though it isn't a friendly one. I am a wolf in a barrister's robe. 'I want to take a minute to go over the information you just gave the court.' I gesture towards the jury, making sure they understand I am about to reveal how he has lied to them. I want it to feel personal. 'On the twenty-second of November last year did you expect Peter Taylor to be in his home when you entered it?'

'I did not.' He shakes his head and I can tell he has no idea where I'm going with this. He thinks I am lost and playing for time.

'When Peter did indeed turn out to be home, and he confronted you in his kitchen, can you tell the court again what transpired?'

'Sure.' He shrugs. 'He attacked me.'

'Can you describe the attack for the court?'

'He rugby-tackled me to the floor and we fought a while, he kept trying to grab me round the neck but I managed to get away. I was trying to leave, had my back to him, when he must have grabbed the iron from its board where it stood at the side. The next thing I knew, I felt a searing hot pain on my left shoulder.'

'He burnt you with the iron?'

'Yes.'

'But he didn't hit you with it? It's a heavy object.' I watch his eyes flit to his defence barrister, Rose Ballard, before answering me. She hadn't prepared him for this line of questioning.

'Well, he was quite far away from me at this point. I was trying to leave. I guess he lunged and it caught me.'

'And what happened next?'

'I spun around. He was much closer to me by then. He had the iron swung back as if he was about to whack me with it again.'

'Can you tell me what was going through your mind when you realised he'd burnt you and was still holding the iron?'

'I thought he was going to kill me.' He looks over to the jury as he says it, all sad and forlorn-looking. What he doesn't realise is he's just delivered me the perfect answer.

'And how exactly did you react to this?'

'I stabbed him.'

'How many times?'

'Five. In self-defence.'

I pause, letting it sink in. Not just once, but five times. 'OK. Can you confirm for me that the reason you stabbed Mr Taylor in self-defence was because he burnt you with the iron?'

'That's right. I had my back turned and was leaving. I'm telling you, he came for me.' I try not to smile, keeping my cards close to my chest for just a little while longer.

'Did you have any injuries as a result of Mr Taylor's assault?'

'We've been over this already,' he sighs, clearly tiring of my questioning. Good. The more frustrated they are, the more likely they are to make mistakes. We wear them down.

'Humour me,' I say, gesturing theatrically and making some of the jurors snigger.

'I have a scar on the back of my shoulder.'

'And this scar was there when the police arrested you one week after Peter Taylor was killed in his kitchen. Correct?'

'That's right. They have photos and everything. I ain't lying.' I raise my eyebrows. He is starting to sweat.

'So you were caught by the iron badly enough for it to scar. And that same burn had healed one week after the injury was first sustained, allowing the police to take photos of the area as shown during the trial when you were arrested one week after the attack?'

'Erm.'

'Just answer the question please. It's a simple yes or no.'

'Yes.'

'During the period of time between the burning and your arrest – just one week – did you receive any medical advice or treatment? Did you google how to treat a burn? Was there anything you did to help it heal?'

'Not that I can remember.'

'The thing is, Mr Jackson, a second-degree burn, which is what you would need to have sustained for it to scar as shown in the photos, takes at least two to three weeks to heal and that's even using the best treatments around.'

'Well not for me,' he says forcefully, the puppy-dog eyes from earlier turning into something a little more threatening. *That's right, I'm on to you.* The adrenalin is pumping faster through my veins now. This feeling, it is addictive.

'I put it to you that it did in fact take precisely the normal two to three weeks for the burn on the back of your shoulder to scar. It could not have been sustained during the alleged assault you were subjected to by Mr Taylor but must have happened before you even entered his home, otherwise it would still have been an open wound at the time of your arrest.

'To be clear, whatever caused you to get that scar must have been inflicted at least – and I repeat, at least – one week prior to the incident you're currently on trial for. In fact, I think given this scar is the only injury you can point to having sustained from Mr Taylor, that there was no attack at all from the victim and you killed him in his home without being provoked.

'Importantly, you killed him not as an act of self-defence but simply because you could.' He doesn't say anything, just gawps looking like a rabbit caught in headlights. 'Mr Jackson,' I raise my voice, 'am I correct? Did you sustain your burn before the night in question?'

I watch as he rubs his hands over his face, leaving red finger marks trailing down his cheeks. He is cracking.

We are going to win.

The robing room sounds a lot more majestic than it is, but the romance of it is not to be underestimated. I always find that I need this time and the camaraderie found here, even between opposing sides, to make the transition from hard-nosed barrister back to functioning human. Without it, I wonder if my marriage would have survived this long. If I'm honest, I highly doubt it. The two sides of me, constantly pulled in opposite directions. One part doggedly determined to win no matter the

4

cost; the other desperate to find stability. I can't seem to make my mind up on what exactly I define as 'success'.

That's why, as Rose asks if I'm joining them in The Ship for Lara's birthday drinks later, I hesitate. Lara works for the same chambers as Rose and I first got to know her from frequenting the well-known barrister haunts of London, such as The Ship, after work hours. Our paths have crossed a couple of times in the courtroom, too. I would bet the majority of people I work with will be out tonight.

Everyone knows that important work still gets done during the hours spent at the pub. As old-school as it sounds, it is still our reality. The problem is that you never know quite when those important conversations will take place, so it's not like you can strategically show up then make a speedy exit. They could happen at ten p.m. Maybe one a.m. Frequently at three a.m. Never before nine. You're in it for the long haul or you might as well not go at all.

And so, instead, I make my excuses, offering my biggest smile to the woman I just spent the past six hours up against in court. I remove my wig that is the same off-white colour as the worn walls and gather my things before heading home. I tell her it's my and Noah's fifth wedding anniversary but decide to leave out the fact he isn't even home for it because he is away on business in Paris; that my evening will be spent sharing a dinner hundreds of miles apart relying on a dodgy Wi-Fi connection to summon some kind of romantic atmosphere.

It's a far-cry from how we spent last year's anniversary – mostly with our bodies entwined at a hotel in Oxford, where they serve only locally sourced produce and have large fireplaces in every room. I smile back at the memory of it – it really was the perfect weekend, spent with my perfect husband. Absurdly expensive for one night, I admit – but given this year is a bit of a miss, maybe next year I'll suggest we stay there again.

'Well done today, Justine,' Rose calls after me, 'formidable as always, but next time I'll win.' I can hear the smile in her voice. Any trace of bitterness is gone. You can't hold a grudge in this business. Not if you want to survive.

'We'll see about that,' I call over my shoulder and smile to myself as I push open the door, though I make sure it doesn't linger too long. I have always made a point not to celebrate my court successes. There's something a little distasteful about being responsible for locking someone up. That's not to say they don't deserve it or that it isn't the right thing to do, but over the duration of a case you get to know the defendant. Not personally of course, but it feels like I become them.

I like to think of it as a character study, doing what I do. You simply can't ignore the nuances of it all, how each event in someone's life has shaped them. What if you could unshackle them from all of it? Start again, reborn. Do people deserve a second chance?

In my line of work the answer is no, but I spend one hour a week with my therapist, Aya, convincing myself that I am deserving of exactly that. Rationalising that I am worthy of spending luxurious weekends away in fancy hotels with my loving husband.

The thing about red wine is that no matter how earthy or smoked it supposedly is, all I can smell as it swirls around my glass is the distinct iron zing of blood.

'Cheers,' we say in unison, all smiles as we pretend to clink our glasses together.

I look at the image of Noah over the rim of my glass; his suit is still on from a long day at the office but his shirt is now open at the collar, his tie discarded, and I think about how different he is to the husband I'd always imagined myself to have. I push it away. Allow myself to be happy. He is handsome, very handsome, and he is kind.

The two don't normally go hand in hand, count yourself lucky, my mother's voice echoes.

And, while my skin crawls at the double standard of it – that a woman should, without exception, be always both beautiful and likeable – she is right. I am lucky. From the moment I opened the front door this evening, Noah has clearly been on a mission to make tonight feel special. A bottle of champagne – Bollinger, no less – delivered to the house along with a bunch of white roses (my favourite), and instructions to turn on a new Spotify playlist he has made with songs from our wedding.

I'm allowed to be happy. I am worthy. Do not push Noah away.

It's a trait of mine, when things feel like they are spiralling out of my control, to push Noah away. As though the easiest way to deal with my fear of losing him is to not have him in the first place. That way no one can take him away from me. Or, worse, him decide he no longer wants me. The problem is, I have been feeling overwhelmed a lot recently.

I hear a knock on his hotel room and a small voice announces room service.

'Ah ha! The pièce de résistance,' he exclaims before dashing off-screen to open the door and retrieve his apple crumble. Noah is not normally the type of man to exclaim, nor dash, and I can tell he's trying to make an effort, even though we are apart.

While he is away, I sneak a look at my phone. I'd promised him a phone-free (meaning work-free) evening and true to my word had put my work phone in the office drawer, but I'd kept my personal one tucked under the screen, out of sight. I'm not sure why – I suppose I've fallen victim to constantly needing to feel connected to people rather than happy in my own company.

Aya suggests the noise of social media helps keep my own

thoughts at bay. She labels it 'unhealthy'. I feel the itch creep along my fingers and before I realise I'm doing it, I've logged on to Instagram to see how my colleagues are getting on at Lara's birthday drinks. There's nothing on my newsfeed. In fact, there's nothing new at all since the last time I looked, and I find myself absent-mindedly typing into the search bar at the top of the app.

Jake Reynolds.

It's a habit I haven't been able to shift. Nearly eighteen years ago, it was only Facebook I would find myself searching through but now there's Instagram and Twitter too. Each time, I'm presented with a long list of Jake Reynoldses but not one of them is him.

I don't know why I still do it. It's not like I expect him to suddenly show up at the top of my screen after all these years. But just like unlocking your phone or checking your emails become habits, typing his name into search bars has become ingrained in my muscle memory. I don't consciously do it, but I can't stop either.

I feel the guilt worm its way in, that on my anniversary it is Jake who I am searching for. I love my husband, I really do, but your first love never leaves you. And Jake was no normal first love. He saved me. And then he left me. I suppose that's one of the reasons the next guy I fell in love with was Noah. In some respects, the two of them are similar; they both made me feel safe, but the ways in which they achieved that were entirely different.

Jake made me feel safe enough to be myself, to let loose, to free myself from any shackles of expectation. I was allowed to feel big. Being with Jake was like putting loud music on and finding yourself dancing to it without a care in the world.

With Noah it is different. He is steady. Secure. I feel safe he will not abandon me. It isn't an explosive kind of love – we aren't the most flamboyant couple in the world – but it is just as strong in a different way. It is secure. Steadfast. Real.

We've even started thinking about trying to get pregnant. Well, Noah has. The thought of being a mother doesn't feel the most natural thing for me. That title, 'mother', and everything it would mean. It's not an easy thing to be.

What if I fail? Not everyone is cut out to be a mother. I know the harm that can be done if you don't do it well. Would I be a good one? I'm not so sure. If I'm honest, I think Noah talking about having a baby soon has fed into my feeling overwhelmed recently. It has reminded me of my own mother. Of her short-comings. Of everything I would hope not to be.

Noah returns to his laptop full of gusto as he shows me his plate of food from across the ether and I push my phone further out of sight. Take a large gulp of my red wine and tell him it looks delicious. That I wish I were there sharing it with him. He smiles back at me and I push away the encroaching doubt; the voice inside my head asking, 'But is that really true?'.

Chapter Two

I lie in the dark staring at the seductive text Noah sent me precisely four minutes ago. I know what he wants and that it must feel like an eternity to him as I type then delete. Type then delete. Not too long ago I would have found it exciting, sexy, the slow burn of desire working its way from the tips of my toes through the rest of my body as we texted through the night while he was away on business. But tonight, I simply can't find the words.

He is good. We are good. Noah is good.

I repeat it over and over again in my mind, willing myself to press send. Before I do, the voice rears its ugly head again. It has been getting louder in recent months, hissing at me when I least expect it.

But are you good enough?

What am I afraid of? I know he isn't about to reject me. Yet I can feel my anxiety eating away at us, pressing into the corners of our marriage and darkening the edges. The more I panic about what to reply, the faster my heart beats and then I'm back there.

Trapped. Locked in. Darkness.

I am gasping for breath.

Last week, just after Noah had once again brought up starting a family, Aya told me that in times of extreme stress, traumatic events we thought we'd worked through can resurface.

Are you particularly stressed right now, Justine? Has something happened?

No. I'd lied. Not quite ready to discuss it with her. Keen to avoid talking about my own mother as much as possible but knowing that is exactly where she'd take the conversation.

The pain in my chest is tight and there's a dull ache spreading from the base of my skull. I swing my legs over the side of the bed, needing the sensation of the floor beneath my feet to bring me back to reality. Slowly it begins to work and, as the fog clears, I pick up my phone from where I'd left it lying in the middle of the bed.

Justine: *I'm sorry. I'm really tired. Speak tomorrow. Happy anniversary. I love you x*

I type it fast, pressing send before I can change my mind.

It's eleven p.m. on a Wednesday but, reasoning that many of my colleagues will still be ordering last drinks at the bar, I pour a large glass of wine and fire up my laptop. That's the thing about being a criminal barrister. Crimes never stop, so neither does our work. It's been fifteen years since I took a holiday – a real one, where I stopped being Justine the barrister and was just Justine. Wife. Lover. Friend.

I scan over the twenty emails which have made it into my inbox in the three hours since I last checked and my eyes are quickly drawn to one from the Head of Chambers, Charles Cole. The subject line simply reads URGENT. I race to my work phone which is still lying in my office desk drawer.

Three missed calls.

I toy with the idea of returning Charles's call but Aya's voice echoes in my head, reminding me that some boundaries need to be drawn, and instead I skulk back to my laptop.

Justine,
Big case just in. We need someone to take the lead on this urgently. Mike's already been recommended to the clerks for it but I was thinking of throwing your name into the mix. If

you want this, you need to get back to me fast. This case isn't going to hang around. Preliminary details attached.
Charles

Sorry Aya, some boundaries do need to be broken. I don't bother opening the attachment, there's no more time to waste. I pray to God that Mike has enjoyed a few too many tequilas and is still stumbling around The Ship regaling junior staff with tales of his courtroom successes.

Charles answers on the third ring. 'She's alive then.'

'I'll take it,' I shoot back.

'It's a big case, Justine.' Charles warns, 'Ones like this don't come along often and it would be your first murder case. It's make or break. Are you ready? The media are going to be all over it. Every sentence you string together will be pored over, examined, analysed and most likely splashed across the front pages. Can you handle it? Better than Mike could?'

I search frantically for what to say next. Why didn't I read the case file? I grab at something, take a chance, knowing that there are certain cases I am better at than Mike and hoping this is one of them.

'Mike can be flashy and sharp, I'll give him that. He can woo a jury, but I can tell a story. Get them not to fall in love with me, but with the victim. Some cases need a shark. A Mike. Others need the jury to be strung a delicate web, to make sure they see the full picture. This case, it needs me.'

Charles's laughter barks down the phone at me. 'OK, Justine. This isn't a closing speech but I'll see what favour I can pull with the clerks. It helps that Mike's still drowning in tequila but I like the fighting spirit.' The call clicks off and I close my eyes. It's not a done deal, not yet, but if anyone holds sway with the clerks, it's Charles. He's been a KC for more than thirty years and won many high-profile cases.

Only moments later, as I'm pouring myself a second glass of wine, my phone lights up.

Charles: *It's yours. If you want to go through the file with me, I'll be in Chambers at eight a.m. tomorrow.*

When the Head of Chambers offers you their advice on your first murder case, you take it. I inhale deeply and slip my feet out of my slippers so I can feel the cold wooden floorboards against the soles of my feet. This is it. The case I've been waiting for.

This is *my* moment.

Chapter Three

Charles is already seated when I knock on his office door at seven forty-five. No matter how hard I try, Charles is always one step ahead.

I give a little wave and make a show of the pastries I bought from the gloriously Insta-worthy bakery that recently opened next door.

'Fuel,' I say.

'I knew I liked you more than Mike for a reason.' He smiles back at me. Charles strikes fear into every other barrister he comes up against, a fact widely acknowledged, but as soon as the wig is off the transformation is complete. No wig, no bite.

'Right. Down to business then I'll leave you to it. You're going to need all the time you have to prepare for this one.' He taps his middle finger on the file tied with a thin pink ribbon before pushing it across his desk towards me.

The email last night hadn't given too much away. Brad Finchley was a thirty-five-year-old white man with two charges of murder against him. I haven't led on a case this serious before and Charles is right: the media love a murder trial, but two bodies? It will be feasting time for the sharks.

The plea and trial preparation hearing has been set to take place in five weeks' time. This is where I will be required to state our case against the defendant, and he will plead either guilty or not guilty. I suspect, with a case this serious, the defendant will have been advised by his barrister to plead not guilty, hoping at the very least to bring the murder charge down to manslaughter. I am already preparing myself for a six-month trial. To battle it out.

My adrenalin is fired up.

This is why I became a KC.

I draw the case file closer, full of anticipation. The first page is always a mugshot with factual details about the defendant. Seeing who is accused of committing the crimes we are prosecuting them for intrigues me. In my job as a criminal barrister working for the prosecution, I do not care who you are or where you are from.

Of course, it would be naïve of me to claim I'm not aware that our justice system is intrinsically flawed, but my job is always the same, no exceptions made: I follow the case and put together the facts in a way that is the most *persuasive*.

We are master manipulators.

I present the prosecution case regardless of whether I think you did it or not. That's what they teach us, it's what our judicial system relies upon – a fair trial. For that to happen, both sides of the argument need to be presented with equal conviction.

During my career, I've often marvelled at how many different ways the same facts can be presented and wondered what that says about the truths of our own lives and the ways in which we interact. The gaps and misinterpretations which must happen on a daily basis. When you do my job, you see just how grey even the most devastating scenarios can be. It only works if both the prosecution and the defence put their best foot forward.

Over the many middle-class dinner parties I am subjected to, I have heard the majority of my colleagues answer the question, 'What part of your job do you enjoy the most?' with the same generic answer, 'Winning.' To me, this answer has always seemed frightfully dull for people whose whole job it is to put on a show in the courtroom. We all like to win, it's a natural instinct – survival of the fittest. I am more fascinated by the people behind the cases. The psychology of it all. Who they are. What they have done. Why they have done it; it's my secret weapon with the jury. I'm a storyteller, and to tell their story I need to know them.

Who are you, Brad Finchley? What have you done? And why did you do it?

I untie the ribbon.

Begin the puzzle.

And there is Brad Finchley. Staring at me with his strong jawline and deep brown eyes. I drop my glass of water a little too forcefully, and a splash escapes over the rim, landing on the page and blurring the ink.

I cast my eyes over a small scar on his right cheekbone.

I follow the line of the scar down to the curve of his lips, where I'd trace my finger over his Cupid's bow, so perfect I'd joke he must not be real.

And then just below the left corner of his mouth, another smaller scar you would miss unless you knew to look for it. I'd spent hours, probably time amounting to days, studying this face; I knew to look for it.

Because I am certain, with every fibre of my being, that the man staring back at me is not Brad Finchley.

It's Jake Reynolds.

My heart begins to bang against my chest. Hammering. Desperate to get out. And then all of a sudden I'm back there again.

Alone. Trapped. Surrounded only by darkness. This time it's not my heart hammering to get out but my fists. Loud and clear. Unanswered.

Jake Reynolds. Where have you been? And why did you leave me?

* * *

'Now, the interesting thing about this defendant is that he legally changed his name from Jake Reynolds to Brad Finchley almost two decades ago.'

Charles's words pierce through me. *Interesting*. As though Jake is the villain in a television drama and it's an intriguing plot-twist rather than news about the man who broke my heart and never came back for me. Who, it turns out, changed his entire identity to ensure I would never find him. Did he really hate me for what I'd done that much?

'Justine?' Charles asks. 'Are you all right?'

I blink and force myself to tear my eyes away from the photo staring up at me. I look directly at Charles and say I'm fine, that I just feel a little sick, and then I feel my body rise out of the seat and walk towards the door. I hear my voice declaring I just need a 'quick breather'.

It all happens as though I'm watching the scene play out from the corner of the room. I'm saying these things, acting as if everything is normal, still able to put one foot in front of the other, but at the same time it's not me. The real me has shattered into a million pieces.

The last time I saw Jake was after my dad's law firm's Christmas party in 2005. That night changed everything – and everyone. I know I'm not the same person I was back then and thinking about Jake now – or should I say Brad – I wonder who he has become. A murderer?

I've thought about him a lot. Imagined what he might look like. In the quiet moments of my marriage to Noah I have felt guilty for it. Everyone says there's no love quite like your first. It doesn't mean you don't love anyone after, but it is a different kind of love. Less all-consuming. Healthier, perhaps.

Jake and I, we were the epitome of first love. The kind you see in films and read about in books. The sort inevitably ravaged by tragedy. It's the only rightful ending. That kind of love, it can't keep going forever.

At least, that's how I rationalise it to myself. Like Romeo and Juliet. An explosive ending for an explosive love before it burns out. That way it stays alive and vibrant forever. Romeo and Juliet wouldn't be Romeo and Juliet if they'd grown old and boring together, bickering about what to eat for dinner.

If Jake hadn't left, maybe we would have diluted ourselves over time. Become something else. Something smaller.

I push open the toilet door and look at myself in the mirror. Knuckles turning white as I grip the basin. *Jake Reynolds, what have you done*, I whisper.

I don't think I've said his name aloud since the day I realised he wasn't coming back. That had been a very bad day. It had also been the start of a new chapter for me, and I suppose you could say that from it I had been born: the Justine who was now married to Noah.

They say you need to hit rock bottom before things can get better. Well, I hit rock bottom and then some, but things did get better. Nearly eighteen years later, except for the occasional search on my internet history, I have successfully erased Jake from my life.

Something tugs at my memory. *Finchley.* Finches was our favourite restaurant.

Brad Finchley.

Is it a coincidence? Some kind of sick joke? Does it mean something?

I feel the urge to splash my face with cold water but, seeing as I'm not due in court this morning, I've taken the liberty of wearing a sharp red lipstick as a *fuck-you* to the patriarchy, so I gracefully kick the wall beneath the basin instead.

I had somehow managed to navigate my way back to Charles's office, finish the briefing with a lot of nodding and generic reassurances, and am now sitting in my office spinning slowly in my chair. The file is closed and pushed to the edge of my desk, as if touching it might burn me.

I'd searched the internet for Jake Reynolds and never found a single trace of him. Not so much as a photo on Google or a LinkedIn account. But I'd never searched for Brad Finchley. I stop spinning and open my laptop. I type it in, taking my time as I punch each letter of this strange unfamiliar name into Facebook, and hold my breath.

The results load and there he is, fifth account down. His page is set to 'private' but I can still see his profile picture. He is tanned and wearing a simple white T-shirt. His eyebrows are low-set; he has just the right amount of stubble – the kind that says purpose-fully roguish rather than can't be bothered – and a slightly crooked smile as though he knows something I don't. That smile drove me mad.

He doesn't look like a murderer, but you don't have to be a barrister to know it's not only inherently evil people who end up committing evil acts. I know too well that things can happen in people's lives to trigger a kind of snowball effect where finally you find yourself acting in ways you'd never considered yourself capable of.

Shattered glass. A sea of red. Overflowing.

According to the file, his permanent residence is listed as Maldon, Essex, the same place we both grew up in. Why haven't Max or Mum said anything? Did they know he was back? How long has he been living there for? Why change your name, and then return somewhere everyone already knows you? None of it makes any sense.

I read on to learn Brad Finchley has been released on bail and is staying with a friend in Letchworth ahead of the hearing. Not considered a flight risk and with a clean previous record, he has an ankle tag, curfew and regular police check-ins.

My headache is back. I open my drawer, scrambling for the stash of paracetamol I keep there, and quickly wash down two tablets. I tell myself that anything could have happened to Jake in the eighteen years since I saw him last. He has quite literally reinvented himself.

No, I don't know this Brad Finchley at all.

Which is a good job really, as legally I should have declared I know the defendant the moment I saw his picture.

But I didn't.

If I'm found out before I take myself off the case, I risk losing everything. Being sanctioned by the regulator would certainly tarnish my reputation – most likely my career – depending on how far I let this go on.

And as for Noah? How could I explain it all to him? I couldn't, which means I am also risking my marriage. The thought of it terrifies me. I have already done so much, told so many lies, to protect us. You could say I've sanitised my past but I had no choice.

And yet, it has taken me eighteen years to find Jake and so, despite it all, I find I cannot simply let him go again. Not straight away.

It helps to think of Jake and Brad as two separate people and, knowing I can't put this off forever, I once again draw the file towards me and open it up. This time fully aware of what horrors await me among its pages.

Mark Rushnell and Beverley Rushnell were both sixty-seven years old, living in the affluent area of Epsom, Surrey. Almost one month ago, their bodies were found: dead in their home, a place which should have been a safe haven but in so many of the cases we deal with is all too often the heart of the crime.

A report circulated round chambers recently showed that an estimated 2.3 million adults experienced domestic abuse last year; a shocking two women are killed every week by their part-ner or ex-partner. But in this case, both husband and wife were found dead in the house they called their home.

I flick through to the most graphic part of the report in front of me. I find it important to tackle the violence head on. Over the years I've realised there's no point darting round it; it always finds a way to creep up on me. If I don't confront it now then the effect it has is worse, it becomes more personal somehow – shad-ows dancing in the corner of the room, phantom footsteps behind me at night. No, I cannot run from it.

The photos show the aftermath of the murders and there is no part of it that is pretty. Mark Rushnell was killed at point-blank range. It does not leave much to the imagination. Beverley Rushnell was also shot in the head but from further away. The forensic report estimates they were killed within the same time frame, but who was killed first is too difficult to determine.

I think of all the times Jake's fingers cupped my cheek or brushed the small of my lower back, and instead try to imag-ine them closing around the trigger. Twice. Bullets aimed to kill.

It was purposeful, calculated, undeniably violent.

Not only was the murder weapon found in a bag in Jake's possession, but it was discovered alongside a cap stained with the Rushnells' blood. Damningly, fibres from the exact same cap were found on both victims' dead bodies.

I can already hear the words the prosecution will say in court, condemning Jake to a lifetime of imprisonment.

Both Mark's and Beverley's times of death are recorded as somewhere between two and two fifteen p.m. A lot can happen in the space of just fifteen minutes. The job of the prosecution is to decide which version of events will make the most sense to the jury: did Jake kill Beverley first, maybe even making Mark watch, or did it happen the other way round? Was there a gap between the shootings or did they happen in quick succession?

I scribble my thoughts on a notepad:

1) Order of the killings?
2) Why was Jake in the house?
3) Why did he kill them?

And then I add a fourth:

4) Mark and Beverley RUSHNELL

I find myself writing their surname in capital letters and circling it. Who were they? And why does their name sound so familiar to me?

Chapter Four

The clock on my office wall says 08:38. Before today, Jake Reynolds had been absent from my life for eighteen years, but it has taken a total of fifty-three minutes since he re-entered it for him to turn my whole world upside down. Again. I try not to think about what that says about me and the life I've built for myself.

In one of my early sessions with Aya she told me about kintsugi, the Japanese art of visibly mending broken pottery with gold along the cracks. It's steeped in a whole philosophy about celebrating the imperfections as much as the beauty of the object, along with the notion that the piece is all the stronger for having been broken and then mended. I loved the idea so much that I started collecting kintsugi to place all around our house. If you open our kitchen cupboards you'll find plates, mugs, glasses and even our teapot with beautiful, delicate gold lines running through them. Her whole point, of course, was that I myself am a piece of kintsugi. Stronger and more beautiful for everything I've been through. I wonder now if I had instead simply stuck myself back together with PVA.

I slam my laptop shut and hastily pack it into my wheelie suitcase along with the case folder and my notepad. I do a quick sweep of my office, making sure to take anything else I might need, and then I head for Charles's office. Knock urgently on the door.

'Come in,' he calls, and I push the door open.

'I just got off the phone with my mother. Terrible timing, I know, but she's had a bit of a funny turn. My brother, Max, would normally be able to stay with her but he's had to go away for a while. I'm going to work remotely from hers for the next few days. I've packed everything I might need –' I grimace apologetically towards my wheelie – 'and I'll put together a list of potential witnesses and start the ball rolling with forensics while I'm gone. I've got the prelim for that ABH case I told you about, the one where the guy bit the arresting officer, on Tuesday over at Blackfriars, so I'll be back by then.'

He frowns. 'Well, it's not great timing, but I understand family is important.'

'Thanks, see you next week,' I say as I start to close the door, quickly.

'Justine?' he calls after me and I pause. 'Just don't mess this one up, OK.'

'Of course not. Number one priority.'

Do I feel guilty about lying to Charles, the man who just helped hand me the biggest opportunity of my career so far? If I dwell on it, then yes. But I am quite literally trained in the art of manipulation – I hold a first-class degree in it, in fact.

I decide it's not worth dwelling on, there are bigger things at play here. If Jake is going to be sent to prison for murder, I need to know the full story. Not just the version the prosecution determines is the most persuasive to tell in court.

This time, I need the real story.

Finally, nearly eighteen years later, it's time to go home. Back to where it all started.

Back, in many ways, to him.

BEFORE

JAKE – THE BOYFRIEND

The first time Jake saw Justine, really saw her, was on a dreary day in February. It had been his mum's 48th birthday and his dad had booked a surprise dinner at the Blue Eagle. It was Jake's job to fetch her from the office. He'd chosen the scenic route into town, through the prom, rather than the quickest – his dad would have rolled his eyes at that, he was much more practical than Jake. Less *emotional*, as he liked to declare whenever Jake disappointed him or said something in front of his dad's friends that made him feel uncomfortable.

Usually, Jake would brush it off, happy enough in his own skin, but today as the clouds darkened he admitted it had been the wrong choice. He should have followed his head. Not his heart.

He knew of the Stone family. Everyone in Maldon did. Gerard Stone was quite the pillar of the community and, unsurprisingly, he was running for the town council once again. His face lined posters stuck to lampposts, flapping in the wind. You couldn't miss him if you tried. God, sometimes Jake hated this small town, where it felt no one ever escaped.

Generational, that's what it was. You were born here, and you stayed here. Even the lucky exceptions who disappeared to university often returned years later, a young family in tow, to start the cycle all over again.

University wasn't written into Jake's future. His family fell firmly into the generational camp. He would leave school at the end of the academic year and the expectation was he'd do his accounting qualifications sponsored by a local company, likely end up marrying someone he'd been to school with – though, God knows, he dreaded to think who – and buy a terraced Victorian house like the one he grew up in just around the corner from his parents.

He shoved his hands further into his pockets and wove his way down the short-cut public footpath. The hedges loomed high. Today the path seemed to stretch on further than he remembered. One long straight road ahead of him. No room for diversion. He scuffed his shoes in the mud and, feeling the first drop of rain, pulled his hoodie up over his head and began to run.

Finally, the path opened on to the prom and he breathed in the sea-salt air. This town was small and oppressive, but even he had to admit it could also be intoxicating. He rounded the path by the water and let himself imagine that maybe one day he would in fact live in one of these houses. He could more readily accept his fate then.

No one could deny just how beautiful it must be to live looking out over the estuary. In Maldon, the big houses with land down by the water's edge were a little enclave to themselves. A semicircle of council and ex-council houses lined the edge of the prom, closing them in.

The geography of it seemed a little threatening if Jake really thought about it. It was a sort of maze, with the prized desired houses smack bang in the middle of the less desirable streets. It made for a funny mix: those with enough money to escape London's rat race next door to those who had never had the opportunity to enter it in the first place.

The Stones owned the large pink house with decking all the way around the edge and with a white picket fence, like one of those American houses he'd seen on television. There was an observatory on the second floor at the front – all glass walls and two armchairs facing out, overlooking the water. He imagined Mr Stone smoking cigars and playing chess in there.

Jake turned down the lane from the entrance of the promenade with the ships on his right and the houses to his left, and that's when he saw her. Justine Stone. Red hair, lying in the middle of their front lawn, dress soaked through from the rain.

'Justine?' he called hesitantly. What the hell was she doing? By now it was pouring and the open waterfront provided no shelter from the howling wind. He figured his voice had got lost as it floated out across the water, or maybe, it dawned on him, she was hurt. He started running towards her and called out again. Louder.

This time she turned her head and smiled.

'Doesn't it make you feel alive?' she shouted back, her voice cutting through the wind and rain.

'No. It makes me feel cold and shit,' he replied, and she laughed. Really laughed, a deep belly laugh that didn't match her slight frame or the delicate dress she was wearing. And he saw it then. Just how beautiful she was.

'Do you want a hand?' he asked, stretching his arm out. She smiled and took it, letting him pull her up off the grass.

'Jake, isn't it?'

'That's right. Are you going inside?' He nodded towards the house, his T-shirt starting to stick from the rain.

'Not yet.'

He looked at Justine, standing there so freely in the rain when everyone else he knew would be running for shelter, exclaiming loudly how awful the weather was, and wondered what else there was for him to learn about her.

'OK, well.' He tried to think of something else to say, something to keep her talking, but his mind was blank. 'I better be heading off then,' he said and turned away, kicking himself for not being more interesting.

'Jake?' she called after him. 'Say happy birthday to your mum.' Justine had never met his mum and it took him by surprise how personal it was. He wondered if she wanted to keep him talking, though it was probably wishful thinking.

'Would you like to go for a walk?' he heard himself asking, before he had time to change his mind.

'Now? It's your mum's birthday.'

'Not now. Tomorrow. Noon?'

'Actually, I think we should go now,' she grinned wickedly. 'I can come with you to find your mum. Don't worry, I won't intrude. I just fancy the walk.'

'It's raining and you're soaked through.' He tried not to stare at her, but he couldn't look away. She was captivating. Vibrant. She was the most beautiful girl he'd ever seen.

'So? I'm already wet-through, what does it matter if I get rained on more?'

It was a logic he couldn't argue with.

'OK,' he said, bemused. 'You're sure you definitely don't want to go inside and get changed first? Maybe grab an umbrella? You know, those things someone clever invented to keep us dry?' He laughed.

Justine looked at the house and Jake thought he saw her expression change. She'd seemed so wide-eyed and alive talking to him. But looking back at the house she looked different. Smaller, somehow. Her hands clasped together, in front of her chest.

'Fine. But only to grab an umbrella from the porch. I won't be long. You don't get rid of me that easily, Jake Reynolds.' And all of a sudden she seemed different again, releasing her hands and laughing, face up towards the rain. He convinced himself he'd imagined it. That she hadn't looked scared to go back in that house.

They'd seen each other before, passing shoulder to shoulder in the corridors, but neither had ever really paid attention. They were in different friendship groups. At school, that kind of thing seemed to matter. But today was different, today – they'd both admit later – was the beginning.

It wasn't until towards the end that he thought again about the moment she'd looked towards her house and chosen to stay outside with him in the rain a while longer, and wished he'd asked her what she was so afraid of.

Perhaps, if he had done, then everything that came next could have been avoided.

Chapter Five

I pull up outside our white-cladded house at the top of our cul-de-sac and sit for a moment in silence. This is our house – mine and Noah's. We've worked hard for it. With its blue front-door we'd both spent days agonising over, and the potted plants out the front which Noah has to water because I kill everything. We aren't perfect, I know that, but together we've built a home.

I look at our immaculate, well-loved front lawn with the apple tree we planted the day we moved in, and I know everything is going to change. I wonder how long I can protect Noah from it and realise I am crying. I can't let this life be ripped from me – I will fight for it if it ever comes to it – but even so, as I sit here it feels important for me to drink in every last detail. Just in case.

I enter the bedroom and stare, rooted to the spot, at our wardrobe. It is nothing like the one from my childhood bedroom, and yet, today, that is exactly what it reminds me of.

I crick my neck and tell myself that on the count of three I'll open it. This is my own house. In London. With Noah. Life is different now. I am different.

I pack as lightly as possible, sure I'll be home before Noah returns next week from Paris. As I leave, I hover outside the kitchen doorway, drinking in the dark-blue cupboards with marbled white granite counters. The space was designed with entertaining in mind. A designated area to display our success. It's an impressive kitchen, with hanging chandeliers over the island and a sofa at the far end.

I force myself to keep moving. To close the front door behind me. I tell myself I'll be back before I know it and that when I return nothing will have changed.

I have always been good at lying. Even to myself.

The road leading into Maldon is winding. There is only one road in and out of the town and as the car snakes its way round the corners it feels as though I'm travelling back in time; each corner peeling back another year until finally I'm greeted by the promenade and I'm seventeen again, taking my early walk along the prom to the very tip where a large iron statue of a Saxon stands, marking the Battle of Maldon.

I would sit there watching the sun rise, envisioning what a fantastic sight the Viking ships would have made with their long sleek designs as they stealthily approached the Essex waterways ready for combat. I'd imagine I could hear their rhythmic chant above the seagulls' cries and feel the beat of their drums reverberating through me. How brave they must have been as they prepared themselves for war. I would hope that, sitting there on the water's edge that held so much history, I could absorb some of their courage, bottle it up and take it home with me.

I avoid the turning that would lead to the house we grew up in and instead carry on straight, heading for Max's. I couldn't believe it when he bought a house just around the corner. It made no sense to me that he had actively chosen to stay.

I'm only planning to visit for a few days and I plan on avoiding Mum and our childhood home completely. There's a reason I haven't been back in almost twenty years. Even the memory of that place makes my throat go dry and the air around me feel too heavy, as though it is crushing me. Constricting my ability to breathe. To move. As though I am back there, unable to escape.

And as for Mum? She hadn't been able to get rid of me fast enough. Only one week after my father's death, she entered my room declaring she'd spoken with dad's older sister Aunt Carol. It was decided I was to stay with her and my seventeen-year-old cousin, Charlotte, in South London for a little while. That it would be good for me to 'have a change of scenery' and to spend some time in the city before starting university there.

That 'little while' turned into me living in London for the next eighteen years. I moved Sixth Form and spent the next summer there, before heading off to King's College London. She never came for me. Not once. Never demanded I return. She did not play the part of a distraught mother desperate for her daughter to come back home. Instead, she orchestrated for me to leave, and then she forgot about me.

Since then, our relationship has been confined to the essentials – Christmas, birthdays and big events. My mother has never invited me back into her home, and in return I've never invited her to mine. We function as a family unit – for Max and for show (the Stones have always been good at that) – but there is no intimacy. She is my mother, but there is no mothering. It would be easy to claim it started when she shipped me off to Aunt Carol's as soon as the opportunity arose, but that simply isn't true.

Mother. No, she has never lived up to the word.

It feels unnatural now, to be driving towards her, but I remind myself I'm not here for her, I'm here for Jake.

I shake the thought. No, I am here for the truth.

Every single curtain is drawn. It's the first thing I notice as I pull into Max's driveway. I'm a stickler for details, it's part of my job. It strikes me as odd, particularly on a day as bright and sunny as this. Usually, even when we were children, Max would be the first to declare we should make the most of summer.

I knock on the door, loudly, but there is no answer. Max's car isn't in the driveway so I try calling him instead. It goes straight to voicemail, just as it had every time I tried calling him on the drive here, so I decide to grab a coffee from the coffee shop on the corner; sandwiched between the fish-and-chip shop and the rundown hairdresser's.

We used to love escaping the house on a Friday night to indulge in fish and chips from here, wrapped in greasy brown paper, the smell of vinegar soaking into our clothes. Max had started the tradition, walking me there every Friday night from the age of eight. He had just turned ten. If it was freezing, we'd spend the evening sitting at the white plastic tables playing cards, and on the days when it was warm enough, we'd sit eating on the wall outside before getting up to as much mischief as we could at the prom. I always loved our nights here; the fish-and-chip shop felt like our own magic place.

Looking at it now, through adult eyes, the spell of it is broken. I see the worn, blackened sign and the mould framing the windows. The smell of grease no longer enticing, but rather a warning to stay away.

If nothing else, it is a stark reminder of just how differently we see the world as children. Everything is more innocent. I used to look forward to those evenings with Max, but I wonder now why he took it upon himself to take us out of the house. Even as a teenager when he should have been down the park with friends drinking White Lightning out of the bottle, he was with me, eating fish and chips.

Today I don't go in, instead taking a seat in the coffee shop next door, which I'm relieved to see has had a renovation in the years I've been gone.

When they politely ask me to leave at the end of the day, I move to the car – at least there I have aircon. It is hot this July. Record-breakingly hot. By eight p.m. I've been waiting for five hours. I try Max's mobile again but, as I've come to expect, it doesn't even ring. Whether he's somewhere with no signal or no battery I don't know, but either way it's left me with no choice.

Bloody Max.

She smiles and I'm surprised to see it reaches her eyes. They widen and curve upwards at the corners. Then I see it falter and, although she is still smiling, the moment is lost.

'Hi Mum, surprise,' I say and stretch my smile over my teeth as wide as it can go.

'Don't just stand there, come in out of the cold,' she says, pulling me towards her for a hug. She is small, smaller than I remember, and I can feel each of her vertebrae through her cardigan.

She ushers me in. It's been years since I was last here, but the same sense of claustrophobia pours over me now as it did back then. Funny really, given it's a huge house. As I follow Mum through into the formal lounge, I can almost imagine hearing the swell of the last Christmas party Dad held right before he died. I shake my head and focus on feeling the ground beneath my feet. I am not there. They are not here. *He* is not here.

I don't know if she does it on purpose or if I'm taking it all too personally, but it feels deliberate; as though she is making a point that I am a guest here. That this is no longer considered my home. The other, less childish part of my brain reasons with me that perhaps she's just trying to be a good host.

Whatever the reason for it, I wish with every bone in my body we were sitting in the snug instead. The formal lounge is too big; its vastness swamping us and my mum's small frame. This room used to be full to the brim with Dad's laughter – surrounded by his friends, of course – I was rarely included but would sit on the stairs and catch as much gossip flowing out of the door as possible.

I break the silence first. I am the one, after all, who has turned up uninvited at her door. There are already too many lies dividing us; I can't bring myself to add any more into the mix, so I decide the best way forward is to keep it simple.

'Would it be OK if I stay a few days?'

'Of course. You're always welcome here, you know that. Now, I'll just put the kettle on and you can tell me all about that fancy case you were working on a few months ago. We were all very excited to see you make the news.' She makes to leave the room but before she's reached the door she turns back. 'Just a couple of days, you say?'

Technically, I'd said a few, and again I wonder if it is intentional. I don't correct her, confirming instead that I'll be out of her hair by Saturday and not bothering to argue that being on the very edge of a press conference shown on BBC news after a politician was sentenced for sexual assault does not qualify as being the new town celebrity. I wasn't even lead on the case.

I hope Max is back soon – I'm not prepared to leave without answers, but I also don't know how long I can bear being in this house. I make a mental note to ask Mum where he is tomorrow, deciding not to mention it tonight; I'd rather she didn't know she was second choice, although I'm sure she's already worked it out.

After tea I make my excuses and head to bed. Mum assures me I'm welcome to stay in what used to be my old bedroom and has since been converted to a guest room.

Unusually, this doesn't fill me with a sense of abandonment but instead I am reassured. Relief floods through me and although I can feel the tell-tale signs of the hammering in my head returning, I tell myself that while certain aspects of the room will still exist, I will not find my younger self still in there. I am here. Standing on this side of the door. I am free.

It means I am unprepared, as I enter, to see the wallpaper is unchanged. A yellow and lilac floral print on one wall. I haven't been home in eighteen years and I assumed she would have changed it. That 'converted to a guest room' meant there would be no trace of it as my old room. More importantly, no trace of the night of the Christmas party all those years ago.

I close my eyes. Count to ten. *I can do this*, I tell myself. I have no choice. I head to the en suite but as I run the tap the basin becomes stained with red, rivulets running down the side. I turn the tap off, fast, but the blood keeps flowing, filling the sink until it overflows, dripping on to the floor.

I slam the door behind me, grabbing the duvet and pillow off the bed. I knew it would be hard to return and I had prepared myself for the psychological challenge, at least as much as was possible, but I realise now I was not ready for the physical assault of it. How being back here, in this room, would force the blood to pump so violently round my body that my eyes would sting.

Perhaps I'll try again tomorrow if Max still hasn't shown up – a bit like getting back on the horse after a nasty fall – but for now, I'll have to put up with the sofa.

Chapter Six

I start the day with my usual two paracetamol before calling Noah to tell him where I am. His voice sounds silky-smooth as he answers the phone.

'You're in Maldon? Can I ask why?'

'Work is quiet and you're away.' I try to bat it away, but I also know this is huge news. Noah knows I've never come back here.

'So, how is it?' he asks, taking it in his stride. He sounds jovial and intrigued, as though me being in Maldon is exciting rather than terrifying. As far as Noah is aware, my career has grounded me in London but I'm still close with Max. I've kept him away from the family get-togethers as much as possible, so he's not been witness to the awkwardness that pervades my mother's and my relationship. Distant but not dysfunctional, is most likely how he thinks of me and my mum. How wrong he is.

'It's nice. A bit weird,' I admit. 'I'm staying in my old room.' It's a white lie – I stayed on the sofa the entire night but that would be impossible to explain to him.

'Ah, surrounded by teenage memories. God, I don't miss those days.' He laughs lightly. If only he knew just how right he is. I do not miss the past.

'One second, I'm just putting you on speakerphone. I need to pull my suitcase out from under the bed,' I say, crouching down and stretching my arm out.

'You still haven't unpacked? That's not like you.'

He's right, normally the first thing I do when we go away is unpack and diligently hang everything up – I claim it makes somewhere feel more homely. But here it is different.

'I know, I've just been so busy since I arrived. Right, so sorry, I need to jump in the shower but have a great day. I love you.'

'I love you,' he replies, his voice deep and sincere. It makes me feel dirty, as though I need to scrub off my guilt. The lies are already stacking up.

I get to work pinning the case files in some sort of order on to the wall in what used to be Dad's study. I can hear Mum creeping down the stairs and wonder why she still does that: walk around the house trying to be as inoffensive as possible. Dad is gone. There's no one left to tiptoe around. I want to tell her to put loud music on, to throw things, to let rip. Scream. I am sure she needs to.

Not once have I ever seen her lose control. I heard Dad. I felt the aftershock of their arguments. But I never once saw her crack. It didn't impress me. Instead, quite the opposite. How could she be so cold? So detached. Did she not know we felt it too? Did she not care? She was there, in the house with us, but she wasn't. Always creeping. Always quiet. I just wanted her to wake up and show me it was OK for us to make a fuss. But she never did. She simply kept going. Day after day. And so we all had to.

I cannot forgive her for that.

She pops her head around the door, like a puppet on a string.

'Justine. What on earth are you doing in here?' She looks from me to the wall, where Jake's mugshot is pinned in the centre, and I see her face visibly pale.

'Why didn't you tell me?' I try to keep my voice as level as possible but I can't stop it from rising higher at the end.

'What is this?' She is completely still. Her control, compared to my lack of it, unnerves me.

'The new case I'm working on.' I just got off the phone with Belinda, the head police media officer, and know the story is going to break on this morning's BBC news nine a.m. slot. I glance at my watch. Eight seventeen a.m.

'Brad Finchley,' I say with a smirk. I am being unkind but I am angry. 'Or should I say, Jake Reynolds, was arrested one month ago on account of murdering two people. He was arrested where he was living, in Maldon.'

She stays silent.

'When did you find out?' This is what I really want to know. Right now I don't care if he did it or not, I care when my mother found out Jake had returned and how long she has been keeping it from me. 'Why didn't you tell me he was back?' And this time I am shouting. Proof, once again, that she forgot about me long ago.

I see a flash of something across her face. Hurt, anger, indignation, pride. I can't work it out and it's gone before I have time to process it. She lowers her eyes and then looks up at me, slowly.

'As far as I know, he turned up about three months ago. I wanted to protect you. That's all I've ever wanted to do.' She says the last part quietly and I know it's the truth, but she failed. On every account. Parents aren't meant to fail at keeping their children safe.

This is new territory for us. She shipped me off so soon after Dad's death that we haven't learnt how to exist as a family without him, even after all this time. He had always been there. Commanding attention. Giving attention. Taking it away. It feels strange now, without him.

No one tells you how to grieve your father at just eighteen years old. A police report will tell you that on the sixteenth of December 2005 my father died while driving under the influence. He lost control of his car going too fast round one of the country lane corners, hurtling down a bank before smashing into a tree. As if that hadn't caused enough damage, the car caught fire.

I am surprised when Mum stretches out her hand and places it over mine. I try not to flinch.

'I'm sorry, maybe I should have said something.' It is a concession. 'Should you really be working on this case, though?'

'No, but I need answers.'

She nods, biting her bottom lip as she does so. 'Then what?'

'I don't know.' And it's true. I have absolutely no idea what happens next; it depends on what I find.

I pick up my cup of hot steaming coffee and let it burn my hands. While I wait for the news segment to air, I rake over the witness statements again, first turning to the full statement from the Rushnells' neighbour.

My name is Elizabeth Smith. I'm 79 and live at number 32 Cherry Tree Grove, Epsom, Surrey. My neighbours were Mark and Beverley Rushnell. My semi-detached house is linked to theirs so that my living room runs parallel to their kitchen-diner. On the 15th June I had brought over a Victoria sponge for them around midday.

I didn't stay long but Beverley seemed upset and a little jumpy. They hadn't told me much but over the past week I'd heard a few disturbances: raised voices and a lot of crying, which was unusual. I'd never really heard much before. It had always been something I told friends and family when they came over. That although it was semi-detached, I couldn't hear the neighbours. So I knew something was up and that's why I'd made the cake. I was trying to be a good neighbour, I suppose. Community isn't what it used to be when I was a girl.

I left my house to go to my weekly book club at five p.m. The road was mostly empty. I remember seeing a big white van, and a few cars which I'm afraid I can't remember very well, but nothing that seemed out of the ordinary – mostly they were neighbours' cars, and a motorbike which I'd seen a couple of times before parked further up the road. There was nothing that stood out as strange. I returned home at seven fifteen p.m. and decided to check in on Beverley again. I was still a bit shaken up from how nervous she'd seemed earlier. I thought perhaps if I caught her again and Mark wasn't in, she might open up to me a little more. Not that I thought Mark was to blame, he was such a gentle man, but it can be difficult to talk when someone else is listening.

Anyway, I rang the doorbell and there was no answer. It was unusual as all the lights were on and their car was in the driveway. Mark and Beverley were both very keen on clean living. Everything from being vegan to recently buying an electric car. It just wasn't in their nature to go out and leave all the lights on. I rang twice more and then I started to get a bad feeling so I peered through the front window. I couldn't see much as there was furniture in the way but I could make out a man's leg – I could tell by the shoe – as though he were lying on his back on the floor. That was when I dialled 999.

The fact their neighbour wasn't in so didn't hear anything isn't particularly helpful. In general, this statement could be difficult for the prosecution. I take out a highlighter and mark through 'over the past week I'd heard a few disturbances'. Could the defence argue Mark killed his wife then shot himself? Would it account for the point-blank range?

I can feel myself wanting to believe it, and not for the first time know this is exactly why I shouldn't be working on the case. That I am jeopardising everything. Still, I need to know.

Why did you do it Jake? What drove you to kill two people?

But even as I think it, I question if what I really want to find out is why he left me when I needed him the most.

I let a little more time pass after the news has gone live before getting ready, allowing for the latest gossip to ripple through the town. I figure people will have looser tongues now they potentially know a real-life murderer. The news segment referred to him as Brad Finchley as it's now his legal name, but it also revealed he'd previously been known as Jake Reynolds. As I'd known they would be, journalists are all over his name change. Why? Who was Jake Reynolds? What was he running from? It will draw the press here, I am sure of it. I can't stay too long.

I'm sure the locals would have recognised him anyway, but there's no doubt now that the town will be riled up. They'll all pretend to be horrified of course, but I bet at least half the people I talk to today will secretly be revelling in it.

There's a reason why true-crime documentaries are so popular. I used to be surprised by the crowds that would turn up to watch the most gruesome displays of human depravity play out in the court of law, rustling their sweet wrappers in their pockets as if they were simply at the cinema. Now I barely notice them; they've become part of the package.

I also know I need to strike now, before the media circus arrives. No doubt the Rushnells' friends and family will also descend on the town. People will start to alter their memories to fit in with those of the newcomers; the targeted questions the media ask will shape what they think they know; the friends and family will make Mark and Beverley feel more real to them. Their deaths even more tragic. All these things will change and mould what they believe to be true about Jake. I have no time or need for their distorted memories. I need to act fast.

When in chambers or court there are all sorts of convoluted rules around appearance and I'm so used to wearing perfectly ironed white shirts, court heels and black suits which cover my knees that I'm a little lost when it comes to blending in with the fashion. But blending in is exactly what I want to do today.

I pull on a pair of loose mom jeans I bought purely because all my friends seemed to be wearing them, and a pale-green cotton top. My hair would normally be scraped back into an unflattering ponytail but I leave it loose. It's not the way I'd usually dress to meet with potential witnesses but nothing about how I'm handling this case is the way I usually would – or should – do things.

I decide to try the pub on the other side of town first. It's the closest one to Jake's house and it seems as good a place to start as any other. I couldn't sleep last night thinking about the gun they found hidden in a bag under a floorboard below Jake's late mum's bed.

It was found buried at the bottom of a gym bag. His mum had recently died, only two months before the murders, after a short battle with cancer, and his dad passed away six years prior from a heart attack. Jake was an only child. His fingerprints were found both on the gun itself and on the outside of the bag. Not only that, but fibres from one of the caps he owned were found on the dead bodies of both victims.

It isn't conclusive but it's pretty fucking *persuasive*.

Over the years, I've become pretty expert at leaving my emotional reactions aside. People do awful things. All the time. But the thought of it being Jake who pulled the trigger? Who hid his gun under his dead mother's bed after coldheartedly murdering two people? It turns my insides out, as though my body is rejecting the very idea of it. The small voice inside my head is back again, reminding me that this is exactly why barristers are not permitted to work on cases where they know any of the people involved. It is why I cannot keep doing this much longer.

Before I leave the house, I jot down another note:

Was he scared? Was the gun for protection?

I think again about Mr Rushnell, killed at point-blank range, and know it is wishful thinking. It was purposeful. Violent. Whoever shot him made sure they left no margin for error. Did Jake really have it in him to be that callous? I close my eyes and count to ten, feeling my legs turn weak at the possibility.

Usually, I'd turn to Noah to ground me and keep my emotions steady when it feels like the universe is too cruel. When I feel like the darkness is going to consume me, too. I face it often in my job, and Noah always manages to calm me at the end of the day. But he isn't here, and even if he was, this is something I have to face alone. I breathe in deeper and slowly unfurl my spine, back to standing tall.

Aya has equipped me for this. I can do it.

Chapter Seven

None of the witnesses listed in the case report mention the Blue Eagle but that doesn't mean it isn't a missing piece of the puzzle. The detectives have done a thorough job, I could tell that as I read through the investigation, but they were working backwards from the murders, whereas I am moving forwards – from eighteen-year-old Jake towards Brad Finchley. My hope is that the two will balance each other out, kind of like how a prosecution and defence set-up is meant to result in a fair trial, and I'll end up with the truth.

I realised, as I read and reread through the case that I kept waiting for the pub to turn up somewhere and the fact it never did bothered me. The Blue Eagle had always been Jake's local and he came from a family where those kind of things were passed through the generations. His grandad had worked there, then his dad spent every Friday night perched on a stool at the right side of the bar.

As soon as Jake turned eighteen that September, he worked part-time there and every weekend he and his dad played pool until the early hours. If Jake had been back for three months prior to his arrest, as Mum claimed, I'm certain he would have made at least a few visits here.

I swing open the heavy oak door and my senses are flooded with déjà vu. I push it away, and purposefully stride towards the bar. I'm risking a lot being here. What if someone recognises me and works out that I am also working Jake's case? What if they report me before I'm able to spin my own version of events to Charles?

Even though on first look it seems as though everyone here is too young to remember me – it has been eighteen years after all – I am confident every single one of them will know of my family. That any mention of the Stone family will be closely followed by sympathetic looks as well as an anecdote or two about how they, or someone they know, used to be close to my father.

Maldon is a small town. Too small. And my father was well respected – twice elected town councillor. Every year, Maldon hosts its famous mud race across the estuary on the first Saturday of August. No one can remember when or why the tradition began. After my father's death, it was changed to be held in his honour, raising money for the local youth club he'd got planning permission for before he'd died. Even people who never knew him are confronted annually with banners of his face staring down at them and asked to contribute money in his name.

I feel eyes on me but keep my feet moving towards the bar. These people don't know me. They know my family. But they don't know me. I remind myself they are simply staring because they *don't* know me. That's the twisted thing about a small town like this: everyone either looks at you because they know you, or they look at you because they don't.

The barmaid clocks my approach and diverts her gaze. I let out a small laugh. Avoiding eye contact with customers was Jake's number-one tip for getting through his shifts. Undeterred, I perch on the bar stool furthest right, just as Jake's dad would have done.

The interior has changed. What were once stained grey-blue walls now resemble something straight off my Pinterest board with deep, rich blue panelling running along the bottom half of the walls. There are industrial-style hanging lights and large gold mirrors. I bet the toilet walls are lined with small potted cacti on floating wooden shelves. The gentrification of Maldon's historic seaside high street has clearly begun.

I'm pleased to see there are still two pool tables round the back and the bar is in the same place, anchoring it in the past. It may be spruced up, but it's still the same old Blue Eagle.

I order a ginger ale and sit back, biding my time. I want to observe the bar staff a little more before I dive straight in. Figure them out, work out the best strategy. I am good at reading people and changing tack accordingly. You have to be when trying to convince a jury. It's important to find out what makes each of them tick and then, as you go through the case, make sure you're catering to each one; giving yourself the best chance of a unanimous vote: guilty or not guilty.

I notice how the barmaid touches her hair when she's talking to the guy she's working with. She also seems to get louder whenever she's near him. There's an edge to it that tells me she's hoping he's paying attention even though she isn't talking directly to him. Perfect.

'I bet you two can't stop hearing about it today?' I say, making sure my voice is loud enough for him to hear too, including them both in my conversation from the very beginning. 'I imagine news becomes very old news fast when you work behind a bar.'

They look at each other and I'm surprised to see them frown, then look away. 'I guess, a bit,' the girl says and then turns from me. This is not what I'd expected at all. I thought they would jump at the opening to gossip. That once I'd lifted the lid, it would all come pouring out. Clearly, I'm going to have to work harder than I'd first thought.

'I imagine working here is a real skill. Being able to read the punters. Not just what their favourite drinks are but also predicting how the night might go. Staying one step ahead of the customer at every turn.' I draw the conversation away from Brad

Finchley back to safer ground while giving her the opportunity to impress me – more importantly, him.

'Oh absolutely. This one time we had a group of lads in, right, and I clocked straight away they were right pricks. When they started asking for shots, I watered them down.'

'So smart.' I draw the words out, slowly, my eyes widening in admiration. 'I bet you've learnt all the tricks. What about Brad Finchley? Did you think he was a right prick too?'

She hesitates but doesn't immediately turn away, unlike before.

'I worked as a barmaid one summer and punters always underestimated me.' I make myself relatable but it's also meant as a challenge – have I underestimated her, too? Will she rise to it?

'Well,' she says, leaning in but keeping her body open enough so the guy she's desperate to impress can still hear her. And that's how it's done. Hook, line and sinker. 'I saw him here twice,' she continues. 'First time he seemed all right, kept himself to himself, sat right where you are now actually. But the next time I saw him was a proper disaster. He was violent.' Her voice weakens as she barely whispers the word 'violent' and for a second I panic she's about to cry. 'God, what if I could have saved that couple? I told my manager but maybe, like, I should have reported it or something.'

'It's OK, nothing could have stopped what happened. You are not to blame.' I say the last part forcefully, allow her to compose herself and then press on, 'What was so odd about him, that second time?'

'It wasn't him that was odd, it was the other one.'

'He was with someone else?'

'Yeah. The other guy was a right creep. He kept looking at me every time I came too close. Maybe he thought I was listening in. They ordered drinks then sat in the corner over there.' She points to two armchairs tucked away in the corner. 'I went down to the cellar, just for a second mind, and when I came back, that Brad guy was holding the other one against the wall by his neck. I shouted and he let him go. The other guy picked up his coat, downed the rest of his beer and walked out. But he was smirking. He'd just been pinned against a wall by his throat but he was smirking. Creep.'

'What happened then?'

'Brad picked up the rest of his glass and threw it at the wall. Why'd he have to go and do that? The other guy had left and now I had to bloody clear up their mess. Anyway, he looked at me, said *Sorry, I'll go* – too bloody right, I said – and then he left. Didn't come in here again as far as I know.'

'And when was this?' I check myself – this is not a cross-examination – and try to soften my questioning. 'Sounds pretty scary. You did well not to let it escalate.'

'I know, right. I remember it was my first day back from holiday. So the fourth of May.'

'Do you have any idea who the other guy was?'

'Nah. Never seen him before but I'm not really from round here anyway. We moved a year ago. My manager acted well weird about it though when I told him. Usually, he'd have got the right hump and sworn blind he'd kill the guys who dared mess up his pub. But he just put his head in his hands and told me to get back to work. Then, this morning, he called me into his office and said there was no need to ever say Brad had been in here. To distance ourselves from it all. So when you came in here asking questions, I didn't say anything. You ain't the first person to try to talk about it to us today.'

'Right. And who is your manager?'

'Jimmy Falcon. Do you know him?'

When I think of Jimmy Falcon, I think of fumbling in the garden bushes at Max's eighteenth birthday party. As my older brother's best mate, before Jake came along, I'd had a crush on

Jimmy for most of my teenage years. When he was the DJ for Max's birthday and kept filling my glass up with vodka he had stashed under his decks, I thought he was the coolest guy I'd ever met. Jimmy Falcon with his too-tight leather jackets, flannel shirts and Vans. Jimmy Falcon – my very first kiss back when I thought idolising someone you didn't really know was what love felt like. More like fancying a celebrity than anything else. Naïve, but certainly less painful.

'No, I'm not from round here,' I say.

Just before I leave the pub, I tear a page out of my notebook and scribble down my mobile number. No name. I hand it to the barmaid and ask her to call me if she thinks of anything else.

'Wait. Are you a journo?' Her face has turned grey and she looks genuinely frightened. What of? I wonder. Me?

'I'm not a journalist. You can trust me. I promise.'

'No, no, no, I thought you were just a nosy customer.' She starts clawing at her neck.

'Just call me, OK. I'm looking for the truth, that's all,' I insist.

As I walk out on to the street my words bounce around my head. *You can trust me. The truth.* I made it sound so simple and easy. I clench my teeth. Count to ten. When I reach seven my phone starts ringing. Surely she can't already be calling me? I pull it out of my jacket pocket and see Noah's name lighting up my screen. I hit the red button to cancel the call. Not now, Noah. I don't want him to sense something is wrong, and I'm not sure I can push away the panic engulfing me enough to keep it from my voice.

I can already feel myself beginning to spiral. The sharp decline into what can only be described as a black cloud of impending doom. It's such a strange phrase, 'impending doom', it feels melodramatic, but when Aya first used it to describe the anxiety that sometimes paralyses me, it fit perfectly. It is the closest I think language can come to describe the whirlwind of fear whipping up inside me.

Aya.

I close my eyes and smile. Forever my life raft, I realise that this afternoon is our weekly session, which means I only need to make it through the next few hours before she can help me. I fire off a quick text, checking she's OK for today's session to be over Zoom instead of in-person, but I don't yet reveal that – after all these years – I'm finally back here. I wonder how she'll react. I want to see her expression when I tell her. She replies 'of course' immediately and I roll my shoulders back.

I am not alone.

I repeat it as I walk until my pulse begins to slow. Normally I talk everything through with Noah. I've always been in awe of his ability to keep his own feet on the ground when mine are doing somersaults. It's one of the reasons I was first drawn to him and why we work so well together. In among the chaos, Noah always remains anchored. Not being able to lean on him right now is taking its toll, not least because I could do with his strength through this, but because I can also feel it distancing me from him, inserting a wedge between us. All my secrets are resurfacing, threatening to tear us apart.

I see them as soon as I round the corner away from the high street. The vultures are descending, just like I knew they would. The journalists are huddled together outside the police station, no doubt waiting for a statement from DS Sorcha Rose. She didn't arrest Jake and I doubt she even had anything to do with the case – it would have been handled by the Met police – but she's the face of this town. They'll want her to comment.

Soon they'll spread themselves further, trying to build up a better picture of who Jake was. What his life was like – no doubt digging to find a reason for why he turned into the monster they believe him to be. Was it something from his childhood? I'm sure it's the reason they're here. It's part of our fascination with true crime: what makes a murderer?

Everyone knew we were a couple back then, I'm sure my name will end up being mentioned. It won't be long before they come knocking on Mum's door. I need to be prepared.

What will they ask? What should I tell them?

BEFORE

JAKE – THE BOYFRIEND

Justine didn't change her mind about going back inside the house. Just as she'd said she would, she simply ran to fetch an umbrella from the porch and rushed straight back to where Jake was sheltering under a tree, her dress still soaked through. Her hair hanging wet against her shoulders. Rain dripping from her chin.

'Ready.' She grinned and he laughed as he ducked under her umbrella and took the handle from her.

Justine didn't stop talking as they walked from the prom to his mum's office, looping her arm through his as if they were old friends. The strangest thing about it all was that it didn't feel awkward or forced.

'You wouldn't dare,' Justine laughed, realising what he was doing – as for the third time he purposely strode straight towards the biggest puddle he could find, forcing Justine to either walk through it or sacrifice the umbrella. This time, instead of running round it, she walked straight through and then kicked the water towards him.

Jake pretended to look furious, before joining in.

What were they doing? He'd not acted this childlike in years. It felt freeing.

Was this it? Was this what falling in love felt like?

He knew he was a romantic – his dad always told him so – but he didn't think he was imagining it, nor building it up to be more than it was. He could see the way she was looking at him. It was electric.

Shit, his dad was going to be so mad if they were late for dinner.

'Truce. I call a truce,' he shouted, holding his palms up, and Justine raised her eyebrows threateningly at him. 'As much as I would love to do this all day, I do need to get to Mum before Dad kills me.'

'Yes sir, sorry sir.' Justine curtsied and ducked back under the umbrella.

Jake's mum spotted them through the office window and her mouth fell open at the sight of them. Both drenched through.

'What are you doing here?' she asked, rushing to usher them through the door into the warmth. Always so mum-like.

'I'm under strict instructions from Dad to march you back home as dinner is booked for seven p.m. and, in his words not mine, *You know she'll take bloody ages to get ready.*'

'The cheek!' His mum looked towards Justine, pretending to be outraged. And then she looked back towards him, where he could see the curiosity sparkling in her eyes. He'd never introduced a girl to his mum before. Was that what this was? It had been one walk, but he was pretty sure it was going to be the first of many. 'And Justine? Will you be joining us for dinner?' she asked.

Jake felt himself stiffen awkwardly, suddenly feeling vulnerable. His mum could always be so forward.

'Oh thank you, but I really don't want to intrude on your birthday. I was just keeping Jake company. Plus, as you can see, I am soaked through and there's not time for me to go back home and out again.'

'Well, if you don't mind borrowing something then I'm sure I can find a dress for you back at our place?'

Justine looked towards Jake questioningly and he shrugged, grinning, as if to indicate this was complete madness but absolutely, of course.

'OK then, yes please. I'd love to join you,' Justine gushed and Jake's whole body filled with butterflies. She'd said yes.

'Brilliant, that's settled then. I've got just the thing for you. You'll look divine.' Jake thought he'd never seen his mum looking so pleased with herself, but this time, he really didn't mind her being so meddling. As the three of them headed out the back and clambered into his mum's car, she winked at him, and Jake realised he'd inherited his romantic side from his mother.

Chapter Eight

I'd tried therapists before Aya, but none of them stuck. With their stark wooden chairs and overbearing silences – the way they'd deflect every question back to me – it was boring. It showed me they'd never understand.

The ones who came before Aya had all diligently stuck to their textbooks and their processes. They wanted to fix me, I'd decided. But I wasn't sure I wanted fixing. I just wanted to be heard. Not straight away. And maybe not everything. But I wanted to feel that one day the option might be there, if ever I needed it. That whoever was listening at least had the capacity to try and understand the nuance of it all. How that night – the night of the Christmas party – was a culmination of everything that had come before it.

Aya had shown me very early on that she wasn't a stickler for the rules, that she was also capable of blurring boundaries. Those beginning sessions were purely a safe space for me to tell my story. No active therapy took place. She asked no questions. Not even how things made me feel. She just listened. The dissecting it all would come later.

The last thing I'd told her before our time ran out was that Max had returned home from university for the Christmas break. I knew the next part of my story was always going to be the hardest to tell, and the day before I was meant to meet her, I got scared and convinced myself I couldn't go through with it. I didn't trust myself not to say the wrong thing, so I called her and told her the process had already made me feel much better – thank you very much – so I was ending our sessions because I didn't need them any longer.

I hung up and that should have been that. Except it wasn't – just two days later, Aya turned up at my door. She looked at me and declared, 'I'm here to listen, when you're ready to trust me with it,' before walking back down the driveway. A month later I called her to schedule another session and, from then on, I've never missed a single one.

'Afternoon Justine.' She smiles out at me from behind the screen and already I feel a little warmer. 'Do you want to start by telling me where you are?'

I wet my lips before saying, 'I'm at my mother's house.' This is not going to be small news for Aya and I feel a little thrill run through me in anticipation of her reaction. We've discussed many times the fact I've sworn never to return, that what happened here is not something I want to revisit, yet she barely blinks at my big dramatic revelation.

How often do clients surprise their therapist? Perhaps the mark of a truly good therapist is to know what their client's future holds before they do. Preparing them for it. Maybe my being here isn't a surprise to Aya at all. I find myself disappointed.

'That must be really difficult for you. How are you feeling?'

'I'm not sure how to explain it,' I say. Scared. Angry. Sad. Everything in between. None of those.

'That's understandable. Perhaps we can talk about the *why* later? For now, I'd like for us to try and unlock more of an understanding of *how* you're feeling, first. Then you can begin to process it better. Why don't we start with you simply telling me about your mum's house. Can you describe it to me?'

I've set myself up in my old bedroom as it provides more privacy than the study downstairs and I force myself to look straight at the floral wallpaper. To finally let my eyes linger over it. The colours start to run and the flowers no longer look like flowers; instead they morph into faces. Open-mouthed. Screaming.

'I don't know where to start,' I confess as I crick my neck. First left. Then right. Blink hard. I'm not doing very well today.

'Well, as the saying goes, start at the very beginning. In this case, why don't you start with the front door. I'd like you to describe the rooms but to also think about how each room makes you feel now you are back there.' Her voice is calm and soft – a gentle nudge. I wonder if she thinks she's started with something easy. If she doesn't realise she has, in fact, pushed me straight into the deep end.

'The front door is red,' I start. 'It is big. I always think it looks bigger than your average door. Imposing even. But I've never found out if it really is or not. Straight ahead is the kitchen. It stretches along the whole back of the house. Glass doors opening out on to the sloping garden. The kitchen is bright. Sometimes I think it is too bright. Even when the sun has gone down there are far too many lights than are necessary. You can't miss anything. Every spill. Every detail. You can't avoid it. The rooms at the front of the house are darker. Much darker. It's a south-facing garden, you see. Mum is proud of that. She says it helps with the gardening. To the left is the formal lounge leading into a dining space. There is a big oak fireplace. It's ornate. Black carvings. Growing up I thought it was impressive, but now I think it was intended to be and that makes it less so. The act of trying so hard. Then, to the right of the hallway, is the snug. It's supposed to be the cosiest room in the house. Sandwiched between the snug and the kitchen is the study. Being in there I can't help but feel afraid, though I'm unsure of what. And that's the downstairs. Unless you're interested in the toilet.'

Aya smiles in a way that tells me I do not need to describe the toilet unless I want to. And then she crosses her hands neatly in her lap.

'You didn't tell me how the snug makes you feel. Only that it's supposed to be the cosiest room in the house. Is it? Are you spending any time in there?'

I close my eyes. 'No,' I whisper.

'That's understandable. And what about upstairs?'

It is dark. Too dark. I am alone. Hugging my knees.

There are some things Aya knows – like what transpired in the snug – and others she does not.

What about upstairs?

It is obvious to me now that Aya knew all along she was throwing me in the deep end. Waiting to see what lifelines I would give myself. She was never interested in the front door. She knows how I feel about the downstairs and what happened there. It's the upstairs she's interested in. The upstairs that holds the most secrets. Ones, I'm guessing, she suspects she still isn't privy to.

Because a house is never just a house. A house holds all your secrets.

'How about your bedroom?' she continues, on a roll now. I fumble for something to say but she dives in first. 'How about that wall behind you. I can see a hook and the wallpaper is slightly faded. What used to hang there? Was it a picture? A photograph?'

I turn to face the wall – careful to rotate away from the wardrobe rather than towards it – although I don't really need the reminder; I know exactly which picture used to hang there.

'It was a photograph of me and Jake,' I say. 'It was taken on my eighteenth birthday.'

'If I remember correctly, you had a lovely time with him that day. Do you know where the picture is now?'

'It smashed.'

'That's a shame. How does that make you feel?' I'm relieved she's gone down this route, instead of asking what caused it to fall off the wall and smash into a thousand pieces in the first place. This is an easier question to answer. There is no need for me reveal I'd thrown it on to the floor the day I was shipped off to stay with Charlotte and Aunt Carol. One week after Jake left me. One week after Dad died.

'I don't really care. It was all a lie, anyway.'

'What was a lie?'

'That night. My birthday. It was all one big lie.'

BEFORE

JUSTINE

Blood ran down Justine's shin where she'd cut it on the branches by the river, but she couldn't feel it. The adrenalin of being with Jake anaesthetised the pain, even as he scooped her up in his arms and carried her up the stairs. She squealed in delight, wrapping her arms around his neck.

'Thank you for the best birthday,' she said as he placed her down carefully at the top. They needed to be quiet. Her father was supposed to be out for the evening but she was worried his plans might have changed and didn't want to risk waking him in case he was, in fact, home. She understood that as a girl her dad was always going to be more protective of her than Max, but increasingly it felt like the string was pulled too tight. Sometimes she needed space to breathe and to make her own decisions – and that included dating Jake.

The disapproval of her having a boyfriend was palpable. The questions he asked, the looks he gave, it made both her and Jake feel uncomfortable. Was this what every teenage girl felt from their father when dating? She supposed perhaps it was and she was simply imagining it to be worse than it was. That she was, as usual, the problem.

You have too vivid an imagination. It'll get you in trouble, her father used to tell her growing up.

'I do have one more surprise,' Jake said, mischief tugging at his eyes.

'Another?'

He had already presented her with the perfect present earlier that evening over dinner at Finches. She stroked it now, the natural cut simultaneously rough and smooth against her thumb. A gorgeous gold necklace with an irregular green pendant. *Like your eyes*, he'd said. She'd always been conscious of her green eyes and red hair. Aware it made her stand out from the other girls at school. She didn't look like the women in magazines. Too-big eyes. Too-wild hair. But Jake made her feel beautiful.

'Don't get your hopes up,' he warned. 'Your next gift is nothing expensive, and actually I'm not sure it's a good idea.'

'You do not get to do that Jake Reynolds. I demand my present, now,' she pouted, hoping it looked cute rather than childish, but really she had no idea how to play this game where she was meant to be both desirable and conservative. Beautiful but modest.

'Fine, but promise you won't laugh,' he said seriously.

They spilled into her bedroom as one, the two of them too wide to fit through the door, but neither wanting to be separate from the other. All shoulders and limbs, squeezed together.

She realised, as Jake turned round to face her and the moonlight caught the side of his face, that he really did look a little nervous. It was cute.

He fumbled in his jacket pocket before pulling out an envelope and then thrust it sheepishly in her direction. Her name was sprawled on the front in almost illegible handwriting.

'What's this?' She turned it over in her hands.

'I wrote you a letter. I'm not always very good with words, I know, so I wanted to try and let you know how I feel. This was the best way I could think of doing it. Then, whenever you need to, you can read over them.'

She'd never had a letter before. Texts, WhatsApps, emails, yes. But there was something different about a handwritten letter. It was more intimate.

'Can I read it now?'

'If you want.'

She moved to open it but just before she did, she looked up one more time, and the sight of him standing there with the rain outside her window made everything else fall away. All the pain, all the hurt. None of it mattered anymore. It was just Jake and her.

Instinctively, she moved towards him, the unopened letter still clutched in her hand. Something in the way she moved must have seemed different, as Jake looked at her with an intensity as if he understood.

She was ready.

Slowly his fingertips brushed her shoulder. Delicate. Soft but purposeful. She placed her hand on his and then guided him to slip her top off. Never once did he look away, embarrassed or shy. She loved him for that.

She'd heard plenty of friends talk about their awkward firsts but nothing about the way they were moving together felt awkward. She had thought her first time would make her feel vulnerable, but she felt the complete opposite. In control. Strong. Jake, she realised, made her feel fearless. It was a feeling she'd been searching for her whole life, one which until now had always seemed just out of reach.

'Are you sure?' he asked her, stopping for just a moment.

'I'm sure. Stay with me,' she whispered as he lowered her on to the bed. He hadn't stayed over before, and she wanted him to know that this was OK. That she wanted it. Needed him.

'Justine Stone,' he kissed her neck in reply, 'I'll never leave you.'

Chapter Nine

I always find myself in desperate need of some air after my sessions with Aya – a way to reset and prepare myself for the rest of the day – and today is no exception. I didn't set off in this direction intentionally, but subconsciously I've walked myself to the top of Max's road.

I continue until I'm looking directly at his house, hands on my hips, sweat trickling down my spine, and note the curtains are still perfectly drawn. I try his phone and once again it rings straight through to voicemail. We've always been close and, as I hang up, I realise it's been an unusually long time since we last spoke – a couple of weeks at least.

I go over in my mind again our conversation from a couple of months ago. He hadn't made a big thing out of it, and typically he hadn't pushed when I'd said no, but he had asked, and I had ignored him. I should have listened. It has been eating away at me ever since. After everything he's done for me, I should have been able to come when he asked. Instead, I'd put myself first again. I squeeze my hands into fists until my nails push uncomfortably into the flesh of my palms.

I think you should come home, he'd said.

I can't, I'd replied.

And Max being Max – always kind, always my big brother – hadn't asked me again. Why hadn't he pushed me on it? And why, after all these years, had he been asking me to come home?

*   *   *

'Mum, Mum,' I shout as I tear back through the house, letting the front door slam behind me. I find her in the observatory, a glass of wine in her hand, looking out across the water.

'Mum?' I repeat. She smiles sweetly at me but there is something missing in her eyes. As if she's not quite in the room with me but still gazing out to sea. She looks sad. Empty. 'Where's Max? I can't get through to him.'

'Oh, I'm sure he's fine.' It strikes me that I never suggested he wasn't. 'He told me he was going away for a couple of weeks. Maybe he's switched his phone off or something. He deserves a break from always looking after me, I told him I'd be all right here.'

'Did he tell you where he was going? When did you last see him?'

'I'm afraid I can't remember now. He did say. It's, it's on the tip of my tongue . . . It's a shame you'll miss him.' Is that a little dig? A reminder I told her I was leaving tomorrow?

This complicates things. If Max told Mum he was going away, the police will say he isn't a missing person. But I don't understand why he would go on holiday and not tell me. Besides, who turns their phone off on holiday these days? Half the value of holidaying is in the number of 'likes' your photos receive.

Fear begins to crawl under my skin but before I leave, I remember I had something else to ask her. I don't know why I feel the need to ask her right this minute. But something isn't right. I feel it tapping at the base of my skull. A feeling that we are hurtling towards disaster. I just don't know why yet.

'Mum, does the name Rushnell sound familiar to you? I mean, apart from being all over the news?'

'No.' She shakes her head. 'Why do you ask?'

'Just wondering,' I say noncommittally, pulling out my phone. I begin to scroll through Max's socials. The last post I can find is from June. Almost one whole month ago. The guilt gnaws at me.

I think you should come home.
I'm here now, Max, I want to shout.

Because what kind of sister doesn't come when their brother asks them to? When did I morph into this worse version of myself?

I begin to run.

BEFORE

JUSTINE

The water was on the turn, more cold than warm, and the candle wax had started to run over the sides. Still, Justine was determined to savour the peace for as long as she could. Her parents were out so she had the run of the house. She should have been revising, but instead she was taking full advantage of the fact no one was around to witness her procrastination.

She closed her eyes, took a deep breath in, and sank lower into the bathtub; submerging herself entirely before forcing her eyes open so she could see her red hair floating on the surface above her. Small bubbles escaped from her mouth, rising to the top.

She didn't hear it, instead feeling the tub vibrating slightly. She pulled herself up, gasping for air, to see her phone screen lit up on the side displaying a call from Max.

Another day, another slice of university gossip from her brother. He liked to keep her updated with the latest college antics. He felt bad for leaving her at home, and Justine enjoyed the escapism of hearing about his time away. Soon, that would be her.

'Hello,' she sang down the phone. But he didn't reply. She couldn't make out any words at all, just gut-busting cries. She imagined them violently shaking his body. Bent over, hunched, trapping his words deep down in his stomach.

Justine had never heard Max cry before.

She shot out of the bath and the momentum forced the water to flow over the edges.

Max was less than two years older than her, and they had grown up the best of friends. He was, she knew, her better half – stronger, wiser and generally more sensible – it was he who had always taken on her pain so that she didn't have to. Justine wasn't quite sure what to say now their roles were reversed. His pain seemed to travel through the ether and worm its way across her skin.

'Lily is gone. She's broken up with me.' Finally, she managed to work out his words. At least he was safe. The worst-case scenarios, of him lying hurt somewhere, ruled out.

A broken heart. His first broken heart. Justine had never experienced one herself; she'd never been in love before Jake. Listening to Max now it was only by imagining her life without Jake in it that she felt perhaps she could understand how he was feeling. As if Lily had left and taken all the best parts of him with her.

Still on the phone, she dried herself off as fast as she could and jumped in the car; wet trickling down her spine, large patches seeping through her clothes.

'I'm coming,' she reassured him. 'Stay right where you are.'

Cambridge had an energy about it unlike anywhere else she'd been and, as she fought her way through the streets – weaving past hordes of students and dodging out the way of cyclists – it struck her just how small and insignificant their lives really were. It felt unfair that the world would not stop for them. That no matter how awful things got, good things would carry on happening to those around them.

She supposed she should take solace in it but all she felt was anger. That to all these swarming bodies, Max's grief did not matter. It was unjust, yes, she thought, that was the word for it.

'You see Justine, we called you that because we knew you would always fight for what was right, fair and just. Justice is the very glue that holds our society together. It must never be compromised.' She'd heard the speech about her namesake more times than she could remember, her father telling her with swollen pride that they had named her after the values they knew she'd grow up to uphold.

It seemed to her, aged only eighteen, that they'd overestimated her. She wondered if it wasn't for this legacy her parents had already forged for her that she might have chosen to study a different subject at university. Psychology perhaps. But her dad had worked his way up to owning his own law firm and she was, apparently, destined to follow in his footsteps.

She found him on a park bench. True to his word, he had not moved.

'Max?' she called gently and, as he slowly lifted his head from his hands, she felt a wave of emotion envelop her.

'It's OK, I'm not going anywhere,' she said, taking her place beside him on the bench. His breathing shuddered, threatening to spill over into tears again. This time she silently placed her hand in his.

It reminded her of all the times they'd hidden under the stairs together playing hide-and-seek as children. Side by side. Hand in hand, until Max would declare they'd won the game and could emerge once more.

She couldn't fix it, couldn't force Lily to take him back, but she was with him. Just like they'd always promised each other, it was still the two of them against the world. Most importantly, Max had not been alone.

Loneliness – isolation – they both knew, made things feel scarier. It's why they'd always chosen to hide together.

Chapter Ten

It is raining. It's that hot sticky summer rain where you can't quite distinguish what is rainwater and what is sweat. Mingling together. Cloying. I'm scrambling around on my knees overturning every large stone I can find lining the back of Max's house. Our 'weird aunt', as she is commonly referred to, bought us both a stone key holder at Christmas one year and as much as we laughed about it at the time, I still use it and I'm hoping Max does too.

After ten minutes I give up, instead reaching for the largest stone I've managed to find. After a count to three, I hurl it at the back door. The glass shatters, scattering into tiny fragments at the base of my feet. The sound makes my head swim and I am transported to another night. A much colder one with shards of glass embedded in my feet.

I take a moment to pull myself back to the present and press down firmly on the pressure building at the base of my skull, providing only a few seconds of relief. I imagine what Aya would say and list one thing I can see, one I can hear and one I can smell.

A discarded beer bottle.

Seagulls.

A barbecue.

I am standing in Max's back garden. I am not there. I am safe.

Now what? I remember a case I worked on last year where the defendant had broken into five houses in one night. He was sentenced to fifteen years. But this is different. I'm not going to steal anything, I just want to take a look inside and check Max is OK. But staring at the jagged edges of the glass now framing a gaping hole, I'm not quite sure what my next move should be. How exactly I get from here to inside without shredding my arms into little fleshy snakes. I have a cushion in my car which I use to support my back when driving and I'm sure there are at least a couple of jumpers lying around on the back seats. It's time to get creative.

When I am finished, my arm resembles something out of *Dr Who. I am a Dalek, exterminate.* I use the cushion to push through the loose jagged bits of glass and make the hole wider, before very slowly and carefully lowering my arm through. I am praying that Max left a key in the lock.

Voilà.

I turn the key and more glass crunches underfoot as I transfer my weight. I am in. I know it's against the law, no matter how much I convince myself I'm just a concerned sister, and yet I feel a jolt of excitement – of triumph – pass through me.

I've had many defendants claim a life of crime is addictive and while I certainly don't plan on making breaking and entering a habit, I can see the sweet appeal of the rush that comes with it. Perhaps it takes a certain kind of person to feel excited rather than afraid, but I know myself well enough to not be surprised that I tick those boxes. If not all of them, then at least a few.

I take in my surroundings and am frozen to the spot. I can't believe what I'm seeing and, as reality sinks in, my breathing quickens. While the décor and furniture itself is tasteful and expensive-looking, almost every surface is covered with dirty plates, takeaway cartons, and beer bottles. This is not the Max I know. Max who carefully looks after everything and everyone around him. He is the sturdy one, the reliable one. He's an investment banker for God's sake. I close my eyes, willing the tears not to fall.

I think you should come home.

And I know, in this moment, that this time my fears were not just products of my overactive imagination. Something has gone horribly wrong. Not only can I feel it, deep down in the pit of my stomach, but the evidence is right before my eyes: I have left it too late. Worse than that, I left him alone. 'I'm sorry,' I whisper, hoping that wherever he is he can feel it, but still the guilt crashes through me. A tidal wave.

I open the fridge and am relieved to see there are a few bottles of beer left. I open one and lean against the wall, letting the cold drip down my throat before I get to work. Methodically, I move through the house room by room, as if by tidying the aftermath I can undo the cause.

Two hours pass before I find myself in the office upstairs. I stand at the entrance and stare. I can't see the colour of the carpet for the coating of shredded paper. Somewhat optimistically, I pick up a handful and see if I can make out any words. No such luck. What I do spot, though, is a slim shiny laptop waiting stoically for me in the middle of his desk. I wade through the paper and fire it up.

Password.

Shit.

I try everything I can think of: birthdays, names, places, combinations of all three, but each time I'm greeted with a little red cross. It is laughing at me.

I will not be defeated. I pull out my phone, find the number I'm looking for in my contacts and make the call.

'Hello?' Otis's voice is gravelly and Northern. It always manages to make me smile.

'Hi Otis, it's Justine.'

'I know, it bloody says so on my screen. What do you need?'

'I have a laptop. Password encrypted. Can someone come get it? I'll text you the address.'

'I can collect it tonight. Doesn't sound too complicated to me. What am I looking for exactly?'

'Well, to be honest, I'm hoping you'll be able to tell me that.'

'I'm going in cold?'

'Yes, I'm afraid I'm right at the start of this one.'

He laughs. It is low and staccato. 'You know I love a challenge. I'll get straight on it.'

Otis has always been the guy I can rely on. He is quiet and serious but in a 'you can count on me' kind of way. Stereotypically 'the tech guy' in the best way possible. Verifying evidence, checking for any anomalies that might be used against us in court. The police do a great job, but Otis does it better.

He'd been down on his luck when our paths first crossed. The last trial he'd worked on hadn't gone as planned, with the case he'd helped put together crashing down in a spectacularly disastrous way. After that, his name was doing the rounds as one to avoid. Rather than seeing him as someone to steer clear of, I saw my opportunity – I was a junior but I knew careers were forged by finding yourself a guy like Otis. I needed him and it seemed he needed me. I gave him his job back, and he gave me the chance to build mine. We say our goodbyes and I sit back in Max's chair; my feet trailing in the shredded paper.

What is all this?

It seems frenzied to me and I imagine Max, standing in front of me, swaying from too much beer, a little plumper than the last time I saw him from the looks of the takeaway cartons downstairs. He is moving wildly. Fast and frantic. Pulling open the desk drawers so hard the right one crashes to the floor. He finds what he is looking for and destroys it. It is important to him that every last piece is eradicated. It isn't enough that it's contained in the shredder. He wants evidence of its destruction. He opens it, tips it up and lets a sea of paper flood the room. It is over.

Or was it just the beginning?

I feel small sitting here, in Max's house, without him beside me. I've never contemplated a life without Max in it. He always felt so steady, so constant. But there is a thrum of energy in this room that I can't ignore. It does not feel steady. Or constant. I fold myself up into the chair. Knees bent, as though I am a child playing hide-and-seek in their parents' office.

Come back, Max, I want to shout. *I'm here. Come and find me.*

Chapter Eleven

I know that I can't get away with staying on this case for much longer but, instead of going back to read over the files while I still have them, I decide to follow up on the shiny new statement I unearthed this morning.

I use my best no-nonsense barrister voice and ask the guy serving behind the bar if I can speak with Jimmy Falcon.

'Do you have an appointment?'

'No but I really do need to speak with him.' I didn't expect it to be quite so difficult to speak with a bar manager but after what feels like a brief staring competition, the guy escorts me out back. Taps lightly on the office three times.

'Come in,' a voice from my past calls from behind the door.

I don't wait, pushing it open myself.

'Justine Stone. Am I imagining things?' Jimmy smirks, but the shock is etched across his face. I can see it in the way he stands up immediately. How he indicates with the swipe of his hand for the other guy to leave us. He is wearing a dark-green plaid shirt rolled up at the sleeves and if it wasn't for how good it looks, I'd be tempted to make some quip about how he hasn't grown up.

'It's Justine Hart now,' I say, for some reason feeling the need to clarify I am married. 'And it's good to see you too.'

He removes his glasses. One eyebrow raised. 'Justine Hart.' He whistles, 'I didn't peg you as one to take someone else's name.'

'Well, people change.' I don't elaborate. Refrain from telling him that by the time I got married I was desperate to shed the last part of me tying me to my past.

'So what can I do for you, then?' He is intrigued. I'm not surprised. He hasn't seen me since we were teenagers.

'I have a favour to ask.' I decide to play my cards slowly.

'A favour? After all this time. I was hoping you might want to go for a drink first.' He laughs and I realise that Jimmy Falcon is flirting with me. Fifteen-year-old me would have fallen weak at the knees.

'You'd be so lucky, no, but I do need your help. Do you have CCTV footage of Jake getting in a fight?'

He looks more wary now and moves back behind his desk, as though it is a shield. I wonder why he feels the need to hide behind it, or maybe it just makes him feel more important, reinforcing his position as manager.

'Yes, but I don't see why that should concern you.'

'Concern me? Don't give me that crap, Jimmy. It's Jake. Let me see it.'

'It's my bar. You can't just come in here demanding to see CCTV footage. Can you tell me why, at least?'

'No. I don't really know what I'm looking for yet.'

'Well then, unless you can give me a proper reason my answer is no.'

I'd been expecting this response and have come fully prepared. It's the next card up my sleeve.

'OK I guess, as long as you don't mind Max knowing you kissed his little sister when she was underage.' It's a low blow – Jimmy is a good guy and we both know I was desperate for that kiss – but I'm hoping he still cares as much now as he did back then about Max never finding out he kissed his best friend's little sister. Thankfully for me, apparently there are some 'bro codes' that shouldn't be broken and kissing me remains one of them.

*   *   *

I watch in silence as Jake enters the frame. He is wearing a black cap, skinny jeans and a plain grey jumper. There is nothing extravagant about him and yet he is enchanting. He moves in exactly the same way he does in my dreams. He may have changed his name, but there is no denying it is Jake Reynolds on the screen in front of me. He takes a seat at the far right of the bar, just as I'd expected and just as the young barmaid had described earlier, and then he waits.

I wait with him, more than two months apart from each other, and as the minutes tick by I wonder how it would have felt to be sitting right beside him again. We don't have to wait long before the other man – the 'creep' – can be seen walking towards him. I don't know why I do it, as he has his back to the camera, but I squint and lean in as if it'll help me see him better.

I carry on watching as they are handed their drinks and when they turn around, I already know they are headed for the table in the corner. I still can't see the other man's face; he is turned to the side talking to Jake. And then, as if he can sense me looking at him, he looks straight at the camera.

I'd prepared myself to see Jake, there is something different about seeing someone on video rather than in a photo, and as weird as that was, I knew it was coming. What I was not prepared for was to see that the 'creep', as he is now rather unpleasantly nicknamed, is my own flesh and blood.

It is Max.

I shake my head as though that might alter the picture in front of me and ask Jimmy to rewind and pause, but there is no denying it: Max met with Jake and he never told me about it.

It doesn't make any sense he'd keep it from me. And it makes even less sense to see them fighting.

Max and Jake loved each other.

I can't believe what I'm seeing. How did the three of us get here? How far we have fallen. I crick my neck, left then right, as

Jimmy replays it for me. Even on second viewing I still cannot recognise this man as my brother. I really wish the CCTV had audio.

I look sharply, accusingly, at Jimmy. 'Is this why you didn't want me to see the tapes?' I demand.

'I didn't want you to see the CCTV of my pub because it's none of your business.'

'It's Max and Jake; it's my business.'

Jimmy doesn't bother disagreeing and instead he moves towards me, placing a hand on my arm. His touch feels surprisingly soothing. A connection back to the past I've fought so hard to leave behind.

'I'm sorry, it can't be nice seeing this,' he says, and there's a softness to it that shows me he remembers. Jimmy knows how important these two men were – are – to me.

'Do you know what they're talking about?'

'No,' he sighs.

'Did Max speak to you about Jake at all?'

'No.' I can tell he's losing his patience. He removes his hand.

'Did you know Jake changed his name to Brad? Shit, did you all know? Was it just me who didn't?'

'No. God, Justine. Calm down. None of us had seen or spoken to Jake since he left that Christmas. Not until his mum died. I don't think he told anyone he'd changed his name. I only found out on the news this morning. He was definitely going by the name Jake when he was back recently.'

'I guess that would make sense. People here already know him as Jake, and it means it would be easier for him to disappear again as Brad when he decided to.'

'This whole thing with that poor couple though. I just can't believe it. Do you think he did it?'

'I have no idea but you don't get arrested for double murder over nothing. Are you sure Max didn't mention anything to you?

You're his best friend. And this happened in your pub. I find it hard to believe he wouldn't tell you about it.'

'Jesus, Justine. Why bother asking me questions if you're never going to believe my answers?'

I don't tell him I never believe anyone's answers unless they're on the stand, and even then I always have my doubts. It's amazing how many answers change once they've sworn an oath to tell the truth, the whole truth and nothing but the truth.

'Fine. One more: when did you last see Max?'

'I don't know.' He pauses, ruffling his hands through his hair as though trying to remember. 'A couple of months ago, I think. Before the fight, which was early May. You know how it is, you have friends but your life no longer revolves around each other the same way it used to. Why do you ask? Is he all right?'

I don't know if it's because it's the first time I'm admitting it aloud or because the CCTV footage suggests there's a lot I don't know about my brother, but suddenly the full force of it hits me and I have to fight to stop my voice from cracking as I say, 'No, I don't think he is. I'm pretty sure Max is missing.'

It can't wait until I'm home. I race out of the pub on to the busy road and call Otis from where I'm standing, no longer able to put one foot in front of the other until he picks up.

'Hello?'

'Have you found anything on Max's laptop yet?' I don't have the patience for pleasantries right now.

'I'm afraid not, but that's not because there's nothing to find. In fact, I'm pretty sure your brother was hiding something.'

'Why?'

'He's installed Tor software, the sole purpose of which is to hide your search history. It's practically impossible to break through.'

'Calculated too.'

'Exactly. You want me to carry on?'

'Of course. I think he might be in trouble, Otis. We really need to find something and soon.'

'Don't worry. I'm on it, I promise.'

'Thanks.' I breathe a little easier and remind myself I can trust Otis.

But the thought that Max has secrets – big ones, from the sounds of things – hangs heavy over me.

You do not install software to encrypt your search history unless you are doing something you know you shouldn't be – something you think somebody might come after you for.

But evidence of what?

And did that somebody already come for him?

Chapter Twelve

While I'm waiting for more news from Otis, I try to distract myself by raking over the details in Jake's file instead. I've promised myself I'll hand the case back tomorrow. This has gone on long enough.

While I still have all the details, I try to work out what story the prosecution might spin the jury for the most effect.

Name: Brad Finchley
Age: thirty-five
Height: six feet four inches
Weight: fifteen stone.

It is a win for the prosecution. Jake – or rather Brad, as he's referred to throughout the case files – is imposing. By nature, he will come across to the jury as threatening before the trial has even begun.

I can feel it just out of reach. The scene has almost come together for me but there's still a missing piece of the puzzle. It's like an itch I've forgotten to scratch. I turn to the detailed crime-scene report and this time one detail feels more important than the others. I hadn't paid enough attention to it before – the violence of the scene overshadowing the smaller observations.

But it is precisely in the details where a case is won, where you can spin a story: the house phone was in the kitchen on the wall above Mr Rushnell's crumpled body. It was noted to be hanging loose off the hook. I close my eyes and let Mr and Mrs Rushnell come back to life.

The attacker is dressed in a long black jumper. He doesn't plan on hurting anyone, it's why he isn't wearing any gloves. There'll be no need for that. He doesn't plan on actually using the gun. It's just there in case of a disturbance.

He didn't think anyone was in, had wanted it to be a simple robbery. In and out. No cars on the driveway. And he certainly hadn't expected Mr Rushnell to make it into the kitchen before him. To pick up the phone and start dialling. He is shouting for him to stop, but the man won't listen. He does the only thing he can think of. He brings out the gun, the one he never intended to use but which made him feel safer to have it on him. He holds the gun to Mr Rushnell's head. Tells him, forcefully, to hang up. But the man is bolder than he'd given him credit for. He tells him again. Wills him to stop. This is not what he came for. Again, he does not listen. The attacker is panicking now. He knows there's no way he'll make it out without the police finding him. The pressure is getting to him. He can feel his hand shaking. The finger pressing against the trigger. Mark Rushnell turns to look at him, and he knows there is nothing more for it.

Blood splatters up the cupboards. A sea of deep red spreads out on to the kitchen floor. It had been such close range that the devastation is horrifying.

And that's when the screaming starts. High-pitched and far too loud. Someone is going to hear. Mrs Rushnell has collapsed to the floor on her knees. She is reaching out towards her husband. He must make the noise stop. And so he does the only thing he can think of. He shoots her too. Just as her fingers reach her husband's.

Finally, it is silent.

And there I have it. A story for the jury.

Is it the truth? Probably not.

Does is sound persuasive? Absolutely.

All that is missing is why Brad was there in the first place. I've used the age-old excuse of a robbery, but even I know I'm grasping at straws. Until the murders, Brad's record was squeaky-clean. You don't go from strait-laced citizen to gun-wielding burglar in one fell swoop.

For a bullet-proof case, the prosecution needs to provide a motivating factor for the murders. We already know there is forensic evidence placing Brad at the scene of the crime.

Still, I keep coming back to the fact the police weren't able to gather any footage of him in the area on the day of the murders, and there is still no known link between him and the Rushnells. Of course, there is no denying that the case against him is strong but, and this is crucial, it is not a smoking gun.

And then the penny drops. I pull my notepad out with an urgency I haven't felt in a while and write it down with such force I can even feel the indent in the paper as I run my fingers over the words.

When did Jake get hold of the gun?

I think back to the CCTV footage from earlier. The way he moved. It was as though I could still feel him. If only I could reach into the screen and back in time. I cannot claim to know Brad Finchley or what he is or isn't capable of, but being back here, I'm starting to wonder if Brad was still just Jake.

And Jake Reynolds I did know.

Jake Reynolds is not capable of murder.

Which means if Jake did not kill the Rushnells, then who did? And how did he end up with the murder weapon and a load of forensics placing him at the scene?

Chapter Thirteen

I surprise myself with how cautiously I push open the door of the Blue Eagle. I can feel my confidence starting to slide. It's unnerving being back here and I can feel the past gnawing away at my edges. I glance around the room checking for any sign of the Rushnell family, aware they could turn up any day now. We often see a victim's family drawn to the place where an arrest was made; desperate for answers and to give context to a crime that seems to have no reason.

It's not like they'll know who I am, but still it's hard enough just thinking about Mark and Beverley as real people with family who loved them, let alone actually witnessing that grief. Or thinking about Jake, supposedly responsible for the pain that'll no doubt be etched on their faces. To be honest, I'm not sure which is better – to imagine Jake capable of murder, or the possibility of him being falsely imprisoned.

And that is, really, the root of why I'm here. Setting myself up in the corner of the Blue Eagle where the CCTV showed Jake had once sat with Max. I'm ready to call Charles and come clean – or at least my version of it. It's a Saturday but the longer this goes on, the worse it's going to sound.

I've always known it would come to this. I couldn't stay on Jake's case for ever, but I also couldn't simply let him go. I needed time. And, if I'm completely honest, I needed access to the full details of the case. But the longer this goes on, the more I'm risking the course of justice and if Brad is still just Jake, if he didn't do the things he is being accused of, then he needs the best possible shot at a fair trial. It was always going to end like this but still, it feels momentous; like I am severing my link to Jake. It feels unnatural.

Jimmy brings my hot chocolate over personally and the comfort of seeing him – knowing that he is within arm's reach, still living and breathing here in this very town we grew up in – is suddenly overwhelming.

I pick up my phone to call Charles when I see the first part of Jake's transcript was emailed across late last night. Technically, at this very moment, I am still the lead prosecutor on a double murder case.

I breathe in for four, hold for five, out for six.

Try not to open it.

Remember why I am here.

Look back at Jimmy as he disappears into the back room.

I press the palms of my hands into my eyes but the pain takes me back there.

I am drowning in the darkness again. Alone. The floor hard beneath me. Why won't someone come?

I open my eyes, letting the light flood back into them. I am free. No longer trapped. No longer eighteen and afraid. I can do what I want.

I make up my mind and click Open Attachment.

BRADLEY THOMAS FINCHLEY
PART 1 OF RECORDED INTERVIEW

Date: 17/06/2023
Duration: 12 minutes
Location: Chelmsford
Number of pages: 6

Conducted by officers of Essex police DC Murray and DC Grainger

I thought seeing the name Bradley Thomas Finchley at the top might help me once again separate Jake from Brad – convince me he had changed and to not get myself so emotionally involved – but there is nothing quite like a police interview transcript to capture the very essence of a person. This document *sounds* like Jake, there is no escaping it.

It starts as any other police interview, going over his rights, his personal details, that he knows what is happening and where he is. And then the real interview begins.

DC Murray: Can you tell me when you arrived in Maldon, most recently?

Finchley: Sure, it was the nineteenth of April.

DC Murray: And where were you living before?

Finchley: I'd been living in Scotland.

DC Murray: Can you confirm where exactly?

Finchley: Glasgow.

DC Murray: But you grew up in Maldon, is that correct?

Finchley: Born and bred.

DC Murray: So after years of living so far away, what suddenly made you want to return?

Finchley: Well, my mum, she passed away and I needed to come back to sort the house out. Sort through her and Dad's things, get it ready for sale. That kind of thing.

DC Murray: You weren't planning on staying? You just wanted to . . .

Finchley: No, I came back just to sort through the house.

DC Murray: But, three months on, you were still living in Maldon?

Finchley: That's right.

DC Murray: Did anything happen when you returned that changed your mind? Made you want to stay longer?

Finchley: With due respect I haven't finished sorting the house out. There's a lot to do and I'm the only one around to do it.

DC Murray: And that's the only reason you're still living in Maldon?

Finchley: Correct.

DC Murray: OK let's go back a bit, shall we? How about you tell us why you left eighteen years ago.

Finchley: No big reason, there was nothing left for me in Maldon. It's a small town.

DC Murray: Unlike Glasgow.

Finchley: Exactly.

DC Murray: What about friends? A girlfriend? A job?

Finchley. Nope. No one.

DC Murray: So would you say you were a bit of a loner? Do you find it hard to make friends?

Finchley: Not really.

DC Murray: OK, let's move on. When you were living in Maldon you were known by a different name. Can you confirm that name for us, please?

Finchley: I was Jake Thomas Reynolds.

DC Murray: Can you tell us why you changed your name?

Finchley: I didn't like mine.

DC Murray: Your father's name was also Jake Thomas Reynolds. Correct?

Finchley: Yes.

DC Murray: It must have meant a lot to your parents for them to name you after your dad. Did you not like your father?

Finchley: I loved my father.

DC Murray: So, now I'm just going over all this again to make sure I've understood. You loved your father, with whom you shared a name, and likely that held a lot of emotional significance for your parents, would you agree?

Finchley: Probably.

DC Murray: OK. What month did you leave Maldon?

Finchley: December.

DC Murray: Finchley, did something happen that December
   to make you leave?

Finchley: No comment.

Did something happen that December to make you leave?

The words blur together and swim in front of my eyes.

I've always thought something else must have happened the night of the Christmas party to make him leave. I've never been able to accept that he would simply abandon me. But here it finally is, in black and white – confirmation that what I did drove him away. That on December the sixteenth I shattered everything we had into so many broken pieces he felt he had nothing left to stay for.

What about friends? A girlfriend?

No one.

I feel the sting of it scorching my skin. The thing is, that Christmas, he didn't just leave me. He left Max, too. Is that what they'd been fighting about?

BEFORE

MAX – THE BROTHER

The route was familiar by now. A short walk following the river out of Maldon and they'd reach a clearing by the water's edge perfect for summer days of doing not much but everything all at the same time. Barbecues, paddleboards and Frisbee. This was what summer was made for and it helped him leave behind the worst parts of his year at Cambridge.

He'd been wary of Jake at first, and had purposely kept a close eye on them. He felt it was his job. It had always been their dynamic, ever since he could remember. He protected Justine. Always. The only people they could rely on were the two of them. It had been difficult at first to let Jake in, but quickly they'd become an easy three.

He watched them from the grassy bank, both out on their paddleboards, Jake edging closer to Justine's board, threatening to knock her off. She was laughing with her head thrown back, carefree, desperately trying to paddle away from him. The freedom of being out here was palpable in comparison to being back home. In that house. He could feel the change within himself, and he could see it in Justine, too. They felt more alive out here.

It wasn't just the summer air; it was also the effect Jake had on them – he was their magic ingredient. Jake and Justine were perfect for each other; everyone could see that. Max knew Justine had a tendency to be her own worst enemy; the thoughts

89

in her head could threaten to drown her: Dad restricted her. Mum avoided her. But when she was with Jake it seemed to Max as though she relaxed, she broke free from everything at home – she became larger than life.

'Give us a hand,' Jake called to him.

'Don't you dare!' Justine howled, starting to paddle faster.

Max leapt up and raced to the grassy edge, barely stopping before jumping off and swimming towards her. She turned; panic mixed with joy. A bit like a child playing hide-and-seek, knowing they're about to be found. Jake cheered him on. As he reached her board all he had to do was grin, wickedly, threatening to tip her off before she jumped off the side, into the water. Choosing to escape rather than be caught; even though she'd end up in the water either way.

Max knew that was how Justine would play it.

They'd been made that way – him and her.

The Stones were wired to always remain in control. Even when the odds were stacked against them.

Chapter Fourteen

Charles answers after the very first ring. It takes me by surprise, and I am momentarily lost for words.

'Hello?' he repeats, agitation seeping into his voice.

'Hi Charles, sorry I'm here.'

'Everything OK, how's the case coming along?' There's never any small-talk with Charles, he doesn't have the time. I breathe in deeply and then rip the Band-Aid off.

'I'm sorry—' God, I hate that word. It feels too simple, using one word to encompass how I actually feel. No one is ever completely sorry for their actions. Or at least, they're not solely sorry. It sounds uncomplicated. I never trust anyone who begins with 'I'm sorry'. 'I've realised I've made a huge mistake: I know the defendant.' I force myself to spit the truth out.

'You know Brad Finchley?' Charles sounds incredulous.

'I do, but not as Brad. He used to be called Jake Reynolds. I haven't seen him for eighteen years and I had no idea he'd changed his name. I promise you, it's as much a shock to me as it is to you.' I'm using a bit of creative licence, but it's not entirely a lie. I was genuinely shocked to see Jake accused of murder.

I can hear Charles's intake of breath on the other end of the phone.

'I really had no idea until this morning,' I repeat, hoping it's not overkill.

'This is very serious, Justine, you should have told us days ago.' He says it slowly, emphasising the 'very'.

'I know, and I promise you if I'd have recognised Brad as being Jake I would have said so straight away. The last thing I'd want to do is jeopardise the case, but you have to understand, I hadn't seen him in years and we were children back then. I barely even knew him, we're just from the same town.'

'I see.' He pauses, as if he doesn't really see at all. 'Have you told the solicitor?'

'Not yet. I wanted to explain to you first.'

'Obviously you'll be removed from the case and who knows which chambers will get it now.' He sounds annoyed – likely at the logistics of what happens next as much as the embarrassment of having the case taken from us. If we'd secured a conviction it would have done wonders for attracting new cases our way.

'I really am sorry. You know, more than anyone, how much I wanted this to be my big break.'

'What's done is done, Justine. I trust you wouldn't have put us all in this situation knowingly.' I can imagine him raising his eyebrows at me, peering over his glasses. A look that tells me while he is saying he trusts me, he doesn't believe it one bit.

'No, I wouldn't have.' I stand my ground and we both let the silence settle between us. I try not to break first, but perhaps it's the guilt that makes me weak as I crumble, adding, 'Thanks for understanding.'

He hums down the phone, his silence maintaining his authority. This is the side of Charles that makes him formidable in court.

'OK well, I'll see you when I'm next in chambers. Sorry for letting you down,' I repeat again – wishing I hadn't – before hanging up.

I hate disappointing people. Men, in particular. Aya tells me it's because I'm projecting the need to please my father. Dad – even after all these years and hours of therapy – still impacting how I act. I shouldn't be so surprised.

Chapter Fifteen

My skin flares with the heat as once more I turn the dial on the shower even hotter. It is almost at its maximum. I hold my breath until my body adjusts to the new intensity, waiting for the sting to subside. Relaxing into it, I reach for the hit again. The steam rises, something like an exorcism, and with it I find myself transported away from here; from Mum; Max; Maldon; Jake; up, up and away I rise. I ignore the almost suffocating stench of alcohol seeping out of my pores and let the heat carry me away.

I'm not sure how much of my story Charles believed this morning when I told him I'd only just realised I knew the defendant. Charles is anything but gullible, but for whatever reason, for now he has decided to let me live out my lie. To accept it as the truth, at least on the face of things. How it goes from here, we'll have to see. Often the worst punishments are the ones doled out slowly; so subtly you can't even argue they are there. But you know they are. You feel them in the details. It always comes back to the fucking details.

I pick up a sponge and start to scrub at my skin. Hard.

Until I hear it.

One of Jake's dad's favourite stories to tell was about when his dad, Jake's grandad, had run across the road in his dressing gown to save their neighbour who was being assaulted by her husband. Jake's dad was just a boy at the time and described the screams coming from their neighbour's house as being like those out of a horror-film. *You knew she wasn't just in trouble. She was being murdered*, he'd said. I'd always wondered what made that noise so distinctive, so animalistic.

This is what it must have sounded like . . .

Is the first thing I think when the screaming comes.

I race down the stairs, my towel wrapped round me exposing the red raw skin on my legs, before coming to an abrupt halt at the sight of two police officers at the front door.

They've found me . . .

Is the second thought that comes to mind.

Mum spins in slow motion, as though her body is struggling to move as it usually would.

The screaming has stopped now.

We've never been one of those mother–daughter acts who claim to have the closest bond. Half the time I have no idea who she is or what she's thinking. But from the very moment she looks at me, I know.

I know that Max is dead.

The realisation arrives immediately, but time simultaneously slows down. Together, it means that the truth of it, the horror of it, doesn't hit me all at once, but slowly. Breaking me apart as it travels through my body. Painfully. First arriving in my brain – for I register it straight away – the pain is etched so clearly across my mother's face you couldn't miss it. Then, torturously, it creeps through me. Finally, as it reaches my toes, my whole body now burning with grief, I feel myself begin to sway, knocked off balance.

The taller of the policemen moves towards me, his arms outstretched. I feel his hands grab my arms, and I realise I must be falling.

My own guttural cry now replacing my mother's.

*   *   *

They guide us into the kitchen, and I notice how adept the police-men are at taking control in a stranger's house. Cupboards open-ing, kettle roaring. How many other homes have they entered after just tearing the family apart? It is a skill, I think as I watch them, to suddenly be unfalteringly in charge in someone else's space.

As a steaming cup of coffee is placed in front of me, the other officer emerges with a dressing gown they must have found upstairs and hands it to me. It makes me acutely aware I'm still in my towel and I wrap it around me quickly over the top.

'Now,' the shorter, kinder-faced of the two says, 'we will need to take statements from you both but first, is there anything you'd like to ask us?'

Mum looks to me, handing the responsibility over. Am I up to this? Max is dead. Now what?

'You said Max was found at sea. So, he drowned?' I ask, desper-ate to try and gain back some sense of control. To prove to myself that I am capable. But the words sound broken as I force them out.

'We're waiting on the autopsy report still, I'm afraid. We don't yet know the official cause of death but Max's body was found by local fishermen off the coast of Mersea. Our initial thought is he's likely been in the water a few days.'

'Since when, do you think?' I ask. It takes all my strength not to shout at them for more answers. To explain it to me. How has this happened? Why has Max been taken from us?

'We're not entirely sure yet. Much more than a few days though and the damage to his body would likely have been more significant.'

Damage to his body. It makes me visualise all sorts of things. Different versions of Max. This is not how I want to remember my brother. I pinch my thighs. It clears my mind.

'But long enough to float?' I know enough about drowning to know it takes a while for the body to release the gases which make it rise to the top.

'It would seem so, yes.'

'Do you have any idea what might have happened? You can't come here without any answers at all. It's not fair,' I say although I know I sound like a whiny child. I look to Mum for support. Surely she wants to demand more from them too? But she is just sitting in her chair, silent. Her head bowed. 'Mum?' I snap. 'Do you have any questions?' But she just looks at me as if she's completely lost.

I know I should feel sorry for her, but it angers me. She was like this when Dad was around, too. Quiet. Pathetic. Useless. She let the world simply happen to her without fighting back. Once again, I am reminded of my determination never to end up like her: a puppet with no agency of her own.

'I'm really sorry,' the officer says. 'In situations like this there are certain steps that have to happen first before we can put the whole picture together. Rest assured, we are doing our very best. The first thing we need is for you to come to the station and identify the body. Mrs Stone, would you like to come?'

'No, no. I can't. I just can't.' Her shoulders crumple and she starts to cry again.

'I'll go,' I volunteer, my voice clearer now. This is something I can do. A way to be of use. To help. To matter. To prove I am nothing like my mother.

Max was there when I needed him, and now it's my turn to be there for him.

You need to come home.

If only I'd realised it sooner, would he still be alive?

The police officers wait downstairs for me to get dressed. I know I should hurry, but I take a moment first to speak with Otis. As soon as there's a body involved, I know the clock starts ticking. The sooner you start, the more likely you are to find answers. I already know I won't be able to bring myself to say Max is dead out loud, so I text him first instead – warning him Max's body has been found and asking him to call me. As is his usual style, my phone starts buzzing only minutes later.

'I'm sorry Max is dead,' he says immediately. He is the first person I've spoken to since the news and I'm grateful for him. He is not afraid to say it how it is. He does not dart around it. Death and murder fill Otis's every day; he can treat this matter-of-factly, which is exactly what I need right now. I can't let myself crumple. Push it away. Force it down.

'Thank you, I'm about to head to the station now.' I pull on my khaki shorts and a loose top, balancing the phone between my shoulder and ear. 'Have you had any luck yet?'

'I haven't, but I did do some more digging after you sounded so worried yesterday.'

'And?'

'Did you know he lost his job six weeks ago?'

'What? You're sure?' More secrets. Max's. Mum's. Mine. When will it end? When did it start?

'Definitely.'

'Did they say why?'

'Apparently he was turning up drunk. They gave him warnings, followed procedure, but he didn't pull himself together.' I think of the beer bottles found discarded in every corner and crevice of his house. Of the Max in the Blue Eagle's CCTV footage. It is all fitting together, but right now I only have one corner of the puzzle and no idea what image it's all meant to add up to.

'Thanks. Promise you'll tell me the moment you find something more?'

'You have my word. Is there anything else I should know?'

I think about Max's fight with Jake and I know it could be important, but I also feel an overwhelming instinct that I should keep the two cases separate for now. Not least because I'm off

Jake's trial completely – another thing I should tell Otis – nothing stays secret from him for very long anyway, but if Otis thought it might be connected to a case I'm no longer on, I'm not sure he'd be so keen to help me out. Max is dead and I need all the help I can get, for as long as I can get it.

'About Max? No. I've told you everything I know,' I say, trying my best to avoid directly lying to him.

'OK, well, I'll keep digging. And Justine, I really am sorry.'

'Thanks. Actually, just one other thing while I have you.'

'Yes?'

'Can you also look into the Rushnells for me? Who they were? Did they always live in Surrey?' I don't ask him what I really want to know: did they ever live in Maldon and why can't I shift the feeling that I know them from somewhere?

Chapter Sixteen

Swollen, bruised, cold. This is not the first dead body I've seen, but it is certainly the most personal. I fight to push away the wave of grief threatening to drown me. Remind myself I can be Max's sister later but that right now he needs more from me.

I thought I'd be stronger than this; I know being emotional only makes you careless. I need to be sharp. Observant. Smart. Everything I am trained to be. *I can do this*, I steel myself. I owe it to Max. But still my feet feel rooted to the spot. It takes every effort to place one foot in front of the other until I'm standing right beside him. My tongue is sticky in my mouth. I feel too hot, but rationally know they must keep the room cool to preserve the bodies. I try to focus my mind on the facts. Anything to distract myself from the fact that this is Max, my older brother, lying on the table.

In victims who have drowned, the putrefaction of flesh causes gases to be released, inflating the body. It is this which caused Max's body to float and be spotted by a local fishing boat. Taking into consideration the temperature of the water and the decomposition of his body, the police have suggested he entered the water three to five days ago, but we'll know more after the full autopsy.

'It's him,' I say, confirming what the police liaison officer needs to hear. He exits the room silently, leaving me alone with Max for a few minutes longer.

I know I shouldn't but, before I can stop myself, I reach out and pull the sheet which was resting just below his chin, back to his waist. I've already been shown photos, so I know what to expect, but I still breathe in sharply as I expose the sunken right-hand side of my older brother. The bruising is visible and I can see where they've pulled the skin taut over the damage and jaggedly stitched him back together from his hip bone to his clavicle.

Whether this was foul play or caused by rocks or other debris once he was already dead, we do not know yet. All we know so far is that Max Stone, aged thirty-seven, was found dead at four thirty a.m. floating four hundred metres from Mersea's shoreline. Mersea, with its picturesque colourful beach huts where we'd spent many summers building speedboats and volcanoes in the sand. Those are, without a doubt, my happiest childhood memories. The sea air seemed to blow everything else away when we were there; I remember once looking over at my mum and dad and seeing them laughing together. I was struck by how pure that laughter sounded down on the beach compared to when we were at home. My mum was sitting on a stripy sun lounger with her red-painted toes buried in the sand, laughing as my dad struggled to light the barbecue. So postcard-perfect they seemed almost unreal. I remember staring at them at the time, thinking: where had my real parents gone?

The liaison officer is back.

'Are you ready?' he asks gently, well-practised at his role.

I place the sheet back as carefully and as lovingly as I can. Before letting myself be led out the room into the starkly lit white corridor, I look at where he is lying one last time and make a promise: *I will make whoever did this to you pay for it.*

DS Sorcha Rose is waiting for me just outside the examination room. She is wearing a pristine black trouser suit with her hair scraped back into a high bun. This woman means business. More big city boss than regional police force.

'Shall we go for a walk?' she suggests as she passes me a lukewarm coffee which I assume is from the machine down the corridor.

'I thought you said a walk?' I'm confused as she clicks a set of keys and the headlights flash on a black Škoda in front of us.

'I did, but how about we get away from here first? The sun is out, which I have quickly learnt means this place will soon be heaving. I thought a bit of quiet might do us both good.'

'OK,' I relent and slide into the front seat. 'You're fairly new here then?' I had already clocked she wasn't local, not with her accent.

'I transferred from Manchester six months ago.'

She doesn't give me a reason for the move and I don't pry. I know there's usually a story behind why a detective transfers from a big city to a smaller town two hundred miles away but I just don't have it in me today. Normally I would scrutinise her for clues but instead I simply stare out of the window as the car speeds away, leaving Maldon behind us.

We haven't gone far before DS Rose pulls into a small car park on the side of the road. I smile and feel a surge of respect for this woman. She may not have been in the area long, but she clearly knows her stuff. This is the perfect place for a walk away from prying eyes.

I know we are just a stone's throw away from the waterways of Tollesbury Wick. If anywhere was going to convince someone they were safe to reveal their secrets, it would be here. Vast and exposed with the wind whipping through you as you follow the intricate crisscross of waterways, this place never fails to remind you of how small you are; reducing your fears and worries until they seem almost insignificant. So small, perhaps, that you forget to hold them close to your chest. It is a clever move, but I am no stranger to playing games.

We walk in silence along the main road and, as we peel away down a narrow track, I notice her inhale. Long and slow. Then, just as the view opens up ahead of us, she hits me with, 'I am so sorry for what's happened to Max.'

The combination of being confronted with a sight so beautiful mixed with her words so sad causes me to have a physical reaction, and I have to use all my willpower to keep my hands hanging limp at my side instead of raking over the throbbing at the base of my skull. It is so perfectly executed, so exquisitely timed, I wonder how many people she has brought here before me, taking them through the exact same routine.

I am a little jealous.

'Thank you. We loved him very much.'

'I know you've already given a statement at the station and really this is just a casual chat, but I wanted to ask if there was anything else you've thought of since that you didn't put in your statement? It's so hard to think of everything especially when you're at the station, and it's perfectly normal for other things to come to mind after.'

'I'm quite used to police stations. I'm a criminal barrister. I really don't have anything more to add, but if I think of anything you'll be the first person I tell.'

'Ah yes. I saw. Working for the prosecution at One Eight Seven Chambers.'

She's read up on me.

'That's right.' I keep it simple.

'In your statement you say you came back to visit your mum on the thirteenth of July. You didn't think it was unusual you couldn't get hold of Max? Your brother wasn't reported missing before he was found on the fifteenth.'

'With respect, my brother was a grown adult and it had only been a few days. I was here to visit my mum.'

'I understand. I'm just trying to get the full picture. There is something else we discovered today though, and I wanted to wait until after you'd identified the body before telling you.' The way she says 'the body' feels so impersonal I try not to shudder. She continues, 'I'm afraid there is evidence of a break-in at Max's house.'

Of course, the moment they pulled Max's body out of the water I knew they'd find the smashed door panel at his house.

I stop in my tracks. Eyes wide.

'Sorry, this is just a lot to take in. Do you think it's connected? Did they take anything?'

'It's hard to know if something was taken without Max being able to tell us. I know it's a lot to ask, but it would be really help-ful if you could look round and see if you notice anything out of place once the team is ready for you?'

'Yes, of course. Whatever you need. Does this mean you're considering foul play?'

'I'm sorry, I'll be better placed to answer that once we have the full autopsy report, but I don't want to rule anything out too early.'

I let the silence between us settle for a while and then I say, 'It could just be a coincidence? An empty house is an opportunity.'

'Well, whatever the link, I'll find it.'

I remind myself there is no reason to feel guilty, not least because I didn't kill my brother.

We are nearing the end of the circular walk when she asks me the question which I suspect is her main reason for bringing me here.

'Look, I know you're used to how this works and so I'm going to be frank with you. The other officers, well, they aren't particu-larly experienced with cases like this. You could be a huge asset to me if it comes to it. If – and I mean if – we end up opening a full investigation, I want to be one step ahead. Worst-case scenario and your brother's death wasn't an accident or suicide, who would you suggest I start with?'

I've been asking myself the same question over and over again, ever since I learnt Max was dead. Two days ago, I could have hand on heart said everyone loved Max and that he didn't make enemies. But the Max I saw in the CCTV footage wasn't the Max I knew. I can't bring that up without dragging Jake – and myself – into it.

'Honestly, I wish I could say. But Max was the guy everyone loved. I can't believe someone would want to do this to him.'

DS Rose looks disappointed with me.

'OK,' she says slowly. 'Well, as I'm sure you know, these things are often committed by someone close to the victim. Can you write me a list of people from the town he's friends with?'

'Of course. I'll bring it to the station tomorrow.'

'I'd appreciate it.' She is looking at me differently now. I know she was expecting more.

'And I'll have a think about your other question. You're right, I've already been going over it again and again in my mind, but I'm just not coming up with any answers. I promise I'll let you know the moment I think of anything. I'm sorry I couldn't be of any more help today,' I add, hoping to please her, to claw back her respect.

'That would be wonderful, thank you.' She smiles gratefully but her gaze lingers over me a little too long and I wonder if I have finally met my match.

Chapter Seventeen

Mum's back is hunched and from here I can see the curvature of her spine. Her arms are surprisingly strong for her delicate frame, sinewy in a way I hadn't expected. As she digs the shovel into the ground then levers it up, I see her muscles flex beneath the skin. Mum has always loved gardening and it is no surprise to me that on a day like today, instead of being curled up in bed, she is out here.

Every part of her has been poured into this garden over the years. All her pain, all her grief, all her love. The thought of it raises the hairs on the back of my arms; all the days of my childhood when I needed her and instead of holding my hand, I'd look out of the window to see her here. Tending to her flowers. Attentively weeding and dead-heading, cutting out the decay before it took hold of her precious garden, while leaving the rot growing inside her own home. It was only a matter of time before its vines would encase me and pull us all under.

I'd wanted her desperately back then, but she always seemed distant – as if half of her was off somewhere else. Physically she was there, in that house with us, but as for the motherly side to her, it was as though she was always holding back. A ghost in her own house. Growing up, I was mad at her for that.

I needed my mother.

'What are you clearing? Do you need a hand?' I call.

She wipes the sweat off her brow with her gloves and then shoos me away.

'Just an overgrown patch. It's time I got rid of this mess. I'm fine. You go in, thanks.'

I think about ignoring her. Pulling on Dad's gloves which are most likely still in the shed and busying myself next to her. Showing her we are in this together. That she is not alone, with a husband and son both dead; she still has a daughter. But I have never been a keen gardener, and my vision of us side by side clearing away the weeds that have tangled our lives, thorny and dangerous, quickly morphs into something else. The weeds take hold, tightening around my waist, squeezing the breath out of me. My mum could cut me loose, she has shears right there in her hand, but she does nothing. Watching, she lets me die.

Yes, growing up I'd needed my mother. She wasn't absent from my childhood. She was always there. In this house. Watching. Quiet. Too quiet. That was her crime. It's what I cannot forgive her for – she was there. Yet she didn't protect me.

'OK, well I'll put the coffee on,' I say and head inside.

As the kettle roars, I flip my notepad open and start on the list for DS Rose.

Justine Stone (sister)
Evelyn Stone (mother)
Jimmy Falcon (school friend)

It is performative. The only name I can think of is the one I can't write down: Jake Reynolds. It swirls round and round my mind forming a loop as if I am watching the footage of him pinning Max up against the wall in the Blue Eagle on repeat.

One of the conditions of Jake's bail is that he can't leave a one mile radius from where he is staying. He has an ankle tag on. If he had broken bail any time in the past week it would have been all over the news. Still, I make a note to ask Otis to check.

It is too much to handle and I lower my head into my hands. Close my eyes. Grind my teeth. How did I get here? Is this really happening?

There is only a sliver of light underneath the door. I spread my fingers out so the light shines on them. And then I make a fist. Flex and fist. Flex and fist. The longer I'm in the darkness, the more it consumes me.

Yes, I remind myself, anything is possible. I pull my phone out. I'm struggling right now, my grief threatening to pull me under, but I need to remember who I am and what I can do. I made Max a promise – I will find who killed him and I will make them pay. I must pull myself together and fight my way through this, just like I did all those years ago.

Justine: *Any chance you can fit me in for an extra session? Max is dead.*

I'm fully aware it's the wrong way round to do things. To tell my therapist my brother is dead before I tell my husband, but Aya isn't going to suddenly turn up in Maldon. She will stay contained just where she's always been, in a perfect Aya-shaped box which has been carved out neatly for her. But this, Max's death, is going to change my marriage forever.

As soon as Noah knows, he will take the first flight home and come as fast as he can to be with me. He'll think he is doing the right thing, and there is nothing I can tell him to explain why I don't want him here. That he is, in fact, the very last person on earth I want by my side right now. I cannot tell him that blurring the lines between my life with him and my life here is something that up until now I have fought so hard to prevent.

When I met Noah fourteen years ago, I wanted nothing more than to reinvent myself. I'd not long finished university and was back flat-sharing in London with Charlotte. I was determined to be better. To be the person I knew I could be – and not let everything that had happened here, in this town, in this very house, ruin me. The Justine Noah married? She isn't the same girl who grew up here. I don't want him to find that out. I look down and see the fleshy gap between my thumb and index finger has started to bleed where I've been scratching it.

The collision course is set; realistically I can't avoid it. Not now Max is dead. I count to ten. Decide to take a third paracetamol first. Tell myself today is an exception. And then I dial my husband's number. On the call Noah doesn't say a single thing wrong. He is kind and compassionate. He doesn't presume to know how I am feeling. He offers to fly straight over but I manage to convince him I just need him back for the funeral. I couldn't think up an excuse plausible enough to keep him away longer, but at least it gives me a few more days before my worlds collide.

My before and after.

Noah: *I love you.*

He sends the text as soon as we've hung up. It is thoughtful and kind. It makes me want to throw my phone across the room. To pretend Noah isn't about to leave Paris and make his way here. For now, as his text says, Noah loves me.

But for how much longer?

The kitchen door crashes in the wind. She moves so quietly, I hadn't heard her come inside. Without a word she turns the radio on and the kitchen is flooded with the operatic crescendos of *Tosca*. Soil streaks her face where she's wiped her brow. I guess I never was going to be able to avoid her forever.

I'm not sure why I'm so reluctant to talk to her about Max. Maybe because it requires a certain level of vulnerability. An emotional conversation. Something deep and meaningful; all the things we've both striven to avoid over the past eighteen years – our relationship reduced to formalities and niceties.

There is no way to talk about Max's death politely.

'I assume it was him?' she asks and I nod. 'Was he—' she struggles to go on – 'was he . . .' Another pause. 'Was it bad?' She finally finds the words.

'It could have been worse.' I can't bring myself to lie but I also know she needs to be given a glimmer of something good to hold on to. I am not a monster.

'Did you speak to him recently?' Mum asks and again I am flooded with hot guilt.

'Fairly recently, but not as much as I should have,' I admit. 'Was something wrong?'

'Not that I know of. Why do you ask?'

'I went to his house.' Mum looks surprised. 'I think something might have happened before his accident.'

'Like what? What makes you say that?' She sounds tired. Exhausted, in fact. I feel bad for putting this on her, but Mum saw Max more frequently than I did.

'I don't know exactly, but the house was a state. Messy. Drink everywhere. You know Max he isn't – wasn't – the type. He was always whipping out facts about unhealthy eating and drinking. He read mindfulness books and thought tidying up was therapeutic.'

'I hadn't been round in a while,' she muses, 'and clearly I missed something. Oh God, I'm so sorry, Justine. I'm so sorry.' She has wound her arms around herself and it strikes me that there is no one left to comfort her except for herself. I'm not sure me hugging her would do the trick. Actually, I'm pretty certain it would have the opposite effect – too awkward and confronting for the both of us.

'I did know he was drinking too much,' she sniffs, 'I should have stopped him.'

'There are a lot of things we all should have done,' I find myself saying, and it's true. There are things I missed. Things I didn't do. 'But what started the drinking? That's what we need to find out,' I press her.

She sighs and shakes her head. It is all too much, and she seems to be shrinking under the weight of it.

'It's OK. I'll find the answers, don't worry. I owe it to Max,' I reassure her.

'I believe you will,' she says, smiling sadly.

Chapter Eighteen

The clock in the kitchen says it is eleven fifty-seven a.m., and though the kettle has just boiled, and technically it's still only morning, I decide caffeine won't cut it and so I give in and traipse upstairs instead. I pour myself a glass of white wine, warm from where I left the opened bottle on the side by my bed last night, and gulp it down before logging on to speak with Aya. Savour the burn, rather than the taste. Max is dead; I think a little erratic behaviour should be forgiven.

As the screen reflects my image back to me, I am struck by just how white I look. Gaunt. Shell-shocked.

'Oh wow, I look like I've just seen a ghost,' I exclaim, before breaking into slightly hysterical – some might say manic – laughter. 'Well, I did just see a dead body,' I continue, trying to quell my laughter by grabbing for my thighs and pinching the flesh hard between my thumb and forefingers. It's a bad habit of mine, covering up my emotions with humour.

'I can't imagine how tough today must have been for you, Justine.'

My laughter dries up and I find myself sniffing instead, trying to stifle the tears threatening to follow.

'I'm used to dead bodies. I didn't realise quite how hard I'd find it.' The word 'hard' sounds hollow. Running a marathon is hard. Or revising for your final exams. Seeing Max's lifeless body? That wasn't just hard. That was fucking impossible. So much so that I shut down. Went on to autopilot. I'm sure Aya would have a lot to say about that.

'Well, I'm glad you reached out to me. It shows a lot of strength. Look how far you've come; you should be so proud of yourself. You are taking control of your emotions, recognising when you need help and not being too stoic to ask for it. I'm really impressed. How about we agree that over the coming weeks you reach out whenever you need me, and I will do my best to fit you in.'

'Thanks.' It's a very kind offer. I know Aya is in high demand. She's right though, I am proud of myself too. Sometimes it's easier to allow yourself to fall back down again. To simply let the tide take you away. It's harder to swim.

'I imagine there's a lot going on in that mind of yours today. Have you thought about anything specific you'd like us to talk about?'

I shake my head.

'No problem. I was thinking about this having happened while you're back in Maldon and it made me realise how affronting those two things must feel for you. I know you stayed close to Max after you left, but you've told me many times before that whenever you'd meet it was always in London. That, although you've seen him over the years, you haven't ever seen him back in your hometown. And now you're back, he has died. Has it brought up everything from the last time you were there?'

'You mean, is it not lost on me that the last time I was in Maldon there was also another dead body?' I guess this is where she's going. I already knew she'd link the two.

'It can't be easy. The mirroring of it,' she replies slowly, cautiously.

'I never saw my dad after he died,' I say.

'I know, but you left only one week after his accident, didn't you? Now, a few days after finally returning all these years later, your brother's body is found.'

My palms are sweaty and I have to remind myself this is not an interrogation. There is no direction of blame. No accusation.

Aya is simply acknowledging this can't be easy for me. I close my eyes as I struggle to find the words.

'I don't think I can talk about him yet. Max, I mean. I, I—' My voice begins to crack and visions of his bruised, broken body swarm in front of my eyes.

'That's fine. How about your dad? Could we talk about him?'

'I can try,' I say, forcing my eyes open. Brush a stray piece of hair away from my face. Usually, I find it almost impossible to speak about Dad but today it feels the easier of the two.

'How about we talk about the last time you saw him. The evening of the Christmas party.'

'Why? Because today is the last time I'll see Max?'

Deflecting my anger, she says, 'We don't have to talk about anything if you don't want to.'

I look at the clock. We're only halfway through. I can't sit here in silence for the rest of the hour, and besides, I'm here to swim.

'OK. What do you want to know?'

'It's not about what I want to know, Justine. We've been over this. It's about you exploring the words.'

Exploring the words.

It's a phrase Aya often uses. What she really means is exploring how I feel. Unravelling the knots that have become tangled and tied up inside me with words. Finding a way to give meaning through language to all those complicated feelings I can't make sense of.

'So, how about you start with describing your last interaction with your dad?'

'We were in my bedroom. Here, in this room. I'd just told him what had happened at the party and he was angry. Furious. I'd never seen him quite so angry; I was afraid of what he might do next. It wasn't directed at me. He was angry at *him*. His anger made me feel safer, able to tell the truth. As though it meant he would protect me. He told me to stay in my room until the party was over. He forgot to give me a kiss goodnight but I forgave him because I knew he was distracted by how angry he felt.'

'And after that?'

'There was no after. A few hours later the police knocked on our door.'

'How do you feel about your last conversation with him?'

'I feel guilty.'

'What about?'

'I feel guilty that right before he died he felt so much anger. That if I hadn't told him what happened, perhaps he wouldn't have drunk so much. Or maybe, even if it didn't change the accident, that if he hadn't been so angry then maybe he wouldn't have forgotten to give me a kiss goodnight and the last thing he'd have told me was that he loved me.'

'The only thing we're in control of are our own actions, no one else's. And even then, we cannot try and move the chess pieces too far ahead. There are too many variables. You have no idea what your last conversation would have been if your own actions had been different. Maybe someone else would have said something. Maybe, just maybe, your last conversation would have been worse. Not better.'

'I know.' We've been over this idea before, how there are so many sliding-door moments running simultaneously at any given time that you can't even indulge in the 'what ifs', because they aren't real. They are simply fantasies.

'You did not do this, Justine. You can't control everything.'

I look over my laptop screen at the floral wallpaper of my bedroom. The flowers still resemble open mouths and I wonder, if walls could talk, how differently they would have answered Aya's question.

Chapter Nineteen

The path by the river is overgrown. Starting at the shipyard and leading away from the centre of town before looping back, this is one of the walks I'd often do with Jake. After the intensity of my session with Aya, I am desperate to put some space between me and that house. The brambles are scratching at my arms, clawing at me. I imagine they are hissing at me to turn around and go back home. To London. To Noah.

I used to find this walk peaceful but today the quiet is too loud. The aeroplanes roar in my ears, and the heat feels so suffocating I have tied my T-shirt up above my belly button in a knot – something I haven't done since my early twenties on a night out, probably somewhere like Infernos in Clapham South, classy establishment that it is. But I'm willing to do anything to help me cool down in this heat. The colours are bright. Too bright, as the sun sparkles on the river. Instead of feeling at one with nature I feel apart from it. It is all too vivid, and in its vibrancy my own colour feels washed out.

As the river bends, I am forced to climb over a fallen tree trunk blocking the path. My leg snags on a branch. *Shit*. I look back at the offending branch as if it can feel my wrath. My shin is bleeding but that's not what draws my attention. There is a heart carved into the trunk. My legs collapse beneath me. A different tree, a different heart, but the memory won't let go. We were just kids, really, but back then all my emotions felt bigger. All-consuming. Now they are held steadfastly in place, fastened tightly by experience and pain, no longer allowed to expand so big they can hurt me. That wasn't the case when I was with Jake.

The day we carved a heart into a sycamore tree had been on my eighteenth birthday and it was the first day Jake had told me he loved me. *I'll never leave you*, he'd whispered in my ear that evening. Only months later, he disappeared from my life.

I trace the heart in front of me now with my finger and I close my eyes. It is too painful to think about the old Jake when I know what he has gone on to be accused of. Seen the faces of the people he is supposed to have killed.

I've come on this walk to try to escape the pressure roaring in my ears ever since Max's body was found four days ago. Maldon is a small town where major crime is not something that happens often. Our newspaper headlines consist of stories about graffiti and excessive chewing gum. They are not filled with blood and death and murder. One local murderer is gossip. But another body, floating out to sea? The CCTV footage? I know it cannot be a coincidence.

There is more to uncover here. I know it, and I'm pretty sure DS Rose knows it too. I can feel her circling above like an eagle. Hunting me.

On my way back to town I call Otis who confirms that Jake's ankle tag has not been activated, meaning he has stayed in Letchworth all this time. The relief rushes through my body and the weight that's been crushing my ribcage feels a little lighter. It's still there, but I can fill a full breath for the first time since I was told Max's body had been pulled from the water.

The police station is at the top of the high street. A wall of cold air hits me as the door slides open. It is both refreshing and affronting.

'Hi, I'm here to see DS Sorcha Rose,' I announce myself to the man in uniform sitting behind the front desk. We are separated by a glass shield with just a small opening at the bottom for me to present my ID through.

'Hi Justine, I'll let her know you're here. Please take a seat and I'm so sorry for your loss. I hope your mum is holding up OK,' he says without even glancing at my ID before pushing a visitor book in my direction. I think I recognise him, but Dad's friends all blurred into one all those years ago. I could never keep track of all the new people. The changing faces at our door. At the time I thought he was just a people person. To my childlike eyes everyone seemed to love him, and why wouldn't they? The parties, the dinners with police friends, the weekends shooting with local farmers, late-night pub gatherings with other business owners. Dad was friends with everyone, and I saw it all as confirmation he was the man that I desperately wanted him to be. That everyone else saw it too – he was charismatic and charming. Smart. Good – if you looked hard enough.

But now I'm older, and arguably wiser – myself part of the world he once inhabited – I realise that wasn't the case at all. Everyone knew Dad, and Dad made it his business to know them. I think of all the people who would turn up to his Christmas party each year. Too many to keep track of – faces I'd never seen before would suddenly appear at our door for one night only. No one needs that many friends, not unless you're getting something out of it. No, Dad didn't have many friends, he just had his finger in every pie.

The chairs are a reddish-brown and sticky. I'm hoping it's just from the heat but still I wish I was wearing a long dress instead of shorts. To while away the time, I people-watch, making up backstories for everyone I see. There's the wife who caught her husband sleeping with her best friend and stabbed them both;

the grandma who runs a local knitting group but is suspected of laundering money through her bakery. And then there's Jimmy. No, really, it is Jimmy, being led out by DS Sorcha Rose. He tips his cap at me as he walks past and then DS Rose is almost on top of me. Smile wide. Wolf-like.

'Justine. Thanks so much for coming. Follow me.'

She leads me into a small room off a narrow corridor. Unlike the waiting area, this room is stuffy and approximately three times hotter than outside. I wonder if it was designed like this on purpose. There are plenty of ways to apply pressure on an unco-operative suspect, all of which are technically legal. Our physical and mental states are intrinsically linked. Affect one and you'll alter the other.

I pass DS Rose the list of everyone in the area I know Max was in close contact with.

'Have you heard back from the autopsy report yet?' I ask. 'Or toxicology?'

'I'm afraid not. The autopsy report should be back by the end of the week but the toxicology report may take some time. If the autopsy shows we have to open a full investigation, it'll speed things up with toxicology. But let's hope it doesn't come to that.'

'Thanks. And I've been thinking about what you said, about looking round Max's place? We should do it sooner rather than later to limit the potential argument that something was taken after Max's death instead of before it.'

She narrows her eyes, 'You make an interesting point. Go on.'

'Well, if I were defending someone and they were linked to the break-in but couldn't – without doubt – be placed at the murder scene, I would try to argue that the burglary took place after the event of death, by someone simply preying on an empty house, rather than presenting the case as having happened before an attack and with a specific personal motive. Or even a burglary gone wrong. If this does turn out to be foul play, I want the case against the bastard to be as strong as possible.'

'They do say you're good at what you do. I'll let you know as soon as we're ready for you.'

'Perfect.'

As I leave the station, I can feel DS Rose watching me from the doorway. Uncooperative, kiss my arse. I expect a room with aircon next time.

'Hey.'

I am not easily frightened but since coming back to this place I've found myself more jumpy than usual. Spinning on my heels I come face to face with Jimmy.

'Have you been waiting for me?'

'I have. I'm so sorry about—' It's like he can't bring himself to say Max's name and I remember most people aren't as used to death as me. 'How are you doing?'

'I'm not great. Mum is worse. How about you?'

He looks at the floor and then back up. 'I just . . . I can't believe it. I keep thinking, what if I'd been there for him more. You know?'

I think you should come home.

I try to push the guilt away. Focus on Jimmy.

'I'm sure Max knew he could always come to you. Like you said, friends drift, you have nothing to feel guilty for.'

My words are intended to soothe, but instead he looks even worse. His eyes are red-rimmed, eyelids puffy as though he's been crying.

He clears his throat, 'I have some ideas for a memorial service. I thought maybe I could talk to you about them over lunch?'

'Now?'

'We—, we—, well—' He stumbles over his words and the clear display of emotion makes me uncomfortable.

'Lunch would be lovely,' I interrupt.

Mrs Salisbury's café is as quirky and quintessentially cosy as it sounds. Low ceilings, creaky floorboards and cosy wooden booths with worn red leather seats where people huddle together gossiping over scones and tea. Once again, I feel like I no longer belong here, sitting among the delicate china and buttercream cakes. I am too damaged. My soul too dark. I must look as awkward as I feel as Jimmy asks again if I'd rather go back to his place, but I decide that would be even worse. Too close to Max. It's not that I don't want to feel close to him, but I'm certain my pain would spill over. I'm aware enough to know I still need some distance. To keep it at arm's length. Here, I can almost pretend we're just two old friends catching up over a lovely lunch – not discussing how to bury my brother and Jimmy's best friend, the din of the other customers quietening my grief.

Before they've even brought our food, we've already covered the memorial plans – the music, the photographs, the pallbearers, the buffet food in the Blue Eagle afterwards. Now, as I bite into my sausage sandwich, I struggle to find something else to say. To fill the silence.

An eruption of cheering bursts from the booth at the back of the room and I peer round to see what all the fuss is about. It's a small group of women – a range in age – and the varying sashes across each of their outfits make it clear to every passer-by that they are on a hen do. Bride. Mother of the Bride. Bridesmaids. The innocent hope of a happy marriage. Then, with the pop of a champagne cork, the table bursts into howls of delight and clapping. A clang of a knife against a glass, the familiar marker of the beginning of a toast.

I feel dizzy with the tug of nostalgia.

'My family always loved a toast,' I say. 'It was Dad's thing. He always had the same speech lined up for any and every occasion.' It's a strange feeling, to be consumed with nostalgia at the same time as disgust. My family has been ripped apart by tragedy twice now. But what kind of family were we to begin with?

'You know Max carried the tradition on?'

'He did? I haven't heard that speech in eighteen years.' I don't tell Jimmy I haven't missed it. Nor do I admit the thought of Max repeating it makes me feel physically sick. More than that, it makes me angry. Confused. Why would he repeat it? Whose side was he on?

Jimmy shrugs. 'Maybe he didn't want to remind you of what you'd lost. I think he found a comfort in it though. A memory of your dad he could keep alive.'

I force myself to stay silent. To not shout that's exactly what I'm so angry about – why would he want to do such a thing?

'Max wasn't exactly one for traditions, but I think he always respected that your father was. It's probably what drew your dad to the Freemasons. Even though that wasn't for Max,' Jimmy continues.

'I'm sorry, what?' My sandwich suddenly feels thick and stodgy in my mouth. I force myself to swallow it down.

'You didn't know your dad was a Freemason?'

'I had no idea.'

What else don't I know about my father? The fact he was a Freemason doesn't actually surprise me; he always had a flair for the theatrical, and he loved anything that felt elite and exclusive. What better fits the bill than being part of an all-male brotherhood dating back to medieval times? One with secret handshakes, rituals and passwords. No one really knows what goes on within the Masonic lodges, but their involvement in historic moments is the subject of speculation throughout the world. I rather suppose it's now mostly reduced to 'I'll scratch your back and you scratch mine', but the legends and mysteries of the Freemasons remain.

'But you say Max wasn't?'

'Nope. He got invited to join after your dad's accident but turned it down.'

'And Max definitely said no?'

'I'm sure. He said it wasn't for him. Caused quite a stir to be honest.'

'Why?'

'Well, your father was so respected in Maldon I think every-one just assumed Max would follow suit.'

'Why does that have anything to do with the Freemasons?'

Jimmy raises his eyebrows at me as if he's suddenly realised he knows something I don't know. 'Because here almost every-one is a Mason.' He says it conspiratorially, almost in a whisper.

'Men.' I sit back defiantly in my chair.

'Pardon?'

'I assume by everyone you actually mean the men.'

'Sorry, yes.'

'So not everyone.'

'No.' At least he has the decency to look sheepish, a little red creeping across his cheeks.

'And you? Are you part of this exclusive club?'

He rolls his eyes at me as if I'm being childish. 'Absolutely not. You know I always copied Max.'

He did. Max always had that effect on people – he was a natural-born leader of the pack. A trait inherited from our dad.

We finish the rest of the lunch filling the space with small talk but on my walk home it is all I can think about: the fact Dad had secrets. He was a member of a notoriously secret organisation. One, according to Jimmy, which has taken over this town.

I came here looking for answers, but I'm beginning to wonder if I'm up against more than I realise? A town steeped in traditions: a family built upon them.

BEFORE

JAKE – THE BOYFRIEND

The summer had passed all too quickly, and it was already time for Max to leave again for Cambridge. Jake could hardly believe he'd only known him a few months. Over a short period of time, they'd become so close that Justine had taken to referring to them as 'double trouble'. It made him laugh, the pair of them the least likely to stray from the rules.

If anyone were to cause trouble, he'd have placed his bets on Justine. He loved her, but he also couldn't quite place her. He supposed that was partly why he loved her. She intrigued him – she was full of dichotomies.

He'd noticed that about her the first time he'd seen her lying in the rain. Quiet, but you couldn't take your eyes off her. Bold, yet cautious. Carefree, but with something steelier at her core. It was that inner fire he loved so much. Hoped it would never be extinguished. He knew she didn't even know she had it, but it was the very essence of her.

Jake had noticed the whole day felt a little off. Gerard was being exceptionally talkative, and Evelyn – while she never spoke much anyway – seemed so withdrawn it was possible to forget she was there at all. He'd asked Justine quietly as they'd moved from dinner into the snug if everything was OK and she'd smiled and slipped her hand in his, but it hadn't gone unnoticed that she hadn't actually replied.

They were now all standing in the snug, a fire roaring in the old-fashioned fireplace. He wasn't sure it was quite cold enough for one yet, but the weather was on the turn and lighting the fire was a very British way of trying to make the wet feel cosy rather than depressing.

Jake found himself drawn to looking at Evelyn where she sat across the room from everyone else. A bystander to her own family. The more he watched, the more he realised she wasn't even blinking. A smile was plastered across her face, but nothing lay behind it.

He looked again to Max and Justine, who were deep in an animated discussion about what 'Freshers' week' entailed, to Gerard who stood near them, content just listening in on their excitement, and then back to Evelyn. Apart. Her limbs were folded in on herself, each hand wrapped round the opposite elbow, legs bent over one another and her feet tucked under the chair.

He felt caught in the middle. It was as though all the different pieces didn't fit together, as if Evelyn didn't belong in this particular scene. He decided to ask her if she was OK, but before he reached her, he heard Gerard declaring it was time for a toast while clapping Max on his back. Immediately, Evelyn sprang up from her seat and set about filling their glasses. Back into action, Gerard's voice rousing her from whatever dream-world she'd been in.

He'd learnt fast that toasting for the Stones was somewhat of a tradition. Never just a simple affair, the rule was that you'd go around the group each making your own toast before finishing off with the same short speech each time by Gerard. In some ways it was nice, but Jake couldn't help thinking it was also a little cultish.

'To Max,' Justine cheered, kicking things off, 'I was worried you'd come back a posh git but you didn't. So that deserves a toast.'

'To my son,' Evelyn went next, raising her glass seriously, 'stay safe and kind.' And then she looked at Jake, readying him to go next. She had the same piercing eyes as Justine and he wanted to remember to ask her if she was OK after.

He always hated this part, could never think of anything clever to say, although Justine assured him that was not the point. 'To Max, for welcoming me into your family and only ever *threatening* to push me into the river but never actually doing it.'

'Yet,' Gerard added and they all laughed along with him, though his own laugh was quiet as he watched Evelyn once again, noting how when she laughed she lowered her eyes. As though she were caught in a lie.

'And to Jake,' Max chimed in, taking him by surprise. 'Look after Justine while I'm away, although I already know you will. She's found her person in you, we can all see that. But what I didn't expect this summer was to make a new best mate. So, that's enough soppiness for now, let's drink.'

'And finally,' Gerard began.

'Let us raise a glass to those whom we love,
to those standing here and those up above;
Let us toast to our promise for as long as we live,
we'll have the courage to love and we'll fight to forgive.'

They all drank, finishing their champagne with a final flourish.

Courage and forgiveness: the pillars of the Stone family motto. The thing that had always intrigued Jake about it was that up until then, he'd have said he couldn't see anything they would need the courage to overcome or to forgive. But tonight had been different. Tonight, he realised there were more layers to this family than Justine had showed him. Layers which didn't seem quite so shiny and perfect.

After all, as his own mother liked to remind him, all that glitters is not gold.

Chapter Twenty

It's like a carousel round here, as though people have set a reminder in their diary to check in on us this Sunday, two days before the funeral. Not so close to Max's death as to encroach on our private grieving time, but not so long that they run the danger of us thinking they don't care. It turns out most people have decided today, nine days after they found his body, is the perfect balance.

The doorbell rings – again – and I open it, barely bothering to see who it is; assuming another of Mum's friends.

'Is now a bad time?' DS Sorcha Rose asks. She is accompanied by the police liaison officer who showed me Max's body and my heart starts to race faster. Gearing up. Readying for battle.

The four of us are sitting round the small kitchen table – my mother, me, the detective and her officer.

'The good news, Mrs Stone, is the autopsy report did not show anything suspicious. The damage to your son's right-side was most likely caused by the swell of the water moving the body forcefully across rocks and debris under the sea. It is very common in cases like this. You can read here that the pathologist found fibres and organic material across the surface of the wounds to support this conclusion.' Mum gasps and I surprise myself by clasping my hand over hers.

'It's OK, it means Max had already passed away. It's better this way,' I reassure her, trying to make myself believe my own words.

She rolls her hand over, interlocking her fingers with mine and giving a little squeeze. The intimacy of it catches in my throat. I force myself not to pull away.

'Now, we do still have the toxicology report to come back which will potentially fill in a few other gaps.' Mum's grip tightens again. 'During the autopsy the pathologist took samples from Max's organs, urine and blood. The toxicologist will study those for any sign of toxins such as alcohol. Right now what we *do* know is that all of Max's physical injuries were sustained after he entered the water.'

DS Rose pauses briefly, letting it sink in. 'I know it's a very difficult conversation to have but a few of the people I've spoken to have mentioned Max didn't seem himself the last few times they saw him. Is there a chance he was depressed? Particularly stressed with work? A relationship gone wrong?'

'I'm sorry, I can't do this. I – I need a minute.' Mum holds a handkerchief to her face and runs out of the kitchen.

Max didn't seem himself the last few times they saw him.

Who have they spoken to? The barmaid?

'Justine, is there anything you can think of?'

I can feel myself about to tell all, that Max had a fight with Jake six weeks before Jake was arrested. Now I'm wondering if Max's death is somehow connected to what really happened to the Rushnells. How could these two men, whom I knew never to harm a fly and whom once were the closest of friends, have ended up arrested and dead only one month apart from each other?

But I catch myself just in time, forcing the words back down. Now is not the time to do anything rash, even if the truth feels itchy on my tongue. No, I need more answers before I decide how much to say. Once that box is opened, it will be almost impossible to shut again. Most certainly, it will dredge up the past. Do I really want to spill all our family history if none of it is important?

There is no point risking everything simply on a whim, fuelled by grief.

So instead, I bide my time. I think of all the interview transcripts I've read over the years. The hardest ones to manipulate are those which give the least away. *No comment.*

'No, I'm sorry.'

'Very well then.' I note she seems disappointed in me again but no longer surprised. 'Mark here is going to stay a little while longer, answer any questions you or your mum might have. If you think of anything else then please let me know. Like I said, we still have the toxicology report to come back but I wanted to let you know Max's official cause of death has been deemed as drowning. You can read over the report details if you so wish in your own time.'

She opens her briefcase and places a copy of the autopsy report on the table. Pushes it towards me and then taps at a section titled *Conclusion to support death by drowning.*

Silt and weeds found in airways.

Watery fluid in stomach.

Heavy lungs.

I look her in the eye and neither of us look away. This is not standard procedure. There are some things the family of the bereaved do not need to see. Is she trying to goad me into talking?

Am I one step behind or in front?

I hear Mum returning and hurriedly I pick the report up, stashing it behind my back. A mother does not need to read this.

'I know it's not the perfect time, but we have a team down at Max's house at the moment. Justine, if you're feeling up for it, are you still happy to take a look around?'

'Of course, I'll come right now,' I say, as sweetly as possible.

DS Rose is very impressive. I like her – in a messed-up way. I blame Mum and Dad for that.

'Do you know what type of laptop it was?' DS Rose asks. We are standing in Max's kitchen.

'A Mac, I think. I don't know if he got a new one recently though, so please don't take my word on it.'

She makes a note, flips a page, looks back at me.

'What about his phone?'

'I have no idea, I'm so sorry. Was it not on him? I assumed it had been given to Mum with his personal belongings.'

'No, but that's not unusual with drownings. The tide can do all sorts. I just thought I'd ask, and the laptop reminded me.' She flaps her hand dismissively and makes it sound so casual that I don't believe her for one second. This woman is calculating and meticulous.

'And there was nothing else you noticed missing? No family heirloom or special watch or photograph. Nothing?'

'Just the laptop as far as I can tell. But, as you know, I haven't actually been here before. I've seen the house on Facetime but I'm not really the best person for this job.'

The laptop would have been obvious to DS Rose from the beginning. A home office with a charger but no laptop. She did not need me for this.

As we make our way back on to the street and I'm readying myself to leave, she starts again. I notice it's a rhythm she has. To hold back her most important question until the end, disguised as an afterthought, hoping to catch you unawares. It's clever but I'm too smart for such games. 'Just one more thing. Do you know what day the bins go out this side of town?'

'I don't, sorry. Like I said, it's been years since I stayed here for any amount of time.'

'I thought you might say that. I asked Jimmy yesterday and he said Mondays.'

Perhaps I'm not quite as smart as I think.

DS Rose scratches the side of her head with one finger, and I know it is just for show, 'The confusing thing is that the rubbish was found empty. But if the bins were collected on Monday, Max was already dead. Now, he could have put them out a couple of days early, say, but you'd expect to find at least one thing that had been used and needed throwing away since then if he'd been living here. But there's nothing. The place is as clean as a whistle.'

'What are you suggesting?' I keep my tone calm, curious. As if I simply think she's including me in the investigation, that I haven't cottoned on this is her way of telling me she's watching me. That she knows I have my own secrets.

'At this point in time, nothing. I'm simply asking a question. Thank you for your cooperation today, it's been much appreciated. Have a nice day.'

In my defence, it is not a crime to clean your brother's house, and at that point I didn't know he was floating out to sea. I had no idea that my family was about to be ripped from me once again.

But it serves as a reminder that DS Sorcha Rose is still the eagle and I her prey.

Chapter Twenty-One

Being dressed in my robe and wig feels wonderfully safe and comforting. I am transformed. The physical act of getting ready is also a mental one, and I need a break from being me right now; from the weight of deciding how much of my own truth needs to be told in the face of Max's death.

It's my first day back in court, ten days after Max's body was pulled from the sea. My first since I was taken off the biggest case of my career. I'm sure I could have got someone else to cover today's hearing for me. Max's funeral isn't until tomorrow and Charles isn't expecting me back in chambers until after the weekend, but I could feel this was exactly what I needed after yesterday. It is empowering standing in court.

At least, that's how I was hoping it would feel, but as the judge once again rules 'sustained' to an objection against my cross-examination of a witness, I can no longer think of a different way to phrase my question. Even worse, I can't remember a single thing about the case I'm meant to be prosecuting. I am no longer in the courtroom; I am suspended in time.

One thousand pieces of tiny glass. Each one with the ability to hurt. One thousand possibilities to cause pain.

I remain out of my seat, poised to address the witness box. I am dressed head to toe to play the part. The wig, the robe, my extraordinarily expensive shoes buckled tightly with just the right heel height to clip-clop as I walk, but still modest enough to allow me to stride through the courtroom. And I am failing;

quite simply rendered speechless. I squeeze my fists together, hoping the sharpness from my nails digging into the palms of my hands might bring me back to the courtroom. It doesn't work. In my mind, I am no longer in court. Instead, I am standing, blood running from the soles of my feet, staring at my father's lifeless body.

I am aware of Lara rising from her seat beside me, and with every ounce of energy I force my body to obey and sit down.

'Can you please describe, in your own words Miss Nightingale, the scene of the crash when you first arrived,' Lara continues seamlessly.

'There was glass. So much glass, and I could see all the windows had caved in.'

I pick up a pen and pretend to look as though I'm still in control. Lara carries on impressively from where I left off; finally having a chance to shine after her last two years working alongside me.

The next witness fails to turn up, meaning the court is adjourned soon after what I'm now referring to as my 'blackout', and as I sweep the papers into my wheelie and walk out of the courtroom, I do my best to avoid eye contact with any of the other legal professionals. We all know each other, inside and outside the courtroom. What is rivalry in court quickly morphs into comradeship outside of it. But not today. Today I need to avoid their questioning glances.

The courtroom door has barely swung shut behind me before my phone rings. The name on the screen flashes 'Charles'. Even the appearance of his name on my screen seems to convey a furious urgency, although I know it is just in my imagination. Still, the anger in his voice is undeniable.

He doesn't tell me how he heard, but my guess is it was from Andrew Marsfield, the prosecuting barrister on today's case. He has always been a little weasel, with his thinning floppy hair and small eyes knitted too close together. He hit on me once a few years back when I was already engaged to Noah. Men never deal well with rejection; it wouldn't surprise me if he's been waiting all these years to exact his revenge and I've just given him the perfect ammunition. Without a doubt, it has worked. I have been summoned. Apparently immediately, back to chambers.

I watch, mesmerised by the muscles as they protrude in wild circles out of the side of Charles's jawline while he speaks. To describe him as angry doesn't cut it. He says it reflects badly on the entire chambers.

'We pride ourselves on being the best representation out there. It's simply unacceptable. You have a duty to provide a competent standard of work to the client.' It is the second time he's said it, and I wonder if it's a line he'd been rehearsing before my arrival. Stolen from the *Bar Standards Board Handbook*.

'I'm sorry, I'll make sure it doesn't happen again.' It sounds no more sincere now than it did the first time I apologised. I wish I meant it. That I was as mortified at myself as Charles is, but I feel nothing. No shame. No guilt. No sense that I've let Charles, or myself, down. It's not that I don't care, but part of me is stuck there — as if I never fully returned to the courtroom – and I'm still staring at the broken glass. The blood trailing from the soles of my feet. Dad's eyes, looking up at me. Lifeless.

I wonder when reality will hit. Logically I know I've just jeopardised my entire career, but I cannot feel it yet. Is it self-preservation? Or have I finally lost myself to the past completely?

'No. It won't,' Charles says, finally taking a seat behind his big oak desk. 'The other silks have been talking and we think it would be best if you take a step away from your cases for a while. A month perhaps. Give yourself some time to grieve.'

Now he has my attention.

'I can't do that. I'm self-employed. This is my livelihood you're talking about.'

'We know. Look, you've gone through a lot – clearly are still going through a lot – and these are people's lives we're dealing with here. Their futures. You cannot fuck it up, and you're clearly not ready to be back in court yet.'

'I'm fine,' I protest but he interrupts me. His hand held up as though I'm a naughty schoolgirl.

'Justine, I strongly advise that you take some time away and then we'll go from there. I'll leave it up to you to let the solicitors on your cases know.'

Go from there. It is distinctly lacking in any promises. I remember the creases around his smile when I turned up at chambers with pastries ready to celebrate my biggest case. It was so clear he shared in my excitement at this breakthrough in my career. He had been proud of me, his protégée. I look at him now. Deep furrow lines staring back at me. No trace of a smile. The stress makes him look more tired than usual.

Well Charles, I am also tired.

I am really fucking tired.

I have been tired for eighteen years.

Chapter Twenty-Two

It takes three hours to escape the London traffic and drive to Maldon. I don't want to go back to sit in a house I hate and face the fact my whole career is disappearing before my eyes. I know what this means. Even if in a month's time I do get assigned new cases, there's no way my reputation won't be scarred by this. I am losing control.

Cracking.

The past is intruding on my present more and more frequently every day. I can be walking along the street and then, without warning, I'm back there. In a small dark space. Unable to escape. Locked in. The flashbacks have always been there, but they're getting worse.

I have never done well standing still, it allows too much space for my thoughts to swell. To press into the corners of my mind and grow roots where they shouldn't. No, I cannot go back to nothing. I need a distraction. A task.

By the time I'm pulling up in front of Max's house it is already starting to get dark. Jimmy has spent the past week organising the memorial and has asked me to bring some framed photos to be displayed on a table next to the casket. All the photos at Mum's place are of us as children but I saw some when looking round with DS Rose that would work perfectly.

All traces of Max's house as a crime scene are now gone. There is no yellow tape billowing in the wind and the back door has been replaced. This time I let myself in the front with Mum's spare key and there's something disastrously sad about it. A finality to it; the fact there is no point knocking on the door – no chance Max will be here to let me in.

Opening the fridge, I'm disappointed to see there are no longer any beers left.

I start with the lounge, sweeping the mantelpiece and bay-window ledge for anything suitable. There's a photo of him with a group of friends on holiday a couple of years ago in Corfu, hanging their bare feet over the edge of a yacht, the sparkling blue sea looking inviting below them.

Silt and weeds found in airways.

Death by drowning.

I do not pick it up. There are others, and I sweep them straight into my bag: a photo of the two of us at Max's graduation; him and Jimmy at the BMX track as teenagers; Mum and Max in her back garden.

In all these photos he looks so vibrant. He always did live life to the fullest – sometimes a little too wildly – but at the end of the day he was always there when you needed him. I used to wonder where it came from, his ability to let go and have fun. I wanted to know his secret, how he didn't let everything weigh him down like I did. Perhaps he simply didn't see what I saw?

Swollen.

Putrefaction.

Heavy lungs.

Or maybe it finally all caught up with him. *Max, what happened? How did you end up in the water?*

I'm about to leave when a call comes in from Otis.

'Hey, just the guy I want to hear from,' I say, hopeful he'll have some answers for me.

'I heard you're off your big murder case.' Flat. Monotone.

I'm not really surprised; I knew word would get around fast. I had just been buying myself time.

'Who told you?' Immediately I realise it's a futile question. Otis never needs to be told anything and he certainly never reveals his sources. 'Actually, no need to answer.'

'Does it have anything to do with me digging around your brother's laptop?'

There is no point lying to Otis, as he always finds the truth, but evasion is a different skill altogether.

'Can we meet? Please, just give me the chance to tell you everything and then if you want out, I understand.'

'For you, fine. I'll pick you up in two hours.'

'Thing is—' I know I'm really pushing my luck with this one, but it's true, and I'm supposed to be working on setting boundaries. 'I can't meet tonight. Noah is expecting me back, he just flew in from Paris, and then tomorrow is the funeral. Can you wait until the day after? I promise, I'll tell you everything.'

'Fine.' He sounds reluctant but at least he's not pushing it. I wonder how understanding he'd have been in different circumstances. One where I'm not grieving my dead brother.

'I'll pick you up. I assume you'll want to go somewhere private?'

'Ideally, yes.'

'OK. But the truth, Justine. If you want me to keep helping you, I'm going to need the whole truth.'

I almost laugh at the notion of it coming from Otis's lips. He's just as well-placed as I am to know there is no such thing. People like to think the world can be divided into fact and fiction, but I have seen first-hand how facts can be manipulated and used, moulded so much that you can no longer distinguish what is real and what is not. Everything in this world is subjective, examined through a lens, the facts we view distorted by our own experiences.

I have spent many dinners debating this with Noah, convincing him there is no such thing as the truth. Just a gap between one person's experience and another's; one we can fill with any number of different truths. I see it play out in the courtroom every day. But still, I promise Otis just that. The truth. Because, while I may no longer have any new cases from chambers, I still have my own answers to find.

Chapter Twenty-Three

I know Noah has arrived at Mum's safely because he's kept me updated every step of his journey back from Paris. It was sweet, making sure I knew he was on his way – imagining I might be waiting impatiently for his arrival when the truth is, I have been dreading it. I want more than anything to feel the touch of Noah, to feel the security blanket of him wrap around me, keeping me steady.

And yet, I do not want any of those things to take place here in Maldon, not least back in that house. I don't even know how I'll react to him being physically present in this place. Whether all the safety he normally provides for me will even work here, or if he too will become tainted.

Yes, I know to expect him – he cut his business trip short to be back in time for Max's funeral – but still, all my senses feel confused seeing him in Mum's lounge. He is wearing the dark-blue shirt I bought him last birthday, open at the neck, and cream chino shorts with loafers. Round, thick black-rimmed glasses. It is so overtly London in style he looks comedically out of place. A visual reminder that the before and after stages of my life were never destined to come together like this.

He leaps up from his chair as soon as he sees me. The first thing I think is that he should not be sitting there. That chair does not belong to him. It is *his*. Dad's. He needs to change seat. But how do I tell him that? Instead, I let him kiss me, and try to focus on the fact he is my husband.

Noah is good. We are good. Despite it all, we are here together and that should be enough.

'You've been OK with Mum?' I ask.

'Of course. Why wouldn't I be? In fact, I may have promised her I'll cook dinner tonight.'

'You what?' *Please God no.* I was hoping to keep them as separate as possible during his stay.

'I thought it would be the right thing to do. And besides, it'll be nice to get to know her a bit more, even in these circumstances.'

These circumstances.

I try not to flinch at the coldness of it. Remind myself that this is Noah. He is not unkind – he hasn't said it intentionally, it's just who he is. Always trying, sometimes too hard, to smooth over his edges. Too loud, to counteract his insecurities. Too funny, to fill in when he feels vulnerable. Too clinical when it all gets over- emotional for his boarding-school background to cope with.

'That's really thoughtful of you,' I force myself to say, because it is true and I am trying not to lash out at him when all he's doing is turning up for me. He isn't perfect, but he is kind.

It is not Noah's fault I do not want him here – in this place – this house – with my mother. It's almost as though I can feel the poison dripping from the walls, from her lips, and sliding its way towards him; readying itself to infect us.

I know I can't get away with sitting on the toilet for much longer before they start asking questions. As promised, Noah has cooked dinner and Mum has set up the big oak table in the dining room instead of having us eat on our laps in the snug. Before now, Noah and I have never eaten a meal with my mum. Not even on our wedding day. We married on holiday precisely so I could avoid the awkwardness of having a 'top table' dinner.

Of course, Noah doesn't know that's the reason. I sold him the dream of it being romantic, away from the fuss of a big do that distracts from the promises we were making. We spent the money we would have used on a ridiculously overpriced day all our guests would remember as a 'party', on two months in the Mediterranean. To be fair, he didn't take much persuading, not once I'd shown him the type of villa we could afford to stay in. He's met Mum before of course, although how many times can be counted on one hand, and never back in this place.

Knock-knock.

'All OK in there?' Even Noah's knock is slow and steady. His voice, soft and concerned. The control he has not to bang the door down and demand I tell him what is going on sums up everything I respect about him: everything that is the opposite to me. The real me – hidden deep down below.

There's no reasonable response to someone like him other than being calm back. That's the thing about Noah, he always keeps his emotions in check, everything in order – no word out of place. It keeps me grounded. It keeps me level-headed, quietening the swell of feelings threatening to burst out from inside me.

It's one of the things about him I love the most: how he helps me be this person too. But today, the night before Max's funeral, I can feel the pain inside me needs a release. It does not want to be quelled.

I close my eyes and tune into what he's saying from the other side of the door, hoping it will calm me as it usually does. He's talking about what he's made for dinner. The ingredients he used. What part of India the dish originates from. It's a tactic Aya has helped us implement, a way of pulling me out of my own head and having something else to focus on. I know he presumes I am simply overwhelmed by my grief.

In part it is true, but it's not the whole story. In this moment I couldn't love Noah more, but instead of helping me, the very thought that I might lose him one day – that he might not like what he finds when he realises who the real me is – makes the pain in my chest worsen. I pull open the cabinet door over the sink and find a packet of Mum's codeine.

Open it.

Noah has fallen silent, but I can still hear his breathing. He is waiting. Patient as ever. And so, instead of tearing the house down like I want to, I call, 'I'm coming. Thanks. You start plating up,' and then wash down a pill with tap water.

'You really do have a talent, dear.' For what feels like the hundredth time, Mum compliments Noah on his cooking.

Anyone would think he has served up an exquisite five-course tasting menu rather than a simple curry. Granted, he cooked it from scratch, but Mum isn't usually one for giving compliments and certainly she isn't one for going overboard. Enthusiastic is not a word I'd use to describe her, but since Noah's arrival she's seemed to have all this energy I've not seen before.

If I'm honest, it's pissing me off.

'So, Noah.' She puts down her knife and fork. Wipes her mouth with a napkin. 'Banker, son-in-law, chef extraordinaire.' *Dear God, make it stop.* 'I just want to say that I'm so thankful you're here and we can all be together at this time. It means a lot.' She reaches out across the table and puts her hand over his.

'Excuse me a moment, I won't be long.' I scrape my chair back, in need of some air.

I'm resting against the front of the house. Right next to the dining room, but slightly out of sight. I can still hear their conversation as it wafts through the open window; I haven't done it on purpose.

'The thing is,' Mum carries on, 'I'm not entirely sure that being here is the best thing for Justine. I know she feels like she should stay with me but being back here, in this house, and what with everything with Jake, I'm worried it's not good for her.'

'Who is Jake?' he asks.

I want to smash my head on the wall over and over again. Instead, I ball my hands into fists. I could knock on the window and interrupt before she can answer, but we've been hurtling towards this moment ever since I opened the case file. It's inevitable, one way or another. It might as well happen like this.

'Brad Finchley *is* Jake Reynolds, dear.' She says it with such emphasis as if suddenly the penny will drop for Noah.

'Brad Finchley? The guy who killed that couple?'

Accused. He is *accused* of killing them. I don't hear Mum's reply, but I can imagine her tight-lipped nod of the head.

'OK. And Jake Reynolds is?' He leaves it hanging and I can't resist peering in through the window. Noah is sitting with his broad back to me, but Mum is in full view. She clocks me and I can see her stricken face as she looks at me, back to Noah, then back to me.

She wipes her mouth with the napkin again even though she hasn't had another bite.

'I'm sorry, I shouldn't have said anything.'

'Please, go ahead. Say whatever you need to. I just want what's best for Justine.'

Mum looks towards me again. Her eyebrows knitted closer together, in question. I nod, giving her permission to continue.

'Jake Reynolds is,' she stumbles over her words, and I find I'm intrigued to hear how she'll sum us up. 'Well, he and Justine, they loved each other very much. Many years ago.'

It's not a bad try. We did love each other, very *very* much. Perhaps too much.

Noah is pacing up and down the bedroom like a gazelle. Third step in from the left wall and the floorboard creaks. I wish he'd move half a metre closer to the bed; it doesn't make a sound there.

'What I don't understand is why you didn't tell me you'd had a serious boyfriend before. Why pretend I was your first? I wouldn't have cared. I don't care. We all have pasts, that's fine. But why lie about it?'

'Things didn't end well. I just wanted to forget about it. At the time I really didn't think it mattered. I didn't mean it to come out now as if it was this big lie.'

'It was a' – *creak* – 'big lie.'

'It was, and for that I'm sorry.'

'I feel like I'm still missing something. Why didn't you tell me about leading your first big murder case if you didn't know straight away it was Jake? It doesn't make any sense. You would have told me. I know you would have.'

Creak.

I look at my husband. The man who has never said a nasty word to me: always so thoughtful and considered. He doesn't act on impulse and he cares about doing the right thing. He is everything I am not. Everything I wish I was. I can see he is hurting. I have caused him pain.

And so I start to tell him. Not everything, I'm not careless. Just enough. I tell him Jake was my first serious boyfriend and that after almost a year together he left Maldon and ghosted me from his life. I never heard from him again. Four years later, I met Noah at one of Charlotte's friend's birthday party in Clapham and my teenage romance didn't seem important.

Through this part of the story, I can see him softening. Told like this, it doesn't seem too big a lie. There was a long time between the two of them, and we were only young. I've even almost convinced myself that by the time I was twenty-two Jake seemed too insignificant to mention. The next part is trickier to wade my way through. There's not really any sugar-coating it.

'Fuck.' Noah isn't one for swearing, which is how I know he really isn't happy about the fact I didn't disclose I knew Brad – Jake – the defendant, straight away. I resist the urge to smile, satisfied to see he is just as fallible as the rest of us.

'I know. Honestly, I don't know why I didn't say anything. I guess I was just so shocked it was him.'

'Is that why you came back here? Reminiscing about the past?' I almost scoff at his use of 'reminiscing', as if this place and Jake hold good memories for me.

'I don't really know. I think maybe it just made me want to come home. It was a bit of a shock seeing him accused of killing that couple.'

'I suppose I can see why. I just wished you'd told me the truth straightaway.'

'I know. I just didn't know where to start.'

'And what about Charles? What did he say when you told him? Seriously Justine, you were risking a lot.'

'I wasn't thinking properly, it was all just so out of the blue, I acted on impulse. But Charles seemed to believe that I told him as soon as I realised. Or at least, he pretended to. For now.'

'OK, well that's good. That's good,' he repeats, as if convincing himself.

'There is something else I need to tell you, though. I messed up today in court and I was –' does bullied sound too childish? – 'it was suggested I take a break for a while.' I can feel my own disappointment in myself begin to swell in my stomach. Trying to burn its way out.

I force myself to look at Noah and prepare myself to see the same disappointment reflected back in his eyes, but there's no trace of it. His whole demeanour has softened and I'm almost shocked to find him lunging over to envelop me in a hug.

'I'm not happy you've been keeping secrets, but don't be hard on yourself about today. You've been through a lot, it's no surprise that your first day back in court was going to be hard. And with the Jake – Brad – situation, you did the right thing in the end. That's what matters. It will be OK. We'll be OK. Let's just go to bed. We can talk more in the morning. Maybe a break from court is exactly what you need.'

I kiss this kind husband of mine hard on the lips and close my eyes tight hoping when I open them again, we'll be back in the comfort of our own home. It doesn't work.

'Just no more secrets, OK?' he whispers into the nape of my neck.

'No more secrets,' I repeat, hoping maybe this time I can stick to it.

We get ready for bed in silence. There's a softness to it. Something delicate lying between us. This man loves me. The truth of it hits me as I climb into bed and I wrap myself around him, face buried in his chest, willing my breathing to stay steady.

The last – and up until now, only – guy to lie on this bed with me was Jake.

I feel for Noah's hand under the covers and entwine my fingers with his. Our wedding bands rubbing together.

'Are you OK?' Noah murmurs groggily.

'I will be,' I say and he tightens his grip, securing me in his arms. It makes me want to cry. Noah was never meant to be a part of this world. There's no holding back the tears any longer and they roll freely down my cheeks.

I am crying for the old Justine.

The Christmas party: the dividing line of my before and after.

BEFORE

EVELYN – THE MOTHER

Evelyn had spent the past month organising the firm's Christmas party. Every year she found the pressure mounted as the expectation seemed to be for each year to improve on the last – bigger and better. She shouldn't have been surprised really, it was this competitive determination of Gerard's which had got him so far in his career, now owning his own law firm with a number of partners – not all of whom she liked. As expectations rose, so did the consequences of failing to meet them.

Consequences.

She hated she had to think this way, with her whole life thought out in terms of action and reaction – Gerard's, not hers. This wasn't what she'd signed up for when she'd made her vows for better or for worse. Of course, that's not what they stood for either. No one would blame her if she left him. But it was more complicated than that.

In the beginning she'd made excuses for him. How had this man who'd loved her so fiercely, who'd made her feel alive, turned into someone completely different? No, that wasn't right. He wasn't completely different. That's what scared her. He was still charming, affectionate, loud and intoxicating. But over time he showed other sides to him. Crueller sides.

Surely there must be something wrong with him, causing him to act this way. He hadn't treated her like this at the start. What

148

had changed? She desperately wanted there to be a reason. Something other than – it was just him.

Or worse, that it was her. That she was the cause of the hate she could feel pulsing from him. He hadn't always been filled with such hate. They'd loved each other once. She was sure of it.

She'd researched everything in that first year, when the consequences had started. PTSD, brain tumour, depression, bipolar disorder. In the end, she'd finally accepted it was just plain old cruelty. Narcissism.

It had taken a long time to admit it to herself though; it was not easy to accept responsibility. Because that's what it felt like to her. A whole mix of confusing guilt. That she loved him. That she married him. That she angered him.

When he'd proposed, she'd never felt more alive. It had been the easiest yes in the world. No hesitation. They'd only known each other a few months, but it had been a whirlwind romance full of big gestures and riding the high of falling in love.

She hadn't stopped to get to know the man behind the charisma and charm until it was too late. 'You married me. You love me.' He'd caress her neck as he said it. It was something he'd started doing the night of their wedding and it had enthralled her back then, as if he was turned on by the fact she wanted him. It had made her feel powerful. How naïve of her. It had morphed, over time, into feeling like it meant he had all the power, and she none. That shift had happened slowly, and gradually. But now when he touched her like that and whispered those words into the crevice of her neck, it only made her fear what was coming next.

She'd do anything to turn back time, but that was the one thing she had no control over. This was her reality. Perhaps she should have seen it coming. But you never expect it to happen to you. For the man you fall in love with to turn out to be one of the monsters you hear about. Never expect it to look like this – like Gerard.

It wasn't a marriage filled with hate. Most of the time Gerard was still the man she'd chosen to marry. That's what made it so difficult. At first, she'd had a husband who she loved, who had made her feel loved back. But then he had chipped away at her, inch by inch. Was she to blame for that? Or was this guilt she felt imposed on her by Gerard? Is this what he wanted? To reduce her sense of worth until she blamed herself? She tied herself up in knots over it, the pain and confusion so internalised she no longer trusted her own feelings.

When she forced herself to think about it, she wondered if at first she'd forgiven him because her entire sense of self by that point relied on him. She had been lonely when she first met Gerard. And young. She'd never had a father figure in her life and her mother had fallen into a drink-fuelled depression after he'd died. She'd only been a child, left to fend for herself. Never good enough, the full force of her mother's grief with all its pain and anger had been directed at her.

When Gerard entered her world, everything had shifted. He made her feel desired. He made her feel as though she had something worth loving. Had it all been a trick? A way of making her reliant on him? Not just practically (because he'd certainly ensured that financially), but emotionally too?

The only thing she knew for certain was that while he had a hold over her, one she couldn't quite break, she would never let him touch her children.

Max and Justine.

Her lights in the dark. Because sometimes her world was pitch-black and she would feel she was in the darkest, longest tunnel. For days on end. The world continuing around her, but she couldn't get out. The fog imprisoning her while she could only watch.

She knew they felt it too. That they thought she wasn't a good mother. But she could only do what she could, and some days just getting dressed took all her strength. They didn't know how hard she worked to get out of bed for them every day.

All of this made this year's party feel particularly important to Evelyn as it was the first year Gerard had deemed Justine old enough to join them. She saw it as her chance to show her daughter what she was capable of – that she really did exist as a full person.

A mother's strength did not have to be seen, it only had to be felt, she knew that. Lived by it even. But it didn't stop her relishing in this opportunity to show her daughter that she too could have an impact.

She took a final walk through the house, making sure everything was in place; every room sparkled and glowed. Christmas trees – big and small – adorned almost every corner. But the magic was in the details: a Christmas-tree-shaped cheese board, a hot-chocolate bar at one end, a mulled-wine station at the other. She'd even arranged for a wreath-making table to be set up in the snug for those who wanted to make a keepsake and escape somewhere quieter for a while.

She'd done it – there was no way this party wouldn't be a success. From the colleagues and lawyers to the policemen, businessmen and Freemason friends (though often you couldn't separate the two – the Masons could be found everywhere), there was something for everyone. No wonder the guest list was growing year on year. As she turned on the lights in the final room, she smiled.

The scene had been set.

Chapter Twenty-Four

I lie on the bed listening to the tick of the clock hanging above it. The sound, normally almost imperceptible, is as loud as a drum this morning. I know, with every passing second, that we are hurtling towards Max's funeral and it all feels too final. I am not ready to say goodbye.

The car is due to arrive in twenty minutes but my body still won't move. I don't *want* it to move. I am sitting on the edge of the bed with my clothes piled next to me, skin exposed; I am raw from another too-hot, too-long shower. My arms feel heavy, my chest tight. I do not have the energy to get dressed; it is taking all my effort to simply keep breathing.

In for four, hold for five, out for six.

Usually the counting helps focus my mind but this morning it's not working. Like an old cinefilm on loop, I see Max looking up at me from the Blue Eagle CCTV; him lying stone-cold dead with a sheet pulled over his sunken body; and then Dad's face swirls into view. It starts again. Over and over.

It feels like it is physically crushing me: my emotional pain evolving into the real, tangible, physical sort. My throat constricts and my breathing quickens. Short bursts of breath become harder and harder to grasp. I can hear I'm making noises with the effort of it all, yet I feel disconnected from the noise, like it is coming from someplace else and not from inside of me. A deep long pain radiates out from my chest. If this hadn't happened to me before I would genuinely think I am dying.

Instead, I try to remember that I am in control. This feeling will pass.

As the light glares and dances in front of my eyes, finally I know I am coming to the end of it. It always happens like this, a surge of light-headedness just before it eases off. The eye of the storm.

I don't always know what causes them but I'm certain today's panic attack was triggered by hearing Noah having a shower in the en suite on a day when my emotional barriers are already worn thin. I tried to suggest he use the main bathroom instead, but I couldn't really come up with a convincing reason as to why. He'd just laughed it off. What he hadn't realised was that the sound of that particular shower would pull me back to another day. One where the water ran red and wouldn't stop.

As I feel the worst of it pass, I'm aware of the shower clicking off and the door opening. Noah emerges, takes one look at me and the pile of untouched clothes, and gently he begins to dress me.

'You'll get through today,' he tells me. 'I'm right by your side.'

Again, I feel my love for him swirl up, mix with my fear, and transform into anger. It takes all my strength not to shout at him to leave me alone. To leave this place and wait for me at home. I do not want him here, where the past threatens to infect him – us – too. He is meant to be my 'after'. If our marriage and the life I've fought so hard to build for myself since comes crashing down, then what was it all for?

Was I ever really free?

It cannot all have been for nothing.

Grasping for something to keep me in the moment and not let the pain rip me from reality, I scratch fervently at the fleshy space between my thumb and index finger as I watch the casket approach down the aisle. Max's body is carried by Jimmy and three other friends. I recognise them from the yacht photo at his house.

Mum has not let go of my arm since we clambered into the car to take us to the church. It is a white-hot excruciating pain to lose a brother, so I cannot imagine how it feels to lose a son. Our family of four is down to two. I let her cling to me even though I usually avoid her touch as much as possible.

It's an emotional barrier presenting itself as a physical one, Aya tells me. Not directly about my relationship with Mum, I haven't spoken to her about that – I don't know how I could tell some and not all of the story without getting in a muddle, so it's best to keep it all locked up – but something I struggle with in general.

It isn't a recent development; it has been a part of me for as long as I can remember – the way someone else's hand on my skin makes my throat tingle. A bit like a metal spoon being scraped across the bottom of a saucepan. I've learnt to live with it and am fairly good at knowing when to push through the barrier for the sake of the other person, but it is a conscious effort to ignore the physical need to pull away. Usually, I find myself counting down until I think it has been long enough for me to move without causing offence.

I'm self-aware enough to know that today is one of those times I need to let the other person take what they need from me and, on the day she is burying her son, my mum needs to hold her daughter close. I can give her this.

My difficulty with physical closeness is always what set Jake apart from the rest – touching him felt good. And then along came Noah, all those years later, and finally I'd found someone else who I never wanted to pull away from. That first time Noah had placed his hand on my leg and I hadn't held my breath uncomfortably had been a shock. I glance at him and lower my hand on to his knee. Desperate to hold on tight to him. Afraid that he too will be ripped from me.

As the casket is lowered on to a stand in front of us I try to catch Jimmy's eye, but he doesn't look towards us. I'm surprised. I would have thought he'd at least acknowledge Mum. The rest of Max's friends do. A nod of respect to Max's family.

Watching Jimmy's every move I see him take his seat the other side of the aisle, before rubbing his hands roughly over his face. I remember what he said outside the police station about feeling guilty for not being there more for Max, and I realise we all have our crosses to bear. Nothing is ever as simple as it first appears. Just take Mum and me, for example: without doubt we are the two people in this room to have loved Max the most, and yet we both have our own secrets – of that I am quite sure.

And as I look around this room, at everyone gathered to say goodbye to Max, I think about the town being riddled with Freemasons and I wonder how many more secrets are being held here.

I wonder which one of them killed my brother?

Chapter Twenty-Five

Max's wake is being held at the Blue Eagle and I bet more than half the town has turned up to pay their respects. My dad was once the pillar of this community – his death is still commemorated by a charity mud run across the riverbed every summer. I question how many people here actually knew Max, and how many are simply here to witness the Stone family's latest tragedy.

I am standing by the buffet table. It's always the best place to stand and observe; most people are drawn to the food at some point during an evening. From here I can see Noah expertly working the room. He is the perfect husband, but I wish he'd stop. I do not want him talking to these people. The lack of control fills me with dread.

The other great thing about standing here is that I have a clear view of the pub door, and I've not been here long before it opens and DS Sorcha Rose swoops into the room. I can't say I'm surprised. It's a small town, and as the new detective in the area it's polite to show her face given the circumstances. But I'd be surprised if there isn't also another motive. That, like me, she knows despite the lack of evidence of foul play, Max's death is still suspicious. That when a crime is committed, it is most likely perpetrated by someone close to the victim. Someone in this room.

She spots me straight away and strides over. 'I'm sorry for your loss,' she says.

'Thank you.'

Pleasantries thankfully out of the way, I'm eager to hear what she has to say. Instead, she simply stands next to me. Shoulder to shoulder. Observing the room. I can't help but smile. We make for an uncomfortable duo.

'Any news from the toxicologist?' I ask.

'The report hasn't been written up yet, but I spoke to him this morning. I'm afraid Max's alcohol levels were significantly high. Your brother was, without doubt, severely inebriated.'

'So, what's the verdict? That he fell into the estuary drunk and drowned?'

'The evidence certainly points that way. Once the report is written I'll be closing the case.'

We stand there a while longer, silence settling between us, and then she says, 'Justine, we both know evidence only ever tells part of a story.'

I let out a long slow breath, unsure what my reaction should be. I'm relieved someone else is on my side, and I am not the only one who thinks there is more to the story than a drunken accident, but I am also wary of saying too much. I know once she starts asking questions, she might never stop.

'So I ask you again,' she carries on, 'what else do you know? Anything you can give me might help keep this case open. But right now, I'm under pressure to close it, and then there's nothing more I can do for you and your family.'

Do I want her to close Max's case? I'm not sure. I want answers. Need answers. Max is dead and every time I close my eyes all I can see is his body lying in that awful, stark mortuary, cold and broken on the table. But at what cost? Demanding what sacrifice? There's no bringing Max back, no matter what truths I spill.

'The thing is, Detective Sergeant, it's only ever just that. A story. No matter how much you think you understand, it's never the full truth. We both know that.'

'I agree. But as I'm fairly new around here, I'm making it my business to get to grips with some of these – stories – as you like to put it. And I thought perhaps you could help fill me in on your family.'

'My family?' I repeat in disbelief. Is she really doing this? Here, on the day we bury my brother? I can't work out if it's genius or rude. I think it's both. Perhaps that's what makes it such a powerful move.

Before either of us can say anything more, Jimmy is by my side. Has he been watching us? It feels protective. Like he is trying to save me.

'DS Rose.' He dips his head slightly. 'I didn't mean to eavesdrop but is this really the time? Some might say that in her grief, Justine is extremely vulnerable right now. Maybe she isn't able to think clearly.' I hate him for weakening me but I can also see it's a smart angle, particularly if for now I want to keep my secrets, so I refrain from contradicting him.

'Of course. Don't mind me. I'm very sorry for your loss, Justine. Perhaps I'll drop in in a few days and we can pick this up then.'

As she moves away, I thank Jimmy for getting rid of her.

'It's true though, she shouldn't be talking to you right now. You're in no fit state.' And the reality of it feels like a slap in the face. It wasn't just a move from Jimmy. He really does think I'm vulnerable right now. *No fit state.* The bloody rudeness of it, who does he think he is?

I'm about to argue when my mother stands on a chair – *dear Lord, how many wines has she had?* – and what she says next sends a shiver down my spine.

'I'd like to make a toast,' she says above the noise in a voice so loud I barely recognise it as hers, and the room quietens. She finds me in the crowd and, without taking her eyes off me, she begins.

'Let us raise a glass to those whom we love,
    to those standing here and those up above;
    Let us toast to our promise for as long as we live,
    we'll have the courage to love and we'll fight to forgive.'

I down the rest of my wine. 'Excuse me,' I say to Jimmy, and make my way out of the pub, using every ounce of strength left in me not to break into a run.

I do not forgive, and neither should she.

BEFORE

JUSTINE

At first, Justine had been nervous about joining the party. She'd spent years up in her bedroom wishing she was old enough to be allowed downstairs, but now it had finally arrived she'd felt exposed, anxious about making small talk with all these people she'd heard her dad talk about with such admiration. What did she have to contribute?

As the clock had struck seven p.m. she wished she could hide in the comfort of her duvet reading books, listening to the hum of the party in the rooms below and only imagining what it would be like to be a part of it. Instead, she was staring at herself all glammed up in the mirror which was propped up on top of her desk. She looked older than usual, with her hair scraped back into an elegant bun and a burst of the red lipstick her mother had given her the night before.

After her first mulled wine she'd started to get into the swing of it a little more. She was sure if Jake has been there too she'd be enjoying it more, but it was his nan's birthday and she understood it was too important to miss. Besides, there would be other Christmas parties, and she had Max who was back home for the holidays. She watched him from across the room and hoped she too would gain his easy air of confidence once she was at university.

'And this,' she heard her father before she saw him, 'is my daughter, Justine.' Her father was weaving his way through the crowds with a man she knew to be one of her dad's partners striding behind him.

'Austin MacNeil, it's nice to meet you,' she said, and she could see the fact she already knew who he was had bolstered his ego. *Typical.* He tipped his head to the side, raised his eyebrows as though impressed and gave a slight nod.

'Clearly you talk about me as much as I do you,' he said to Gerard, eyes narrowing, and there was something about it that made Justine's insides crawl. A chumminess which felt insincere, as if it was laced with poison.

Keep your friends close, but your enemies closer, her dad liked to tell her. 'Do you have many enemies?' she'd once asked him, to which he'd replied, 'Darling girl, I certainly don't have many friends.' And then he'd laughed. She hadn't believed him at the time; her dad was always surrounded by others – people were drawn to him like moths to a flame.

Charismatic, yes, that was the word. But seeing him with Austin now she wondered if her dad had been telling the truth, and the more she thought on it the more she came to think the room held a kind of electricity. Something more than simply a room full of good friends.

It was not a comfortable energy but rather an underlying buzz and it dawned on her as she watched Austin that it was a performance, a balancing act, and the energy she felt was simply the feeling they were all just teetering on the edge and could at any moment fall off. But into what?

'Would you care to show me around?' Austin asked her. 'Rumour has it there may be somewhere to make a wreath. Perhaps you can help me? I'd love one to take home to my wife.'

Justine looked towards her dad, who exclaimed it was a great idea before turning around to find someone new to chat with.

'Of course. This way,' she said, leading Austin out of the room.

Chapter Twenty-Six

I needed to drag myself out of bed this morning knowing Otis would already be on his way to meet me. The majority of my and Otis's business together is conducted over the phone but when we do meet, I'm always reminded of how unassuming and ordinary he appears on the outside. If anyone is the perfect example of the saying 'Don't judge a book by its cover', it's him. It's part of what makes him so effective, of course. Everyone always underestimates him.

I'm already waiting halfway down the road by the time he pulls up; giving my mother another thing to question me about or, even worse, to watch in judgemental silence, is the last thing I need right now. The door of his Land Rover flings open, and I slide inside.

'There's a quiet lane surrounded by fields out the back of Maldon, usually with just a light footfall of dog-walkers doing a circular walk to Beeleigh Abbey. I'll park there,' he says, taking control in a way his slight frame and hunched shoulders would never imply.

As we drive, I take in the smaller details of him: his shirt, though oversized and a slightly off-putting creamy colour, has been meticulously ironed and though I'm certain they are the same trainers he was wearing the last time we met they still look brand-new.

Despite first appearances, this is a man who cares about the small things. He pays attention. I wonder if the stoop and questionable fashion choices are all simply part of a carefully curated plan, but I am certainly not one to judge.

It has been ten months since we last spent time together in person. He had some very sensitive information that helped us go on to win a very long and complicated attempted murder case I'd been assisting on. We'd gathered in the nook of a pub back then but this time, hiding out in his car, everything feels a bit more clandestine. I know this isn't really the right time for it, but a small thrill runs through me.

We park up in a small bay down the lane and Otis pushes his seat back before turning to me.

'You know I love a challenge, but in this job I also need to draw a line. So, if what you're asking me to do with your brother is linked to this murder case you're now off, then I need to know why and how. Shoot.'

I push my chair back to mirror his and begin. I tell him Brad Finchley used to go by the name Jake Reynolds, and that Jake and I started dating when I was seventeen. It's more than I'd let on to Charles but from there I spin him the same story, explaining I haven't seen Jake for eighteen years and wasn't aware he'd changed his name so didn't immediately recognise him or make the link when his case file turned up in my hands. I'm sure he is already aware of all of this, so I skim over it and move on to the part he is really interested in – whether I think there's any connection to my brother.

'The report says Max's death was an accident with no sign of foul play. But these two men were the most important people in my life at one point, both from a small town where nothing out of the ordinary normally happens. And now, one is dead and the other accused of murdering two people. I just can't get it out of my head that there must be a link.'

'You think Jake is also behind your brother's death?'

'Well no, that's the thing.' I pause, readying myself to admit it, and then bite the bullet. 'I'm not convinced Jake is guilty at all.'

Otis doesn't reply immediately, but I can see he is processing it, letting the implication of what I'm saying sink in. It's the first time I've said it out loud myself, and hearing it now makes it feel more solid.

Jake is innocent. I'm sure of it.

'Is there anything linking the two? A reason someone might want to cause them harm?' he asks after a few minutes.

'Not that I know of. Jake has been out of our lives for so long.'

'What about before he left? Did anything happen back then?'

'No,' I say. It is the first time I have ever properly lied to him, and it strikes me that Otis was the last one left. The last person in my life who I'd not lied to.

I comfort myself with the thought it is only a white lie; what happened then didn't affect Max and Jake. At least, not in the same way it affected me. I can tell he's still thinking it through and so I carry on, lowering my tone ever so slightly, but there is enough of a shift so he knows I am being serious. 'Otis, I really need your help with this,' I say.

We lock eyes and from his rapid blinking I've clearly got my point across. It's not intended as a threat, rather a reminder that when we need help, we're there for each other; I've been there for him when he needed someone to take a leap of faith, and now I'm asking him to do the same for me.

'OK. If you think there is more to his death, then let's go find the proof.'

I stretch out the tension that has been building in my fingers and unscrunch my toes. There is no way I could find the link between Max's death and Jake's arrest without his help and all the resources he has at his fingertips. This is good news. But I'm also hyper-aware the stakes just got even higher. I cannot get sloppy.

'You're the best,' I announce, coming very close to throwing my arms around him. 'OK, did you get any further with looking into the Rushnells? There is plenty of evidence building against Jake, but the glaring hole in the prosecution is *why* he killed them. What links Jake to Mr and Mrs Rushnell? It's the thing that the more I was putting the case together, the less obvious it seemed to me that Jake was guilty. It's our biggest chance of finding out if he did it or not. Very few people kill with no motivation, not unless they are clinical psychopaths, and that's just not the Jake I knew.'

The Jake I loved.

'I haven't yet found any links between the Rushnells and Maldon, but I'll look into any connection they had with Jake or Max. And I'll carry on trying to crack Max's security encryption. He's hiding something, and with time I'll find out what.'

My skin tingles and when I look down, I can see goosebumps covering my arms. I could describe it as fear, but deep down I know it's excitement. I've always loved the thrill of the chase. Fight or flight. There's nothing quite like it. It helps too, to have a focus; something to distract myself from the raw pain of Max's death.

You are not guilty. You did not do this.

I repeat it to myself, just like Aya taught me to, hoping it will somehow make it true.

I tell Otis to let me out of the car where we are. There is an urgency pulsing through my veins which needs releasing, and the best way I've found to regulate myself over the years is by running. It's midday and as I get out the heat hits me like a solid wall. It hasn't rained in months and climate change protestors are gathering by the day in London. Personally, I enjoy how uncomfortable it is. It is purging me, one bead of sweat at a time.

The prom is busy when I turn into it. The locals have flocked here to make the most of the coastal breeze. I find it hard to see this place so full of life. It feels wrong, as if there should be a period of mourning. Instead, children whizz by on scooters, dogs bark at ducks and queues of people stand waiting for ice cream.

There is lots to watch and yet my eyes are drawn straight to him – Jimmy is sitting on the wall outside Mum's house. I wonder how long he has been waiting for me. What does he want? Before he notices, I turn and head in the other direction. I hadn't planned on a longer run, but I do not have it in me to face Jimmy today. After meeting Otis, I need longer with my own thoughts before plastering my mask back on.

I run faster. But as I gain speed, instead of feeling freer like I usually do, I feel worse. Today, I can't outrun the pain. The further from the prom I run, the more intense the feeling. I am not alone. I check over my shoulder, but there's nothing – and no one – of note. I carry on running. Faster. One foot in front of the other. The pounding on the pavement sends shocks through my knees with every step. There's no proof, but the feeling isn't going away, and I have learnt to trust my instincts. Is the witness lying or trustworthy? I reason with myself that maybe this time it is just my guilt, the paranoia that I'm going to get caught cloaking my skin. But no matter how hard I run, or how many turns I take, I cannot escape the feeling someone is watching me.

Finally, I make it back to the house, my arms so weak I struggle to push the heavy front door open. I find Mum in the kitchen. She's seated at the table with a small glass, still full, in front of her, a bottle of bourbon next to it.

'Max's favourite,' she says quietly and her mouth turns up sadly at the edges. 'Would you like one?'

I am hot and sweaty. Definitely dehydrated. The last thing my body needs is alcohol. 'Sure,' I say and she looks so relieved it makes me wonder if she couldn't bring herself to drink it alone. How long has she been sitting here, staring at it?

She hands me a glass and we look at each other as we take the first sip. It is hot and comforting as it slips down my throat.

'I thought you might be leaving today?' she asks and the hurt floods my body.

'No! We just lost Max. I'm not ready to go yet.' I leave out the fact I think there are more answers to find before I do. 'If you don't want me here though then I'll get a hotel.' My tone is sharp and I try to wash it away with the rest of my drink. When I look back towards Mum I regret it immediately. She has turned grey.

'What an awful thing to say. You are my daughter. Of course I want you here.'

I swallow down my need to retort; to not bring up the fact she shipped me off to live with Aunt Carol only one week after Dad's death. She did not want me here then.

'I'm sorry, I'm just tired. I'm going to check on Noah, he texted to say he wasn't feeling well.'

As I turn, she catches my elbow and says, 'I just meant please don't feel you have to stay here for me. You can leave if you need to.'

It catches me by surprise and for the first time I find myself wondering how much she really knows, this quiet mother of mine.

I tiptoe up the stairs, knowing although it's still the afternoon, Noah has gone to bed. I'm surprised he doesn't stir when I creak open the door – usually I joke Noah sleeps with one eye open. His breathing sounds laboured and I decide to wake him. To make sure he is OK. He rolls away, groaning.

'That bad?

'Not great.' He grimaces.

'I know you want to be here for me but honestly, I'm OK. I think you should go home, there's nothing worse than being sick in someone else's house. I can call you a taxi.'

'You don't mind me leaving?'

I shake my head. 'Are you still OK if I stay here a while longer though? I know you also need to go back to work soon.' I cannot believe I am asking to stay longer in this house – where the memories press in on me wherever I look – but Max's death has changed everything.

'Of course. You need to be with your mum right now, stay as long as you need. I'll be fine.' He reaches out and clutches my hand. Guilt pulsates through me. Not just at leaving him, but also for lying. Again. I remind myself that yes, I am Noah's wife but that is not all I am. I'm also a KC, Max's sister and Jake's . . . well, I'm not sure what I am when it comes to Jake but I'm hoping I might have some answers soon.

'If you get worse then call me, I'm not far away.'

'I love you,' he says.

'I love you too. I'll be home soon,' I reassure him – or maybe myself – before pulling out his suitcase from under the bed, hoping it doesn't come across as my being too keen for him to leave.

I've barely made it back downstairs before my phone rings. I almost let it ring out without glancing at the screen. I am tired. I just need a breather. But years of working in a competitive field has ingrained in me a need to be responsive and available at all times – at least, according to Aya – and even now, though every part of me wants to bury my head in the sand and spend the rest of the day bingeing Netflix, I cannot resist flipping it over and checking who is calling.

Otis.

Well, that was fast.

'What have you got for me?' I say, rushing into the study and picking up a pen. I bite the lid off while flipping open my note-pad with my free hand. Poised and ready.

He tells me the Rushnells recently moved back to the UK after eleven years spent in the Algarve. 'It seems Mark Rushnell became somewhat of a businessman over there, forming a number of differ-ent companies under which he bought and sold properties. On further investigation, over the past five years, not just one but three properties which had all been bought under different company names were the subject of terrible and accidental home fires – all, now this is the key part, with expensive insurance payouts.'

'Have you been able to find if there were any ongoing investi-gations into him? Were the fires ever flagged up as suspicious by the police there?'

'Not yet, but you know as much as I do that once you find something like this it's always just the top layer of what these people are involved in. Maybe he thought the police were start-ing to get suspicious and they quit while they were still ahead and moved back here, or maybe he pissed people off in the process and they came back here trying to flee them. They weren't exceptionally rich, not from what I can tell. Which means they must have been loaned the money to buy these prop-erties by someone. The dodgy thing is that I haven't been able to trace where all the money came from yet.'

'Perhaps those same people could finally have found them.'

'There's no proof yet, but it's a lead and there's room to argue motivation.'

'You're starting to sound like a barrister.'

'I'll take that as a compliment.'

'You should. What about any links between my family and the Rushnells?' I still can't shift the feeling of familiarity every time I hear their names.

'There's nothing as far as I can tell.'

'OK, well let's keep looking.'

We hang up but my excitement is hard to contain and I can feel my energy start to seep back through me. Maybe this is it? Is this as far as the story goes, with nothing particularly original about it? A small-time criminal who made the wrong people very angry and failed to hide out in the Surrey suburbs. Maybe Jake had got himself into some trouble of his own while he'd been away? I'm not usually wrong but I indulge myself with the thought that maybe this time I am. Perhaps there is, in fact, nothing to connect Jake's arrest to Max's death. To our family. To me and the past.

It feels like a step in the right direction. I'm so quick to link everything bad, everything tragic in my life back to that Christmas party but I'm allowing myself a glimmer of optimism that Max's death has nothing to do with it. And if it's not linked, then I don't need to feel guilty for keeping my own secrets from the detective. Maybe, just maybe, this time I'm not to blame.

Chapter Twenty-Seven

Only two days after we buried Max, and just after Noah's taxi has rounded the corner, DS Rose pulls up in her Škoda. She is dressed in a tailored black suit and I wonder how she can stand it in this heat. Is it that important to her to dress the part? I can't help but wonder if she has been watching the house all morning, waiting for the opportune moment to confront me.

The wolf always did know how to hunt its prey.

I push my panic far down and plaster a serene smile across my face. Infallible, that's me.

'Come in,' I say, leading the way through into the kitchen. 'Can I get you a coffee or tea?'

'I'm fine, thank you.' Boundaries established and message safely received. This is not a social call. We are no longer on the same side.

We take our places at the table. I sit purposely in the same chair she had sat on last time we were gathered in this kitchen. We're creatures of habit, meaning we look to establish order in everything we do. Today, I feel like disturbing that security a little. Before she can say anything, I launch straight into it, taking her by surprise with my readiness. 'I assume you're here to ask me about the night Dad died?' They are small power moves, but I learnt from the best that the consistent use of subtle actions no one can call you out on is often the most effective way of chipping away at a person's confidence.

'That's right. As I said before, I'm going through all the big historic cases from the town to give me some context and a better sense of the place and people here.' It's a nice line, but no part of me believes she hasn't intentionally dug out our family's old file.

'Is there anything in particular you want from me?'

'The thing is, I've been told the previous DS knew your dad well, and apparently all the officers working the night he died would also have been very familiar, friends even, with your family. Am I correct?'

'Most probably, Dad was well loved.'

'Well, I didn't know Gerard Stone and I don't know your family. Can you tell me about him?'

'I don't understand why it's important?'

'Character profiles, background checks, they're a huge part of putting together a history on a victim. I don't have that here. I'd like your help with filling that context in for me.'

Victim. I swirl the word round in my head. Is anyone ever just one thing?

'Dad was a big character. He helped the town in many ways; he gave money to local causes and employed lots of people from here for his firm. He always did what he could for other people. I think the fact a mud run is held in his honour is testament to that, DS Rose.'

She smiles but looks uninspired by my description.

'The thing is, in my experience people are never wholly good. But all I'm ever told about your dad – your whole family, in fact – is how good you all are. It's a funny word, really. Good. It's something fully dependent on meeting the expectations of the person describing you, but who knows what those expectations were or are? A good friend, a good boss, a good lawyer, a good husband, a good father.'

I fight against a stiffening in my shoulders.

'He was all of those things, I assure you.'

There's a short pause while neither of us looks away.

'Well then,' she says, 'you are very lucky to have had a father like that.'

'Thank you. Is that everything?'

'There is one more thing. It's not really a question, just something that's been preying on my mind.' Here we go – I've come to anticipate it now. I brace myself. 'The report says your father's car caught fire causing substantial damage to the body. They were lucky to be able to perform a toxicology report at all. Had the fire services been any longer arriving, there may not have been that possibility. What's interesting to me, though, is how and why the car caught fire in the first place. You see, contrary to popular belief it's actually fairly uncommon for a car to catch fire like that. To do so, it would need to be the result of significant damage to the petrol tank. Which makes the situation of your dad's car fire very rare indeed. There was some damage to the tank, but when compared to other car fires, the impact is noticeably less.'

'So, you've come here to tell me my father was unlucky?'

'Maybe. Or maybe there's another explanation.'

'Like?'

'Did your father have any enemies?'

It is the second time DS Rose has asked if my family had any enemies. The first was in relation to Max, and now my father. I think back to the funeral and how she'd also started to link Max's death with Jake's murder trial. Clearly, like me, she doesn't believe in coincidences. Likes to look for the patterns. They may be years apart, but I agree with her – there is a pattern here. We just haven't found it yet.

'I'm afraid I'd find it very hard to believe.'

'OK, well, thank you for your time.' She stands abruptly. 'I'll be back in touch if there's anything else.'

'Anything else? With respect, DS Rose, my father's case is closed, is it not?'

'It is, yes,' she says, 'for now. But Justine, a word of warning' – by which I know she really means what she's about to say next is to serve as a threat – 'while I may be bound by rules and regulations, those same boundaries don't apply to the reporters.'

What she's impressing on me is that, while the case is officially closed, she still has other sources. That she is still circling.

I close the front door firmly behind the detective and find myself locking it with both the key and the chain. She is good. Better than I'd anticipated. Suddenly I feel the urge to confirm that Noah is still heading away from this place and pull out my phone. I track him on 'Find your friends' and let the satisfaction of his mark on the map pulling further and further away from Maldon settle over me.

I may be staying here, but it is not because I didn't want to go with him. It's the very opposite. I need answers so I can go back to being the Justine he married. I know the less time he spends in Maldon, the more likely it is that I can go back to him when all this is over. I want that more than anything. Otherwise, what has all this been for?

Max. Jake. Dad.

It must have been for something.

I chant it over and over again. Pull out my notepad. Write it down. Circle it.

Surely not.

But what if I'm right? What if DS Rose is right to be poking her nose into Dad's old case? What if, somehow, everything that's happened with Max and Jake is also connected to Dad's death?

I pad my way into what is now only Mum's bedroom, the cold floorboards sticking to the soles of my feet, and open the side of her wardrobe which was always Dad's. Perhaps I do know her better than I think. There, hanging untouched, are Dad's clothes. I close my eyes and breathe in the scent of them.

On the far side hangs his navy dressing gown and I slip it off the hanger and slide my arms into it slowly. Tie it up at the front in a double knot, the way he used to. At the bottom of the wardrobe are his shoes, neatly lined up – he always prioritised order – and I find his slippers, stuff my feet into them. I can feel where they had moulded to Dad's shape, the arches and indents in all the wrong places. I shuffle out and into the study. Slowly, I pull open the drawer on the top right. If his clothes remain where he left them eighteen years ago, then I'm banking on the likelihood of his cigars remaining where they were too.

I fumble around and my hands clasp something cold. It's a strange shape and I pull it out. It's a silver brooch. The edge looks like a compass, and in the middle is a giant G. I can't ever imagine my dad wearing something like this. What is it? Why does he have it? I place it on the desk in front of me and force the drawer open further, determined to find the cigars I know must be here.

This time, I find them. They are buried under a pile of paperwork in a polished wooden box with a gold clasp. His prized possession. I slip one into the pocket of his dressing gown, pour myself a bourbon and make my way to the first-floor observatory overlooking the estuary. From here, the harbour is lined with vessels: industrial fishing boats and the odd smaller rowing boat.

I sit back in his favourite chair. Light the cigar. Breathe it in. Let it out. Before coming back here, it had been a long time since I'd thought of the Viking ships and the warriors making their way to shore, but I imagine them again while I sit.

It's obvious now; it all comes back to Dad. Everything always did.

BEFORE

JUSTINE

There were only two other people in the snug, who Justine suspected were there for a reason other than making wreaths, given they left with no wreath in hand as soon as Justine and Austin arrived.

'Marvellous,' Austin said, but Justine wasn't entirely sure what was so impressive. Mum had done a great job, but at the end of the day it was just some leaves and decorations in bowls on a table.

'It's nice to have a bit of peace and quiet, don't you think?' he said, pulling out the chair next to him and indicating for her to sit. She really didn't want to be rude; she knew Austin brought in a lot of money for the firm and had just secured their latest big client. One, her dad said, which would take the firm to new heights.

So she sat, tucked her dress over her knees and scraped the chair back towards the table. She thought about Max, chatting so effortlessly away in the other room – 'networking' he called it – and desperately tried to think of something to say.

'Are you having a nice evening?' she asked as she reached towards the middle of the table for some ribbon, leaving her chair slightly as she stretched.

She thought she must have imagined it, but his hand lingered there, cupping her bottom where it had left her seat. She didn't say anything, couldn't think of the right thing to say – she'd never been taught this at school – and instead sat down quickly. He moved his hand, *thank God*, and she swallowed down her fear. Her imagination always got the better of her. But then without warning, without *invitation*, he slipped it on to her knee.

The silence stretched between them.

Deep down she knew she should say something. She tried to peel her tongue away from the roof of her mouth, to force herself to say 'no', but she couldn't seem to make a sound. Not a single one. Fight or flight. She thought that was the phrase. But neither of them applied here. All she could do was freeze.

Why was there no one else around?

Why had her mum thought this was a good idea?

No one wanted to make a stupid wreath anyway.

After what seemed like forever, Austin took his hand away and finally she thought it was over. He must have felt her body tense beneath him and realised she did not want the same thing. That this was all one big misunderstanding. But then he placed it on her shoulder and, whereas Jake's hand had felt like it belonged there, Austin's hand scalded her skin. He smelt of whisky and cigars.

She wanted to be sick.

Yet she remained still, and she hated herself for it. Where was her courage? She had none. Put to the test, her worst fears had come true. She was weak, more like her mother than her father.

She started drifting off into her own head, realising her skin could become numb to his touch, and it was only when she couldn't smell his breath anymore that she noticed he'd removed his hand, having been disturbed by a couple pushing the door open overenthusiastically. She could not have been more grateful for them at that very moment in time.

They were around her parents' age but far less glamorous. The woman had mousey, bushy hair – like it should be curly but she hadn't ever learnt to style it – and the man was thin. Wiry thin, with glasses and a moustache. They looked like something out of a seventies sitcom. Still, they were today's heroes as she took her chance and raced out of the door, frantically searching for Max. She spotted him across the room and, using her shoulders and elbows, she jostled her way through, not caring when she made some old lady spill her wine.

'Max,' she interrupted, but he ignored her, clearly slightly embarrassed by her forcefulness. 'Max,' she said again, louder this time. She was practically shouting but she could no longer control it.

The commotion had started to draw attention and the room fell noticeably quiet, all eyes on them. Austin appeared at the door, and it crossed her mind that perhaps he was blocking it intentionally.

'What's happened?' Max asked as soon as he turned to look at her. Good. She knew she could count on him. That he'd take one look at her and believe she was telling the truth. Ridiculous, really, that it was one of the first things running through her mind. Not: I can't believe this happened to me, but: will people believe this happened to me. Just a few words changed, but the meaning was entirely different.

'Austin—' but she didn't get to finish her sentence before her dad's voice boomed across the room. He had appeared in the doorway next to Austin and she wondered what the snake had already told him.

'I'd like a word upstairs, please. Now,' her father commanded. And there was something in his tone that echoed the poison of Austin MacNeil: his words were kind enough, followed by a smile, but the threat buzzed between them.

And I've just fallen off the edge, she realised as she followed her father up the stairs.

Chapter Twenty-Eight

A ship horn blares, bringing me back to reality, and suddenly I'm acutely aware it's still bright daylight and I'm sitting here in a dressing gown and slippers smoking a cigar. Not any old dressing gown either – my dead father's dressing gown. It's a far cry from busting my way up the career ladder in court. How far I've already fallen.

I take another puff. Hold it in my mouth until it makes me cough. Part of me is tempted to sit here until sundown, working my way through the entire box, but I also keep seeing Max's face disappearing under the waves, pulling him down, down, down. Did he struggle? Did he fight it? I am not here to drown too. Max needs me to swim.

So, instead of scarring my lungs further, I pull out my phone and text Aya asking if she has any availability today to fit me in. Quick as a flash she replies saying she has the time now if I'm free. She's efficient, I'll give her that. Maybe too efficient – I still wanted time to wallow and fester a little longer. But no, as usual, Aya is pulling me out of the darkness faster than I'm ready.

I force myself to tell her I'll be ten minutes, and peel Dad's clothes off me. I return his belongings to their rightful place, taking extra care to put everything back exactly as I found it – as if he might arrive any minute, furious to find I've been through his things.

*　　*　　*

'Are you OK? Has something else happened?' Aya asks, and I think back to when she'd posed the same question to me only a few months ago. How I'd lied then, saying it hadn't, when really Noah talking about having a baby and Max asking me home had already started to dredge up the past. To seep through my cracks, to make me question everything all over again.

'Not exactly, but there's a police detective here asking questions about the night Dad died and now I can't stop thinking maybe it's all connected in some way. Max, Dad, even Jake being arrested.'

'I see. And what makes you think there's something to find? Other than this detective, of course.'

'Because I'm crazy.'

'We don't use that word,' she says. Lips pursed.

'Sorry. Honestly? I don't know. I feel useless but I also think the detective might be right. There's something I'm missing.' I bite down on my tongue, reminding myself to tread cautiously. It's a hard line to walk; to be open and truthful while also guarding your own secrets.

'Well, our brains are very good at repressing memories. Perhaps this is stirring something up for you. Something you are struggling to remember properly. Be kind and patient with yourself. If there's something there, and we put in the work, it'll come back.'

I smile. It is very generous of her to give me the benefit of the doubt like this. The world could do with more Ayas in it.

'Do you want to do that?' she asks and I assume she means do I want to 'put the work in'. To see if there's something lurking deep-down in my core. I could tell her there most certainly is, but telling my own secrets isn't going to bring me any closer to uncovering Max's. And that is why I'm here. So I say, 'Of course,' and consciously unfold my arms. Look willing.

'Great. You've spoken about Max, Jake and your dad, but you haven't really mentioned your mum. Have you spoken with her about any of this? Asked her what she thinks of this detective?'

'No.' I say it curtly. Fine, so maybe I'm not ready for this.

'Why not? What is it you're so angry at her for, do you think?'

'Everything,' I say. 'My entire childhood. The fact she was so weak. So distanced from us all the time. So judgemental all the time.' I'm not sure why but this time I find I can't stop, my voice rising higher and louder with every new reason. I've opened the floodgates and it's all rushing out. 'And I blame her.'

'For what?'

I know it won't make any sense to Aya. I've left out too many details. But I also can't hold it in any longer. I blame my mother, in more ways than one, for my father's death.

'For not protecting me,' I reply. I've jumped ahead. I know I have. But my brain is moving too fast.

'From Austin?' Aya asks and I shake my head. 'Then from who?'

'My dad.' Realising what I've just said, I look up and see Aya with an expression I haven't seen her wearing before. She is confused.

I have made my first big mistake.

It lingers between us for a moment, while we both register what's just happened. And then Aya takes the lead again. Professional as ever.

'Why did you need protecting from your dad, Justine?' she asks softly.

I scratch at my thighs.

'Why don't you tell me again about the last time you saw your dad?' Aya prompts, once again proving that she's worth every penny.

'I've got to go,' I say, logging out of our meeting before she – or I – can say anything more.

It's very common for therapy patients to cover up their truth at the beginning of starting therapy. It's all part of the process: breaking down those walls to expose what they're meant to be protecting.

Aya once told me that working out where the lies are is just as important as knowing the truth. You need to find out what a patient is lying about to work out why they might be lying in the first place – to be able to identify which parts of them need healing.

Which parts are they hurting over too much to tell you about?

The thing is, we're six years in – Aya and I – we've been through that process. I wasn't supposed to have any more secrets.

Certainly not ones I'd ever intended exposing.

BEFORE

JUSTINE

'This is my fault,' Justine's father turned and said to her once they were back in her bedroom with the door safely closed behind them. His tone was measured, and the fact he was taking the responsibility took some of the pain away. Justine allowed herself to sink down on to her bed.

'I thought you were mature enough to join in tonight but clearly I was wrong,' he continued, and it took Justine a moment to register what he was saying. If only he'd let her explain; surely he must simply have misunderstood.

'But Dad, he—'

'No buts, Justine. Austin is a friend of mine. He is a good man. Whatever you think happened, I'm sure you misread the situation. That is my fault. You are still so young.'

A friend of the firm's more like, she thought.

'I know what happened, Dad.' If only she could make him listen, let her tell him the truth, then she was sure he would march down there and give Austin MacNeil everything he deserved. He was her father after all. She, his daughter.

'Justine.' Gerard's voice changed, no longer containing just a trace of poison but this time purposely laced with it. His normally charming open expression resembled more of a snarl. And right then, as she sat looking up at her father towering above her, she lost her voice completely. She knew that tone. Had heard it through the walls, but it had never been directed at her before.

'If you can't be trusted then I'll have to take matters into my own hands,' he said, looking around the room before opening the walk-in wardrobe. The one he'd built her for her sixteenth birthday. When he turned to face her, his eyes looked different, as though there was enjoyment there. Justine would remember this moment for years to come. 'Remember, Justine. I don't want to be doing this, you have made me become this father.'

She wasn't sure what he meant. What on earth was she making him do? Why had he opened the wardrobe? Did he want her to change out of her dress? Fine by her, she was finished with the goddamn party anyway.

'In,' he demanded.

'In?'

'That's what I said, is it not?' His voice sounded clipped and sharp.

Justine willed for the Viking chants to fill her head with bravery, but no matter how hard she tried she couldn't hear them. Couldn't find the words. Instead, she stood up and walked into the wardrobe. Watched in silence as her father closed the door and heard him scrape and prop her desk chair up outside the door, blocking the handle. Stood in silence as she listened to his footsteps retreat out of the room.

It wasn't until she was certain he'd gone back downstairs that she slid down the wall and wrapped her arms around her knees. Hugged them tight, burying her face in her dress.

Finally, she allowed herself to cry into the darkness.

Chapter Twenty-Nine

The river is alive. A sea of bodies crawling, writhing, clambering over each other. Whistles blow, crowds cheer and horns blare. All the people from our town, and even those from neighbouring towns, have come to watch the annual river mud race now held in honour of both my father and my brother.

Although it is a day's event held in their memory, there is no sadness today. Yes, there are banners with their faces on hung throughout the prom, but today is more about celebrating the town and raising money while we're at it. Not only does it make me feel physically sick, but it also makes me feel like there is something wrong with me. That my own memories and experiences must not be real – as if my mind has lied to me and the rest of the town is right to celebrate this man. My father. And I am mistaken.

I have been tasked with manning the registration desk, signing everyone in for the next wave and handing out their race numbers, which are to be carefully pinned to their chosen outfit. Some have come in old clothes, others in gym wear (taking it far too seriously in my opinion), but the majority have taken the opportunity for fancy dress – the incentive being a magnum of champagne awarded for best costume.

It's a little ironic, if you ask me, to be handing out alcohol in memory of not one but now two people whose cause of death has been linked to the alcohol levels found in their bloodstream. Regardless, alcohol seems to always sell. So far today the most memorable effort has been by a group of teenagers who have attached themselves together to resemble the Jamaican bobsleigh team from *Cool Runnings*. I'd taken a selfie with them and sent it to Noah as if it were proof of me holding it together; today a cathartic celebration in honour of Max and Dad.

The whole aim of the race is to make it to the other side of the thick, muddy riverbed as fast as possible. Five hundred metres may not sound like a long way, but in mud that acts more like quicksand, you'd think they'd run a marathon by the end of it. It's the kind of thing Max would have loved – in fact, if I remember correctly, it may have been his idea to set it up in the first place. It's a chance to be free, for the adults to act like children on their bellies squelching in mud.

Everything about today is so bright and happy. Laughter booms across the promenade from every corner. I look over to the banner hung between two trees opposite my station, my dad's enlarged face beaming down at me, and wish I could get in my car and drive back home to Noah right this minute. My skin feels tight as though I myself have just emerged from the riverbed caked in mud; now drying in the sun, shrivelling my skin. It is the uncertainty making me anxious. I am unsure what happens next or how much DS Rose already knows.

The feeling only worsens when I see him. He's a journalist, that much is obvious, with his head whipping round and notebook in hand. He's standing next to an older couple who I recognise as Mr and Mrs Green who lived across the street from Jake's family. How are they still alive? I thought they'd have kicked the bucket long ago. What's most unnerving, though, is that they are looking straight at me. Caught in the headlights I smile and wave. *Be amenable. The more someone likes you, the more they trust you.* Dad's words bounce around my head.

I'm relieved to see the stragglers from the last wave make it to the halfway mark and am grateful to have something to keep me busy; hopefully it will ward the journo off from coming over. I begin calling forward the queue in front of me to prepare for the next race. Luckily this is the last race of the day. After this, the live music starts and the whole promenade turns more into a festival venue for the rest of the evening; at which point I will be making a speedy exit.

The queue snakes its way towards me and I catch sight of a familiar face. It is the barmaid from the Blue Eagle. I smile at her and see her eyes fill with panic as she recognises me. I'm trying to register a very annoying, entitled man dressed as Thor who no doubt thinks he looks hot – he does not, he looks like a wanker – while also keeping one eye on her. She's turned to the guy she is with and it's clear from the way she's jaggedly moving her hands that she is worked up. I wish everyone else would be quiet so I can hear what she's saying, but she's too far down the line.

'Hello? My number?' fake Thor demands, his impatience clear. Rude. Still, I apologise and bend down to reach for it from a box below. When I look up again the barmaid has left the queue. My eyes search desperately to find her, but she's lost too readily in the swarming crowds.

I think back to her reaction when I handed her my card and how she'd clawed at her own neck. I wish I had my notepad with me. I must not forget to find her again and find out why she's so desperate to avoid me. What else does she know?

Just as I clear the last of the participants and they are led away to the starting bank, the survivors from the previous race appear around the corner, making their way back from the other side of the river now bruised, bloodied and covered head to foot in thick mud. Jimmy stands out at the front of the crowd, one of the first to return. Of course he'd have been one of the quickest to complete it. His red wig is streaked brown, large clumps matting together. I can't help but laugh as he heads towards me, grinning.

'Was it really that fun?' I ask.

'Absolutely. You should try it one year.' He shakes his head to one side, as if he's got mud stuck in his ear.

'Yeah, I'll pass, thanks.'

'Suit yourself. But letting go once in a while might do you good.'

Harsh, but probably true. I don't find it easy to relax and have fun. I never have done. Not until Jake came into my life. And certainly not since he left it. I'm afraid that if I peel my layers off, I'll never be able to put them back on again.

Bare for everyone to see.

To judge.

No, that's not for me.

'I do have a question, though.' I'm hoping he can at least tell me the barmaid's name.

'You always do, I'd expect nothing less,' he says. His tone isn't mean, it's familiar. As if he knows this about me, and he likes it.

'Well, I do hate to disappoint.' I cringe. Am I the one now flirting?

'Fine, but I'm going to need a shower first. I can barely hear you with all this mud stuck in my ear. Why don't you knock off now and we can chat more back at mine once I'm cleaned up?'

I agree – any excuse to escape the banners with Max's and Dad's faces staring down at me, and so I get up to leave as he slings a towel round his shoulders.

Chapter Thirty

Photos of Jimmy and Max line his bookcase. The shelves are stacked with impressive author names and hardbacks only belonging to a serious reader. I find I'm a little surprised and tell myself not to be so judgemental. Just because Jimmy seems more the hands-on DIY type of man, one who runs his own pub, doesn't mean he isn't also interested in literature. I remind myself we are all full of surprises. If Jimmy knew all of me, I doubt he'd still want to help me. And if Noah did? I shake it off. Push the possibility away. Noah never will.

In the corner of the room stands an old but beautiful record player with the whole bookcase next to it dedicated to his record collection. There must be at least five hundred different vinyls here. Floor to ceiling, the different coloured sleeve edges create a tapestry that lures you towards it.

I can hear the shower is still on upstairs and run my finger along the records until I find the album I'm looking for: 'Parachutes' by Coldplay. 'Yellow' was Max's favourite song for as long as I can remember. That summer, when it was mostly just the three of us – me, Max and Jake – we'd listen to it on Max's portable CD player almost every evening down by the water. It became almost like a ritual, signifying the transition from day into night. I slide it carefully out of the case intrigued to see it is a special edition with a translucent yellow vinyl, and place it in the record player. Move the needle, just as Dad had once taught me. Savour the crackle as the music fills the lounge and close my eyes.

I can see Max's face again, animated as he laughs along at something – most likely me – with Jake, and can feel the sun beating down on my arms. But then, as the music gains momentum, the image darkens and transforms into a tornado of other memories: of Dad's face watching over me all day in the prom from a banner six feet long and three feet wide; of Max's face which now flies on a matching banner alongside his.

I want to stay strong but as the song comes to an end, the music withdrawing into silence, it feels as though it takes with it every last drop of strength I have left. I have always avoided the mud runs for this exact reason – an event held in Dad's honour is too complicated for me to process. Even after all these years of therapy, I'm not there yet. And now Max flies high with him, as if they were literally cut from the same cloth. But Max was nothing like Dad. I want to rip those banners down. Tear them up. Burn them.

I hear the creaking of a door and am aware of a presence behind me. Slowly, I open my eyes.

'Max loved this song,' Jimmy says with a small, sad smile, moving past me to play it again.

Although I am nodding, I am no longer concentrating on the music. Jimmy is only a few feet away, his white towel wrapped around his waist. He is still wet from the shower.

I'm conscious that I still haven't said anything as he takes a step closer.

He is within touching distance now and I know I should move away. I love Noah. I am his wife, and he is my husband. For better and for worse. Those were the promises we made to each other, and I meant them.

But I recognise the sadness in Jimmy's eyes. It tells me he is hurting just as much as I am. That this day hasn't just been tough for me, but for him too, and it occurs to me that, if we work together, if I can rid him of his pain, then maybe he can rid me of mine.

Without another thought, I am kissing him. Hard and purposefully. It is not soft and it is not loving. I am ravenous. I am hurting. I need to feel something else. Something other than a constant anger boiling in my veins. Jimmy bites my lip and lifts me against the wall, telling me this is something he needs too.

I don't think of Noah again. At least not for the next hour or so. I have always been good at pushing the truth away.

We are lying on the floor of the lounge and Jimmy is playing 'Yellow' again. I wonder if it's a kind of acknowledgement that what's just happened between us was caused simply by our grief.

'So how about some dinner?' I say as I trace my finger along his chest.

'Now that's some master manipulation right there.' It is a joke, but something inside me snaps back into place. As if it was broken but now it is fixed. He is right. I am great at what I do – I am an outstanding criminal barrister. I didn't get given a double murder case as my first murder lead for any reason other than the fact that I am good enough. And while I may no longer be on the case, I still have all the skills to find the truth and work out how Jake's arrest and Max's death are connected. I have no proof, not yet, but I can feel it at the very core of me. More importantly, I have a promise to my brother to keep:

I will make whoever did this to you pay for it.

Chapter Thirty-One

I leave Jimmy's the next morning with the barmaid's name and address written on a piece of paper in my pocket. *Alice Myers*. She's local, which is no surprise, and checking it's not still too early to make a cold call, I decide it's worth a short detour.

Their house is an old Victorian terrace with beautiful large bay windows at the front. It's the typical style here in Maldon, an original two-up two-down but since extended far out at the back, making them deeper than they are wide. The pretty door-way is framed by an arch and stained-glass windows form a semicircle above the white front door. It is quaint – no, it is more than that, it is beautiful.

I ring the bell but there is no answer. I try again but there's still no movement from within the house. It feels odd. I am sure I saw someone in the upstairs window when I first arrived.

I step back and move further down the front path to peer up to the top window again. My hand frames the sun out of my eyes. It is already so bright this morning, it is going to be another scorcher. There's no one there but I'm usually good at the details and I'm certain I was not imagining it. Did Alice Myers spot me coming and choose not to answer the door? If I'm right, then I need to find out why.

I try the door once more, but the house remains eerily still. I give up and start walking back to Mum's house. Towards the end of her street, I see a woman with her dog coming in the opposite direction. I don't recognise her at first but, as she draws closer, she starts to smile enthusiastically. I rack my memory for any recollection of her.

'Justine?' She beams. 'Is that really you? My goodness, how you've grown.' She's right in front of me now and I'm pretty sure I remember she used to work in the local library.

'Mrs Hicks?' I take a leap of faith.

'That's me, dear. Oh, how wonderful to see you again. Your mum must be pleased to have you around, particularly right now. I am so sorry my love. Such dreadfully awful news about Max. It has hit the whole town, you know.' I try not to roll my eyes, the hyperbole diluting her sincerity. 'And how is your mum?' She raises her eyebrows as if she's about to gossip conspiratorially with me about my own mother. 'Is she still seeing that lovely man? Oh, I can't remember his name now, but he wasn't from round here. I do hope so. Your mother is a good woman. She deserves to find happiness after all she's been through.'

It knocks the wind out of me. I am trained in not letting any new information seem to be a surprise – *never let your opponent know you weren't aware of a detail in court* – but even I am struggling to process this calmly.

'Sorry, which man?' I ask, trying to keep my voice level.

'Oh dear. I shouldn't have said anything. I've probably got the wrong end of the stick. It's just that they looked so cosy. Maybe it wasn't Evelyn. My eyesight really is terrible.'

And then, before I can say another word, she's hurrying away, leaving me with more questions than answers. Cosy? I've never seen Mum look cosy with anyone before, not even her own children. And certainly never with Dad when he was alive.

She'd reminisced with me once, back when I was a child – not yet a teen – and I think she'd had a few too many glasses of wine one summer's day. She told me she'd married my dad in a whirlwind of fast love. Apparently, they'd only known each other for six weeks. She said they had been the best, most invigorating six weeks of her entire life. And then she'd taken a long drag on her cigarette, looked me straight in the eye, and told me never to marry.

At the time it had made an impression on me, not because of her warning, but because she'd described how, before marriage, they hadn't been able to keep their hands off each other – and quite frankly, it had revolted me.

I rush back home and, as I break into a run, I think again about Mrs Hicks's description of my mum.

Your mother is a good woman.

What does that even mean? What constitutes a woman being good? Whatever it is, good certainly isn't a word I would attribute to my own mother.

BEFORE

JUSTINE

Justine's eyes had adjusted to the darkness inside the wardrobe and she'd managed to roll up some jumpers to make an impromptu cushion. Larger than average and built into the corner of the room, the wardrobe had a rail running the whole length of it with just enough space to walk along selecting your outfit for the day. It wasn't particularly fancy – nothing like the real walk-in wardrobes or dressing rooms she saw on TV – but still she'd been so excited when, for her sixteenth birthday, she'd come back to find part of the room partitioned off. Never could she ever have imagined one day it would become her prison.

She wasn't sure how much time had passed, but the thrum of the party was still loud below her when she heard the bedroom door creak open and light footsteps creep across her floorboards. Straining to listen, she traced the noise and imagined whoever was there was now sitting down on her bed, most likely facing the wardrobe she was curled up in. Trapped in. They would have seen the chair propped outside blocking the handle.

'I'm in here,' she called. But there was no answer. She strained to listen again and once more was certain she could hear someone the other side of the wardrobe.

'It's Justine. Let me out.'

Again, the person did not move. Did not help.

'Please, please, just let me out.' This time she pleaded with them to free her but still no one came to her rescue.

Who were they? Who was sitting there ignoring her need for help?

Shit, she thought, what if it was him? Austin MacNeil? Come to finish what he'd started. Revelling in her torment.

She scrambled around the floor trying to find something she could use as a weapon and clung on to a pair of stilettos. She guessed from the silky feel of them that they were her red ones. One she let drop to the floor but kept the other clutched close to her chest. Just in case.

Still no one came for her. There was no shadow looming closer from under the wardrobe door. Whoever it was had stayed on her bed this whole time. Justine closed her eyes and tried to focus her hearing to find any clue as to who it was. Why wouldn't they help her?

She decided the person on the bed sounded like a woman; it would match the light footsteps which had danced across the floor. She was surprised, yet certain, that the woman was softly crying. Relief spread through her body.

Until another thought hit her and it was one which, if she was right, felt like a different kind of menacing to Austin, but menacing all the same. She held her breath and listened to every sound as carefully as she could. Yes, she was right. The warm feeling of relief deserted her body again as quickly as it had filled her.

The woman keeping her locked in the wardrobe – perhaps even keeping guard – was her mother.

Chapter Thirty-Two

I run home and through Mum's front door wrapped in a tornado of emotions. It has been eighteen years and before coming home again I openly accepted – was secretly proud of the fact, even – that I no longer had a relationship with my mother. At least, definitely not a close one. Ours was formal and minimal – civil and polite. At the birthday dinners and family get-togethers organised by Max our conversation never exceeded small talk.

I didn't want to share details of my new life, the life she'd forced upon me, with her. I didn't want to give her the satisfaction of knowing it had turned out so well. And she never probed. So why am I struggling so much with finding out now that she hasn't told me she's in a new relationship? I shouldn't care. Yet, there's something about Mum being in a relationship again that feels strangely complicated.

Who is this man?

What is my mother like with him?

Is she happy?

They aren't all selfless concerns; if I'm completely honest with myself, I don't even know what I want the answers to be. How awful of me, her daughter. I like to think I rose from the ashes to find and marry Noah. Forged a respectable successful career for myself despite the odds. That I am happy. But the first thing I felt when I heard Mum had a new man was anger. Anger she's moved on while I am still broken. That she had managed to find her own happiness while mine had been taken away from me in the space of just one evening.

Perhaps it is this dawning of reality about how I really feel about my life which is hitting me harder than the fact Mum is in a relationship. Being home is quickly tearing down the image of myself I'd carefully curated these past years, stripping away the layers of paint I'd applied week after week with Aya until I'm simply the same Justine I'd always been once more. The girl I'd fought so hard to leave behind, resurrected.

And while that is dangerous, maybe it is also powerful. I know things no one else does about the old Justine. Most importantly, I know just how much she is capable of. Perhaps it's time I no longer push her away. Enough of the new Justine has already been broken; perhaps it's simply time I accept it and stop running; stop trying to pretend I'm someone else.

It was always going to be too hard to carry on the pretence being back here; it's exactly why I'd never come home before now. But Jake is standing trial for murdering two people and Max is dead. These things were out of my control, and I am now back home whether I like it or not. As soon as I saw Jake's face again in the case file, I knew nothing was ever going to be same again. Not even me.

I can hear Classic FM playing softly from the kitchen. Mum always put music on when she was planning on a big clean, and from the sound of things nothing has changed. I should go in, ask her more about the life she now leads. See if she'll open-up to me about this new man and try to build some bridges over the gaps still keeping us apart. I know this is what I should do, and yet I am unable to bring myself to move even an inch closer to her.

Was he at the funeral and I didn't realise?

No, I am not ready to hear it. Instead, I head straight for the office upstairs. The door bangs behind me and the throbbing in the base of my neck tells me I am overdue my painkillers. Last night's escapades have thrown my whole routine and it is already taking its toll. I know it's not a healthy habit, and one I can't deny has escalated since being back here, but I tell myself now is not the time to punish myself. I just need to survive, to find out what happened to Max and if Jake is really guilty of murder or not, and then I can go back home. Back to Noah, my husband. Back to who I used to be.

Panic fills my limbs as it dawns on me just how much I regret last night with Jimmy. Only a few weeks ago I was a happily married KC on the brink of the largest case of my career. Now I'm a cheating wife whose entire professional reputation has been tainted. And for what?

At first there was only a little bit of blood.

Then a pool.

Before long it felt like I was drowning in it.

Chapter Thirty-Three

Driving home to London, I try to emulate the same feeling I had when first approaching Maldon – this time in reverse. I am willing each turn in the road to cloak me again with my armour the further and further away I drive. It doesn't work. It seems unfair that it should only work the other way; as I drove towards Maldon it stripped me back, but it doesn't work its magic to protect me when I leave. Part of me remains anchored in Maldon; I can feel it bubbling under the surface.

Tonight is Charlotte's birthday dinner and while I know everyone would understand if I don't join in, for my own sanity I know I must cling on to my life here if ever I am going to regain it after all this is over. Charlotte lives further south than us, in Richmond, where the houses are as beautiful as you would expect for the price tag. No one buys a two-million-pound house and then is happy for it to look tacky inside.

Tiled porches, stair runners, real wooden floors which require you to take your heels off at the door and fancy large mirrors propped up in the most random of spaces. It is undoubtedly an exquisite house made to house a perfect couple. Long legs covered classily and yet seductively by beautifully tailored clothes, blonde blow-dried hair and freshly manicured nails.

This used to be my world too, once the robe and wig came off, and yet here I am, standing nervously in the porch feeling profoundly out of place. Charlotte's dad came from a lot of money and although my family were well-off and respected in

Maldon, in contrast to the lifestyle my cousin led in London it barely compared. Living with Charlotte I'd learnt to mould myself on her. To finesse my edges.

I still look the part now, of course. I'm wearing a mid-length black silk dress with a ruffled hem down a modest thigh split, which I've paired with strappy heels and the delicate gold necklace with a blue topaz stone Noah bought me last year for our fourth wedding anniversary. Yes, I look the part, I reassure myself, and when Charlotte opens the door I make sure to smile my bright white smile as I exclaim 'Hello,' and plant two air kisses either side of her cheeks. She welcomes me into their house, as though I belong there. But I know the truth.

That much blood should have been followed by screams.

No, I don't belong here. I may look the part; I may act graceful and put-together, but I am only playing dress-up. I have buried the real me out of sight. I like this newer version of me – but standing here now after driving back from Maldon, I am confronted with the reality that I never really belonged here.

The old Justine, though perhaps it's more truthful to say the real me, is messier, not just in terms of style but deep down. My emotions, my thoughts, the way I see the world. It is not black and white. It is a swirl of colours. Murky. It is loud. This world Noah and I have created for ourselves with our pristine house and wealthy glamorous friends, it is too contained. Too organised. Where are the blurred edges? With it comes the pressure not to reveal my own blurred edges. I too must remain perfect.

I am tired.

The hug Charlotte envelops me in is full of warmth and the sincerity of it almost makes me want to cry. These are good people. Overtly posh, certainly, but no one can deny they are kind and generous.

'I'm so glad you could make it. We've missed you so much, and especially with everything you've been going through. You know we love you, right?'

'I know, thank you.' I smile graciously. 'But today is your birthday, and I brought wine,' I say, trying to lift the mood. If I have to spend the evening talking about myself, I won't last the whole night.

'Ooooh, Chablis. Thanks darling,' Charlotte coos as she whisks the bottle away towards the kitchen, and I follow her in. I'm slightly apprehensive about seeing Noah again. I will myself to be normal; recognisable as the woman he married. Pray he can't tell I've cheated on him simply by looking at me. It has been a week since I stayed over at Jimmy's but the hot guilt still feels rough and raw across my skin.

I don't know if it's just my imagination, but the air seems to shift when I enter. Noah and Rob were clearly mid-conversation, but they stop suddenly as soon as they see me. It is true that in this country we don't know how to act around grief. There is a short, but noticeable, pause before Noah heads towards me. I kiss him lightly on the lips. The guilt inside me starts to burn. Rob follows after, exclaiming loudly how good it is to see me and how sorry they are for my loss.

I dig my index finger into the flesh between my thumb and scratch at the scab there. Noah has remained standing close to me. The space between us feels awkward. I know I'm overthinking it, but I force myself to thread my fingers through his hoping it'll make him feel more solid again. To remind myself that we are real – him and me. My guilt makes me acutely aware of my hand in his and I want to pull away. I force myself to stay. I've been so absorbed in my past, I know I've made mistakes. I need to remind myself that this is my world. I belong here. Noah is mine and I am his.

'Right, ladies and gentlemen,' Rob announces, full of his usual energy as he claps his hands together. 'Game time,' he sings. We groan, but it is only for effect. We love a games night. It's the foundation of our friendship with Charlotte and Rob. 'Good old middle-class fun,' Jake had once teased when I suggested we stayed in to play Monopoly. The memory shoots through me and momentarily I am frozen to the spot, Noah's hand tugging me towards the lounge. His fingers slip from mine as he walks on ahead.

'Seriously? We haven't played this since we were in our twenties,' I hear Charlotte exclaiming from the other room.

'What are you making us do now?' I force myself to say, plastering a grin on my face as I round the door, following Noah.

'Never Have I Ever.' Charlotte rolls her eyes, but I can tell there's a sliver of excitement. Something alluring about acting young again. For them it's nostalgic, to relive the years they were full of recklessness and naivety. I was robbed of those years. My university years weren't full of drinking to have fun. Instead, I drank and acted out in order to forget.

'I'll go first. Now, remember you drink if you have in fact done the thing described. So, never have I ever danced on a table wearing a gold sequin dress,' Rob says and Noah drinks as we all laugh, remembering a particularly fun New Year's Eve in our late twenties.

'My turn,' Noah continues, wiping residual wine from his lips. 'Never have I ever streaked naked on a golf course.'

Charlotte and I raise our eyebrows at each other and as she takes a swig from her glass I pretend to do the same – as designated driver I am keen to make my one glass last as long as possible. But it was a dare we once lost to the boys and so I must be seen to drink. And then they're all looking at me and I realise it's my turn. My mouth is dry and I suddenly have stage fright. I can't think of a single memory. At least, not one suitable to bring up.

'Never have I ever.' I pause. Start to sweat. I can feel the blood rushing to my cheeks. 'Never have I cheated.' The words are out before I can swallow them back down. They stare at me and I force my drink to stay firmly rooted in my lap. What have I done? This is what guilt does to a person. It simmers. Waiting for an opportunity to boil over.

'Thought we needed a break from drinking, did you?' Rob says, more enthusiastically than necessary, and I am grateful to him for it.

'Sorry, I panicked!' I try to laugh and avoid looking in Noah's direction though I can feel his gaze upon me.

'How about we play something else?' Charlotte chimes in. 'Guess who? I'll go fetch the Post-its and pens.' She is out of the room before anyone can object and the relief floods me. I can't remember the last time we got together for a birthday dinner and didn't play this game. The familiarity of it, and the fact it is something so firmly rooted in the 'after' part of my life, feels nicely safe and secure. I allow myself to relax a little. Perhaps tonight will be fun after all.

I find my rhythm again and by the end of the evening I am constantly slipping my hand into Noah's without even thinking about it. The awkwardness of my arrival has dissipated. Noah fits, and briefly I allow myself to enjoy it before the guilt closes in again. He looks at me, a flash of white teeth as he laughs at another of Rob's jokes – really, they are relentless – and I pull him closer for a kiss.

It takes him by surprise; five years married, we're far past this kind of public display of affection. Realistically, I haven't kissed him like this in private either for longer than we'd like to admit. He grins. Leans in again. He has definitely had too much wine.

'All right you two lovebirds, get a room,' Charlotte quips and I feel strangely proud of us.

'Wow, is that the time, thank you so much for having us.' I glance at the clock. Two a.m. It really has been surprisingly good to be back.

'Don't be silly, darling. Always a pleasure. Just look after yourself, OK?' she says, making me wonder if perhaps I wasn't as smooth this evening as I'd hoped. It makes me feel as though they can see right through me and I tug on Noah's hand, practically dragging him towards the door. Charlotte and Rob stand with their arms around each other waving us off as we walk hand in hand towards my car. To anyone else walking by, I'm sure the four of us look a picture of happiness.

I am always amazed by just how deceiving appearances can be.

Designated driver, I drive us home and we spend the journey regaling each other with our thoughts on the evening; reliving every funny moment, laughing again at Rob's jokes, commenting on Charlotte's tenderness. I can tell we are proud of ourselves. That we'd both been anxious about the evening given everything that has happened and now want to revel in its success. Noah had no doubt been worried about my fragility and me, my guilt.

As we pull up in our driveway, the dread that has started to become so familiar seeps back through me and I no longer want to set foot inside our house. I am struck this evening by how perfect the life we've built for ourselves here is. It is too perfect. I'm afraid that once I go inside those walls, I'll never want to leave again.

The problem is, I know I have to. I must finish what I've started. For Max. He deserves answers. His death cannot have been for nothing, simply pinned on him as a drunk. And for me. I need to keep going, to regain control of the situation and of the sharks circling. Of DS Sorcha Rose.

Sitting here, with the moon reflecting off Noah's profile, it dawns on me the extent of just how much I stand to lose. After this wonderful evening with our friends, with my husband, now looking at our beautiful house, the full force of how far I could fall hits me. How far I've already fallen. And I don't want to let go.

It has been a few months since Noah and I have slept together but as his hand reaches for the car door, I stop him. Place my hand softly on his chest and wait for him to look at me before I climb over the handbrake until I'm straddling him. We haven't had sex in a car since before we were engaged, and we haven't had sex at all since Noah brought up starting a family – I'd felt as if it would require a decision, one I haven't been ready to make. But this evening I'm fed up with always being in control. With everything being so carefully planned out. And so I let go.

I feel Noah's body hesitate beneath me and he pushes me back ever so slightly. 'Where's this coming from?' he asks. I can tell he's enjoying it but he's also torn by how out of character it is. I don't answer him, unwilling to pollute this moment with more lies, and instead reach for the lever to lower his chair back. He doesn't ask me again and simply hikes up my silk dress.

Noah is my husband. I have no other family left. My mother does not count. She made her decision eighteen years ago and for that, I cannot forgive her. That was her choice, not mine, but I do have power over this – I will not let my husband go. What kind of wife cheats on her husband? What kind of mother abandons her daughter?

BEFORE

EVELYN – THE MOTHER

Two hours and thirty-eight minutes. That's how long Evelyn sat on the edge of her daughter's bed, listening to the whimpers escaping from her own body as she kept her eyes focused on the wardrobe. The sounds from the party below rose in crescendos every now and then, and in those pockets of time she allowed herself to cry a little louder, hoping Justine wouldn't be able to hear over the noise.

When she'd realised Gerard had locked Justine in, she'd felt it break: her last thread of love for him. She was surprised it had lasted this long, but that had always been part of his power. The balancing act between fear and love – tenderness and pain – a delicate recipe. But finally he'd got it wrong and she'd felt her tie to him snap beyond repair.

So she sat there and wept as she thought about what to do next. How best to protect Justine. If she let her out, she was afraid how it would all unfold. She'd lose control over the situation. At least with Justine in the wardrobe, she knew where her daughter was and that, for now, she was safe.

Evelyn kept track of the front door opening and closing, each time trying to estimate how many guests were left, racking her brain to remember who had arrived with whom, until there was no more chatter from below and the music was abruptly turned off.

Silence.

Everything always felt worse in the silence.

Evelyn squeezed her hands together tightly. Part of her willed Max to come upstairs and witness what was going on. The other part hoped he didn't. She'd protected her children for years. Tried to keep all the worst parts of Gerard from them – her own secret – and yet here was Justine locked in a wardrobe.

She'd failed.

There was no going back now, not for Justine. She knew all too well how this would change her. Max, though? She'd heard Gerard tell him earlier that Justine had left to go and find Jake. Yes, maybe there was still a sliver of hope for Max.

Evelyn stood and padded softly to Justine's en suite where she dabbed her eyes with cold water and held a wet tissue to her lips for a count of ten. She pinched her cheeks once each side to bring the colour back, and then practised her smile in the mirror. Quietly she left and headed downstairs. A well-oiled routine.

'I'm going to go and find Justine and check she's OK,' Max called from the bottom of the staircase.

'Great idea, love,' Evelyn cooed, keeping her voice even. Desperate for him not to sense something was wrong.

'Well done this evening.' Gerard clapped Max on the back loudly, making her clench her fists. 'I'm proud of you, son. Now, you go and carry on the night. You're young and free. Enjoy it.' His use of the word 'free' stung. Was it intentional? Was it cruel? Did Gerard know Evelyn had been sitting up there all this time, watching, knowing Justine's freedom had been taken away from her?

'Thanks. And well done, Mum. Great party, a real triumph.' Max grinned before opening the door and walking down the driveway without a single glance back. Evelyn closed her eyes, hoping the image of him smiling would stay forever etched in her memory as vividly as she could currently imagine it. And, as she let herself relax into the knowledge Max was safely out of the house, the air felt a little lighter.

If only for a moment.

The relief lasted for as long as she watched him disappear down the path and out of sight. As soon as the door was shut, everything felt even worse than before. Max had been Justine's only chance, and now he was gone. The only person left was her, and Evelyn knew how this could go. She weighed up the different possibilities, working out what her best move would be. The children had never seen this side of their lives before. She'd sacrificed so much to make sure of it. Bore the scars.

Gerard had used Justine and Max against her over the years, threats fizzing through the air when he'd had too much to drink. He'd assumed they were her weakness. What he failed to understand was that they were the very opposite. Justine and Max had always been her strength. Her love for them was the one thing that had kept her from completely falling under his power. They had kept a small part of her alive, all these years, despite his best efforts to squash out all of her. To make her purely his.

The most important thing now was to try and defuse the situation. Yes, Gerard had locked Justine away, but she knew things could get far worse if she didn't tread carefully. She understood that if she put herself into this scenario; if it became not just about Gerard and Justine, but Gerard against her, too, then he would do everything in his power to win. So she looked at him – the monster she had once loved – in silence. She allowed herself to imagine him one last time as the young man who'd walked on to the train all those years ago, before letting her hatred of him finally consume every part of her, and then she walked away, into the kitchen.

She was banking on the fact he would think she was weak, and that would make him glow. He did not need to know it took every ounce of strength inside of her to place one foot in front of the other and walk away from her daughter.

Evelyn hoped that if Gerard thought he'd already asserted himself once that evening, he'd be gentler on Justine. Forcing her body to obey her brain she sat at the kitchen table with her head in her hands and, for the first time in her life, Evelyn prayed.

Chapter Thirty-Four

I am woken in the morning by Noah's arm as he rolls over and encases me in it. It is heavy and strong. At first, my eyes flash open in panic. *I am trapped.* I feel an urge to break free, but then I take in my surroundings. I am back home, with Noah. This is our bedroom, with its grey panelling round the bottom half of the walls and parquet flooring we spent far too much money on. Rustic artworks adorn the walls. The decor is perhaps more appropriate for a holiday escape than a South London town-house, but I love it here in this room. No floral wallpaper in sight.

This is the very room Noah asked me to marry him in. It wasn't a fancy affair, but it was perfect. He proposed on the very first night we moved into the house. The room was mostly bare except for a mattress on the floor, which is where we promised each other we would build our life here together. That we'd make the house ours. And we have succeeded. The thought is physically painful.

I've always found the scariest feeling in the world to be happiness. If you're happy, it just shows how much you have to lose. And I know all about losing everything. I've never trusted myself to stay happy, and here I am having proved it all once again – I destroy the things around me that make me happy. Maybe I am only ever destined to experience happiness fleetingly.

Maybe it's all I deserve.

'Good morning,' Noah's sleepy voice whispers behind me and I know I have a choice to make. Now I'm back here, I could simply stay. I've done it before; I know I could do it again. It is tempting. I could lie here forever in Noah's arms and stay wearing this mask of mine. But it is exactly that. A mask. If the past few weeks have shown me anything, it's that there never was an 'old' or a 'new' Justine. I was always there. Always the same Justine. I've just been hiding.

If I'm ever going to truly belong here in this life with Noah, then I need to find a way to move on from the past. And that means I need answers. Ones I'm not going to get unless I return to Maldon. I owe it to myself and, more importantly, I owe it to Max.

What I'll do with those truths is yet to be decided – how many of them do I need to tell? But without answers I am out of control. And DS Rose cannot be underestimated. Information is power. How much does she know? I need to make sure I'm always one step ahead. That I remain the most powerful.

Power is everything, Dad used to say.

I roll over, still wrapped in Noah's arm, to face him and kiss him softly. I try to drink him in. It was easier to leave the first time because he was away in Paris. It is harder now, knowing for certain that I'm going back to face a past I would rather keep running from.

'I have to go,' I say.

'Already?' Noah groans but I can tell he isn't angry. He still thinks I'm the caring daughter, looking after my grieving mother. 'I was hoping we could at least go for breakfast at our favourite café.' He smiles at me, cheekily, and the urge to stay is so overwhelming that I worry if I don't leave right this minute then I never will.

'Sorry. I'll be home soon,' I say as I pick his arm up and sidle out from under it.

'Fine, but at least let me make you a breakfast smoothie for the road.'

This man deserves better than me, I think, as my memory of Jimmy resurfaces and the guilt flares up again.

'Can you just grab me some shorts out of the wardrobe?' Noah asks and I freeze. I can't do it. I realise, with absolute horror, that I cannot bring myself to open our wardrobe and I want to crumple right here on our bedroom floor. It has happened. Everything I was hoping to protect. My past has followed me here.

'Sorry actually, I can't stay. I really need to leave right now.' I don't even bother trying to smooth my panic over.

'Is everything OK? What's happened?'

'I just need to get back to Mum. Sorry,' I lie. 'I'll be home soon. I promise.' I lean over the side of the bed to give him a kiss goodbye, and this time it's not a promise to someone else – I'm far too aware how easily I break those – it's a promise to myself.

I keep making that same promise over and over again as I once more drive away from my husband and our home. Away from the city that once held so much promise for my career. Everything has changed.

Chapter Thirty-Five

Back at Mum's once more and I can't resist looking her up.

Christina Lang.

She has straight blond hair which is clearly dyed and a look about her that exudes ambition: something she now has the chance to fulfil, given she's been allocated Brad Finchley's case.

I stare at her bio and headshot on the chambers' website. Apparently, given the circumstances, the entire case had to be reassigned to a different – rival – chambers. Another strike against my name. I'm pretty sure I recognise her from networking events, but our paths have never crossed professionally.

I look down at my chipped nails where I've started biting them again. It is only four p.m. and I am already changed into sweatpants and a baggy pyjama top. If I'm no longer a barrister then why bother looking like one? I take a sip of my coffee before realising it has turned cold.

I know it's not her fault. I'm even acutely aware that if anyone is to blame, it's me. And yet I can't help feeling like this woman, this Christina Lang with her pristine make-up and sharp suit, has stolen my life. I bet she also lives in a London townhouse just like mine, with a partner waiting for her at home, whereas I am back here staying with my mother having this morning run away from my husband. Afraid of my own wardrobe.

Coffee, even a freshly brewed hot one, is no longer going to cut it but as I pull out the bourbon bottle from the desk cupboard where I have taken to keeping it, I realise just from the unfamiliar weight of it that it is empty.

I leave the sweatpants on but make the effort to at least change out of my pyjama top and into a strappy vest. A quick glance in the mirror tells me I barely pass for looking socially acceptable, but it will have to do. Then I grab the house keys and head to the pub. I'd rather keep avoiding Jimmy for as long as possible, but not at the expense of a drink. Some things are just too important and right now a bourbon on the rocks is the only thing that has even the slightest chance of helping my pounding headache.

The TV on the wall of the Blue Eagle changes channel abruptly and I'm confronted by a news segment with a skinny teary-eyed woman in the centre of the screen. The caption below reads: *Sister of murdered Mark Rushnell pleads public for information.*

'The most important thing is to secure a conviction,' the woman says, 'The more information we have, the more likely that is.'

She's talking as though Jake's guilt is unquestionable – as if an acquittal would simply be a failure of the justice system rather than proof of his innocence.

I finish what's left of my drink.

Three bourbons. That's how many it has taken for the throbbing in my skull to subside, only to be replaced with a dizziness which has sharpened my wit while numbing everything else – something I find I'm particularly grateful for now as I listen to Mark's sister's grief being broadcast round the pub.

My phone vibrates with a text from Noah.

Noah: *Feeling sad you're not here beside me. You rushed off so fast this morning. I hope you're doing OK?*

I know it's the drink talking, unleashing the side of me I usually hide from him, but quick as a flash I reply, pressing send before I have time to reconsider.

Justine: *You're sad? What about me? For the record, no, I am not doing* OK.

I stare at the screen. I'm pretty embarrassed by my rudeness – I know he was trying to be nice, but I'm also a little proud of myself. Tonight, I am not going to pretend to be the perfect person. Perfect Justine, always who everyone else wants me to be.

I shove my phone into my bag and push my empty glass forward, indicating for another. It is a young guy serving me this evening. I haven't seen him before. He hesitates and I drawl out a sarcastic 'please'. Before he has time to answer Jimmy rounds the corner of the bar, giving the server a look even I can't miss, and the boy slides past him, clearly grateful to be rid of me.

'Been hiding from me, have you?' I'm unsure if I'm being facetious or flirtatious.

'Not at all,' he says. 'I might say the same about you, though.'

'I'm sat in your pub, aren't I?' I hate myself.

'You are. But I'm pretty sure that has more to do with the alcohol we serve here than me.'

I don't bother replying. He can be a smart-arse if he wants to be.

'It's on the house,' Jimmy says, pouring a fresh glass of water and sliding it across the countertop towards me.

'It's tap water.'

'Tap water with fancy lime.' He grins, dropping some freshly cut lime into my glass, and I do my very best to remain looking doggedly unimpressed. 'Dare I ask what's brought this on?' he asks.

'Really? As if you can't already think of a thousand reasons why I might want to drink myself into a dark hole at a bar.'

'Then why now? And don't say because of me. I know this isn't to do with what we did. I'm not that big-headed.'

Why now?

As if everything we think or feel should have a clear beginning and end. Jimmy doesn't know about my early-morning paracetamol. Going from two pills a day to three, before deciding it would be better to move to codeine – convincing myself it is smarter to take fewer pills than more, as if increasing the strength doesn't matter so much as the quantity. I've been a swan. Gliding on the surface but frantic underneath.

'I really do want another drink.' I say drily.

'Tell me what's wrong, and maybe I'll get you one.'

'You can't do that. I'm a paying customer.'

'In my bar.'

Touché.

'You really want to know? Everything. My marriage. My career. My brother. My mother. Christina Lang.'

'Christina Lang?' I realise I never told Jimmy I was working on Jake's case and it dawns on me that this is one card I still have up my sleeve in this town: that I do, in fact, know things people aren't aware I was ever privy to. I have seen the case files. I've read the witness statements.

Power is everything. And information is power.

'She's stealing my career,' I say, being careful not to reveal too much. 'So, that drink?' I tip my glass towards him.

'I'm afraid not. You're slurring your words, Justine.'

'It's not your job to look out for me.' I clearly say it too loudly, too vehemently, as the couple next to me can't help but look over. I am beyond caring. Let them stare. I'm already the laughing stock of chambers, I might as well play the part here too.

'Justine.' His voice is lower now, more serious. 'I am not going to serve you, but I am going to make sure you get home safely.'

'Fine.' Clearly, I am not fine about it, but what am I supposed to do? Clamber over the counter and pour myself the goddamn drink? It's tempting.

'Is Alice working tonight? I haven't seen her, but then again you've been hiding from me all night. Maybe she has been too.' My chin is on the bar and I'm twiddling my hair. God, I'm drunk.

'Firstly, I have not been hiding from you, I only just finished a stock-take. And secondly, you've taken a real shine to Alice, haven't you? Why are you asking?'

'I ask questions. It's what I do, remember. Even when I am drunk.' He lets out a little laugh and I find myself glad he isn't too mad at me, despite his refusal to pour me another drink.

'She's been asking about you too. What's the story there?' He says it nonchalantly enough, but it tugs at my memory.

My boss, Jimmy Falcon.

Clawing at her neck.

'There's no story.' I try not to sound too defensive.

'Even drunk, there's no getting past you is there, Justine Stone.'

'I used to be the best,' I slur dramatically, my use of the past tense not going unnoticed.

'Come on,' Jimmy says, sliding his way through the bar hatch. 'Let's get you home.' He is standing right next to me. It is the closest we've been since we slept together and it feels complicated and messy. I can't believe I've put my marriage at risk. I love Noah. I want to spend the rest of my life with him – the life we've built for ourselves. But I can't deny the pull of Jimmy. These two men are now representing the different sides of me – Jimmy, an avenue into my past, and Noah, my future.

'No.' It sounds forceful and rude but I need him to listen to me. 'I'm fine on my own.'

'You're dru—'

'I said no. I'm perfectly capable of looking after myself. I don't need you,' I say. And then I lean in closer and lower my voice so only he can hear me, 'I don't want you.'

I leave Jimmy standing there as I storm – though maybe in reality it's more of a stagger – out of his pub. The night temperature drops round here even in the height of summer, and I wish I'd brought a jacket. I wrap my arms around myself and head in the direction of Mum's house. I still cannot refer to it as home.

The lanes are darker than the night-time streets of London. Fewer cars, fewer streetlamps, and I quicken my step. Shadows dance at me and every time a lone car drives past I find myself stepping further away from the road, as if the driver might haul me into their car as they drive past. I'm sure it's just the stench of death these past few weeks taking its toll, but the feeling I'm not alone has settled once more on my shoulders.

I remind myself it's not the first time I've struggled with the violence encountered in a job like mine. It's why I've learnt it's best to dive straight into the worst parts of a case rather than put them off. I can never escape them. That numbness other barristers talk about, journalists too, that comes from too much exposure to the darkness, hasn't affected me yet. I can still feel all of it. All the pain.

Aya once asked me if it was in fact just my own pain that I was projecting on to the cases. Trauma, like gas, will always find a way out if there is one. She always manages to make everything seem so personal. *Why can't it be that I'm just a very empathetic person? That I feel things more than others do?* I'd replied. To which she'd pointedly knitted her hands back together in her lap and asked me the next question. On this occasion though, the lines are undeniably blurred: the death and darkness of my work have become personal. Very personal.

I look again over my shoulder, for what must be the fourth time since leaving the pub, but all I see behind me is a wall of black. In front of me, fifty metres up the road, the lights from the police station shine brightly and I break into a jog.

I'm still running when she steps right in front of me. I don't think it is a purposeful power move; she looks as surprised as I do that I've almost run straight into her.

'Justine,' she says.

'DS Rose.' I am out of breath and acutely aware of the overpowering smell of alcohol coming from me.

'On your way home?'

I nod, gulping in air, trying to control my breathing.

She looks me up and down, a wall of silence descending between us. I can sense that any hope of working as a team has dissipated. There is no longer a façade of camaraderie between us. The way she's looking at me tells me this game we were playing – it is over. We've moved on to the next level.

'I've been working late. This town has some interesting cases.' She indicates the pile of folders tucked under her arms.

'Right.' I nod, fully assuming she means my father's.

'Right then,' she echoes, though she makes no move to leave. We stand there, neither of us willing to back down.

'All right, DS Rose,' calls a voice I recognise as Jimmy's and he emerges from the darkness.

People seem to make a habit of lurking in the shadows and then appearing when you least expect them to in this town. It gives the whole place a certain sense of unpredictability. I'm reminded of Jimmy's revelation about the town being overrun with Freemasons. Has that always been part of it? Why Maldon has always felt so claustrophobic? A town full of secrets? Suddenly it feels significant, and I kick myself for not asking more questions at the time. I hope when I'm sober I remember to follow up on this.

For now though, I turn to Jimmy. Has he been stalking me? What about the other day too, when I was running? Was that him then, as well? And at the funeral, he was quick to come to my rescue. Is he watching me? Too closely? Or am I seeing patterns where there aren't any? Either way, the spell is broken and DS Rose smiles tightly, giving a small nod to the both of us before walking on.

Once she's out of sight I hiss furiously at Jimmy for following me. I do not need a babysitter. Especially not one who lurks in the darkness convincing me I'm losing my mind. We walk the rest of the way in silence, and I try to stay at least one step ahead of him to prove a point.

Only once we've reached the front door do I address him again.

'It's not going to happen. *We* can't happen. OK? So, if that's what this is all about, then please, stop it. I feel guilty enough already. I'm married. I love Noah.' I'm not sure why exactly, but saying those three words out loud outside Mum's house which is so steeped in memories of my time with Jake makes me feel guilty. But Jake was a long time ago, and I am fighting now to protect my marriage.

'I know. It's not what this is about, I promise. I just wanted to make sure you got home safe.' His voice is soft and there's no trace of hurt or anger. I genuinely believe he means it. 'It happened. We can't take it back. I don't regret it. We were both hurting, Justine, don't be too hard on yourself. But I agree, it won't happen again.'

'Thank you.'

Jimmy gives an almost imperceptible nod before turning around and slinking away back into the shadows of the night. It's what I asked him to do, I know that, but as I push the key into the front-door lock of the house I once swore never to return to, I feel overwhelmingly alone.

I don't know what propels me to do it. Perhaps it's the fact the house feels too big, with only me and Mum in it – the absence of

Dad and Max too loud – or perhaps it's that I feel I have nothing left. Christina Lang is now representing everything I'd striven to be. Everything I've lost. I've been stripped back to the girl I once was. I find myself placing one foot in front of the other until I am facing the walk-in wardrobe in my bedroom – the one I can't bring myself to open. I slide down the front of it and hug my knees, just like all those years before, except this time I'm on the right side of it and not caged inside.

BEFORE

JUSTINE

The longer Justine was locked in the wardrobe, the more it changed her. She and Max had grown up knowing the power being alone had over you. How much more dangerous everything could feel. It's why as children they'd always chosen to hide together, under the stairs, when their mother's cries were too loud to ignore. Max would pretend it was hide-and-seek, and she'd go along with it. Even as a child she'd known it helped them both to remain living in the fantasy world Max had built for them.

This time, there was no Max by her side making up stories and games to keep the truth away. She was alone, and there was no choice but to face it.

By the time her father scraped the chair back and swung the door open, she was barely recognisable. Her desire for courage hadn't simply arrived, it had flooded her and could no longer be controlled. She hadn't become the Viking beating the drum, she had transformed into the drum itself.

She rose from the floor and glared at her father, where he stood smoking a cigar. He was not a big man, but he had an aura about him that made him larger than life. His green velvet suit jacket hung slightly too big on his shoulders and his brow was sweaty – probably from all the whisky.

'How dare you?' Justine demanded, surprising even herself. 'I am your daughter.' She sounded confident and righteous but inside she was shaking. Broken. Abandoned. How could he do this to her? Her own father.

'Exactly. I cannot have my daughter making false claims about my most valued partner. Do you know what that would do to us? You almost ruined this entire family tonight.' He is speaking quietly, nonchalantly, as if he hasn't just completely shattered Justine's entire world, and it only infuriates her more.

'They are not false claims.'

'Everything is open to interpretation, Justine, you'll learn that one day.'

'Not sexual assault.'

They were still facing each other. Head on. Charging into battle. He was meant to be protecting her. Why wasn't he? She wanted to make him see. Perhaps it was still just one big misunderstanding.

'Did he kiss you?'

'No.'

'Did he make you touch him?'

'No.'

'Did he rape you?' Justine noticed he didn't even flinch as he asked her that one, and it shook her to the core. How callous it sounded out of her own father's lips. She knew he could be cruel, had heard it through the walls, but he'd never aimed it at her before.

'No.'

'Well then,' he said, smirking. 'Yes, I'd say it's open for interpretation.'

Not one big misunderstanding, then.

Gerard turned from her and started heading towards the door. That was it? He wasn't going to ask for her side of the story? The sight of him striding away from her was too much to bear. He was really going to leave her, again? Why wouldn't he fight for her?

It made Justine feel small. So small. How could she matter this little to her own dad? She couldn't resist drawing him back into combat. At least arguing was better than him leaving her. It was worse to feel discarded, as if her pain did not really exist. As if she'd just made up what had happened, and it was no longer worth talking about.

And so she dug deep. Anything to get a reaction. To keep him there.

'What about hitting your wife? Is that open to interpretation?' She regretted it as soon as the words left her mouth.

Fast strides then, closer and closer. His chest puffed out, rage consuming his entire posture. He was no longer smirking. It was his eyes that told her she had gone too far. They had somehow darkened.

It dawned on her that he didn't intend to stop.

Not this time.

Justine could tell it was no longer just a game to him that he would smirk about winning while puffing on a cigar later. She had pushed him too far. She should have let him win.

She watched, as if in slow motion, as he drew his hand back. He kept looking at her the whole time – unashamed as he hit his daughter. The force of it still took her by surprise, even though she'd known it was coming. The sting burned. Her cheek was on fire. One thousand needles were pricking her skin.

She gasped as her eyes filled with tears. And then she drew herself back to standing tall and willed the tears not to fall. She was a Stone, after all. But as she rose back up with her hand clutched to her cheek, she wondered: now the line had been crossed, would he ever stop? The role he had been playing – the one of the hero father – there was no going back to it. Tonight, he had relinquished his part. Would he fully step into this new role? The one of the villain? Previously hidden behind closed doors. Reserved only for her mother.

There was a moment of stillness as they watched each other. A gap in time. Would this silence mark the before and after? It was as if they knew that whatever happened next would define everything. Who would make the first move? Where did they go from here?

After only a momentary pause, Gerard calmly removed his cigar from where it hung limp between his lips. She knew then he had chosen to be the villain. That the slap had just been the beginning.

She'd seen the circular burns on her mother, in places easy to cover up, but nothing stays secret from a child. They're too in-tune, too small, too observant. Adults forget what it's like to be so plugged into the world around you with no other distractions – no work, no responsibilities, pulling you away from experiencing the present. Children are sponges. Adults are clumsy.

Her parents had thought they were being clever, but Max and Justine hadn't played hide-and-seek for no reason. They knew when it was best to stay out of the way. To hide in places where they could neither see nor hear their mother's pain. Their father's cruelty.

No, Justine would not let him burn her too.

She dropped the stiletto which was still clutched in her hand and she pushed him. Hard and fast. She was only small but she used all of her strength. She would not let him turn her into her mother.

Justine watched as he crumpled right before her eyes. As his head clipped the side of her desk, whipping back with the force of it. And the blood.

She hadn't expected the blood.

It all happened so fast. All she'd wanted to do was to strike first. To let him know she was not her mother. That she would not take it quietly. She would fight.

She hadn't meant to kill him.

Chapter Thirty-Six

A baby bird. Or a sick child. That's what Mum reminds me of as she climbs into my bed at five a.m the next morning. I'm not a big woman, normally I'm described as fairly lithe, but next to my mother's skeletal frame I feel impossibly large. I lie there, unsure what she wants from me.

Even when I still lived here, I never knew how to react in the moments where she'd come to me, broken and small. They didn't happen often, and the pattern seemed to be that her visits occurred a day or two after I'd noticed the air around the house had got thicker. It was never spoken about, and she'd never say a word, but in the early hours of the morning she'd slip into my room and lie there in silence before starting the day as if nothing had happened at all.

I wonder now if I failed her back then by never saying anything. But I was a child. I shouldn't have been expected to speak the first word. To know what words even to say.

I don't have an excuse now. I am no longer a child, and I have plenty of experience of finding the words. And yet. I stay here, lying awkwardly on my back in silence. Perhaps she thought she was protecting me, by not saying anything. But all I ever felt was used. Like a yo-yo. Exposed to the darkness but then expected to pretend, just hours later, that life was bright and sunny.

'Am I keeping you awake?' Her voice crackles and seems to echo around my room. I wasn't expecting her to speak.

'No, it's fine,' I lie. Of course she's keeping me awake. I start to feel the anger rise from my toes. How have I ended up back here?

'I need to get up anyway,' I announce, throwing back the cover unapologetically. She doesn't ask me where I need to be, nor does she move. I hate this house. I hate how the power of silence is used against you just as much as words. It's something I utilise a lot in the courtroom; not saying anything at all. It is surprisingly threatening, and impressively effective. But it doesn't belong in a home.

I pull on a crumpled dress from the floor and before I have time to make a plan, I find myself driving away from Maldon with no idea where I'm headed. All I know is that I need to get away: from Maldon; the house; the bedroom; the wardrobe. From my mother.

I can't pinpoint exactly when on the drive I must have decided this was a good idea but here I am, sitting in a café opposite her chambers, with no idea whether Christina Lang will even show up today or not. I know a stakeout when I see one. It's just not normally something I undertake personally.

I should have been appearing in court myself today. Instead, I'm two croissants down by ten a.m., hiding out with no plan for what happens next. While I'm here I text Otis asking if he's heard any updates on how the case against Jake is progressing. I know it's a lot for me to ask of him – if he got caught snooping into other barristers' cases no one else would ever work with him again. I crick my neck and reach into my bag for more painkillers.

Otis: *What do you want to know?*

I smile. So far he has never let me down. The hearing is edging closer and I keep thinking about it. How will he plead? I don't know why I'm so fixated on it, to be honest. I know that even if he did commit the murders, he'd likely be advised to plead not guilty. But still, it's as though hearing him plead innocent will be confirmation that I am right. That Jake did not kill Mark or Beverley Rushnell.

As I wait – both for news from Otis and to see Christina – I try to distract myself by delving further into the Freemasons. What else don't I know about my dad? My search tells me there is a coded handshake between Lodges and I burst out laughing. Apparently, there are different handshakes depending on your hierarchy within the Lodge. This is exactly the kind of shit my dad loved. Anything to make him feel important. The brother-hood is steeped in secrecy and even my in-depth searching isn't returning much. It's just the same information parroted back to me on each website. One other thing I do find out is that there are a number of objects that symbolise certain values; that a square and compass symbol is used to represent morality and ethics. The thought of my father upholding any kind of morals beyond those which benefitted himself makes a joke of his entire membership. The description jogs my memory, though, and I recall the strange brooch I found in my dad's drawer with a G in the middle and realise this is exactly what I found. I read on and find that the G is supposed to remind Freemasons that their actions are performed in the presence of God, the grand archi-tect of the universe. Is it intended to make their actions more noble? To remind them they are accountable in the eyes of God? If so, I can attest that, in the case of my dad, it failed.

A couple of hours pass before I see her. All sleek black suit and glossy hair. She's glowing and it's no wonder, given the adrenalin that must be pumping round her veins after landing Jake's case. Just like this trial was meant to be my big break, it promises to be a huge career move for Christina too. I can see it in the way she walks. She is hungry for it.

I'm out of the café door before I know it. Following her close behind, but not so close she'll clock me. I'm no professional at this game, but luckily for me it's not too difficult to remain unnoticed in London; everyone is so used to going about their business unaware of their surroundings that they're not expecting someone else to be paying attention to them.

From her pace, the wheelie attached to her hand, and the direction she's headed in, I'll bet my money we're bound for Southwark Crown Court. The more turns we take, the more confident I am of our destination. I feel a buzz run through me. I'm going to get to see her in action. God, I hope she's not as good as I am.

I know I'm smart and I do believe in myself, but simultaneously I've always felt crushingly inept, the sense that I should be successful but also needing other people to tell me I'm good enough. My ego is fragile. Too fragile to withstand watching someone else impress doing a job that once had my name on it.

I take my seat at the back of court ready to make a quick exit if I see anyone who might recognise me – though right now I'm not sure I'd even recognise myself. I don't know the last time I washed my hair, and I have a red-wine stain down the front of my creased dress.

Christina is impressive, I'll give her that. Slick, poised and dare I say a little intimidating. It is an appeal against a previous armed robbery conviction, and it's just getting meaty when my phone vibrates in my pocket.

Otis. Shit. Did I really cross that big a line?

I sidle out of court hoping not to draw any attention to myself. Once I'm in the hallway I answer.

'I shouldn't have asked you,' I admit immediately but he dismisses it, instead telling me excitedly that he has cracked the sophisticated encryption software guarding Max's laptop.

'There's a lot of nothing on there – full of the usual crap you would expect to find saved on anyone's hard drive – but I've combed through it more than once and I think I've found something.'

'Amazing.'

'Don't get too excited. At first nothing stood out to me, but then I found two documents. Both with bank account details saved. One was clearly in Max's name. I checked it out and there's nothing unusual there. But the other was an LLC in the name of The Little Trust Company. Now, any search I do doesn't throw up any link to Max and this company. Do you know anything about it? Or what he might have been trading in under that name?'

'I have no idea. Max never mentioned any side business to me.'

'OK. I'll see what I can find. It's notoriously hard to trace LLCs but I'll do what I can.'

'All you've got so far is a document with bank details on? We don't yet know who is even behind the company or what, if anything, the company was set up for.'

'I know. I told you. It's not much. But we can assume encryption software was installed for a reason, and this is the only lead I have. If it was a public company he was paying into, I'd have expected to find the details of it pretty quickly. But I still haven't.'

'What about deleted files?'

'I've been through those too. Nothing of interest.'

'OK, well let's find out if it was Max's company, or one he was paying.'

The Little Trust Company.

It sounds harmless enough, but I can't help thinking it also sounds exactly like my family's perverse sense of humour. For something to, on first look, appear sweet and harmless only to be intentionally pulling the wool over your eyes.

A sage piece of advice from my father on how to be a success-ful lawyer pops into my head. Even after all these years I can't escape him. Both the good, and the bad.

Always look for the double meaning in things. People might not be lying outright, but that doesn't mean they're not disguis-ing the truth. You have to learn to read between the lines.

I think again about the company name. It is clever. People often call accounts 'trusts', and the use of 'little' makes it feel sweet and charming; as if it's an Etsy user selling homemade boujee décor. But taken separately, the phrase 'little trust' is much more alarming. A harsh, less pleasing truth disguised with sweetness. Yes, it sounds very Stone-like indeed.

'I did also look to see if there was a letter,' Otis says.

'A letter?'

'Just to rule out Max intentionally went into the water.'

'There'll be no letter,' I say it harshly. How dare he. But I know he's just doing his job, leaving no stone unturned.

'I know. And you're right. I didn't find one. But Justine, you know that doesn't entirely rule suicide out.'

He's right but my mind is swirling. The thoughts racing through my head are moving too fast. I know it's at the mention of a letter. Not the kind he's referring to, but the memory of another. The first I ever received, all those years ago on my eight-eenth birthday.

Justine,

Happy eighteenth birthday to you! I'm not very good at this, I know, but you deserve the world, so this is me trying! You've made Maldon feel bigger. Like, before I met you my life was small and now instead of feeling boxed in, I'm excited about my future because I know you'll be in it.

I know you also think you're trapped here, but you're not. You have bigger wings than you think. You're going to go on to do great things, and I can't wait to watch you do them. Or help you – if you'll let me!! And I don't mean that you'll do everything your parents want you to. I know that's part of why you feel so caged up and seriously, I understand. My family is different from yours but we both feel trapped by them. You're expected to fill big shoes and me little ones. But you're already smashing it. You've already changed my life and I know you'll go on to change other people's too.

I love you, Justine Stone. I'll never stop loving you. No matter what. That's what this last gift is meant to be . . . My promise to you that for as long as I live, no matter where I am, I will love you and protect you with all my heart.

Jake xxx

'Justine? Are you still there?' Otis's gravelly voice pulls me back to the present.

'Sorry, yes. I just had an idea. Well, less of an idea – more just something I could really do with your help with.'

'Another favour?' he jokes.

'Come on now, who's keeping count?'

'Is it above board?' he asks. And I know he's still a little on edge about working on the case after I've been removed. That this notion of favours being exchanged between us isn't entirely fiction – after all, it's how our partnership began in the first place.

I hesitate.

'Not exactly. But I just need another set of eyes. That's all, I promise. I'll be doing all the dirty work.'

I hear a groan from the other end of the phone.

'You're impossible, Justine Stone. Do you know that?'

'I do. And you're the best. I know that for sure.'

He laughs. Before we hang up, I give Otis strict instructions to find out when Christina Lang is due in court three days from now and to be ready to meet me in London. Because the thing about letters is that they are powerful. For some unknown reason people find themselves more willing to open up in them. To reveal their true selves.

I think it's about time I wrote my own one. I'm not planning on exposing my secrets – no, I've not lost sight of what's really at stake here – but maybe I can entice them out of someone else.

For all these years, I've naively, perhaps even arrogantly, believed I am the only one keeping secrets about the night my father died. But, if Max's death and Jake's arrest are both some-how linked to that day, then that simply can't be true.

It's too late to find out what Max was hiding, but what about Jake? What does Jake know about the night of the sixteenth of December that I don't?

BEFORE

JAKE – THE BOYFRIEND

For the first time in what felt like weeks it had stopped raining. Instead, the plummeting temperature now threatened to turn the roads into 'icy death traps' as Jake's mum liked to melodramatically warn him. She always catastrophised. It was a defining trait of hers.

The one good thing to come from it was that she told riveting stories. A little fall became a near-death incident; her finally feeling better from a nasty cold turned into a miraculous recovery. Nothing was ever dull or mundane. Just tonight, as Nan had gone to blow out her candles (sadly not eighty-eight of them, much to her disappointment) his mum had exclaimed 'Not too close,' apparently worried all her hairspray would catch light.

It had been a great party, but it was time for Nan to go home and Jake has been assigned getting her into a taxi safely. He felt his phone vibrate as he helped her clamber in. Only a few minutes later, once her taxi had pulled away, did he see he had three missed calls from Justine.

He called her straight back. 'Are you OK?'

'No. I—'

'Hello? Are you there?' She sounded different. He couldn't tell if it was her crying or just crackling on the line.

'He's dead.'

'He's dead?'

'Yes.'

'Who?'

'I killed him.'

Jake stopped and checked his phone again, making sure he'd definitely called the right number. It didn't sound like her, and she was making no sense, but it was Justine's number.

'Who? Who did you kill? What are you on about?'

'My dad. I didn't mean to. It was just a push. He was going to hurt me, I swear, so I pushed him and he fell. Oh my God I really killed him. Jake, help me.'

'You're sure? He's not just, I don't know, passed out or something?' Surely this wasn't real.

'I'm sure. There's blood and, oh God, it's so awful. He fell and hit his head on the corner of my desk. It must have struck him in the wrong place.'

'Is anyone else with you? What about your mum?'

'Max left and I haven't heard Mum. She probably went to bed early. She normally does when Dad's been drinking. Jake, please, I need you to help me.'

Three minutes. That's how long it had taken him to get his nan in the taxi, wave goodbye and call Justine back. He wished now he'd realised how precious those extra three minutes he'd given himself were. Three more minutes he'd bought himself until his life would change forever.

He hadn't fully digested what she'd done, but they didn't have the luxury of time. Instinct kicked in. He knew the longer they waited, the less chance he had of fixing this. He didn't have all the details but the gravity of what had happened was clear: Gerard was dead, and Justine thought she had killed him.

He'd heard such stories before. His catastrophising mother always reminded him of them before a night out as a warning to stay out of trouble. How it can only take one punch to change your life – either for someone to end it, or for you to spend the rest of yours behind bars. He'd always listened, taken heed, avoided trouble where it seemed to stir, never tried out the hero complex.

He was still standing on the kerb outside the pub when he realised he could no longer feel the cold. There was too much adrenalin pumping round his lean frame.

Jake, help me.

But what was he supposed to do?

He loved Justine, but how much?

He combed his hands through his hair and tried to calm down. He needed to think clearly and fast.

Either Justine needed to admit right now what had happened and that it was an accident in self-defence, or they had to come up with a different story entirely; one which didn't involve Justine pushing Gerard at all. First things first, he needed to see what they were dealing with.

He needed to go to her.

Part of him still hoped she was wrong, and all Gerard needed was some water splashed over him to wake him up, and they'd be laughing about it tomorrow.

The other part couldn't stop imagining Gerard Stone dead on Justine's bedroom floor.

It was worse, much worse, than Jake had imagined. Gerard was lying in a pool of thick blood, which was soaking into the floorboards. On one wall, the floral wallpaper Justine had chosen weeks earlier was now splattered with blood.

Jake could see where he'd hit his head on the corner of the desk, just as Justine had described. The corners had sharp metal edges – Justine had once told him it was hipster chic – and the one closest to Gerard's head was still dripping with blood. The violence of it made him want to retch. He'd never seen so much blood before. He forced himself to look closer, to see past all the blood. There, on the right side of Gerard's skull, perfectly placed on the temple, was a gaping, deadly hole.

'Justine?' he whispered. Where was she? 'Hello?' He could hear running water from the en suite. 'Are you in there?' Still no answer, so he pushed it open.

Justine was curled up underneath the blasting shower, her back pushed against the wall. She was still wearing her red dress, which was now soaked through. Her eyes looked hollow. Haunted.

'It's OK. It's going to be OK,' Jake said, reaching in to turn the water off and sliding down to sit on the wet floor beside her.

'Help me,' she whispered, her voice barely making a sound, and Jake felt the responsibility of his love for her break his heart. He would do anything for this girl but now he'd seen Gerard, he knew their options were limited.

'You need to tell them what happened,' he said as kindly as he could, but she whipped round to face him. Fear and shock were plastered across her face. 'It was an accident. They'll believe you,' he tried to reassure her.

Justine shook her head. 'What if they don't? Look at him! He's dead, Jake. He's really dead. And there's so much blood. Why is there so much blood from a fall?' She started shaking.

'I know, I saw. But it'll be OK.' It was true though, he hadn't been expecting so much blood. He knew head injuries could be fatal, but he hadn't prepared himself for how bad the scene would look.

'I can't go to prison. I can't.'

'You won't.'

'You don't know that for sure. You can't promise me they'll believe me. It looks bad. It looks really bad.'

'It does. But they must have seen injuries like this before. What if we say he fell? You just don't tell them you pushed him. Could you do that, if the police asked you?'

'But why would he have fallen? What am I supposed to say?' Her voice is rising with panic.

'Because he was drunk? It's been the party, I'm sure he probably did have too much to drink.'

'But I'd have to lie. To the police.'

'It's barely a lie. Let's practise. Tell me what happened but just say he fell instead.'

'I can't, I really don't think I can do it.'

'Look at me. You can do anything, Justine Stone, I know you can. Either you tell them you pushed him, or you say he fell. They're our only options. That desk is heavy-duty. The corners should be illegal. They'll believe you.'

She turned to look at him again, just as he'd told her to. Her hair dripping wet. Cheeks streaked with mascara.

'What if there's another way?' she said quietly.

'What other way? What do you want to do?'

'We don't tell the police at all. We ... cover it up somehow.'

Jake leant his head back against the wall, banging it slightly, and closed his eyes. Justine never failed to surprise him.

Could he do it?

Should he?

How?

There was so much Justine wanted to do in life. Not like him. He wasn't fuelled by the same ambition. Hadn't been brought up with the same sense of entitlement – Max and Justine had always been told they could do whatever they wanted to in life. Shit, she even wanted to be a barrister. To help prosecute the bad guys. And she was right, they couldn't guarantee anything. Telling the police felt like a risk. Of course she was scared – he was, too. And Justine was right when she said it looked bad. What if they didn't believe her?

Help me.

He loved her. He really fucking loved her.

The 'what if' began to feel too large.

Don't be a fool in love, his mum had warned him. Was this what she meant? That love could make you stupid? Because even he knew, as he agreed to help Justine, that he was going to live to regret it.

Jake had sent her away. If they were going to do this, it was best Justine was seen elsewhere. He'd suggested she go to join the rest of his family at the Blue Eagle. Although his nan's party had officially finished, the owner loved a lock-in on a weekend and there were plenty of people carrying the celebrations on way past closing time.

Now he just had to work out what to do next.

What he hadn't banked on was just how heavy Gerard would be, and how much blood there was to clean up. It had soaked into the rug; spattered the desk, the bookshelf even. The entire floor sparkled with shards of glass from where the mirror which used to be balanced on top of the desk had fallen to the floor.

This was nothing like he'd seen on TV shows. What was he thinking? There was no way he could do it all by himself. His hands shook as he pulled his phone out and called Max.

'All right mate, just the man I need to speak to. Are you with Justine?' Max answered.

'I'm not, but I really need your help,' he whispered, even though there was no one else in the room with him.

'My help? I'm a bit drunk, mate, not sure I'll be much help, but I can try. Where are you?'

'It's hard to explain. I'm at your house. Can you come quickly? And try not to be seen.'

'Not to be seen? What are you on about?'

'Just trust me. I'm being serious. Get here as fast as you can and don't be seen.'

'You're scaring me. Is Justine all right?'

'She is. Or at least, she will be. Your dad tried to hurt her and she pushed him. He's – your dad – he's . . .' But Jake couldn't bring himself to tell him Gerard was dead over the phone. 'Your dad is pretty hurt.'

'The bastard,' Max hissed. It was a side of him Jake hadn't seen before. A flash of real anger. Jake didn't think being on the phone was the time to ask more questions, but it didn't go unnoticed that the possibility of Gerard hurting Justine had simply been accepted. Jake thought again about the night they'd celebrated Max leaving for university. How Evelyn sat apart from the rest of them. How the air had felt charged with something he couldn't quite put his finger on. Had it been fear?

'I'll be as quick as I can,' Max said and hung up immediately.

Jake waited for him on the landing outside the bedroom. He'd spent the past ten minutes rehearsing how to tell Max what had happened.

'Max, your dad—' he whispered again, worried about waking Evelyn, but Max interrupted him. Jake was pretty sure his face showed just how bad it was. To be honest, he wasn't sure how he was still standing.

'Let me see for myself,' Max said, pushing past Jake into Justine's room. For a moment Jake stayed rooted to the spot. He'd imagined a number of different reactions to the news from Max, but none were as cold or as matter-of-fact as the reality. What was going on here?

Jake followed Max into the room and saw him towering over Gerard's body, in silence. Jake had started cleaning up but the extent of his injuries was still clear.

'He locked her in the wardrobe first,' Jake said in a feeble attempt to try and explain.

'He did what?'

'That's what she said. And then. Well. He . . .' How do you tell someone their dad hit their sister?

'He fucking hit her, didn't he?'

Jake nodded, somewhat relieved Max had taken the words straight out of his mouth.

'He was going to hit her again and she pushed him. He fell awkwardly and smashed his head on the desk. Right on his temple. Shit, Max. I'm so sorry.'

'Fuck. Fuck. The fucking bastard.' He was angry, livid, but Jake noticed he didn't seem at all surprised that his dad was capable of hitting Justine. He seemed angrier at Gerard, than he seemed sad about his death. Had this hatred been there all along?

'Where is she?' Max asked.

'I told her to leave. She was in such a state.'

'OK, so now what? We call the police? What if they don't believe her? Dad is fucking dead.'

'I know. I think it's too risky. But, well, I have an idea,' Jake said.

Granted, it wasn't entirely all his plan; Justine had made some suggestions before she left, but he thought it could work if they were careful.

They worked quickly and quietly to carry the body into Gerard's car and place it on the back seat. Jake swore blind he could physically feel the blood being pumped around his body. He'd never felt fear like it before. The whole time he felt terrified Evelyn was going to wake up and catch them red-handed.

Max insisted on driving, saying it would draw less attention for him to be driving his own dad's car in case anyone saw them, and then they drove out along the winding narrow country roads that led away from town. They were dangerous at the best of times, but there was one notoriously precarious corner with a steep hill one side and lined with big thick trees.

It was only while they were driving that Jake remembered how his mum always described the lounge when he split his head open on her new coffee table aged five as being like a murder scene. Maybe they'd overreacted? Perhaps they should have just gone to the police with the truth. But it was too late now, Gerard's body was already lying across the back seats, Max driving and him hiding in the boot. No, there was no turning back.

Jake wasn't sure how he'd managed it, but Max had pulled himself together enough to think about the fact they'd need gloves, which he'd fetched from the kitchen back at the house. Yellow Marigolds, as if they were about to give the car a spring-clean, not drive it off an enormous hill and smash it into a line of trees with his father's dead body trapped inside.

While Max wiped the car down, Jake got to work dragging Gerard into the driver's seat. He positioned him forward so his weight would hold down the accelerator, and he found himself apologising to Gerard as he did so. Then he strapped his body in place and loosened the petrol cap. Just for extra measure. There needed to be no doubt it was the crash that had killed him. He hoped it worked – he'd seen it in a film once.

On the count of three, Max, still with his Marigolds on, released the handbrake and they watched in silence as the car rolled off the road before quickly gaining momentum. Before long, it had disappeared so far down the hillside they could no longer see it in the pitch black.

For a dreadful moment Jake panicked it wasn't going to work. What if the car didn't explode as planned? Would the police be able to tell the injury sustained to his head hadn't been caused by the crash? What if the speed down the hill and the branches from the trees didn't do enough damage? He'd once driven past a crash where a branch had gone straight through the driver's seat. That was the best-case scenario. But what about the worst? What if the car missed the line of trees completely?

It brought a strange sense of relief when all of a sudden there was a loud crash and a lick of flames danced ahead of them. Before long, the night sky was ablaze, and Jake pushed the thought to the back of his mind that the wind carried with it the smell of burning flesh.

They stood there a while, on the side of the road, watching Gerard's corpse burn. They'd done it, they'd really done it. The relief it had worked was quickly replaced with dread. What if it wasn't enough? Jake felt the urge to run down the hill and check but knew it was too risky. They needed to head back while it was still dark. What a strange feeling, to want to run towards a disaster to make sure it was devastating enough, instead of to help the person in trouble. Who had he become?

When the guilt hit it was almost unbearable. He found himself about to apologise to Max – that was his dad after all – just as Max said, 'I think you should leave. And don't come back.'

'Excuse me?'

'Justine can't live with the shadow of this hanging over her. She doesn't know I'm here, right? But she called you. She won't be able to look at you again without seeing this and being reminded of what she's done. Of what she's made you do. You really want to protect her? I think you should leave.'

Leave Justine? Was Max right? He looked at the burning car, with Gerard's body trapped inside, and knew that nothing would ever be the same again, even if he chose to stay. Before Justine, he'd been desperate to escape Maldon. She was the only thing keeping him here. And now? He didn't know how they'd manage to move on from this, each other a constant reminder of what they'd done. She'd killed her dad, and he'd covered it up. At least her crime had been an accident; he'd willingly sent Gerard's body up in flames.

Suddenly Jake had a burning urge to run away and keep running. And if Max thought that was best for Justine too? He could pretend to himself he wasn't abandoning her. He was protecting her.

Yes, he'd leave first thing in the morning.

But where would he go?

He had cousins in Scotland. He'd tell his parents it was a spontaneous trip to see them.

Glasgow. That's where he'd stay. Anywhere but Maldon.

What the fuck had he just done?

Chapter Thirty-Seven

I've driven down for today's session with Aya. My plan is to meet Otis at Blackfriars Station after, although he doesn't need to know I see a therapist. I worry that it muddies the waters. He needs to continue believing I'm sturdy. Robust. Dependable.

I'd started to miss the comfort of Aya's plush cream sofa, the matching drapes that hang in perfect symmetrical scoops, and the aroma of a calming lavender candle. This room has housed the very worst of me over the past years. I am certain that without it, I would have boiled over. It is only thanks to Aya, and the effects of this room, that I have the life I have – or had, up until recently. One where I considered myself happy, safe, and successful.

Aya is perched on a chair I haven't seen before. I don't do well with change at the best of times, but this feels particularly poignant; as if it symbolises that everything else I associate with my life here is about to change. I keep staring at it. It is ugly, too. More like a chair you'd expect in a doctor's waiting room than one designed for you to sink into and lose yourself in.

'Does it bother you?' she asks.

'Does what bother me?'

'The chair.'

'A little,' I admit. 'Life is unpredictable. How I feel is unpredictable. But here, I know what to expect. I didn't think anything would have changed.'

'OK, I want you to have a careful think before answering: is it the change that's affecting you, or the fact you weren't in control of the change?'

I'm aware these sessions only work if I'm as honest as I can be and, while there are some things I cannot tell Aya, I do want to fix the parts of me which are still broken.

'It's that I wasn't in control of it,' I decide.

'It can be hard to relinquish power. To hand over the car keys to someone else. Perhaps we can talk a little more about this, if you're happy to? I'd like to try something.'

I nod. I'm always a little wary of the exercises Aya comes up with. They usually appear much less meaningful than they really are and I'm conscious that it's in these moments I'm most likely to reveal a little too much of myself.

'Great. Now, imagine you're driving that car. The one only you have the keys to. You can go anywhere you want. See anyone you want to. Where would you go? You're in control, remember. Time and space, they aren't factors here. Most importantly – and I want you to understand this one is key to this working – all expectations attached to that person or place are gone. It's just you and that car. Anything is possible.'

Anywhere. Anything. A chance to start over. What she's really giving me here is the opportunity to erase the past. To change it, even. If I want to.

Where would I go?

Who would I see?

I only realise I'm crying when I feel the tears roll over my lips and drip off my chin. 'Home,' I say. 'I'd go home.'

It's the first time in eighteen years I've described the house I grew up in as my home.

*   *   *

The rest of my session with Aya followed a more predictable path. We covered old ground and finished talking about how to handle grief and the many ways it can manifest. By the end of the hour, I felt restored. Back in control. Not just of my own emotions, but of Aya too. I lose that sometimes. She's too nimble, though normally I can claw it back. It keeps me on my toes. Perhaps that's the real reason I keep going back.

I'm mulling this over, sounding out the word 'home' on my lips, when I see Otis appear at the top of the tube escalators. We do not hug and instead walk fast out of the station. I thought he would start by asking more questions about what we're up to today, but he has news of his own he wants to share first.

As we walk, he tells me Beverley Rushnell was the keeper of her own secrets too. According to Otis, Beverley had hired a PI named Grant Aspinall to follow her husband in the two months prior to their murder. The real punchline: she suspected her husband was having an affair.

Now this, I can work with. A lover's tiff – it's a tale as old as time. Love, jealousy, reconciliation, murder. They go hand in hand. I think back over the case file and the fact the time of death for both victims had been assigned the same fifteen-minute window. It's not known who died first. All sorts of possibilities are racing through my mind, and I find myself actually feeling sorry for Christina Lang.

A story like this, rage fuelled by desire, it's something you can guarantee a jury will empathise with. One that, if his defence get hold of it, may well just get Jake off the hook. They could have fun with it. Was it the lover, come for revenge? The husband enraged by a confrontation about an affair only to then be ravaged by guilt? Or, even juicier, a lover scorned seeking to end it all? It also chimes nicely with the neighbour's witness statement claiming things had seemed strained between the couple.

'Do we know if she was right? Was there another woman?' I am hungry for it.

'I haven't found her yet,' Otis says, 'but a guy like Mark, I wouldn't put it past him to turn out to be a cheating bastard, too.'

My saliva thickens, but I try not to react. I remember DS Sorcha Rose's note of warning that no one is wholly good and try to take comfort in it. If no one is wholly good, then surely they can't be wholly bad either. Sleeping with Jimmy, it was a mistake. I am only human. It doesn't mean I deserve for my whole life to crumble around me. Or, in Mark's case, for him to wind up dead.

Thankfully, I'm saved from having to reply by us coming to a stop outside Christina Lang's chambers.

'You're sure your intel is correct? She's definitely currently in court?' I check.

'My intel is always correct, thank you very much.'

'Good. Then I'll see you back here as quickly as I can. Just keep those eyes of yours peeled, OK?'

He nods assertively as though I have nothing to worry about at all, but then he says, 'Good luck,' which seems to me to negate his outward confidence.

Still, we've already come this far and so I turn on my kitten heels, roll my shoulders back and channel all the bravado I can muster. Remind myself I am trained in the art of manipulation. This is my world.

I wasn't wearing the kitten heels in my earlier session with Aya. Nor the black pencil skirt with its fitted jacket which I changed into before heading here. Aya knows I am on what they are publicly deeming 'compassionate leave', and that there should be absolutely no reason for me to dress like a barrister. But if I'm going to pull this off, if I'm really going to sneak into Christina's office and rummage around in Jake's file to find what I'm looking for, then I most certainly need to blend in.

I stride purposefully towards the entrance and smile in a way I hope is both modest and seductive, my eyes tilted up slightly towards the older man who reaches the key-guarded door just before me.

It works.

He says 'Hello,' smiling as he holds the door open for me. I admit, I hate myself right now. But desperate times call for desperate measures. Besides, if they weren't such dirty old men in the first place, then they wouldn't fall for it. It's his own fault, I tell myself to alleviate my guilt. I'm just playing by their rules.

Luckily today seems to be a busy one for chambers. The office spaces are filled with noise – papers everywhere, bodies moving busily between desks and phones ringing. Good. Everyone is too wrapped up in their own business to notice me.

I walk slowly through the space, clocking the names on each of the side offices until I see it. Christina Lang. The office is glass and I know that to pull this off I need to be fast. I check my phone again, making sure there is no warning from Otis, before sliding into her office and clicking the door firmly shut behind me.

I pull out the first drawer I come across and I'm delighted to see Christina is just as particular about organisation and filing as I am. This is exactly what I'd banked on. You don't rise to the top by being sloppy. The files are alphabetised and I quickly find Finchley, B. My hands are sweaty. I had imagined I'd be smooth and seamless, flicking through the pages quickly. Instead, the reality is that I keep fumbling, all fingers and thumbs.

Eventually, I find what I am looking for: 110 Roman Road, Letchworth. It is the address Jake is confined to while on bail. I take a quick picture of it and send it to Otis. I do not trust myself to remember it – we only have one chance at this. And then I make my exit. sweat trickling down my back.

I open the door, stepping out into the fresh air, and the exhilaration of what I've just done hits me. God that was fun. I hurry over to Otis, who raises his eyebrows at me.

'It's quite the rush, isn't it,' he says.

'It sure is.'

Hurriedly, I pull out the envelope from my bag, my letter safe inside it.

'How will you get it to him?' I ask.

'He has an ankle tag and a curfew but his conditions technically allow him to leave the inside of the house after dark as long as he stays within the owned land's boundary. Every Friday his mate has poker night so he'll be alone tonight. I'll deliver it myself. He's allowed to receive correspondence, it's just making sure he feels confident that any reply he gives isn't going to be intercepted or read by anyone else but you. You've given him two days to reply, yes?

'That's right.'

'Good, that's the night before their bins are emptied so he should be able to use it as a cover to go to the bins after dark and leave the letter for me there. There's a covering of trees down the side entrance and I'm confident I can get down to the bins that way without being seen to collect a reply. That way no one ever has to know he's ever sent a letter.'

'You're the best. Thank you, and good luck,' I say, passing my letter to Otis. It's important that Jake feels safe to tell the truth.

'You're welcome,' Otis replies, and it sounds solid. Comforting. He genuinely means it. I cannot tell him how grateful I am that there is still someone left I can trust. Instead, I give him a short hug. The first ever, in all these years, and although he stiffens, he also looks a little red and I know it means a lot to him.

With that, we part ways and head in opposite directions. Me, back to Maldon and him to 110 Roman Road to wait for darkness to fall before delivering my letter.

Dear Jake,

I can't lie and say it's easy to find the words. I have so many questions. I hope you're doing OK – though perhaps that's a ridiculous thing to say. I can't quite believe that after all these years I've found you again. For a while I wondered if you were even still alive. You pulled off quite the disappearing act!

I hope you don't mind me contacting you. Given you legally changed your name to get away from me, I imagine I'm not exactly who you want to be hearing from right now, but you helped save me once and I wonder if I can help you now. I just want the truth. You probably don't know this but I'm a criminal barrister these days and I know I wouldn't be here without you. Let me help you.

Did you do it? What happened?

I also thought you should know Max is dead.

They pulled his body from the sea off the coast of Mersea. The police have ruled it as unsuspicious, but I can't help thinking they're missing something. That I'm missing something.

I saw the CCTV, Jake. I know you met with Max at the Blue Eagle. What were you arguing about? Do you know why he might have died? Was he in trouble? Were you both in trouble?

If you want to reply (and I really would love to hear from you), then leave a letter under your recycling bin in two days' time after dark but before two a.m. I have a contact who can then collect it without being seen. No one need ever know you've written a letter and only I will read it. I promise.

Please, trust me again.

Yours,
Justine

Chapter Thirty-Eight

I see her as soon as I pull into Mum's road. She is sitting on the wall down by the water's edge opposite our house. Her hood is pulled up, even in this heat.

'Waiting for me?' I ask, taking my place beside her, and Alice Myers nods, though I notice she avoids looking at me, as if she's still unsure whether being here is a good idea or not.

The black estuary is particularly breathtaking today. How can something so beautiful also be so deadly? That water killed my brother.

'Do you want to come inside?'

'No, this won't take long.'

'Is everything all right? Do you need help?' I ask, but Alice shakes her head. I have no idea what she's about to say but my gut tells me it's for my ears only and I glance around looking for signs of DS Rose. I'm being paranoid, but I don't like feeling out of control and there's something about the way Alice is sitting, hunched, nervous, making me feel as if I'm about to be knocked off balance.

'I have a brother too,' Alice says, and her words make the back of my arms tingle. 'I just thought I should tell you, in case it is important.'

'Tell me what?' I'm annoyed at the fragile desperation creeping into my voice. I know from years working with witnesses that it's important not to scare her off, but the feeling inside me grows even more certain – whatever Alice is going to say next, is about to change everything. What does she know? There is a part of me – the worst part – that isn't worried just for Max but also for myself. What exactly does this girl know? And who else has she already told?

'Promise you won't tell?'

'Tell me what?' I repeat, avoiding the question. Another important rule when working on a trial: never make promises you cannot keep.

I worry I've sounded too pushy, so I give her a moment, allowing us to wait in silence. It takes all of my strength not to drag her off the wall we're sitting on and force it out of her. But then I catch her nodding a couple of times, as if gearing herself up to speak, and she turns to me.

'Is it true they think Max died on the eleventh of July?'

'That's right. Why?'

'Well, my friend was supposed to pick me up after my shift to go back to hers, but she was late. I got bored waiting around for her and so I walked home. It's not something I usually do, because my parents say I'm not allowed to walk through the prom late at night by myself.' I try not to rush her through her story, but really I do not care what she is or isn't allowed to do. 'Anyway, it must have been gone midnight when I saw them.'

'Saw them? Who did you see? Max?'

'Yes.' Her voice is quiet. She is definitely scared. Of what?

'It's OK. I really appreciate you telling me.' I try to sound as comforting as possible.

'It was Max and he – he . . .' she falters. It's killing me. I'm not sure how much longer my patience can take. 'He was down by the edge of the water, right by the boats. It's dark there but one of the industrial boats had its sidelight on so I could see. Well enough to be sure, anyway.'

'Sure of what? What did you see? Alice, who was he with?'

She looks around again.

Leans closer to me. The information she has, intended for my ears only.

'He was with Jimmy,' she says.

My head is spinning. A black fog creeps in from the corner of my eyes, blurring my vision. Not Jimmy. She must be mistaken. Jimmy told me he hadn't seen Max for around two months before his death. He'd been riddled with guilt over it.

'What exactly did you see?' I ask.

'They were by the big boats on the estuary. I couldn't hear much. It was windy and I was quite far away. But it looked like they were arguing.'

'What made it look like that?' I'm aware I'm sounding like a barrister, my training kicking in, but this is important.

'Well, I couldn't make out what they were saying but I could hear the tone and it sounded like they were shouting. Angry at each other.'

'Anything else?'

'I didn't see much. I'm sorry. I was just walking home.' She starts to break under the pressure and I have to remind myself we're not in the courtroom.

'It's OK. You're doing great. Don't panic. Take your time to think about anything else to do with Max and Jimmy that might be relevant. Clearly, you've been afraid to tell me. Convinced what you saw is something you shouldn't have. Why? What is it making you feel that way?' There's something missing, and I need her to dig deep to find it. That's half the battle most of the time, teasing the details out of the witnesses.

'Well, the day of the mud race your brother's face was all over town on those banners and I realised that not only was he the same guy from down the prom with Jimmy but that he was also the creep – sorry,' she cringes apologetically, aware this time that the guy she's referring to is in fact my brother, 'from the fight. I remembered you'd given me your number that first time we met, and I still had it stashed in my bag. You'd asked me to contact you if I thought of anything else. Anyway, I thought maybe if I watched it again it might jog my memory and I could be more helpful. I went to find the CCTV tape – they're usually stored in the basement before being recorded over – but I couldn't find it. It wasn't there. I couldn't bring myself to ask Jimmy about it. He had already told us not to mention the fight to anyone after the guy's arrest. Usually I do as I'm told, but now there are three dead bodies stacking up. I'm sorry I didn't say anything sooner.'

'Don't be sorry. Thanks for telling me all this.' I force myself to placate her but inside I'm seething. Not at her. But at Jimmy. A missing CCTV tape is calculated. It implies he is hiding something.

At least one thing is for certain: Jimmy lied to me about how recently he'd seen Max. I think again about how he had rubbed his hands over his face at the funeral roughly, as though he needed to rip out the pain.

Riddled with guilt.

I had even comforted him about it. Told him we all could have been there more for Max than we were. That this wasn't his fault. I'd left our conversation reminded of my own guilt for not returning home when he'd asked me to.

Once again, I remember the report about homicide in the UK that recently landed on my desk. Statistically in the UK, while women are most commonly killed by a partner or family member, men are most commonly killed by a friend.

There is no evidence Jimmy was involved in Max's death but he certainly knows more than he's fucking letting on. And that, to me, is a crime in and of itself.

I am pounding on his front door with all my strength, each thump reverberating through my entire body. How dare Jimmy lie to me.

As soon as he opens the door, I force him back inside. Slam the door shut behind me. On one level I know this is not the smart thing to be doing. I should be collecting evidence, readying myself to present a fool-proof case against him. But the other part of me is too full of rage. I feel dirty even at the thought of it. I have slept with my brother's murderer. How can I ever rid myself of it?

'You lying bastard,' I scream, jabbing my finger into his chest as he backs up against the hallway wall.

'What the hell, Justine?' He looks genuinely frightened. Good.

'She saw you. Alice Myers. With Max. On the night he died down by the fucking water.'

'Shit,' he says and I slam my fist into the wall next to his face.

'That's it? Shit?' I take a step back and try to compose myself. Standing there against the wall, running his hands frantically through his floppy hair, he looks pathetic. How did I ever find him attractive. 'Did you kill him?' I don't really believe it, even as the question leaves my mouth, but still, it has to be asked, the possibility ruled out.

'What? No! That's ridiculous.'

'Is it? You've already lied to me about seeing him. Why would you do that if you don't have something to hide?'

'I didn't kill Max, Justine. You know I never would.'

My hand is still resting against the wall, and I stare at him. We are close. I can feel his breath against mine. Is he telling the truth? The silence between us is filled with music emanating from the living room. I recognise it as 'Yellow'. Jimmy is playing Max's song.

Without warning, all my anger seems to evaporate and instead of feeling filled with white-hot rage, I am hollow. Max is dead. Gone. And all I want is to find out what happened to him. I have to find out the truth.

'Why?' I repeat the question again, sinking on to the bottom step of the stairs. After a beat, Jimmy sits down next to me. The two of us squeezed on to one narrow step. I don't even flinch at his proximity, at his leg and shoulder brushing against mine. I simply have no fight left in me.

'I promise you, Justine, I didn't kill Max. But you're right, I did see him that night.'

'Why didn't you say anything?'

'I knew it would make me look guilty.' His voice is full of regret.

A small breathy laugh escapes me. It's clichéd as hell. Everyone is always out for themselves, no matter the cost – just as long as that cost isn't them. I know that better than anyone.

'What about the missing CCTV tape of the fight?'

'What are you on about? It's not missing, you asked to see it and I simply never put it back. I got a bit distracted after Max was found. It's probably still lying on my desk in the office. Go check if you'd like.'

'No, I believe you. But you still lied to me and now, as far as I know, you're the last person to have seen Max alive. You need to tell me everything,' I say, and it isn't a request, it's a demand.

BEFORE

JIMMY – THE FRIEND

Jimmy tried to shelter from the wind using one of the boats as a shield, tucking himself in as close as he could to the water's edge. Even wedged into his jacket pockets his fingers were starting to burn from the cold. He wouldn't be able to stand it much longer.

They'd agreed to meet at eleven thirty p.m. It was the earliest Jimmy could leave the pub – he had even trusted Alice to lock up for him, which was a responsibility he only ever handed over in emergencies. Max had convinced him this was one of those times. And yet, he still hadn't shown up. Jimmy moved his weight from foot to foot, trying to keep warm. He'd wait a little longer.

Max: *I need to explain something. It's urgent. Meet tonight at the prom?*

The last time he'd seen Max was a month or so before he'd strolled into his pub and made a scene with Jake, poor Alice having to deal with it. What had he been thinking? It was so unlike him. He'd left Max a voicemail asking him to call back and explain what the hell was going on, but a couple of weeks since then had passed and he hadn't heard from him until today. The text had annoyed him. He'd asked Max to tell him about the fight weeks ago. Why only now?

But as much as Jimmy was annoyed, he was also worried. He'd watched the CCTV back. Max had been barely recognisable to him; the way he'd looked around, seemingly constantly on edge, and his whole appearance altered for the worse.

Usually, Max drew attention for all the opposite reasons. Certainly, Jimmy had never seen him in a fight before. The more Jimmy thought about it again, the more the anger boiled back over. When Max had texted out of the blue earlier, he'd very nearly said no – how dare he not call sooner and apologise. If it wasn't for the sliver of worry he couldn't quite push away, he wouldn't be here, freezing to death.

He didn't understand why they had to meet here, and so late. But Max had insisted. It had to be private. Very private. *Well, Jimmy thought as he looked around, you can't get much more secluded than this. So where the hell are you?*

He saw his shadow first, looming large against the side of one of the boats, and from the way it staggered he could tell he was drunk before he even came into focus. Jimmy had intended to try and wipe the slate clean, but this was already riling him up the wrong way again.

'You're drunk.'

'I am.'

'And bleeding,' Jimmy said, noticing blood running down his right hand and dripping off his fingers.

'I need your – I need your—' Max began, but he didn't manage to finish his sentence before leaning over the water and dry-heaving.

'Mate, seriously, I'm not here for this. I've been waiting ages and I'm absolutely freezing. Tell me about the fight when you're sober, OK? I'm going home.' He started to walk away.

'Jimmy,' Max called after him and, hearing something catch in his friend's throat, Jimmy turned back around. He wasn't sure if it was just the light from the boat casting the shadows across his face, but it crossed his mind that Max looked haunted.

His eyes were sunken into his puffy face with big dark circles framing them. 'You have to understand, I never meant for it to happen.' His speech was slurred.

'Let's talk about this tomorrow, yeah? Go home, Max. You're wasted.'

'But, I – please.'

'Honestly, it's not that important. Go home and sort yourself out.' And then he walked away, a stride in his step as he desperately tried to warm up again. He wasn't sure if he imagined it, but he thought he heard Max's voice carried on the wind. Two simple words.

'I can't.'

Chapter Thirty-Nine

'You just left him there? Drunk by the water. By himself.' Jimmy doesn't respond, which packs more of a punch. 'He was your best friend.' My voice cracks with the horror of it. Twice Max reached out for help, and both times he was left alone. First by me and then by Jimmy.

'I know. I'm a terrible friend. The worst.'

'You didn't even let him explain? You still have no idea what the fight was about with Jake? Or what he wanted to tell you?'

'No. Obviously, I wish I hadn't left. I was absolutely freezing though, and he could barely string a sentence together.'

'Do you think he did it? That after you left he—' I can't bring myself to finish my sentence.

'I keep going over and over it in my mind. I mean, I've tried not to. I've tried everything in order to forget.' And from the way he says 'everything' I know that includes sleeping with me. 'But I can't.' He moves his hand to hover slightly above my knee and I stare at it, watching in slow-motion as he gathers the courage to place it on my leg. To my surprise, I let him. 'He was the most out of it I've ever seen. I can't even explain it properly. He was drunk, definitely. But I've seen him drunk before. This was different. There was something else. He was in a real state. Whether that meant he fell – we were right on the edge down there – or whether my leaving him was the last straw to whatever was going on with him – I just don't know.

I can't even tell you how sorry I am. I wish I knew what he wanted to tell me.'

'Well, I'm going to find out.'

'I know you will, and I believe you. I'll try to help – properly this time – if you'll let me?'

'You left him there,' I repeat. Letting it sit between us. I won't let him run from the truth.

'I know.'

'You killed him.' I spit the words out slowly. I know I am being harsh but it feels true, whether he pushed him or not.

And yet, I also know Jimmy loved Max. We all made mistakes leading us here, that much I can admit. 'Still, I do need your help,' I relent, heaving myself off the stair and moving into the lounge. I signal for him to follow.

I do not forgive Jimmy, I doubt I ever will, but I am putting myself back together the only way I know how: by compiling a case.

While Jimmy isn't looking, I pop two codeine out of their packet and swallow them down dry. I ignore the fact that I am getting too practised at it and instead focus on how much sharper I feel only a few minutes later.

When I first asked Jimmy to tell me everything he could about Max from as far back as the day I left, he didn't understand. He knew Max and I had kept in close contact, but I tried to explain to him my theory about truth – which is simply that it doesn't exist. Or at least, it does, but only in a way which is full of so many layers and complexities that it is impossible for one person to hold it in the palm of their hand.

I use the Hindu poem of the six men and the elephant to try and explain my point. In the story, an elephant is brought into a dark room and six blind men are asked to touch and describe the animal. They all touch different parts, and each describes those parts perfectly. Their description of the elephant is true to their truth. They are not lying. But it's only when you put all the parts together that the real description of the elephant is accomplished.

'No one is lying,' I continue, 'we are just incapable of capturing the whole truth.'

'OK, and you think I can help fill in a different body part to those you already have? Am I understanding this right?'

'Maybe you're holding the tail,' I say with a shrug. Jimmy looks at me like I've gone mad, but the corner of his mouth is also upturned and he holds my gaze for a little longer than necessary.

You do not forgive him, I remind myself.

The first five minutes of Jimmy's spiel is nothing I don't already know about Max, but I tell myself to be patient and remind myself that even if I think I know this part of the story, to pay attention to the details. And that's when he mentions the Freemasons again.

'Hold on,' I interrupt. 'You said before that almost everyone in this town was a Freemason and you were also invited to join. Does that mean your dad was one too?'

'He was.'

I kick myself. I've been meaning to ask Jimmy more about the Freemasons and what he knew about my dad being a part of it. I've not been my usual self since Charles strongly suggested I took a break from working. I've been falling apart – if I'm not a successful barrister then who am I? My success is the only thing keeping me running from who I really am. Did I drop the ball? Is this the key?

'So, might you have a photo of any of the members from back then?' I ask.

'Sure, I think there is a whole box in the loft full of his Masonic things.'

A shiver runs over me. I can't pinpoint why yet, but I am certain the answer to Max's death begins with whatever is lying in that box.

'The DS dropped by unexpectedly yesterday,' Jimmy calls to me from up the ladder, his head disappearing through the loft hatch before hauling himself up.

'Sounds like her,' I say, hoisting myself on to the ladder. 'What did she want?' I reach the top and drag my knees on to the floor of the boarded loft. The space is larger than I'd expected and I find myself imagining hiding out here for a while. Aya tells me my brain is in a constant state of fight or flight and that I need to rewire my mind to not always anticipate danger. I'm not sure, if she knew the whole truth, she'd give the same advice again. Instead, with the DS still asking questions, I reckon she'd say it's smart to always be looking for ways to disappear. An escape plan, just in case.

Jimmy is rummaging around in the corner and I can see he's already pulling forward a large cardboard box.

'She asked me if I was with Max the night your dad died.'

'What? Why? What did you say?' I reach out for the nearest box to steady myself and my fingers land in a layer of dust.

'I said I didn't see him because it was your dad's party. Everyone that night was either there or at the Blue Eagle for Jake's nan's party. I was at the Blue Eagle. Not influential enough for an invite from your dad,' he quips and I force a laugh.

'Why's she asking about that night? Did she say anything else?'

'She was interested to know if Jake left the party at all.'

'What did you tell her?'

Jimmy looks at me then, curiously, and knits his eyebrows together.

'The truth.' He shrugs.

'Which was? Sorry, another interrogation. Obviously, I have my own questions about Jake and why he left me. Did he meet another girl?' I cringe. Even I know this is a terrible cover-up. Not my best work.

'He left to put his nan in a taxi and I didn't see him again. But I was drunk, and the pub was pretty full even after hours for the lock-up. I wasn't best mates with Jake, we wouldn't have sought each other out in a crowded room. So I don't know. I can't say for certain if he came back in or not.'

Why won't DS Rose just let it drop? Does she have something to prove? Fallen from grace in Manchester and relocated – demoted – to a smaller quieter town. Is that her story?

'Here,' Jimmy says, pushing the box to a stop right in front of my feet and nodding towards it. He slides a key out his jeans pocket and uses it to slice into the tape sealing the box. It clearly hasn't been opened in years.

I've always known that Freemasonry has an air of 'otherness' and 'exclusivity' about it and that feeling is cemented now. It is a brotherhood banded together by secrets, strange rules and traditions. I pull them out, one after another: a soft white leather apron trimmed with light-blue material that is adorned with three rosettes and silver embellishments. A robe. White gloves. What does it all mean?

I find it towards the bottom of the box. Even before I blow the dust away, I can vividly see my dad brought back to life. It's a photograph of what looks like some kind of Masonic ball. Men in suits with white jackets and women in beautiful ball gowns.

I turn it over. Inscribed on the back of the frame are the words *The Knights Templar Charity Ball*. I turn it over again, unsure of what I'm looking for, but I've got plenty of experience in looking at things over and over again until the one detail you hadn't noticed suddenly seems so obvious you wonder how you'd missed it all those times before. I'm prepared to keep staring at this photograph until the penny drops.

That doesn't turn out to be necessary, though. I see him on my first look. The star of the show is Jimmy's dad, smiling broadly, raising a glass of red towards the camera. But if you look closer, you can see him. A grainy figure in the background. He is turned sideways, his legs slightly bent as if he's either about to sit down or has just got up from his seat, and next to him stands a woman. I can tell from her hair that it isn't his wife. His wife has long curly hair, not a short straight bob. It isn't the kind of photo he'd want his wife to find.

His hand is resting on the small of the woman's back. Lurking a little too low to look natural. The short-haired woman isn't facing the camera, but you can see her head is thrown back. Is she laughing? One of her hands is holding his. Is he simply getting up? His hand placement a little too close for comfort? Her laugh an awkward one? We women aren't strangers to unwanted attention.

Or, alternatively, is the movement down, not up? Is she about to sit on his knee? Willing. Complicit. The action isn't clear. That's the problem with just one still photo. But no matter who the woman is, the presence of this man in the photo still takes my breath away. Yes, Otis was right. There was no connection linking Mark to Maldon or my dad's firm but there was another connection that until now we'd missed. And I'm staring at it. Mark Rushnell and my dad were both Freemasons. They weren't from the same area, likely different Lodges, but if Jimmy's dad is in this photo, then it's likely my dad also attended.

I look again, checking there is nothing else I've missed, and then I notice it. The short-haired woman's free hand hangs loose at her side. The back of the hand is turned slightly towards the camera. I squint and hold the photo closer, wishing it was a digital frame so I could zoom in. Still, I can see it. She is wearing an oval-cut emerald ring set in gold on her marriage finger. The stone is so large it's impossible to miss, made even more extravagant by the fact it is framed by a halo of diamonds. It is a beautiful one-of-a-kind vintage emerald ring.

And it is, unmistakably, my mother's.

Before I say anything, I am flying through the front door, the photograph still clutched in my hand. I can hear Jimmy calling after me but there's no time to explain.

'How is your mother? Is she still seeing that lovely man? Oh, I can't remember his name now, but he wasn't from round here.'

Beverley had hired a PI, convinced her husband was having an affair.

I think of Mark's hand placed on my mother's back.

Of her hand, entwined with his.

Has the link between my family and Mark and Beverley Rushnell been my mother all along? And if so, how long has it been going on for?

BEFORE

EVELYN – THE MOTHER

When she was finished, the room looked cleaner than it had done even before the party. The floorboards glistened and the yellow-and-lilac floral wallpaper, well, it practically sparkled. Max and Jake hadn't noticed her watching from a small crack in her bedroom doorway, as they'd carried Gerard away.

She'd felt the urge to stop them. To scream and call the police. Gerard was dead.

Her Gerard.

They'd met on a train. She had been travelling to Manchester from London to meet a friend and he was sitting across from her. It was only when they finally reached her stop that he asked how he could contact her again, admitting he'd missed his stop on purpose to carry on talking with her.

He had her at that.

No one had ever made her feel so desired before.

But that same man had gone on to make her feel smaller and more insignificant than ever before, too.

Gerard held a power over people. He could either build you up or smash you down, depending on his mood. It made him captivating. It also made him cruel.

And now he was gone.

She'd thought about killing him herself plenty of times, but she'd grown up without her own father and she could never quite bring herself to inflict that on Max and Justine.

But what now?

As she rolled her shoulders back, she felt the familiar sharp zing of pain shooting from her shoulder blade and radiating down her back. The burn was still relatively fresh. She hadn't borne all this pain to protect her children, only to now risk Justine's future with the truth.

Being with Gerard had taught her how to stay silent. To keep secrets. To hold her tongue. And so that is what she would continue to do.

Thanks to him, she'd had plenty of practice.

She'd first heard Justine on the phone to Jake, and it had taken everything to stop herself running to help her. But she knew Justine didn't need her mum, she needed someone she could trust. They hadn't built that kind of relationship. It had always been better for her to stay at arm's length. For Gerard to feel Justine was more 'his' than hers.

Instead, she'd stayed out of sight. Waiting. Watching. As always, Justine would think she wasn't there for her, but that didn't matter. Love didn't always have to be seen.

Max and Jake thought they had cleaned up Justine's mess as best they could, and after they'd left Evelyn had finished the job for them. Her attention to detail was better than theirs and there could be no mistakes.

But as she pushed open the kitchen door, in desperate need of a stiff drink, she was filled with the type of fear that shrivelled her insides.

She thought she'd been so careful, but she'd missed something.

They'd all missed something.

Something that was going to change everything.

Evelyn looked at the couple sitting at her kitchen table as if they were expecting her, and knew this wasn't anywhere near the end; this was just the very beginning.

Chapter Forty

I run all the way home, praying Mum will be in when I get back. I need to know the truth. Surely I must be wrong. It is one photograph, and I am jumping to conclusions. But still, I have always been taught to follow my gut. And my gut is telling me something isn't right here. Not least because Mum claimed she didn't know the Rushnells. Which, even if the photo is more innocent than I'm thinking it could be, was still a lie. My parents knew the Rushnells before they were murdered. The photo is indisputable evidence. Have I also met them before? Is that why their name has always felt too familiar for comfort?

I round the corner but instead of Mum, I find a black car parked outside her house. The journalist from the mud race is sitting behind the wheel. I march towards him and knock on the window.

'Can I help you?' My words sound spiky.

'I'm hoping you can, actually.' He keeps his cool as he opens the car door, clearly used to confrontation in his job as a hard-nosed reporter. He is short and even smarmier up close than he'd seemed at the prom. I bet he thinks he's the real dog's bollocks.

'I don't have much time, so you better be fast.' I don't have the energy to be amenable – something I might regret later.

'Let's cut straight to the chase then, I like it.' He doesn't bother pretending to smile either, clearly matching my intolerance for any bullshit today. 'You knew Brad Finchley back when he was Jake Reynolds. Correct?'

'Yes. Though I'm sure you already know we were a couple.'

'I do.'

'So, ask your next question.' I want to hurry this along. I need to get inside the house. Find out the truth from Mum. Had she been in a relationship with Mark Rushnell before his death? Only a few days ago I asked her directly if she knew the Rushnells. If that was why their name was so familiar to me, and she'd told me she hadn't. She'd lied to me. Why? What is she hiding? An affair?

'Do you know why he left Maldon?'

'I don't.'

'It had nothing to do with you?'

'Not that I know of. He broke my heart. The whole town knew about it at the time, so I'm sure they've already told you.'

'They have.'

'Well then, you didn't really need to waste my time, did you.'

'The thing is, I was intrigued by the mud race being held in your dad's honour. Such a brilliant event, unique, I thought maybe our paper could do a separate article on it. I started fact-checking and noticed the date of your dad's death. December 2005, am I correct?'

'That's right.'

'Fascinating.'

'Is it? Why?' I know I'm falling into his trap, asking the questions he wants me to, but I want this over with as quickly as possible. My mind is focused on other things.

'Well, as I'm sure you know, the other story I'm working on – like all the journalists here – is Jake Reynolds and it struck me that your dad died the same month as Jake left Maldon. In fact, when I did more digging, he left almost to the day, I believe.'

'I can't remember the exact timings.'

'But he was your boyfriend, wasn't he?'

'He was.'

'So your dad died. And then your boyfriend disappeared.'

'He didn't disappear. He went to visit his cousins and decided not to come back.'

'But why? Why didn't he come back? Did Jake have anything to do with your dad's death? Is that why you broke up? Everyone tells me you were so heartbroken you ended up staying with a friend. Don't you also want answers?'

He is goading me. I try not to clench my teeth, but I can feel the urge to grind them. I must not give away any sign he's made me angry. Not just that, but afraid too. I'm sure that's what he's looking for – any indication that there is more to Dad's death than everyone thinks. By the time word got around that Jake had left and wasn't coming back, Dad's death had already been ruled an accident. It was never questioned – an innocent Christmastime trip to visit his cousins.

'Eighteen-year-old me cared about finding out why Jake left me but quite frankly, that was a long time ago and I've moved on,' I reply, trying to keep calm, as if the mention of Jake leaving no longer crushes my heart. 'What I can tell you is that my dad died from drink-driving, and Jake spent the evening celebrating his nan's birthday.'

'Only I don't think he was there for the entire celebration. From what I can gather he left just before lock-in, which was around the same time as your father's estimated time of death in the coroner's report.'

'Just a bit of fact-checking you say?' And I wonder how much of his story is true. Did he stumble across this information himself as he claims, or did DS Rose hand it to him on a plate? 'Look, it was a long time ago. People forget things and memories become confused. I suggest you check your sources.'

'Oh I have,' he says with a smirk. 'I've triple-checked them.'

'In that case you didn't need to come and speak with me at all, did you? Seeing as you think you've already got all the answers. Thank you and have a good day.' I'm dripping with sarcasm as I turn away. I am relieved he doesn't follow me towards the house. You never know with journalists – in my experience with other families during big criminal cases, they have very little respect for privacy or boundaries.

Outwardly I think I have successfully kept my fear from showing, but I need to concentrate on stopping my hand from shaking as I put the key in the lock.

The lack of classical music tells me Mum is out, but I check the garden just in case. There's no sign of her so I set to work. I don't know exactly what I might find but I can't just wait idly for my chance to interrogate her. I am looking for proof Mark Rushnell was having an affair with my mother. Whereas only a few days ago I'd been tidying Max's mess away, here I am creating it.

I am frantic.

I am aware that, in this moment, I have lost my sense of control. Usually so calm, so collected, finally, I have unravelled. The destruction I'm leaving in my wake around the house is physical evidence of the fact I have been kept wound too tightly and I can't contain it any longer.

I start with the rooms I associate most with Mum. Her bedroom, the kitchen, the snug. So far, all I've dislodged are memories of my own that I'd hidden deep below the surface. Not the ones I'd recalled when Aya had asked me to describe the house. No, instead now it is other, more painful memories, coming flooding back; the time Mum claimed she'd tripped up the stairs while holding a bowl of hot water from the kitchen up to her bedroom to steam her face and had burned her thighs; the way we'd automatically turn the television up in the snug if Mum and Dad had gone upstairs before us at night.

I know there may not be any physical evidence to find of her relationship with Mark – perhaps it is all stored neatly on her phone – but now I've started, I cannot stop. And so I start on the rest of the house.

There is nothing of note in the office, but that doesn't surprise me. It was always Dad's space; it would feel a little disrespectful to leave crumbs of her new man in his arena. Despite everything, we were the Stones and that mattered more than the truth. We thought it helped us to hide behind the façade and we've been continuing to do so even after his death. Now, as I work my way through the house, turning it upside down and inside out, I am shattering those inner illusions. Room by room, layer by layer, lie by lie.

This house.

Our family.

It is all fake.

None of it exposes the truth witnessed within these walls. The less evidence I find, both of the affair but also of our past here, the more it sickens me and the more I feel the need to shout it from the rooftops. I'd never gone looking for it before, but now that I am, the fact I can't find any proof of Dad's cruelty makes it even worse; as though all this pain I have been carrying around, all the lies, it's almost as if none of it were ever true in the first place.

There are only two rooms left to search: my and Max's old bedrooms. I know he hasn't lived here for years, but I still can't bring myself to open his door. Not yet. And so I enter mine instead. What more can I find in this room that I haven't already uncovered since I arrived back here? It is futile, I'm sure, but Mum still isn't home and I don't know what else to do. I cannot sit still. I have never been very good at waiting for things to happen to me. I like to act first. To remain in control.

As I had suspected, there is nothing here. At least, not in the places I can bring myself to search. Finally, I turn to the walk-in wardrobe. The one I haven't opened since I arrived – my clothes still remain housed in my suitcase. I'm running out of other places to look. It's either here or Max's room. I breathe in deeply. Reach out. Grasp the handle, steady my breathing, and then pull it open with a force so purposeful I cannot change my mind.

My clothes no longer hang on the rail and my shoes no longer litter the floor, but the sense of fear within it has lingered. I can see Mum has used some of the space for storage, with boxes now lining the wall, and so I focus on those, refusing to be dragged back into my memories, and hurl them out into the main bedroom, flinging the door shut behind me as quickly as I can.

The boxes are mostly filled with my and Max's old school-work and childhood badges which Mum has decided to keep. School projects, reports, artwork, swimming awards and netball trophies. I've almost lost myself in the happier memories of my childhood when I find it.

At first, I don't register what it is. And certainly not what it's doing buried at the bottom of one of these innocuous memory boxes. Because that's what it is. Buried, intentionally so, and that part is completely unexpected. I turn it over. It is a black phone. Modern. It must only be a couple of years old. I tell myself it could belong to anyone. Perhaps this is Mum's old phone? One she used to speak with Mark. Perhaps after news of his death she hid it away.

Even as I'm trying to reason with myself, I know it doesn't make any sense. This line of defence would not hold up in court.

For this is not Mum's old phone. As I turn it on, the shaking in my finger betrays the fact I already know exactly whose phone this is. I just have no idea why it's hidden in here at the bottom of a box. As the phone comes to life and the familiar background screen loads, I know for certain why Max's phone was not found with his body: it is not resting on the seabed somewhere, it has been here in my old bedroom all along, just metres from where I've been sleeping every night.

Unsurprisingly there is an onslaught of activity as his phone springs to life. Missed calls, voicemails, text messages. I don't open them. I don't have the energy to, not yet, and they keep on coming. But then there's a vibration and this one isn't coming from Max's phone, it's mine.

I pull it from my pocket to see I have two missed calls from Otis. Usually, we speak over the phone but I can't find my voice, not now, and so I text him instead.

Justine: *Can't speak right now. If it's urgent text me.*

Otis: *I think we should talk on the phone.*

Justine: *I can't. Please, just text me.*

Otis: *OK. But I'd rather have done this over the phone. I couldn't trace any activity on The Little Trust Company but I looked into the Rushnells' finances and found two payments paid into their account. Significant payments. The first was made on the 17th December 2005 and that's the largest amount of £100,000. Then there was nothing more until just over four months ago, when suddenly there was another £50,000 payment received. Both payments were made to them by the same company, The Little Trust Company.*

I stagger back a couple of steps until I'm leaning against a wall. I rest my head, then pull away before forcefully slamming it back again. My phone buzzes again before I've had time to reply.

Otis: *I've also reliably heard Jake is pleading not guilty next week.*

I thought I'd be relieved to hear Jake is fighting for his freedom. To hear it from him that he did not do what they accuse him of. But it's a strange mix of emotions that floods me now. Max and Jake. Fear and relief.

Max, what did you do?

BEFORE

MAX – THE BROTHER

They'd been having dinner when the doorbell rang. Nothing special, but Max tried to make time to spend the evening with Evelyn twice a week. His mother had dabbed at her mouth with a napkin apologetically before leaving the table to open the door.

He didn't recognise the man's voice but he knew from his mother's tone that it was not someone she was expecting – or wanting – to see. Protective instinct kicking in, he hurried to her side. Often, he wondered if it was guilt that made him stick around; to fulfil this need he now had to take care of Evelyn. He hadn't done so as a child, and deep down he knew he wasn't to blame, but still as he'd grown into a man the sense he should have protected her more had shaped who he'd become.

As children, he and Justine had hidden and kept silent. They'd bought into the pretence being performed for them by their parents. But he was no longer that boy. The night of his dad's death had seen to that. He was decisive. He could take control. He had proven he could be both those things and also not turn into his father. That was where Gerard had been wrong: you could be kind and strong. It wasn't one or the other.

Standing in the doorway was a couple, both around his mother's age. The woman was short with mousey-brown curly hair she hadn't tamed, and the man looked her complete opposite

– tall and wiry with a moustache. He couldn't place them, but he had a vague recollection of seeing them before.

The thing that most disturbed him though wasn't that he didn't know them, it was the way that, despite them being uninvited guests at his mother's house, they seemed to take charge of the entire situation. He felt his mother's steely exterior as they both smiled a smile which didn't reach their eyes and stepped inside.

'Shall we?' the man simply said, squeezing past Max.

Evelyn turned to Max. 'You need to go.' And he could feel the urgency pulsing through her every word.

He refused. 'I'm not going anywhere.'

'I am your mother, and I am telling you to leave.' She stepped sideways, blocking him with her small frame in an attempt to stop him following them through the house.

'No.' He was no longer a boy, and there was no one left to protect his mother. Not that he knew what or why she needed protecting, but the air felt icy and his mother's reaction was doing nothing to make him believe he was imagining it. He would no longer leave her to fend for herself.

She stared at him for a few quiet moments while neither backed down and then she relented. As he'd hoped she would. She'd softened in recent years; he'd seen it happen, slowly, but the sharp edges from their childhood had started to fall away.

At first, after his dad's death and Justine leaving, Evelyn had become more withdrawn. Had thrown her energies into gardening and kept herself to herself. But they say time is a great healer, and eventually he'd seen it start to work its magic.

'I'm sorry,' came her reply as her body sagged. She was letting him stay. But why was she sorry? What was going on?

The couple made themselves comfortable at the kitchen table, clearly already familiar with the house. He sat, only noticing Evelyn had remained standing once it was too late.

'I thought you'd moved to Portugal?' His mother's voice was stone cold, cementing in Max's mind that these people were not her friends.

'We did, but we're back now,' said the woman.

'And that concerns me how?' Evelyn asked.

'We saw your daughter on TV last week. Hasn't she grown up. Successful too, by the looks of it. A criminal barrister of all things.' And then the two of them laughed. A barking, hoarse, cruel kind of laugh. Evelyn's eyes flicked over to Max and he saw in them that this was what she was sorry for. That there was something big he hadn't been privy to. Something his mother would rather he didn't know. She had been sorry that he was about to find it out.

'We didn't think it could be her at first. Not after all these years, but we replayed the news segment over and over again until we were quite sure. We looked her up of course, she's got a different surname now – Hart, I saw – I assume she's married?'

No one answered.

'As you can imagine,' the woman continued, 'this opened a whole new world of possibilities for us. Justine Stone. A criminal barrister. You couldn't make it up if you tried,' and the woman laughed again. She was smiling. Shark's teeth.

'Am I missing something?' Max interjected. 'I really do not understand what's going on here and would appreciate an explanation.'

'Oh dear, your mother didn't tell you?' the woman said, looking pityingly over at Evelyn as she shook her head. 'You've grown up too, Max. Last time we saw you, well, how do I put this, dear.' She paused but it felt intentional – a dramatic silence for effect. 'The last time we saw you, you were carrying your dead father's body down the stairs.'

Max's knuckles turned white where he was gripping the side of his seat. He looked, questioningly, towards Evelyn but she wasn't watching him. Instead, her eyes were glued on the uninvited couple in her kitchen who were threatening to tear their whole world apart. And, Max realised, it wasn't for the first time.

'What do you want? Spit it out,' Evelyn barked.

The woman looked towards her husband, as if this was a carefully rehearsed play and it was his line next.

'We know your finances aren't what they once were. We aren't cruel people. We used to be friends and we want to honour that. Be respectful.' The man took over and Max wanted to be sick. 'But you aren't the only one with secrets or problems, Evelyn. We hope you can understand that. We wouldn't be back here unless we needed to be.' It was Evelyn's turn to laugh. 'We need fifty thousand pounds,' he continued, ignoring her. 'By the end of the week.'

'It was an accident,' Max said. 'Justine never meant to hurt Dad.'

'It may have started out that way, but it became a lot more than that, didn't it, dear.' It was the woman's turn to speak again. He had to give it to them, this couple were seamless.

'What if we can't pay it? What then?' Max couldn't help himself, although perhaps it was better not to know.

'Then everything you've worked so hard to cover up will come to light and this life you've built for yourself; your business, your mother's house, the family name, your sister's career, most likely even her marriage, every last part of it will be shattered. What a story: the killer daughter now turned criminal barrister. The brother and boyfriend who covered it up. The mother who lied to the police and paid to protect her children. It will all come out.'

'Who the fuck are you?' Max shouted, unable to contain his anger or fear any longer.

'You don't remember us?' the woman replied. 'We were friends of your father. We're Beverley and Mark Rushnell.'

How could he have let this happen? He had failed to protect his mum when he was younger but he'd always been there for Justine, trying to hide the truth from her – to let the fantasy of their father be her reality. That's why he'd taken her for fish and chips every Friday night, when he knew his father would have started drinking at four p.m. at the office. It was why hide-and-seek had become a regular game he'd instigate, always hiding alongside Justine even though it was only the two of them playing.

When Jake had told him what had happened, how his dad had first locked Justine in the wardrobe and then hit her, he'd felt the bottom of his stomach drop out. He had failed to protect her. Despite it all, finally their dad had come for Justine.

Max had been too smug to see the truth. He thought that night, the night of the Christmas party, he and Jake had succeeded in protecting Justine once more. He wouldn't let his dad hurt her – not even in death. But he had been wrong.

And now he needed to step up again.

Chapter Forty-One

I am staring at my phone in shock when I hear her footsteps treading lightly up the stairs. I wipe the tears from my face and try to pull it together. I remind myself the truth is complicated and that there are still lots of gaps.

I already know this is a jigsaw puzzle I'd rather not complete. Not this time. Still, I made Max a promise, and if I'm going to find out what really happened to him, I have to know everything.

'Mum,' I call out. I have no energy to stand and instead remain where I am, slumped on the floor with Max's phone in one hand, and mine in the other.

She's by my side immediately. Crouched beside me. Stroking my hair. Does she already know? Did she hide Max's phone or did he? What secrets does it hold?

'Were you friends with the Rushnells? Were—' my voice catches and I crick my neck, 'were you and Mark having an affair?'

'What? Absolutely not.' She looks at me, horrified. I can't find the words. She has lied to me again. And so instead I pass her the photograph.

She looks at it, first in disbelief and then she closes her eyes. Sighs. I take it to mean she knows she can no longer lie.

'OK, we did know each other. But this is one photo, Justine. A moment in time. A thousand possibilities of before and after. I can't even remember it.'

'Beverley hired a PI to look into Mark having an affair, not long before their deaths. So the other woman wasn't you?'

'I don't know what was going on within their marriage but I promise, I was not having an affair with that man.' I'm surprised by how full of hate she sounds, unable to even bring herself to say his name.

'But you were friends with them, clearly.'

'For a while, a long time ago. I suppose so.'

'Were they at the Christmas party before Dad died?' I ask, filled with the realisation that perhaps this is why the name has always felt familiar. How could I not remember? But then again, it was the first of Dad's parties I'd ever attended, and I'd spent the majority of the night locked away upstairs.

'Yes,' she says, 'they were there the whole time.'

And it's the way she pauses before saying 'the whole time', how she turns to look at me, that makes me realise it.

My mum knows. She has always known.

My entire world turns black.

I'm not sure how much time has passed but when I'm next fully conscious of my surroundings I'm in the bath, with my mother kneeling beside me. Sponge in hand. The water is hot on my skin and I can see my fingers are purple and prune-like. I wonder how long I've been in here.

'Mum?'

'You're back.' She smiles softly.

'How did I get here?' I feel confused and disorientated.

'It's OK. Try to keep calm. Sometimes our bodies can shut down, it's a way of coping. You've been awake but in a kind of daze. Our brain just needs a moment to process everything without the interference of the outside world. We retreat into ourselves and get lost someplace else.'

'Has it happened to you before?'

'It has. A few times,' she replies, breaking eye contact. 'I find a bath always helps bring me back to reality so I thought I'd try it for you.'

I reach out to hold her hand. Water is dripping on to the floor. For a moment, as the drops land and spread across the tiles, they look red like blood, but I blink hard and when I look again, they're just water.

'You said you weren't having an affair with Mark and I believe you. But I bumped into Mrs Hicks and she mentioned you are seeing someone. What was she talking about?' I ask, picking up where we left off.

'Ah, Mrs Hicks. Nothing ever gets past her,' Mum smiles and her eyes light up. 'His name is Ken. I met him at Bingo last year. We keep each other company and in all honesty it's nice to have someone to go through life with again.'

'Is it serious? Should I meet him?'

'If you'd like. I'm sure he'd love that.' I don't answer. Unsure if it's something I want to commit to just yet. 'Come, let's get you out. You've been in here long enough,' Mum carries on seamlessly as though she knows not to expect too much of me too quickly, and there's something so tender in this moment that it isn't comforting; instead I feel a surge of rage. This is the first time my mother has spoken to me this way in as long as I can remember. Where was she when I needed her most? The pain is flooding back in and I scramble to get out of the bath, to cover myself up and push her away.

'Why is Max's phone hidden in the back of my wardrobe?' My tone is hard again. Confronting. Balance is restored.

'I think he was preparing.' She says it slowly, as if considering every word.

'For what?'

'To leave us.' The pain is so strong now I feel in danger of it cracking my ribcage open.

'Why? Why would he do that?' *Why would he leave me alone?* is what I really mean.

'Justine, I—'

'Tell me what's going on. Tell me right now.' I am getting cold, standing here with just a towel around me, but I can't wait a minute longer. I need to know the truth. I need to know for certain if I am to blame for my brother's death. If, after all this, it is I who must pay for his death.

'It wasn't just Jake who helped you that Christmas.' *So she knew. She knew all this time.* 'You know how close he and Max were, he needed help and he trusted Max. They both loved you very much. The problem was, none of us were alone in the house that night.'

'Mark and Beverley were there too?'

'Yes. They left but then Beverley realised she'd forgotten her handbag. Max must have left the door ajar when he'd come back, as they found it open and let themselves in. According to Beverley, they heard Max and Jake talking about what had happened and when they heard them coming down the stairs they'd hidden in the snug, from where they'd watched Gerard's body being carried out the house and into his car. None of us knew they'd returned, not until it was too late.'

'They knew everything?'

She nods.

'They demanded money. A hundred thousand pounds. I paid them off and that was the end of it. At least, for many years. They moved abroad.'

'To Portugal.'

'Yes. But then they came back and that's when it all started again. They saw you on television not too long ago. It was the case with the politician. His speech was aired outside the court on the BBC news. You were in shot and they recognised you.'

'And they saw their next opportunity.' The penny drops. 'How ironic to see me as a criminal barrister. Am I right?'

'I'm sorry.' Again, I'm reminded how much I hate that phrase. It sounds so hollow from her lips. Meaningless. Sorry for what?

'And you brought Max into it?'

'I didn't mean to, but they turned up on my doorstep while he was here and he refused to leave.' Once again Max had been the person to stay. To show up. Why hadn't I come home when he'd asked?

'And then what? They demanded more money?' I want to know everything. All the details. I don't want to be spared.

'Fifty thousand pounds. Max said he'd handle it and didn't let me be involved. I think he felt guilty. Not about protecting you, no, he never regretted that. But about before. That he hadn't protected you before that night.'

'It wasn't his job to protect me.'

'No,' she says, looking straight at me. 'It was mine.' I don't know how to respond, all I know is that I can't speak to her about this. I am not strong enough to face all the pain head-on, out loud. Instead, I press on with my questions. A cross-examination, now that's something I can do.

'What happened next?'

'I don't know exactly. He cut me out. But I watched it eat away at him, day by day. Week after week. He started drinking and shutting everyone out. When Jake came back after his mum's death, it was all too much for Max. I think everything just imploded. All that pain. All those secrets. He was unrecognisable and ended up losing his job. And then they asked again. Another fifty thousand. A few days later their bodies were found. The following month, Max drowned.'

'Do you think he killed himself?'

'I think the guilt of murdering Mark and Beverley Rushnell killed him,' she says.

Finally, the jigsaw pieces slot together: eighteen years ago Max helped Jake cover up my dad's death, and then Jake helped Max to silence the Rushnells once and for all. That's why Jake had been at the scene of the crime.

He hadn't pulled the trigger, Max had, but just like he'd covered for me all those years before, he had covered – was still covering – for Max.

BEFORE

MAX – THE BROTHER

The third time the Rushnells asked for money, the penny dropped that they were never going to stop. They had relented twice already, and the couple now knew they had the Stones wrapped round their little fingers. While there had been a gap of almost two decades between the first and second payments, this demand had come less than four months after the last.

They'd sat in silence as they'd driven out of Maldon and towards Surrey. Number 34 Cherry Tree Grove. The Rushnells' house was pretty. A four-bedroom semi-detached house out in the suburbs. Perfectly trimmed neat bushes lined the driveway and a doormat embossed with the phrase STAY AWHILE welcomed them. A doorbell which chimed a friendly melody announced their arrival. There was nothing about the house which indicated the owners were responsible for tearing Max's family apart.

This time it was their turn to arrive uninvited, and Max took pleasure in the shock displayed on Beverley Rushnell's face as she opened the door. Her expression was no longer smug or shark-like; the element of surprise had dealt them the upper hand.

'Shall we?' he'd said, sliding past her and following the sounds to find Mark cooking in their kitchen.

He'd spent all morning visualising how the meeting would go. They would be firm in putting a stop to this. They just needed to regain a bit of power. As he'd looked around the house, he'd felt confident it would work – the Rushnells seemed normal enough and he could understand people acting in ways they'd never imagined themselves capable of. He was hopeful that, despite everything, at their core they were reasonable people.

Only the thing about plans is they never go the way you expect, and people are full of surprises.

The air felt thick and charged.

The Rushnells were not harmless suburban people – their strength was that they were simply pretending to be, hiding behind the average normality of their exterior. As the argument escalated, Max felt his fear building. What scared him the most was that the opposite seemed true for the Rushnells. It was as though they thrived off the confrontation. Enjoyed the fight. Rather than gaining control over the situation, Max could feel they were losing it, faster than he'd imagined.

'This has to stop. We can't keep finding huge lumps of money. You've been paid. Twice now. This is complete madness.'

'Madness?' The word seemed to hit a particular nerve with Beverley. 'Some might think a real sign of madness would be murdering your father and then covering it up. Imagine this: one day you wake up and go to fetch your usual coffee from that place at the top of the high street your father used to love. You pick up the paper, just as you do every morning. Only today, your world is about to change. The front page is a photo of Justine. A head-line reads: "Criminal turned criminal barrister".'

'It wasn't murder. You know as well as I do it was an accident.'

'You didn't accidentally carry him into his car. You didn't accidentally fail to call the police. She killed him but it's what came after that I think people will find really shocking. The entire Stone family, not so perfect after all.'

'You didn't call the police either.'

'Should we have? Would you like us to, now?'

'You wouldn't dare. You think you have us cornered but what would happen to you if you told the truth after all these years? Perverting the course of justice. Blackmail. Admit it, you're too late. You missed your window. This is over. We're done.'

'I guess we'll just have to take that chance.' Beverley shrugged, as if what he'd said was nothing more than water off a duck's back.

'What makes you think they'd believe you anyway?' he asked.

'Oh Max, my dear, you treat us like amateurs. You think we played all our cards at once?' Beverley smiled, cementing the fact that he was out of his depth.

It was this loss of control which started to infect all his senses. He felt the twitches return and the saliva gather in his mouth. The sounds of the saucepans boiling on the stove rang too loud in his ear. A too-sweet smell filled his nostrils and made him want to be sick. Would this ever end?

'I'll explain, shall I? You see, we recently came across an old digital camera of ours during our move back from Portugal. You remember when we had cameras in our bags and not everything was stored on our phones. You'd take photos and never look through them ever again. Besides, the camera had been sitting in a box in storage since 2006. Well, imagine our horror all these years later when we realised what we had in our possession. Evidence. Never-before-seen evidence.' As she spoke, she opened a kitchen drawer and pulled out a black notebook. Hidden between the middle pages was a photograph. 'Here, see for yourself. I think you'll be particularly interested in this one, Max,' she said, passing it to him.

The image showed Beverley smiling in front of a Christmas tree in a room he knew all too well to be his parents' snug. Behind Beverley, through the window, you could see his dad's car driving along the road.

'Now,' Mark took over, 'the interesting thing about cameras years ago was I had this brilliant setting with a timestamp and date printed in the corner of each image. Can you see? Right-hand corner. That's it.'

The sixteenth of December. Eleven fifty-three p.m.

'That's your dad's car, is it not?'

'It is.' Max swallowed hard.

'Maybe you can see what we're trying to show you more clearly in this one,' Mark said, and Beverley passed him another photo. The pair of them, so professional. The perfect double act.

Max looked.

This time, the focus was zoomed in on the car through the window.

Of Max, not Gerard, driving it.

The reality of the situation hit. It felt as though he was being put in a box, with the lid tightly shut. No place to escape to, the four walls forcing him smaller and smaller. It wasn't meant to be like this. He needed to find a way out. But he couldn't think clearly; all he could feel was an overwhelming need to make it stop. To make everything stop. Not just the situation with the Rushnells, but the guilt, the pain, the drinking. All of it.

As his adrenalin moved him into fight-or-flight mode, he felt he was no longer part of his own body. He knew he was shuffling from one foot to the other, but he couldn't make himself stand still. Could feel his teeth were clenched down so forcefully it was causing a throbbing pain behind his eyes, yet he couldn't part them.

'But as you say, we'll have to wait and see what the police think, wont we?' Beverley said and Mark moved towards the phone hanging on the wall.

This couldn't be happening. It wasn't meant to be this way. They were losing. He was failing to protect Justine all over again. Not just Justine but his mum too.

And then he was transported back in time, to another night, when he was aged five – the first memory he had of hearing his mother screaming through the walls. Of his father threatening to stuff her mouth with a sock if she couldn't be quiet. 'You'll wake the kids,' he'd snarled, using Max's five-year-old existence against her.

This had to stop.

Max heard the gunshot before he saw the blood. Higher, higher he floated, as the gun was next placed against Mark's temple. As the man dropped the phone where he stood. As he didn't take his eyes off his dead wife's body. As the second gunshot rang out loud and clear.

Chapter Forty-Two

We eat dinner together that evening, something we haven't done since Noah was here to stay. I know we have a long way to go, and I'm uncertain if we'll ever get to enjoy a normal mother–daughter relationship, but something has shifted between us.

It isn't forgiveness, but it's an acknowledgement that life is complicated and messy. That perhaps we've both done our best, despite it all. More than anything, I feel the weight of guilt I've been carrying around with me since Dad's death has lifted slightly. That it can, at least, be shared.

I am not the only one to blame for what happened. My mother knew who my father was – what he was – long before then, and she still did nothing. But she has also protected me – and Max – far more than I'd ever realised. And while it doesn't eliminate her failings, it adds a nuance to them I couldn't see before.

No one is wholly good or bad. If I extend that to myself, I should start extending it to my mother. The truth of someone: it is never just one thing.

'Why didn't you tell us what was going on?' I ask her. 'I thought I had to hide it from you.'

'I could already see you were in so much pain. You never meant for it to happen and I didn't want you to take on even more guilt for all that came after, too.'

'Did Max tell Jake to leave?' Were they both still trying to save me is what I really want to find out. It's the part of the story I've been playing over and over in my mind since I found out Max had helped Jake cover up what I did.

'I wasn't there, so I don't know for sure, but I always assumed that was what happened. They both loved you, very much.'

'So, once again, you lied to me. You let my heart break.'

'Yes,' she says, looking me straight in the eye.

'And I lied to you,' I admit.

'You did.' She does not sound angry.

'For eighteen years.'

'Longer, really. We've both been lying to each other all our lives.'

'Was it worth it?' I ask. 'We barely know each other. Would you do it differently if you could?'

Mum takes a moment to think before answering me.

'There are some things I would change, yes. But I'd never not protect my children. I hope one day, maybe if you have a child of your own, you'll understand.'

The next morning, I pack my things slowly and meticulously. I find I'm no longer in a rush to go home. A part of me feels anchored back here with Mum and Max. I'd always thought of Dad's death as being all my fault, but I can see it more clearly now. What happened, what I did, it was a product of everything that had come before it. Of Mum, trying to protect us by hiding the truth as best she could. Of us, pushing the truth away. Where I had thought my mother had been weak, I see now she'd been strong. In her own way. In, I think, the only way she had known how to be.

And Jake. He'd left because he loved me enough to leave me. Not because he hated me. Brad Finchley. *Finches*. Jake may have left, transformed into Brad, but he never fully left me behind.

I take a final look around my bedroom and smile when I real-ise I can look at my wallpaper and the pattern no longer runs in red rivulets. That the flowers remain looking like flowers. I try it out further and move into the en suite. Turn the tap on and watch as the water runs clear.

It is time to leave.

I haven't warned Noah that I'm coming back, worried somehow it would jinx it. It's a Friday in August and I know he'll be working summer hours from home. I find myself excited to see him. No longer plagued by guilt. I am going home.

He's in the front garden when I pull into the driveway. He stands up and shades the sun from his eyes. I can see he's been pruning our apple tree, loppers in hand. While I was gone from him – in ways I hope he'll never find out – he has been holding us together the best he could. I thought I didn't deserve a man like Noah, but today when I look at him, my love for him no longer turns into hatred for myself. Instead, I look at him and see a future full of possibilities. I open the car door and smile as I pull my suitcase out after me.

'You're staying?' he asks me tentatively, his eyes flitting from me to the suitcase and back again.

'I am.'

'And your mum?' he asks.

'She's OK,' I say, nodding, realising this is the very first time Noah has ever asked after Mum that I've been able to answer him honestly.

'Well then.' He grins, moving towards me and picking up my suitcase, 'let's go inside.'

December 2023

Chapter Forty-Three

The Christmas season always brings with it mixed emotions. Some years I cope better than others. Generally, I try to embrace it for what it is – made easier by the fact that Noah is a full-on Christmas believer. Not of the religious sort. But in its magic. Normally my oh-so-very-sensible husband transforms, for approximately twenty-six days of the year every December, into what I can only describe as a human-sized elf.

Without his infectious enthusiasm for Christmas, I'm not sure I'd be quite so capable of leaving the past in the past. Especially when it comes to the deluge of parties we always seem to be invited to. The annual tradition among our London friends is to mark the beginning of December with the first Christmas party of the season, the idea of it being like the firing of a gun at the start of a race. This year, it is our turn to host and soon our house will be full of laughter.

'All OK in here? Charlotte and Rob have just arrived, so I thought I'd bring you this,' Noah says, entering the bedroom wearing a fetching pair of Rudolph ears. He hands me a glass of champagne.

'Wonderful, thanks. I'll be down in a minute.'

'You better be, Rob has already started on the mince pies, so you'll need to be quick if you want any.' And off he goes, galloping down the stairs just as the doorbell rings again announcing the arrival of more friends.

I look at the champagne, held between my fingers, and without so much as a sip I place the glass on top of the dressing cabinet. I pull open the top drawer. Rummage around until I find what I'm looking for.

It is hidden inside a sock and pulling it out I stare, for what must be the millionth time, at the plain white plastic stick in front of me. On first look it seems harmless enough, but this small piece of plastic has the ability to change my entire life. Do I want it? I know Noah will be ecstatic. No questions asked about what to do next. But what about me?

I haven't told him I'm pregnant yet. I don't want to get his hopes up. I also don't want to tell him until I know what my own thoughts about it are. Am I capable of being a better mother than mine was? What if my child turns out like me?

But I can't keep ignoring the signs, not least because my clothes are no longer fitting as they once used to. From my own calculations I must be around twenty weeks' pregnant already, maybe just over, and I know I am running out of time. I need to make a decision. Partly, I'm worried about a scan and what their measurements might show – that this baby was conceived the week of both the mud race and Charlotte's birthday. I wish it wasn't a question, that I know for certain Noah is the father. But I've learnt, harder and faster than most, that mistakes happen and no matter how much you want to change the past, you have to keep moving forward.

And so I think about that, the pressing need to always keep moving, and finally I decide to embrace it. To push on with the future and not let the past dictate my life.

This baby is mine.

And their father will be Noah.

Chapter Forty-Four

It feels exhilarating to finally be back in the robing room, even if I'm exhausted from hosting last night. It's only a small case, nothing high-profile, and though I'm not even leading it I am still grateful for the new start, which represents a road back to my old life. One which not too long ago I wasn't sure I'd ever get to live again. The day has gone well, at least by my current standards. Today, there have been no snide comments like those of teenagers in the locker room at school.

The temperature has plummeted over the last few days. It is just gone four p.m. but it is already dark outside. I wrap my coat around me and hurry down the stone steps. My chin is dipped against the wind, meaning I don't see him until he's almost on top of me.

'Café stakeout?' I ask.

'Something like that,' Otis replies.

It reminds me of that time I waited obsessively for a glimpse of Christina Lang, and it makes me think how much has changed since then; I am back in court. Nothing spectacularly interesting, and certainly nothing newspaper-worthy, but the foundations of my life are finally back on steadier ground. Noah has even started joining me once a month in my sessions with Aya, and I really do think we're getting somewhere. I am learning, slowly, to let him in. I am committed to making this work, not just for our future, but for our baby.

I wrap my coat around me tighter. Protectively, as if the chill might make her feel cold, too. *Her*. I smile. I'm being presumptuous but I am certain that the baby growing inside me is a girl.

'Do you have time to talk?' Otis sounds worried, but I already knew he wouldn't have come here for nothing. That whatever he needs to tell me must be important.

'I'm dashing between courts so can you chat on our way to the tube?'

'Of course,' he says and we rush towards Blackfriars.

I don't know what he has come here to tell me, but I do know it must be connected to everything that happened during the summer because we aren't working another case together right now – the proceedings I'm currently instructed with don't warrant his talents.

'What have you found?' I haven't asked him to look into anything more since I left Maldon. As far as I was concerned, I had all the answers I needed and it was time, finally, to move on.

'Well, I've been working on this big case and another LLC was involved. Anyway, the point is that I worked out how to trace who had set it up but also who deposited each payment into the LLC account, and it got me thinking about The Little Trust Company.' We're in the station now and Otis follows me through the barriers, down on to the platform.

'But we already know it was Max,' I say.

'You know I'm invaluable because I take nothing for granted.'

'That's true.' I start to grind my teeth, unsure I want to know what it is he's come to tell me. Not this time. I don't want to be thrown back there again, not when I have a job to do: I am going to be a mother.

I hear the rush of the tube hurtling towards the platform and I can feel myself wishing it would hurry up so I can make my escape before Otis can bring everything crashing down around me.

'You said your mother told you Max cut her out once Mark and Beverley turned up on her doorstep having returned from Portugal?'

'That's right.'

I think he senses that I'm going to want to leave straight away. That whatever he is about to tell me will be something I need time to process, because he pauses before speaking again and waits for the thrum of the train to hurtle past us, pulling into the platform, before continuing. 'It's just that it doesn't make sense. I checked and the final payment to the Rushnells was made by Evelyn, not by Max.'

'OK, so what exactly are you telling me?' I'm running through the details again in my head but I can't quite make sense of it. Mum had told me Max cut her out of the dealings with the Rushnells after the second payment. What does it all mean?

'Justine,' he says, 'I don't think Max killed Mark and Beverley Rushnell. I think it was your mother.'

I am grateful for the train's tailwind as it crashes through me, reminding me this is real, that it is happening, grounding me in the present. I step on to the train and turn to face out, watching Otis as he remains on the platform. I can see in his eyes that he is sorry. That it has pained him to have to tell me my mum has once again lied to me.

'What are you going to do?' he asks, but I can't find the words to answer before the doors close and the train slides away from the platform.

BEFORE

EVELYN – THE MOTHER

Evelyn drove while Max fidgeted in the passenger seat. He'd started doing that recently, she'd noticed. It wasn't something that had defined him before, but ever since he'd found out about the Rushnells, small changes had begun to sneak in. Small ones that were becoming bigger ones. She was his mother; it was her job to know these things. Most importantly, it was her job to put a stop to them.

She wondered if it was the guilt or the responsibility that was weighing down so heavily on him. He'd always been such a kind boy, and he had carried that on into adulthood. But with kindness also came a softness at his core. She knew he'd hardened his edges all those years ago, but you could never really change the essence of someone and Evelyn knew he was different to her.

Justine would like to think she was too, but she was more similar to her mother than she knew. Evelyn liked to hope that one day Justine would see her mother in her own reflection and realise what it had all been for. That it had, in fact, all been for her.

But today was not the day for revelations. Today was another day to be the mother she needed to be. She supposed, if she did her job right, the longer it took for Justine to realise, the better a job she would have done.

Number 34 Cherry Tree Grove looked exactly as she'd expected it to. Why wouldn't it? She'd driven past enough times planning the journey over the past four days. The bottom of the road was a cul-de-sac. It was a few houses down from the Rushnells' but it was jam-packed with cars parked haphazardly.

One of the houses was having building work done and there was usually a large white van parked which she planned to squeeze behind, almost out of sight except to those living right at the bottom of the street. She sighed in relief as she pulled into the road and saw that, so far, everything was running smoothly.

She didn't know how the meet would go. She hadn't been able to plan that far ahead, but she knew she'd rather they came and went unnoticed. The fewer breadcrumbs left that could ever link them to the Rushnells, the better. If there was one thing she'd learnt from being married to Gerard for all those years, it was to tread cautiously and to always be prepared: nothing was ever out of the question and people were always capable of more than you thought they were – both the good and the bad.

The day she'd realised her own strength had also been the day she had realised she too was made up of a powerful mix of good and bad. That she didn't have to be one thing. She'd thought when they had Max that Gerard would stop. But what before had been an emotional wearing down of herself had morphed into a whole other beast over the first year of Max's life.

At the beginning, Gerard's episodes (as she'd liked to call them) had been quickly followed by displays of love, like the up-and-down motion of a yo-yo. One minute she would be pinned against the wall by her neck, the next released with a laugh and smile. The same smile which had once made her fall in love with him.

He had been clever at the start, doing nothing that would leave bruises, concentrating on pressure points such as the neck, behind the knees, the wrists. Moments of a loss of control over her own body followed, moments that he quickly released her from, and which left no evidence behind. She'd put it down to the pressure of a new baby. Perhaps it was post-traumatic stress, she'd reasoned with herself. Her labour with Max had been tough on them all. Thirty-six hours, an emergency C-section and three blood transfusions followed by a baby who wouldn't latch; her husband had looked on helplessly as she was hand-milked by the nurses. Yes, PTSD, she'd reassured herself after each episode. She only needed to be kind and patient. She could help him get better. But over time it seemed as though he no longer got the same kick out of the small things. A bit like a drug addict, she'd supposed.

The high of rendering her helpless, immovable, no longer seemed to do the trick. Soon he wanted bruises. Carefully placed, of course. Always so careful. By then he'd started to use the children against her.

She'd thought about going to the police but couldn't forget the scandal splashed across the newspapers in her childhood about how the Freemasons had all but infiltrated the police force. It was years ago, and hopefully things had changed, but it sowed a seed of mistrust she couldn't let go of. Would they take Gerard's side? The only person she could rely on was herself. No other risk was worth it. And so she learnt she could be two things at once – both a good mother and a bad one: one who could not find a way to get her children away from their father and who let a monster transform into their hero, while also being the mother who fiercely protected them, who absorbed all the pain so that they wouldn't have to.

She'd thought it had been the right thing to do. That she could stand them not loving her as much as they did him for as long as he never hurt them. But she had been wrong about that. No matter how much she'd tried, the monster had eventually unleashed itself. She had learnt the hard way that you could not tame a beast, and she would not make the same mistake again.

The doorbell chimed its sickly-sweet melody and she'd followed Max inside, through to the kitchen. It was nowhere near as grand as hers, she noted with pride.

'We aren't paying any more money,' she stated, pleased there was no wobbling in her voice. But while it had started off so confidently, they'd quickly lost control of the situation. The Rushnells had proven themselves to be more formidable opponents than she'd hoped. But the recognition that it had been just that – only hope – had been her strength. This time, she had not underestimated her opponents; they had underestimated her.

She looked over to Max. Her beautiful son. And the sight of him, almost unrecognisable as his eyes popped wide with fear and his anxiety prevented him from standing still, was the deciding factor.

So much of her family had already been destroyed. Not all of that had been the fault of the Rushnells, she knew that, but she would not let them take it all. She could not lose both her son and her daughter.

Her fingers grasped the cold metal butt in her pocket and, as Mark Rushnell lunged for the phone, the decision was made. There was no time for weakness. She had a job to do, and while Evelyn Stone was many things, at her very core she was a mother. No one would take that from her, and her son needed his mother's protection.

Chapter Forty-Five

The journey home passes in a blur, so much so that I'm surprised I don't miss my stop. I walk home from the station, letting my coat blow open in the biting wind. I'm no longer capable of feeling the cold as it whips around my waist. Instead of dipping my head, bowing my chin out of the painful gusts, I keep looking straight ahead, grateful to the icy chill for reminding me that I am still alive and that I possess this body of mine, even when I feel disconnected from it.

My mother is a liar.

My mother is a murderer.

I clamp my teeth down hard on my tongue until I can think of nothing more than the burning pressure and the need to release it.

I am trying to make sense of it, but my brain can't follow one train of thought through to the end before it's derailed by another. If my mother pulled the trigger on the Rushnells and not Max, then did he really kill himself? What else has she lied about? And what about Jake? If he didn't help Max, isn't protecting him, then why is he now accused of a crime my mother committed?

I pull my phone out and dial one of the only numbers I still know off by heart – a legacy from my teenage years. She answers faster than I'm prepared for, and although I am the one calling her, I find myself lost for words.

'Are you there?' she asks.

'I know,' I whisper. It's as loud as I can muster. 'It was you.'

'Are you alone?'

'Yes.'

'I'll come straight over.'

It will be the first time she has visited me in my new life here, something I'd hoped to avoid, but I don't have the strength to argue and simply hang up without replying.

I see her from the window as her taxi arrives and I wonder if I'm seeing her properly for the first time in my life. It turns out this quiet mother of mine has never been very quiet at all.

I open the door before she has a chance to ring the doorbell and she steps inside. We're both silent. It seems to be our trademark. I walk her through to the lounge and pour us both a bourbon. Still, neither of us has uttered a word. Is it a dance? A game? I swallow my pride.

'No more lies,' I demand as I hand her a glass. Leaning in I catch sight of a semicircular scar on the edge of her clavicle where her top doesn't quite cover the full circle my father once branded on her. It is just one of many hidden beneath her clothes.

'I didn't come here to lie to you,' she says, taking a sip.

'I hope not.' Still, I am wary. I myself have made plenty of promises I never planned on keeping.

'What do you want to know?'

'How did you get the gun?'

'Always starting with the practicalities,' she smiles wryly. 'It was your father's. I don't know how he got it. It certainly wasn't registered, but you know your father – he always chased after anything that made him feel powerful.'

'And after his accident you kept it?'

'What was I supposed to do? I wasn't exactly going to hand it in to the police, was I? Besides, I'd learnt never to take my own safety for granted.'

'It didn't keep Max safe though, did it. I need to know why and how he died, Mum. What really happened?'

She closes her eyes and I see how much pain my words cause her. I see them pierce her skin, her body giving a physical jolt at the impact of them.

'He was there with me. Max and I both went to visit them at their home that day. But he did not kill Mark and Beverley Rushnell. Your brother could never have killed anyone, but you already know that by now. I promise you, it wasn't a lie that he was in the house with me. Of course he had no idea I had your father's gun, we both know he was too soft for that, at least not until it was too late anyway.

'It was his softness that killed him, in the end. Maybe that's where I went wrong. He couldn't cope, you see. The Max we both knew, he disappeared before my eyes in the days that followed. He'd already taken the blackmailing badly and this was simply too much for him to handle. I was trying to protect him, to stop him doing anything he'd later regret. You have to believe me. He wanted to give himself up. The guilt, it was consuming him. I just needed to buy ourselves more time. I thought he'd listen to me. That if I took care of him, he'd be OK eventually.'

'And when he didn't listen?' This is the part I'm truly terrified of.

'I took his phone and locked him in his bedroom. I promise you, Justine. I only wanted to protect him. I didn't think he'd climb out of the window.' She downs the rest of her drink. 'I just needed more time,' she repeats.

I inch further away from her. Even though I'm already sitting on a different sofa, it doesn't feel far enough. My dad, my mother. It is bad blood flowing through my veins.

'That's not everything though, is it?' My voice is purposely devoid of emotion. I cannot let myself feel this pain too intensely.

I cannot let it drown me or there's a real possibility I'll never re-emerge. Even I have my limits and somehow thinking I was to blame for Max's death was easier to stomach than the thought it was my mother's fault. I already knew myself capable of such awful things. It's a whole other thing to believe a mother caused the death of her child.

'Ah, you're talking about Jake?' She looks up at me and I can see there is sorrow etched across her face. Sorrow, yes, but I sense no trace of regret.

'If it was you and Max in the Rushnells' house, then why is it Jake standing trial for two counts of murder and not you? You let me believe it was Max and Jake who went to the house that day.'

'You have to understand, a mother's job is to protect her children,' she says with her hands folded tightly into the crease of her dress between her thighs. Her eyes are burning fiercely with a determination I haven't noticed before.

BEFORE

MAX – THE BROTHER

Max couldn't stop replaying it in his mind. The blood. The flesh. The screaming. Two sets of dead eyes which seemed to continue following him. Even now, they were watching him. He could feel it, their eyes crawling all over his skin.

We know what you did.

He hadn't even known his mother had brought the gun with them. What had she been thinking? And then to actually go ahead and use it? Every time he looked at her, it was as though she was a whole new person: someone he didn't recognise.

There were two versions of his mother in his mind now, defined by a before and an after. The mother and the murderer. Surely they were not the same person? He must be mistaken. Confused. Perhaps it was all the drinking, although as much as he knew he should stop, he couldn't.

Everything after the second gunshot was muddled up, a series of images he couldn't make sense of. Still-frames with no context between them. Was this what losing your mind felt like?

He hadn't managed to leave his mum's house since the killings and if he'd kept track correctly, it had been almost a month. At this point, he wasn't sure if it was that he didn't want to, or that he wasn't allowed to leave.

He understood she was worried about him. He hadn't exactly handled all this well. But really, what did she expect? She told him it was for his own good. Just a temporary thing. That until he had processed what had happened, he was better off staying with her. To let everything surrounding Jake's arrest quieten down.

It struck him just how isolated he'd become since the Rushnells had bulldozed back into their lives. He'd scared Justine off, pushed Jimmy away and managed to lose his job. There was no one left to miss him.

He paced around his old room. He couldn't stop. If he stopped, the eyes watching him started to burn through his flesh. Round and round he went, so many times he'd lost count. In fact, he'd lost sense of time altogether. But today, as he walked from wall to wall, his thoughts began to fall into some kind of pattern. If he tried hard enough, it began to make a little sense. Mark and Beverley. That had been their names. They'd had a singing doorbell.

And then there was something about Jake. Now and then, without warning, the memory of what his mother had done – of Jake's arrest – would suddenly all come back to him and he'd double over in pain, the guilt rendering itself physically too painful to bear. Of course, she hadn't told him her plan until after, no doubt aware he'd try and stop her. It was laughable, really, all those years he and Justine had thought their mother spineless, but now here they were – with him the puppet and her as his puppeteer.

No. It was easier to forget. He just wished it would all stay forgotten. He couldn't live with knowing what they'd done. It was during these moments of clarity, when the fog would lift, that he'd try to escape. It sounded dramatic, but it was true. Because, put simply, his mother would not let him leave.

You're unwell.

I'm just helping you get better.

Everything will all go back to normal soon.

But he knew the truth. At least, sometimes he did. Today was one of those days and he repeated it to himself: Mark and Beverley were dead. His mother was a killer. She had framed Jake.

He came to a stop by the wardrobe mirror. A stranger's face stared back at him. Puffy from months of drinking ever since he first found out about the Rushnells, with dark circles around his eyes from the lack of sleep. He needed help. He pulled out his phone and texted Jimmy, the only person left he hoped he could rely on.

He knew Jimmy was pissed off at him for fighting in his pub. Max still felt bad about that. Evelyn had been the one to suggest he meet with Jake. She'd said he should try and persuade him to leave again, worried that Jake hanging around for so long was dangerous for everyone: if the Rushnells caught wind he was around, they might find a way to blackmail him too. Jake hadn't taken it so well; being told to go a second time. He'd replied, 'The past is in the past.'

And Max couldn't explain without drawing Jake into it all – and he wasn't going to do that. But in place of an explanation, his anger – his fear – spilled over instead. He hadn't been able to control it. It wasn't Jake's fault, but Max had cracked and all the anger he felt towards Mark and Beverley came rushing out as he lunged and pinned Jake against the wall.

This was not who he wanted to be, but for the past four months, ever since the Rushnells' reappearance, he seemed to be messing everything up.

Maybe he'd already been starting to lose his mind over all this, even back then – before the murders. Because that's what Evelyn kept telling him – that the stress had made him unwell.

Yes, he regretted fighting in Jimmy's pub, but they'd been friends for years and Jimmy had never stayed mad at Max for long. And this was important: Max knew who had killed the Rushnells.

He should go straight to the police, but from looking at his reflection he knew he didn't exactly look reliable. No, he needed somewhere to sort himself out first. If only he could get out of the house.

She brought his dinner to him on a tray and stroked his face; told him he should drink more water. That's when she clocked the phone in his hand.

'Can I trust you?' she asked. 'What I did, I did it for you and Justine. You have to believe me.'

'You killed them.'

'I think they killed themselves.'

'They didn't.'

'But they did, Max. Threatening to tear us down like that. I didn't make them do those things.'

'That's not how it works.' He heard his voice getting louder. More urgent. Maybe he wasn't the delusional one, maybe it was her. 'I'm going out.'

'You're not well. You need to stay here.'

'I am fine.'

'No. Maxwell George Stone, you are going nowhere. Not in your state.' Max was surprised by how big she made herself seem. Where had her strength come from? 'Now,' she said. 'I need your phone. You're not well, that's all,' Evelyn repeated, softer this time. And once again he felt the dead vacant eyes boring into him from the corner of the room. It made his skin hurt, as if he needed to rip his own flesh off. As if maybe in doing so he could find himself again buried deep inside. He could feel himself weakening, this momentary display of coherence starting to seep away from him.

Evelyn stooped down and picked up an unopened can of beer from by his bed. She cracked it open and handed it to him in exchange for his phone.

'You always were such a good boy,' she said before leaving his room and shutting the door.

Locking it behind her.

Fuck being good. I want to be great! The memory of a fifteen-year-old Jimmy's voice echoed in his mind.

Jimmy. They had made a plan. His mother had his phone, but he still had Jimmy's word that they'd meet after his shift down by the boats.

He watched each tick of the clock on his wall, counting down until he could make his escape. He listened for his mother's footsteps as she made her way to bed.

The wall outside his window was covered in prickly brambles. It wouldn't be easy, but he was sure it was possible. More importantly, he knew he had no choice: he had to leave.

Chapter Forty-Six

My mother remains perfectly still as she recounts how jittery Max had been in the lead-up to the day of the murders and then how broken he was after. She barely takes a breath while she tells me everything she did was to protect him from himself.

Is she holding herself so tightly together because she's afraid of unravelling?

Because I see that in her now: it is not a coldness that shuts her off, making her seem untouchable and aloof, it is fear.

'Were you afraid of Dad?' I ask.

'Terrified. Every day. I was afraid he would hurt you. And then he did.'

'Why did you stay?'

She closes her eyes and begins to cry.

'It's complicated. I thought about it. A lot. I don't know how to explain it other than to tell you I didn't believe I could. Who was I without your dad? He made me think I only existed because of him. That I didn't deserve to live without him. Couldn't. Besides, Gerard would never have let me leave with you. I was afraid of what he would do if I dared try. So I stayed. And I watched. And I hoped that if he had me, then he wouldn't need to take his anger out on you or Max.' She opens her eyes and looks at me, straight in the eye. 'I'm sorry I was wrong.'

'You sent me away.' Even saying the words out loud is almost too painful to bear. To admit that my mother abandoned me.

'To protect you,' she fires back fiercely. 'What you did, it would have killed you too if you had stayed.'

I find myself believing her. Something in me breaks, then. But in a good way, I hope. I think this last piece of me needed to break so I can fix myself with something better, stronger, more permanent this time. I believe her: she had loved me, even when she knew what I had done.

Unconsciously, I move my hand to my belly. I too am a mother. The responsibility of it has already changed me. What I eat, what I drink, how I exercise. Is this what it is to turn into a mother? A metamorphosis of sorts. I didn't think I'd ever be good enough to be a mother and was afraid of letting a little person down. But I've surprised myself.

I am already an excellent mother.

Otis's question reverberates through me.

What are you going to do?

I think about Jake's letter and the decision I have to make; about the need to find whoever is responsible for Max's death; and I think of DS Rose, with her questions over Dad's accident.

Which secrets do I keep? Which ones must I tell?

My hand clings tighter to my belly.

The truth is that my secrets are no longer just protecting me – they're also protecting my child.

NOW

JAKE – THE ACCUSED

Jake sits on the hard mattress in his cell bouncing a tennis ball against the wall. He can't help wondering if she'll come.

Justine.

The trial has lasted just over six weeks and he is about to be led back up to the courtroom for the final time. It is optimistic. Foolish. But he can't stop the thoughts from invading his mind.

There is still time. She might still come for you.

This web is too thick. Realistically, Jake knows there is no way she can save him, not without damning herself, but he had thought perhaps she'd visit him before deciding what she was going to do. It was her family, after all, who put him here.

And as he sits, waiting to hear the final summing-up of the case against him, no doubt once more hearing all the horrific details he was supposedly guilty of, he finds himself wanting to touch her again. To be reminded of why and how he ended up here in the first place.

Eighteen years ago, he'd sacrificed everything for Justine. But eighteen years is a very long time. His silence this time round wasn't so much out of love for her as out of necessity. He couldn't tell the truth to get out of one crime without admitting to another.

The problem is he has no way of confirming just how fool-proof Evelyn's set-up is. If he tells the truth, has she made plans to set him up for Gerard's murder too? At this point, it wouldn't feel like too much of a stretch. Clearly, that woman is capable of more than he'd realised. He was only a boy back then. He's sure he would have made mistakes and left evidence he'd been there – that he'd moved Gerard's body. Certainly, Max is no longer around to corroborate his version of events. And what about Justine?

There is no doubt she knows he is innocent. His letter made that clear to her. Innocent but trapped. The only one with any power left is her. Will she decide to tell her story to save him? A long time ago, he sacrificed everything for her.

He hoped she was happy. That it hadn't all been for nothing. In the beginning, after he'd left, he'd checked up on her every few months, but once she moved in with Noah it became too painful. Finally, he'd forced himself to move on.

He'd left, so she could have a life. One which didn't trap her in a painful past. But now that it is his freedom on the line – his life – what happens now?

Will she choose to save him?

They are running out of time.

There is a jangle of keys and the familiar thud of boots along the corridor.

They have come for him.

Chapter Forty-Seven

The polished wood gives the whole courtroom an elegant golden feel, as though the justice system played out within its walls is in some way of a higher power. Noble. Righteous. If only that were true.

Today I am not here fighting the good fight. There is no feeling of being part of something greater than I am. Today I am simply an observer, seated in the public gallery watching Christina Lang exude charisma from where she stands. It is my first and only day in court watching Jake's trial. I'd walked myself to the courtroom door a few times at the beginning of the trial, but never summoned enough courage to enter. Not until today.

Christina is a force of nature. Would I have been quite so captivating? The adrenalin is seeping out of her, enough to fill the rest of the room. My own skin is absorbing her energy and firing me up.

'You see, ladies and gentlemen of the jury, you have heard from the defence that Brad Finchley entered this trial pleading not guilty. They argue he has no known link to Mr and Mrs Rushnell and no motivation has been uncovered for him to invade their home, let alone to shoot them dead.

'You have heard Mr Murray entertain a number of different possibilities for who may have had more reason to harm this married couple. But let me be very clear: we are not here to judge the misdemeanours or Mark and Beverley. That is not your job as the jury. It is not how this country's justice system works. For that is what we are here to determine – justice.

'We are not here to understand whether they were embroiled in a murky past of insurance claims, nor if there were extramarital affairs. We are here only to find the truth about what happened on the day of their death. Not what came before it. Not even what came after. Simply what happened, *who* happened, on the 15th June. The answer to that question is standing right here before us today.

'Brad Finchley was found in possession of a bag containing the murder weapon and a cap belonging to him. The outside of the bag was covered in his DNA. The cap and gun were found splattered with blood matching that of both Mark and Beverley Rushnell. Fibres from that same cap were found on both bodies of the murder victims. These are not circumstantial arguments nor, unlike Mr Murray's defence, are they simply hypotheses. I provide you with pure indisputable facts. Brad Finchley pleaded not guilty but he has failed, at every opportunity, to provide an alternative fact-based explanation as to why or how these items came to be in his possession. How, exactly, his DNA came to be on the murder weapon, or how his cap could possibly have transferred fibres on to both bodies if he was not at the murder scene. If he did not kill them.

'Not only that, but we must then consider the intent behind the killings. This was no accident. Both victims were found in their own home completely defenceless. This was not an act of self-defence. It was not manslaughter. There can be no doubt that Brad Finchley murdered Mark and Beverley Rushnell in cold blood. I implore you to make the right decision today and to find him guilty of murder to the highest degree.'

I let out a slow breath, controlling its release, and find myself grabbing for my necklace. The one Jake once gave me. I clutch it between my fingers, its ragged edges pressing into my thumb. The courtroom has fallen so silent you could hear a pin drop.

Mr Murray stands up, giving a slight cough as he does so, the squeak of his chair audible from the gallery. It is the turn of the defence to summarise their case in a way that feels impactful and clear to the jury. To present the fact that while their blood was found on the cap, all we can be certain of is that it must have come in contact with the victims' blood after they were injured and before the blood dried. It does not prove he pulled the trigger. He will argue, with as much conviction as he can muster, that crucially Jake's DNA was not found on the gun itself, and he will use this to suggest Jake was framed. He will outline, once more, that there were other people with motivation to kill the couple. The hole in his argument, of course, as pointed out by Christina Lang, is that the defence have been unable to provide any reason for who would frame Jake or why.

That is, of course, exactly why my mother used him. I'm not naïve enough to believe his silence is to do with his enduring love for me – a long time has passed. Yes, he has fought the charge – suggested he was framed – but he has not fought it with everything he has. That is on him. Not me. And that was the ace up Mum's sleeve – because Jake was also complicit in covering Dad's death up. Why confess to one crime and risk that murder also being pinned on you? Three for the price of two. Especially when he had no idea if I'd ever corroborate the truth. Importantly, while Jake knew he'd been set up by Mum, he had no idea how it all connected to the Rushnells.

It was the perfect Catch-22; all she'd needed to do was plan, prepare and execute.

I cling to the fact Jake is also to blame for what we did eighteen years ago as hard as I can in the three short hours it takes for the jury to return with a verdict.

Everyone files back into court noisily and I make sure to hang back until the last minute, not wanting to draw attention to myself. But as I take my seat again, the feeling of being watched seeps over my skin, and I cast my gaze around the room.

I freeze.

Force my face to soften.

When did she arrive? DS Sorcha Rose does not smile, but I can tell she is pleased at my reaction. That she had hoped I would see her. Next to her sits a man I recognise as the journalist from the prom, the one who'd tried to interrogate me outside Mum's house. Is this what she had meant, when she'd said journalists aren't bound by the same rules as the police? Has she followed through with her threat? Continued looking into Dad's case even though it has officially remained closed?

What do they know?

The judge asks the juror cast as foreperson to stand and deliver the verdict, but my eyes aren't drawn to them. Instead, I can't seem to look away from where Jake Reynolds sits in the dock, imprisoned in his glass cage.

For the majority of today, I have been studying his profile. I have watched the way that sometimes he blinks for a flicker longer than necessary, as if pretending when he opens his eyes again this will all be a dream. Just before the juror speaks, some-one explodes into a coughing fit, and Jake's head snaps up to the gallery to see what is going on.

He hasn't looked up before now. I had known he wouldn't like the idea of being someone's entertainment and would avoid acknowledging the gallery. But now he has been prompted to look, I see him start to trace along each row. Is he looking for someone? Is he searching for me?

I am sitting three rows back, second chair in from the right, and it's not long until his eyes meet mine. I wonder if from here he can see I am pregnant. I've grown a lot in the weeks since telling Noah the news, and according to recent scans I'm now halfway through.

It used to be the most amazing feeling to be watched by Jake Reynolds, but today it feels as though my chest is caving inwards. Suffocating me. The electric pulse that used to sizzle through me instead feels like daggers tearing through my skin. And yet, I cannot look away.

Is it a comfort to him that I am here?

The letter Otis hand-delivered to me swirls through my mind and I think perhaps it is more of an insult.

Dear Justine,

Well, this was a surprise although, given the circumstances, I knew it wouldn't be long before you found me again.

I understand you have a lot you want answered but know this – I never hated you and I definitely didn't mean to abandon you. That night was messed up and we were so young. We made mistakes. I wanted to protect you, but I was equally afraid of what we'd done. And so, I convinced myself that by leaving you I was, in some twisted way, saving you. Realistically, perhaps I was just trying to save myself.

I did think about coming home, and I had a few wobbles those first few years, but it wasn't just you who was affected by the party. It changed me too, and every time I thought about contacting you, I couldn't bring myself to do it. As more time passed, the harder it became. In the end I liked the freedom of becoming someone else. Seeing you moving on in London made me want that for myself, too. I never told Mum or Dad I'd changed my name. For them I stayed as Jake. But the rest of the time it was easier to forget the past when I was just Brad.

I can't give you the answers you want, I only have part of the story myself, but if I still know you – which given you orchestrated a way for us to communicate, then I'm pretty sure I do – you can find the answers for yourself and, when you do, you'll have a decision to make.

I know what I did and what I didn't do. I also know what I need to do now. I haven't been given much choice.

But you? You can still decide. You can still change the course of this.

Yours, Jake

We keep looking at each other, even though I'm sure it is as painful for him as it is for me. That my presence here and the very fact the trial has made it this far is confirmation that I have chosen to keep my own secrets. That I decided to gamble with his life. To let the court decide.

The verdict bounces off the walls, 'On account of the murders of Mark and Beverley Rushnell, we find the defendant guilty.'

BEFORE

JAKE – THE BOYFRIEND

Jake hadn't anticipated quite how much his mother had hoarded over the years. It wasn't his fault; he'd never had to clear out a house before. There was so much admin too. 'Probate' and 'executor of the will'. Words he hadn't even heard of until after his mother passed away.

He'd hoped he could be in and out in two weeks, but months later and he was still stuck in Maldon, sorting through childhood memorabilia he'd long since forgotten about. He'd kept in touch with his family of course, but over time their contact had lessened. He couldn't keep up with all the questions. Where was he? Why had he left? When was he coming back? The lies had tied him in knots. They blamed Justine, assuming she'd hurt him so badly that he could no longer stand to be in Maldon. They weren't completely wrong. What they'd done had made it impossible for him to stay.

Two months on and the garage remained full of boxes. He'd been in there for most of the day and was about to give up for the night when he spotted the bag. It wasn't hidden exactly, just wedged between two boxes in the corner. He had assumed it was his father's and was intrigued to find out what it might contain. There wasn't much left of his dad's. It seemed his mother had hoarded almost everything connected to Jake, but had been a lot stricter when it came to his dad's belongings.

He'd pulled it out from where it sat on the floor, not noticing that unlike everything else in the garage, this bag wasn't covered in a layer of dust, and eagerly unzipped it.

The tangy iron smell hadn't immediately registered as blood. Perhaps if it had he wouldn't have handled what was inside it so readily. But, without stopping to think, he'd rummaged around pulling out what he recognised as his own black cap. The one he'd been searching for during the past week and couldn't find. How had it got put inside here? And why? Confused, he pulled the bag open wider and peered inside.

A gun.

There was a real-life gun lying at the bottom of the bag. One that could only have been placed in this garage since he last wore his hat.

What was going on?

He couldn't think. In fact, he could barely breathe. Rushing out of the garage, still clasping the bag, he'd run up the stairs frantically searching for somewhere to hide it. He remembered his dad's old hiding place for their most treasured belongings – a loose floorboard under the bed – and headed towards his parents' old bedroom. He would turn it in to the police, but first he had to find out what the hell any of this had to do with him.

Jake realised far too late that it was no coincidence Max had asked him to meet for a drink and that since then he hadn't been able to find his cap. He hadn't worn it to the pub, but was certain he'd left it on the armchair that same morning. It hadn't been there when he got back. He'd thought it was odd but figured he must have remembered wrong. It was later that he realised Evelyn must have taken the opportunity to enter his home, knowing he was meeting with Max, in order to take something of his.

To frame him.

Premeditated.

But how?

How had all this evidence found its way into his house?

He'd replayed the moment of his arrest – three weeks after his fight with Max – over and over again in his mind as he'd sat waiting in a cold damp room to be questioned. He only had two keys to his mum's house. As the police emptied his belongings and sealed them up in a see-through bag, they had taken one key from him. But, in his memory, and he was sure he was right, as he'd been marched out of the front door and taken a last glance over his shoulder into the house he was leaving behind, there had been two keys still hanging on the key rack. In total, that made three. An extra key was glimmering against the wall. One which hadn't been there before.

The only other person he knew to have ever had a key to his mum's house was Justine. Back when they lived out of each other's pockets. He couldn't bring himself to believe Justine would have framed him. But Evelyn? She must have got hold of Justine's key somehow. He knew Justine had left Maldon in a hurry, never to return. Had she left it behind? He supposed there would have been no reason for her to take it with her. Evelyn must have found it. Saved it for a rainy day.

There was no doubt in Jake's mind that it had been left as a warning. She had wanted him to know it was her. It was a way of keeping him silent; only by knowing it was Evelyn would he realise he was powerless. That this all linked back to Gerard's death, to the one mistake he'd ever made. And now it had come back to haunt him.

Well-played, he thought, sitting in the cold bare cell they'd assigned him.

The Stones had always loved to win. To manipulate and control the narrative. He had learnt far too late that it was what they did best.

Chapter Forty-Eight

From the driveway, I can see a bustle of activity through our large bay kitchen window. Charlotte is standing balanced on one of the bar stools, hanging bunting. They are laughing, and from the way Noah moves around the room I can imagine they are playing music. As Charlotte steps back to view her work, I see the bunting spells out IT'S A GIRL in pink italics. It's too early for a baby shower but Charlotte insisted on celebrating after we found out it's a girl.

'Really there's no need to make such a fuss,' I'd said but she'd claimed gender parties are all the rage these days. An American thing, apparently.

Homemade afternoon tea was the order of the day, of course. The stipulation was that I was not allowed to help set up or organise it. I wonder how much is coincidence and how much fate that today would also be the morning Jake was finally handed down his sentence. That the life he knows has been severed on the very same day I am celebrating the promise of my new one.

Looking at the house now with all the people I love rallying around me, the hole left by Max feels even bigger than usual. Will I ever feel whole again? He should be here. My big brother, celebrating his niece. The pain still holds me like a vice. It's the not knowing that I find almost unbearable. We will never know if he fell into the estuary after Jimmy left, a drunken accident, or if the guilt had boiled over; reached a temperature he could no longer bear, and he'd decided to end it all.

This is what death does to those left behind. How can you find closure without answers? Who am I meant to forgive? Max? My mother? Jimmy? Myself? Without answers, there will be no forgiveness. I think I am destined to be angry – hurting – for ever. Nothing comes without a price, and Max's death is mine.

I am lost in my own thoughts when the front door flies open and Noah stands there, beckoning me to run inside. Run – because by all accounts it is freezing, with Christmas not long away. The house looks warm and happy. Can a house look happy? I didn't think so, not until today. But yes, I have a happy home. I smile, pushing away thoughts of the cold stark cell now inhabited by Jake.

Inside, I am hit by a wall of noise. The house is full of friends I didn't think I had. People who want to be a part of this next chapter in my life. *How was the spa?* They all want to know, and I tell them I've had a lovely relaxing morning. That it was just what I needed. It is only a white lie.

'Good, you deserve to be pampered,' chimes in Charlotte as she takes me by the arm and leads me into the kitchen to admire her set-up.

You deserve to be pampered. For the first time in as long as I can remember, the idea that I am deserving of something doesn't make me short of breath. Instead, I think about the life growing inside of me and know, finally, that I can let go of the past. I can reason with my own guilt; slice it up and hand it out to others around me. Jake did not kill Mr and Mrs Rushnell, but he did still cover up my father's death, setting everything that came after it in motion. He did that. Not me. And while he did not push Max into the water, he did decide to ask for his help that night. For that, I convince myself, I can deem him guilty.

The kitchen is beautifully decorated. Cupcakes and little homemade sandwiches of every variety are stacked on tiered cake stands, covering the marble island. There's a

Sarah Hornsley

pink-and-white balloon arch separating the main kitchen from the sofa area and presents tower high on the dresser in the corner.

This time, instead of looking in from the car, I look out. The kitchen bay window faces directly towards our apple tree. The baby gives a kick and, as I place my hand over my belly, it strikes me how true the saying is that apples never fall far from the tree. Like mother like daughter, I have already started protecting this child of mine as fiercely as only a mother's love will allow.

I'd read Jake's letter over and over again trying to decide what I should do with the truth once I'd found it, but this wasn't just a choice about whether to save my mother or Jake, to explain what really happened to my dad, it was also about my unborn child. About saving my daughter. And, speaking of the truth – saving myself.

Because it took eighteen years but, finally, I can accept my father was right – everything is open to interpretation.

Even murder.

BEFORE

JUSTINE

The longer Justine was locked in the wardrobe, the more it changed her. She and Max had grown up knowing the power being alone had over you. How much more dangerous everything could feel. It's why as children they'd always chosen to hide together, under the stairs, when their mother's cries were too loud to ignore. Max would pretend it was hide-and-seek, and she'd go along with it. Even as a child she'd known it helped them both to remain living in the fantasy world Max had built for them.

This time, there was no Max by her side making up stories and games to keep the truth away. She was alone, and there was no choice but to face it.

By the time her father scraped the chair back and swung the door open, she was barely recognisable. Her desire for courage hadn't simply arrived, it had flooded her and could no longer be controlled. She hadn't become the Viking beating the drum, she had transformed into the drum itself.

She rose from the floor and glared at her father, where he stood smoking a cigar. He was not a big man, but he had an aura about him that made him larger than life. His green velvet suit jacket hung slightly too big on his shoulders and his brow was sweaty – probably from all the whisky.

'How dare you?' Justine demanded, surprising even herself. 'I am your daughter.' She sounded confident and righteous but inside she was shaking. Broken. Abandoned. How could he do this to her? Her own father.

'Exactly. I cannot have my daughter making false claims about my most valued partner. Do you know what that would do to us? You almost ruined this entire family tonight.' He is speaking quietly, nonchalantly, as if he hasn't just completely shattered Justine's entire world, and it only infuriates her more.

'They are not false claims.'

'Everything is open to interpretation, Justine, you'll learn that one day.'

'Not sexual assault.'

They were still facing each other. Head on. Charging into battle. He was meant to be protecting her. Why wasn't he? She wanted to make him see. Perhaps it was still just one big misunderstanding.

'Did he kiss you?'

'No.'

'Did he make you touch him?'

'No.'

'Did he rape you?' Justine noticed he didn't even flinch as he asked her that one, and it shook her to the core. How callous it sounded out of her own father's lips. She knew he could be cruel, had heard it through the walls, but he'd never aimed it at her before.

'No.'

'Well then,' he said, smirking. 'Yes, I'd say it's open for interpretation.'

Not one big misunderstanding, then.

Gerard turned from her and started heading towards the door. That was it? He wasn't going to ask for her side of the story? The sight of him striding away from her was too much to bear. He was really going to leave her, again? Why wouldn't he fight for her?

It made Justine feel small. So small. How could she matter this little to her own dad? She couldn't resist drawing him back into combat. At least arguing was better than him leaving her. It was worse to feel discarded, as if her pain did not really exist. As if she'd just made up what had happened, and it was no longer worth talking about.

And so she dug deep. Anything to get a reaction. To keep him there.

'What about hitting your wife? Is that open to interpretation?' She regretted it as soon as the words left her mouth.

Fast strides then, closer and closer. His chest puffed out, rage consuming his entire posture. He was no longer smirking. It was his eyes that told her she had gone too far. They had somehow darkened.

It dawned on her that he didn't intend to stop.

Not this time.

Justine could tell it was no longer just a game to him that he would smirk about winning while puffing on a cigar later. She had pushed him too far. She should have let him win.

She watched, as if in slow motion, as he drew his hand back. He kept looking at her the whole time – unashamed as he hit his daughter. The force of it still took her by surprise, even though she'd known it was coming. The sting burned. Her cheek was on fire. One thousand needles were pricking her skin.

She gasped as her eyes filled with tears. And then she drew herself back to standing tall and willed the tears not to fall. She was a Stone, after all. But as she rose back up with her hand clutched to her cheek, she wondered: now the line had been crossed, would he ever stop? The role he had been playing – the one of the hero father – there was no going back to it. Tonight, he had relinquished his part. Would he fully step into this new role? The one of the villain? Previously hidden behind closed doors. Reserved only for her mother.

There was a moment of stillness as they watched each other. A gap in time. Would this silence mark the before and after? It was as if they knew that whatever happened next would define everything. Who would make the first move? Where did they go from here?

After only a momentary pause, Gerard calmly removed his cigar from where it hung limp between his lips. She knew then he had chosen to be the villain. That the slap had just been the beginning.

She'd seen the circular burns on her mother, in places easy to cover up, but nothing stays secret from a child. They're too in-tune, too small, too observant. Adults forget what it's like to be so plugged into the world around you with no other distractions – no work, no responsibilities, pulling you away from experiencing the present. Children are sponges. Adults are clumsy.

Her parents had thought they were being clever, but Max and Justine hadn't played hide-and-seek for no reason. They knew when it was best to stay out of the way. To hide in places where they could neither see nor hear their mother's pain. Their father's cruelty.

No, Justine would not let him burn her, too.

She dropped the stiletto which was still clutched in her hand and she pushed him. Hard and fast. She was only small but she used all of her strength. She would not let him turn her into her mother.

She watched as he she crumpled right before her eyes; as his head clipped the side of her desk, whipping back with the force of it.

She didn't know what she'd hoped would happen, she just knew she wouldn't let him hurt her without a fight. He'd fallen at her feet, but was rising now from the floor. Back on his knees. One hand on her desk as he levered himself up. Eyes bulged wide.

Fuck, what had she done.

He wasn't angry, he was absolutely livid. And Justine knew, right then, that he was going to kill her. If not today, then eventually. There was no way he was letting her get away with this.

What her father had not counted on was that Justine was no longer the meek little girl who he had shut in the wardrobe just hours earlier. Instead of weakening her, the ordeal had filled her with hate. She hated herself for it as much as she hated him, her mother too; how had they carried on this long, sweeping everything under the carpet? The rage boiled.

She knew what came next: the displays of affection for days after, the thick air that would trail her around the house wherever she went. The lies. The long sleeves, chosen for practicality and not for comfort. Justine had hated her mother for it and she refused to become like her: meek, quiet and weak. A stranger in her own house.

No, she was the drum.

And so, before he could regain his balance – before he could hurt her again – she bent quickly and swiped the stiletto from the floor where she'd dropped it. She struck.

Once.

Twice.

Then again.

Forcing the heel further into his temple with each stab.

She watched the life flood out of him. He looked at her, eyes full of fear. Good. She'd never seen him afraid before. 'Help,' he mouthed. But she did not move. She stayed as still as possible as he slumped sideways back down to the floor; his head snapping on the corner of her desk as he fell. The impact of it forced the mirror balancing on top to crash to the floor, where it smashed into a thousand shards of glass; each one reflecting the blood as it soaked out of her father's head and across the wooden floorboards.

She stared at her father lying still by her feet and, as the horror of what she'd done sunk in, she was surprised to find it was the opposite of a numbness which infiltrated her body. The crack of his head as it had hit the corner of her desk continued to reverberate too loudly in her ears. The image of his eyes as they glazed over and stopped moving became seared too vibrantly on to her retinas. The blood as it soaked across the floorboards felt too wet against the soles of her feet. He was dead. She had killed him. Would the world ever feel the same again? Would she ever be the same again? Why, after what she'd just done, did she feel so exhilarated. So alive. Was it just fear turned into adrenalin? She wasn't so sure.

She avoided looking at her father's open eyes as she trod as carefully as possible across the room and into the en suite. The glass had spread further than she'd anticipated and with each step shards embedded themselves deep into the soles of her feet.

As she washed the bloody stiletto in the sink, she was transfixed by the water turning red. Even when she could see the shoe was clean, the tap still seemed to run with blood. Would it be like this forever? Would the stain of what she'd done follow her around for life?

She needed a plan, and she needed one fast. For she had transformed into the drum, and she would not stop beating.

Her father had named her Justine, *Justice*, and for the first time in her life she felt she had acted on her namesake. Surely, if nothing else, her father would have been proud of her for that.

Acknowledgements

They say it takes a village. Well, writing *Bad Blood* took a town. It is no exaggeration to say that I would have never written this book without the support of those around me. My parents and husband, who changed their own schedules to make time and space for me to write. And so, the first thank you has to go to Luke, who never even flinched when I told him I was going to write a book, while already working full-time, with a toddler and another baby on the way. His quiet but steadfast belief in me never faltered (at least, not that he ever told me) and for that I feel so lucky.

A huge thanks to my parents, particularly my mum who found every spare minute she could to help out with childcare. I couldn't ask for anyone to champion me more. And thanks to my dad for not only telling me but also for showing me himself that chasing your dreams can actually make them happen.

Of course, this book would never have made it out into the world without my agent, Juliet Mushens. Words genuinely cannot express how much you've shaped my life – not just professionally but also personally. I would not be who I am today without you. Agent, mentor, confidante and friend – thank you for always believing in me, even years before I'd written a single word. Thanks to the rest of the team at Mushens Entertainment for their relentless hard work and unmatched enthusiasm.

And to Phoebe Morgan, dream editor – a huge thank you for your vision and ambition for *Bad Blood*. I couldn't have hoped for a smarter, kinder, more astute editor and I'm thrilled to get to work with you. Again, more thanks are due to everyone else at Hodder who is part of the weird and wonderful process of transforming my little (well, large) word document into something people want to buy; to Kate Norman, Lydia Blagden and Alainna Hadjigeorgiou to name only a few.

There are also certain people that without their love and support, I would have quite simply given up writing – Fran, Sophie, Laurie and Lucy – thanks for the early reads, the cheerleading and the words of wisdom. A special thanks to Cara, too, for riding every single high and low with me. For the memes, the coffees and the laughter.

And finally, thank you to my beautiful two girls, Hazel and Florrie, for allowing me to imagine just how hard a mother might fight for her children. There is no love quite like it.